Wings
LIKE A
Dove

Wings LIKE A Dove

CAMILLE EIDE

ASHBERRY LANE

PRAISE FOR *WINGS LIKE A DOVE*

"Eide delivers a powerful tale of a Jewish immigrant dealing with prejudice. Anna's nuanced inner life and the stakes of her trip make this stand out from similar inspirational fare. [A] harrowing, enthralling tale."
~ *Publisher's Weekly*

"When worlds and cultures collide, friction and conflict are the result...but redemption is also the solution. Camille Eide has written a breathtaking novel of historical fiction that feels like fact in *Wings Like a Dove*. I can think of no greater compliment than I would love to see this story transformed into a feature film. Run, don't walk to get this book in your hands."
~ BRIAN BIRD,
co-creator and executive producer of *When Calls the Heart*

"Camille Eide has done it again with *Wings Like a Dove*! Her captivating characters and riveting plot kept me turning the pages as fast as I could. This Depression-era story takes us from New York City to rural Indiana, on a multi-faceted struggle against shame, injustice, and fear. Just when it seems that bane of prejudice will prevail, Camille works her story-telling magic and raises the stakes even higher for a group of disenfranchised children and adults, who are threatened with losing everything."
~ LESLIE GOULD,
#1 Best Selling and Christy Award Winning Author of over 30 novels

"Once again in *Wings Like a Dove*, Camille Eide takes her readers to places we didn't know we needed to go. She invites us to consider who is the outsider, who responds to discrimination, and who will be carried on wings like a dove. Anna, Thomas, a cadre of children, and an important search for forgiveness marks this compelling story peopled with characters we love. I will take many phrases to encourage my days from this story, the most significant for me being 'Shame is a terrible thief,' and so it is. Enjoy this story of love lost and found!"
~ JANE KIRKPATRICK,
New York Times Bestselling author of *One More River to Cross*

"Rich historical details and three-dimensional characters populate Camille Eide's masterful novel, *Wings Like a Dove*. Eide's beautiful writing draws the reader into Anna Leibowicz's world in 1933, while surreptitiously holding a mirror to the present. One of those wonderful stories that gives you all the feels–including that satisfying moment at the end when you read the last page and know the time spent between the covers of the book was very well spent."

~ CINDY KELLEY, Author & Screenwriter

"Camille Eide's latest novel transports readers back to 1930s America when racial tensions were high and those who showed compassion were persecuted. With Camille's signature style of boldness and grace, *Wings Like a Dove* is an authentic glimpse at the trials and triumph of one immigrant family determined to succeed against the odds. It's a courageous, difficult journey with a beautiful ending that breathes hope into breaking cycles of abuse today."

~ MELANIE DOBSON,
award-winning author of *Catching the Wind* and *Memories of Glass*

"Both gorgeous and harrowing, *Wings Like a Dove* shows the dangers of allowing hatred and racism to grow in a community—and the importance of standing up for right, even when it's dangerous. Anna, Thomas, and Samuel are lovely characters full of depth and strength, and Thomas shows the beauty of a Christian putting his faith in action. With a poignant romance, the story satisfies on every level. Camille Eide has penned another memorable novel. Don't miss it!"

~ SARAH SUNDIN,
bestselling and award-winning author of *The Sea Before Us*
and *The Sky Above Us*

"*Wings Like a Dove* is a beautiful, powerful story. Camille Eide takes you on a journey with Anna that is gut-wrenching and real, and you'll find that you can't tear yourself away. Unafraid to tackle difficult issues, Eide does a brilliant job bringing the characters to life and makes you think long and hard each and every step of the way."

~ KIMBERLEY WOODHOUSE,
Carol Award-Winning and Best-selling Author

"*Wings Like a Dove* by Camille Eide is a gripping, unforgettable novel. Eide writes the kind of story we shouldn't forget, challenging readers about how judging others can lead to racism and how unforgiveness — both of ourselves and others — can destroy our ability to love, to heal. Woven with threads of tenderness and grace, Eide encourages us to think about the choices that mark history...and the choices that are affecting us today."

~ BETH K. VOGT,
Christy Award-winning author of *Moments We Forget*
and *Things I Never Told You*

"With her previous novels, Camille Eide proved herself a talented storyteller. With her newest book, *Wings Like a Dove,* she once again offers a story that skillfully engages both mind and heart. Set during the Great Depression, it's the story of a Polish Jewish immigrant named Anna. Unwed and pregnant, turned out by her mother, she leaves New York for Chicago in search of her missing father. On her journey, she meets six orphan boys, a young former pastor who acts as their guardian, two Catholic sisters, a lonely farm wife and a contingent of Ku Klux Klansmen...all of whom change her life. For lovers of historical fiction, this book is an absolute delight!"

~ ANN TATLOCK, novelist, blogger and children's book author

"Author Camille Eide has a gift for taking the darkest moments of our history and turning them into stories of enduring strength. In *Wings Like a Dove*, she's created unforgettable characters who exhibit grace and courage, even while facing intense prejudice. After reading this beautiful novel, I'm inspired to look around myself and see how little the world has changed—and do my part to make it better. Don't miss this one."

~ KAREN BARNETT, author of the Vintage National Parks series

This is a work of fiction. All characters and events portrayed in this novel are either fictitious or used fictitiously.

WINGS LIKE A DOVE

ISBNs: 978-1-946531-74-2 (Print)
978-1-946531-75-9 (Digital)

All Scripture quotations are taken from the King James Version.

Ashberry Lane, a division of WhiteFire Publishing
13607 Bedford Rd NE | Cumberland, MD 21502

Oh that I had wings like a dove! for
then would I fly away, and be at rest.
~ Psalm 55:6

Beware of no man more than of yourself;
we carry our worst enemies within us.
~ Charles H. Spurgeon

For every muleheaded Sarah

Friday, March 3, 1933
Lower East Side, New York

THE JANGLE OF COINS IN ANNA'S POCKET WAS A SOUND SHE ONLY heard on Fridays, and only from the time she left the garment factory until she deposited the week's earnings into her mother's sugar bowl. Rent was becoming harder to scrape together, but there was always food on the table, even if it was only the heel of last week's challah. And because Mama chose to ignore reality, she blessed every meal, whether scrap of bread or small feast, with the same passion.

The way Mama viewed life through blinders gave her a relentless optimism. If only Anna could wear such blinders. Perhaps then she would not see the invisible walls that made this golden land of promise feel like a prison. She would not know that beyond their neighborhood existed more of the hostility that her mother believed they had left behind in the Pale. Perhaps blinders would put a stop to the shameful memories that churned in Anna's mind like dry leaves whirling in the wind.

She walked on, hands in her dress pockets to quiet the jingling. A chilly wind ruffled the curls at her neck, reminding her that she had traded her long, dark braid for a stylish bob—a foolish choice then, and even more now, since being *en vogue* was about as useful to Anna as a hole in the head.

Anna would be content with no more reminders of her stupidity.

"Late again, Miss Leibowicz?"

Yes, and getting later by the minute...

Gripping her shawl tighter, Anna waved at the apple-cart man but kept going, quickening her pace and holding her breath to block out the mingled smells, which were becoming more unbearable with each passing day. How childish she must have looked, scurrying past the tenements like a truant, dodging food carts, rats, pedestrians, and street muck in her path.

"So late you cannot make *one* small stop?" Hope softened the man's voice.

With a sigh, Anna turned and went back to the reedy old man standing behind his cart, bundled up to his long, graying beard in a tattered coat. He should know that the longer Anna was delayed today, the more annoyed her mother would be.

She looked him in the eye. "Mr. Birnbaum, if I am running late for Shabbat because the payday line was long, what is your excuse?"

The man's shoulders bowed from an unseen weight. "Mrs. Birnbaum is not getting better. But I almost have enough to pay the doctor now. Sales were not so bad today."

Anna smiled gently. He returned her smile, but a deeper worry fringed his eyes. She fingered the coins in her pocket. She was to buy only what was absolutely needed. The Great Crash had changed the entire world in an instant and was the last thing she and her family had expected upon arriving in the Golden Country. Not only had the economic disaster changed Anna's plans, it had made the past four years feel like an endless punishment. Did the feeling exist outside the confines of the tenements? What she would not give to find out.

Mr. Birnbaum warmed his knotty, chapped hands with a steamy breath and waited for her to make a selection.

Perhaps Mama would not mind if Anna spent a little extra, just this once. After all, her sister, Shayna, was working at the factory now, and more money would soon be coming in.

"I am glad you stopped me, Mr. Birnbaum. I had forgotten I promised Anshel a reward."

The man's face lit up. "Yes, good. Little brothers must be encouraged. What will it be today, Miss Leibowicz? A bushel of apples?"

She pulled two coins from her pocket. The quarter would go into her tin to save for college—if she was lucky enough to make the quota. The other was a nickel.

"Just one apple. When his teacher tells us he has passed fourth grade, then we will celebrate with a bushel."

Mr. Birnbaum exchanged her nickel for the fruit. "Anshel is a good boy. He has a clever head on his shoulders. If you continue to tutor him, he will do well."

Anna smiled. "That is our hope."

"You make certain of that, Miss Anna. He is man of the house now."

Her breath seized, but there, on the street, Anna held her tongue. Rumors had circulated in the Jewish community that Papa had chosen to leave the neighborhood nearly two years before his wife and children arrived from Poland to join him. Did the apple man also know something? It seemed everyone except Anna and her family knew what had happened to Papa.

"Your kindness to Mrs. Birnbaum will not go unnoticed," he said softly.

"Thank you."

"Please give your wife our best wishes."

Anna pocketed the apple, then hurried to her building. But as she climbed the stairs, her pace dragged, and by the time she reached the third floor, her legs felt as if they were made of wet sand. Shaky, she paused to catch her breath. In the last few weeks, the three-story climb had been feeling more like thirteen.

Inside the airless apartment, the rich scent of baking bread calmed her wobbly insides.

"Anna!" Anshel crushed her with a hug. "You are late. The sun is almost down."

She hugged him back and mussed his dark mop. "The line was long today. How many times have I told you that good things come to those who wait?"

"Better things come to those who make good trades." His English was improving, and he spoke with so little accent that he rarely needed correction anymore.

While Mama was busy removing challah from the oven, Anna pulled the apple from her pocket and crouched down to look Anshel in the eye. "This is for your lunch at school. Do not trade it this time. It will make your brain smart. You must spend your energy learning, not on sweet-talking your teacher for passing grades."

Anshel's eyes widened. "How did you know?"

"You may be clever, but you do not fool me. Do you understand?"

With a roll of his eyes, he pocketed the fruit and grinned. "Yes, *Madam Teacher.*"

"And that reminds me—you have fallen behind on reading, so you will read *two* chapters to me tonight." Ignoring his groan, Anna kissed his head, then straightened to look around. "Where is Shayna?"

Anshel shrugged. "She is also late."

Anna frowned. "But she left the factory before me." She took off her shawl and kissed Rivka's forehead. At fourteen, Rivka was already a beauty. Mama's matchmaker friend would have no trouble finding the youngest Leibowicz daughter a husband.

Anna kissed her mother's cheek.

"You are *very* late, Channah," Mama scolded in Yiddish. "The sun is almost down. Hurry and take this to Mrs. Feldman while I prepare the table. She will want to talk about her ailments. Tell her you are sorry, but you cannot stay." Mama placed a warm loaf of bread in Anna's hands. "Do not dawdle but come right back."

Would Mama ever see her as anything but a child? Other girls her age were attending college or married and making homes of their own.

She slipped out to the landing, knocked on 12B, and waited, still fuming. If her elderly neighbor still needed bread for Shabbat, then surely it was not *so* late. Anna gave Mrs. Feldman the loaf with an apology for not coming inside.

As Anna headed back to the apartment, Shayna came up the stairs, treading lightly. She froze when she saw Anna, her eyes aglitter like tiny, new flakes of snow.

"And where have *you* been?" Anna asked.

"Me?" Shayna seemed oddly breathless. "Am I late?"

Anna leaned closer for a better look at Shayna's face. The air was cold, but not enough to account for the deep shade of pink that filled her sister's cheeks. "Hmm. It is strange how the walk from the factory gets longer each day."

"Channah!" Mama's voice rang out from inside. "Am I to do everything myself now?"

Shayna grasped Anna's arm and steered her older sister into the apartment ahead of her like a shield. It did not work.

"Shayna!" Mama said. "Now *you* are dawdling. Must you follow after

Channah in everything?" The table was set with candles, Kiddush cups for wine, and two loaves of challah, which Mama now covered with a towel.

As the others took their places, Anna leaned close to Shayna and spoke in English. "I am still waiting."

Shayna glanced at Mama and then met Anna's gaze, the glow on her cheeks making her look younger than her sixteen years. Modesty looked lovely on Shayna. She was the kind of girl who deserved far more than she would ever ask for. There was nothing disappointing about Shayna, nothing reckless or obstinate, and Anna hoped nothing would ever happen to spoil her. Shayna was the kind of girl Anna could never be.

She drew a calming breath to mask a sudden prickle of dread. "That Wasserman boy will make you ill, keeping you out so long in the cold."

"Oh, no, Isaak would never do that." Shayna glanced at Mama again, then lowered her voice. "Anna, will you speak to her? The matchmaker has chosen a boy for me to marry, but I want to marry Isaak. Mama does not like him. She says he is too quiet. He is not a loud talker, but a thinker. He is very smart."

Mama shushed her daughters and lit the candles to begin.

Shayna whispered, "Will you please speak to her?"

For a moment, all Anna could do was marvel at the pure hope shining in her sister's eyes. That Wasserman boy had better be worthy of Shayna, and treat her wishes with respect, because if he was ever pushy or lewd toward her in any way... But Shayna had the good sense to know a scoundrel when she saw one. And Anna was the last person to question Shayna's judgment.

"Yes, my love," Anna whispered back. "And it will go in one ear and out the other. But for you, I will try." She leaned closer and kissed Shayna's cheek.

Mama waved her arms above the candles, as if gathering the light to her face, then covered her eyes and said the blessing. When she uncovered her eyes, everyone said, "Shabbat Shalom." After the washing, all talking ceased as Mama blessed the wine and passed it. She uncovered the challah and said the prayer. Then she tore off a piece, dipped it in salt, took a bite, and passed the bread. Everyone followed in turn, and then the speaking resumed.

"Mama's husband list for *you* is a long one," Rivka blurted out to Anna, as if she could keep silent no longer. "And since you turned twenty, it grows longer every day." She heaved a dreamy sigh.

"I do not need a man complicating things, Riv," Anna said lightly. Her youngest sister could not comprehend why Anna was not pursuing marriage. "What I need is to be accepted by a university, and even then, I will still need to make the quota."

"What is *quota?*" Anshel frowned. "Some kind of bread? Why must *you* make it?"

"The quota is a limit on the number of Jews who are permitted to do certain things," Anna said. Things that non-Jews could do without restriction. Or reprisal.

"In Yiddish," Mama said. "Must I always remind you?"

"*I* would like a man complicating things," Rivka said, switching to her mother's tongue.

"No need to rush things, Rivkele," Mama said. "Someone must stay and help me with going to market and cooking since *both* your sisters seem to have more important things to do than come straight home where they belong." With a sigh, Mama sliced more bread. "I am sorry Papa cannot be here again for Shabbat, but I am certain he will join us one day soon."

Anna nearly dropped the bread that Anshel passed. Many times had she heard this ridiculous claim from her mother in the four years since they arrived in America. Too many.

"When will you accept that Papa has abandoned us?" Anna said.

Her mother's jaw dropped. A thick layer of silence settled over the table. "What a terrible thing to say about your papa."

Cheeks burning, Anna took her portion and passed it. "I am sorry, Mama. But since you rarely go out, you do not hear what I hear. You do not know what the people say."

"So now people in the street know more about your family than your own mother?"

So it would seem. Anna stared at her plate.

Mama busied herself with cutting more bread. "You are just tired and are allowing gossip to affect what good sense you possess. Let us not spoil Shabbat with any more unkind words."

"Yes, Mama," Anna said quietly. She stole a glance at her siblings. Each one kept their attention on their plate, except Shayna, whose glistening gaze met hers.

Let us not quarrel, she mouthed.

For Shayna's sake, Anna held her tongue, but only for now. The time had come for a long, overdue conversation with her mother. Anna dipped her bread in salt and ate in silence.

Once the others were in bed, Anna gathered her take-home work and trudged to her mother's sewing table, barely visible beneath heaps of mending and partially assembled clothing. Unfortunately, as all their Jewish neighbors knew, they would lose their jobs if the work was not finished, Shabbat or not. Mama, Anna, and Shayna were lucky to have garment jobs, as steady work was painfully difficult to find in the years following the Crash.

Anna drew a fortifying breath. "Mama, I know you do not wish to hear of this, but there is talk that Papa went west to make his own life, and this is why we stopped receiving letters from him."

Mama set one garment aside and reached for a new bundle of fabric. "You are right, Channah. I do not wish to hear gossip about your papa. You do not know him as I do. He would never simply leave us to fend for ourselves. How can you believe such lies? Who told you he went west?"

Anna shrugged, hoping Mama would not press the question. The source of that information was something Anna desperately wished to forget.

"Was it those people you insisted on going out to meet? Where are they now, those exciting new friends who you could not even introduce to your mother? They are strangers, and yet you listen to them?"

Strangers... How foolish she was last autumn to think those so-called "friends" were anything special. "Others have said it as well."

"Who—old women who have nothing better to do than sit around inventing stories?"

"It seems as if everyone knows that Papa left us."

"I do not know this, and therefore it is not true."

"Mama," Anna lowered her voice, hoping to soften her words. "Do you only believe what you wish to be true?"

Mama threw down her bundle and turned to Anna. "I am not so blind nor am I stupid, as you think. Have you forgotten living in Bielsk under

Red Army tyranny? What could you know? You were just a child. I lived in the Pale during the pogroms. I have seen horrible things. Though I wished the raids and attacks on our people to end, they did not. And here we are, in the land of opportunity, and yet Jews are counted and spat on and banned from shops and jobs and universities. And yet I still believe—even if you cannot—that God provided your papa a ticket to America and that He kept us alive, and that He will watch over us and bring Papa home."

Anna's cheeks burned. "I remember, Mama. I also remember that when you were out searching for work and the gangs attacked our village, I had to hide my little sisters beneath the floorboards. How can I ever forget that? If God is watching over us, why did I have to keep two babies silent when I was as terrified as they were?" Her body shook as the memory refreshed her terror. "Why did He supply passage for Papa who only sent us half our fares and then vanished? And why did you and Shayna and I have to work until our fingers bled and sell everything we had to raise enough money to come here? Why are we still hated and mistreated? Why have I grown up without a father? If God is watching out for us, Mama, where is your husband?"

Mama burst into tears and waved Anna away.

Shame stabbed at Anna's heart. What had come over her? And twice in the same evening? Her stomach took a sudden and unpleasant turn. "I am sorry, Mama. I should not have spoken to you that way."

Mama sniffled and blew her nose. "You are wrong, daughter, and one day, you will see. I am certain your papa has found work someplace where it is difficult to write."

With a sigh, Anna studied her mother, once striking and vibrant, now pale, wilted. What Anna would not give to see her family free from ceaseless struggle and difficulty. But she held out little hope for that. The promise of a better life in America was nothing but pie in the sky. Perhaps Papa had grown weary of trying to claim a piece of the golden dream and this great, monstrous land had somehow swallowed him up.

"Mama," Anna said gently. "I think we must accept the possibility that Papa is no longer alive."

"He is *not* dead!" She pressed a fist into her bosom. "If he were, I would know."

Anna touched her mother's shoulder. "Then we must accept that he has left us."

"I accept no such thing. Hershel Leibowicz would never abandon his family."

"I wish to believe that," Anna said. "I also wish to understand how men can come to America and then desert the families and communities who need them. But I cannot understand, so I believe it is up to the rest of us to be strong and go on living without them."

Shaking her head, Mama lifted a shirt from the pile. "You are too hard, Channah. There are many things you do not understand. You must have faith."

"I do," Anna said, rising to her feet. "I have faith that as long as you keep getting back up after you are knocked down, you may still have a fighting chance."

She left her mother, then changed out of her street clothes and crawled into bed, too weary to think and grateful for the warmth her siblings had created.

Rivka and Anshel were asleep. Shayna faced the wall, but her shoulders shook.

"Shayna?" Anna whispered. When her sister turned, tears streaked her cheeks. "You heard?"

Shayna's mouth quivered. "I do not like it when you quarrel with Mama. This is difficult for her. For us all."

Anna swallowed hard. "I am sorry. I just do not understand how men can abandon their families. It is shameful to desert your people when they need you most."

"What if he had no choice? Perhaps Mama is right, and he went to find better work where he is not able to write."

What kind of work would keep a man from writing to his family for six years?

Fragments of a puzzling conversation in the dim corner of a speakeasy formed in her mind.

So, doll face—I guess you don't take after your old man much.

What do you mean?

We heard he's been real busy over in Chicago.

Doing what?

Don't you know?

Do you?

Maybe. But questions like that from girls like you only dig up things you don't want to know.

A familiar, sickening sensation crawled up her throat. She inhaled deeply to force it back down.

"You are right, my love. I will try harder not to quarrel with Mama. Go to sleep."

Two

ANNA AWOKE SATURDAY TO THE DULL, METALLIC-TASTING CER-
tainty that she was going to be sick. She scrambled to her feet and reached
the washtub just in time. The sound of her retching broke the silence in the
tiny apartment. It was no wonder her stomach was upset, after her quarrel
with Mama. She wiped her face, then jumped at the touch on her shoulder.

"You are sick again," Rivka said, yawning.

"I am not sick."

"Yes, you are, I heard you."

"I had an upset stomach. It is nothing."

"You have had many upset stomachs lately."

Anna frowned. Had she?

"And I know why." Rivka moved closer and shook her head. "You work
too hard. You will never get better working so much. You should stay home
today and rest."

Anna shook her head, which set off more queasiness. "And then what—
return to the factory tomorrow to find they have given my finishing job to
another girl? What would we do for money then? Thank you, Riv, but I am
well enough."

A sudden wave of nausea struck, and she vomited again.

"Yes, you look *very* well to me," Rivka said, holding Anna's bobbed hair
back.

"I will be fine." Anna rinsed her mouth and spat. She reminded her
youngest sister it was her turn to make breakfast and then slipped outside
to the only place where she could have a moment to think in peace—the
landing in the stairwell.

She lowered herself onto the top step. When she was sick several times a few weeks ago, she suspected she had eaten something spoiled. Then last week was likely from nerves, as Friday mornings were always tense at the factory with the extra pressure of getting all the finished garments bundled for delivery.

And who would not have indigestion after that conversation with Mama last night?

Or, perhaps feeling ill was due to recent changes to her menses. Girls at the factory said the harsh working conditions and the stress on their bodies had altered their cycles. Anna heard that missing one was common, so she had put the missed cycle out of her mind.

Had she missed only one? No. It had actually been more than one.

Her breath caught. Sick several times in the past two months—several *mornings*. Sickness in the mornings sounded like—

No. Missed menses and morning sickness could be explained away.

Or they could mean—

No. Impossible!

But it was possible...

She clamped her mouth with hands that shook.

No, no, no, it could NOT be possible...

Or it could mean that the worst mistake of her life was no longer just a humiliating memory she could quietly bury and try to forget.

Please, no...

A memory of a childish, thoughtless mistake no one was ever to know about. A memory—or fragments of a memory, since she spent most of the evening in a muddled stupor—

Her stomach threatened to revolt again. Anna closed her eyes and willed the nausea to stop. Though she could only remember jumbled puzzle pieces of that night, she remembered enough.

Please...please...please...no!

Nausea rose in another wave. Anna scrambled to her feet but had nowhere to go, so she grabbed the stair railing and retched. Her empty, twisting stomach had nothing more to offer, the heaving only made her gag and gasp for air between spasms.

She steadied herself, then hurried inside her apartment before the neighbors came out to investigate. Rivka stood at the stove stirring porridge. Anna slipped past her and into the bedroom. She dressed quickly, said she needed to get to the factory early, and left.

People swarmed the avenue, all abuzz over the headlines about Roosevelt taking office, their chatter mingling with the cart noise and nauseating smells of food and sewer and trash, everyone going about as if life was grand and today was a bright new day. Anna avoided inhaling the smells and hurried along, crossing Broome Street without a glance and barely missing being run down by a milk truck.

After that wretched night last November, her new friend, Rosie, had never returned to the factory, and Anna had no way of finding her or her gang of friends. Not that she wanted to. She had no desire to ever again see or speak to the college boy who had been assigned her date that evening. All she could do at the time was accept the sting of admitting she had made a very foolish mistake, count it a painful lesson learned, and put the memory behind her.

Why had circumstances fallen into place just so that night? Why had she quarreled so fiercely with Mama? Why had she not simply shut her mouth and gone to bed instead of storming off to meet Rosie and her friends? Why had she been so determined to prove herself an adult? Why had she agreed to go to the speakeasy and drink and laugh too much and too loudly? Why had the flattery gone so quickly to her head? Why had the whiskey, pressed into her hand again and again, muddled her senses enough to let the handsome boy charm her into going "somewhere quiet" to "just kiss a little"? Why did she not disentangle herself before her fuzzy misgivings came too late, before he could no longer hear her slurred refusal, before his hands all over her became too strong?

She closed her eyes, but it did not shut out the tangled memories, could not shield her from the dreadful truth. The soot and stink in the air shouted her dirtiness. Sounds of machinery and whistles and clanging traffic echoed around her, taunting. Mocking.

So this is how you prove you are an adult. So intelligent you are, Channah. So superior.

Someone jostled Anna, bringing her back to the present. Factory workers scurried past. How long had she been standing in front of the brick building, eyes clamped shut like a child hiding beneath the floor, barely breathing, waiting for the nightmare to pass?

But she was not a child paralyzed by fear, and this nightmare would not soon pass. She could no longer count her stupid mistake as a lesson learned and simply move on. Her poor judgment came with consequences. She was not only dirty and spoilt; she was also carrying a child.

A stranger's child.

Monday morning, Anna scrambled to the washtub and lost what little her stomach held. Even with working sunup to sundown on Sunday, she had been unable to eat.

Rivka's voice came from behind her. "See, Mama? I told you she is sick."

The blood left her limbs. What would she say to her mother? There would be no pretending, no hiding the truth. Soon enough, her mother would see for herself.

Her mother insisted Anna stay home from work and see the doctor. Dreading what needed to be said, Anna crawled back into bed while her siblings prepared their lunches and left for the day.

When Mama came in, her face sagged as if she had already worked a full day. She heaved a weary sigh. "I will ask Mrs. Feldman to telephone the doctor."

"I do not need a doctor." Dread numbed her entire body.

"Rivka says you have been sick for weeks. Do you not think it is time to see a doctor?" Mama reached over and felt Anna's forehead.

If only it were a fever.

Anna drew a long, slow breath. "Mama, there is something I need to tell you."

"What is it?"

"Do you remember when I went to the theater last fall with that girl from the factory?"

"Oy, how could I forget? You said such terrible things and slammed the door and did not come home until nearly morning. And then you did not speak to your mother who worried herself sick over you."

Anna's throat seized. How could she ever say the words?

"So, what do you have to tell me?"

"I am so sorry, Mama," Anna whispered.

Mama stiffened. "What? What did you do?"

"We did not go to the theater after all. The girl and her friends took me instead to...a speakeasy. There was whiskey." *Far too much whiskey.* She forced herself to look at her mother, whose expression warred between apprehension and suspicion.

"And...?"

She swallowed hard. "There was a young man, my...date."

"So *this* is the kind of friends you keep now? *Men?*" She gasped. "Channah Tzipporah—what happened? Tell me!"

Tears blurred Anna's vision. Haltingly, she described the evening in the briefest detail possible.

Her mother's face blanched, then reddened. Her whole body shook. "This is what you are now? A *prostitute?* How many men?" Her voice turned shrill. "Are they Jewish? Where are these 'friends' now?"

"Rosie was the only one I knew. I never saw her or any of them again."

Mama's mouth formed an *O* as she stared at Anna. Her trembling hand rose and covered her mouth. "The illness..." Her voice dropped to a horrified hiss. "You are with child."

Anna closed her eyes. "I am so sorry, Mama, I did not know—"

Mama burst into sobs and fled the room. At the sound of her mother's fitful wailing, Anna wiped her eyes with hands that shook and sat on the edge of the bed. All she could do was wait for her mother to work through the thoughts and emotions assailing her.

When Mama returned, Anna held her breath. Swollen patches of pink encircled her mother's eyes.

"I did not mean for things to go so far, Mama. I never wanted—"

"Foolish girl! You are such a *grown woman* now, yes? Then you are old enough to know that you put yourself in that position."

"I know I should not have been there, but—"

"But what? What did you expect? A woman going off alone in such a way with a man—*this* is what happens. There are names for girls like you. You are no better than a prostitute!"

"But I did not—"

"And who will believe you are not? Not our friends or neighbors, certainly not strangers." Mama smeared away tears with both hands. "Do you understand what happens now? If you thought you were mistreated as a Jew before, what do you think will happen to you when people discover you are with child? An unmarried, pregnant woman faces shame and many difficulties. But an unmarried, pregnant *Jew?* You do not know what horrible treatment you will face. Not only banning and name-calling, but abuse of every kind. Or worse!"

"I—"

"And your family? You not only bring trouble and disgrace upon yourself, you bring a curse upon us all. Your sisters will be damaged because of you. What hope do they have for marriage now? They will share in your shame. They are ruined!"

"Rivka and Shayna will not—"

"Think what foolishness this will encourage in them. Wicked, thoughtless girl! Do you not see that your sisters look *always* to you? Follow your example in everything you do?"

Through her tears, Anna whispered, "My sisters would never do such a thing, I promise."

"I accept no promise from you. Your promises and conceited opinions are rubbish. You, with your disdain for your people and need to impress worthless goyim you do not even know. You have not only ruined your own life, but your whole family."

Anna choked on her sobs. Thankfully, her siblings were not hearing this.

Mama left her and paced the apartment, wailing and using a word for the unborn child that Anna had never heard her mother use. Then Mama crossed from the kitchen to her sewing table, sat down, and rocked herself as she sobbed.

Anna rose and went to her. "I am sorry, Mama."

Mama shook her head. "You were always so cynical, so skeptical. Always quarreling, never content. Why could you not be gentle and agreeable, like Shayna?"

A good question, one Anna had asked herself many times.

Mama lifted her blotchy face skyward. "Oy vez mear! What did I do to deserve this? Has our family not suffered enough, now we are to be ruined by such wretched disgrace? I must find a solution, yet I can speak of this to no one. What am I to do?"

"It is my mistake, my problem to solve," Anna whispered.

Her mother kept rocking as she wept and did not seem to hear her. "Your sisters and brother must never know of this. Never."

"Do not worry, Mama. I will tell no one."

"Oy, but I do worry, Channah." Mama's swollen, reddened eyes met hers. "Your life will never be the same now. Ever. And all for what—a night of carousing? And what is to become of your family? We will be completely destitute since you cannot work—not at the factory or anywhere else. Are you happy now?"

Anna ran to the bedroom and buried her sobs in a pillow.

Three

FOR DAYS, MAMA DID NOT SPEAK. NOT EVEN WHEN EVERYONE IN the neighborhood was in an uproar over the new President shutting down all the banks as his first order of business. Mama's silence, Anna could endure, but there were no comforting arms, no woman to ask questions, no one to help sort out her fears and the decisions she needed to make.

Was it possible to hide a pregnancy to full-term? Who would help her give birth when the time came? Would the state welfare people come to take the baby, or would they send the police to do it? Anna had heard stories of unwed girls whose illegitimate babies were seized by the authorities upon birth and placed in foundling homes and orphanages—or worse. She had heard ghastly tales of infants placed in trash cans and left to die. This, she could never, ever allow to happen, no matter what circumstances had brought the child into the world. The child must not suffer. Any suffering to be had was entirely Anna's to bear.

Shayna, clearly troubled by the obvious rift between mother and daughter, tried repeatedly to get Anna to tell her what was wrong, but Anna could say nothing. She could only allow Shayna to believe Anna was sick.

She *was* sick—heartsick. She had expected Mama to be disgusted and even angry about the situation. What she had not expected was for Mama to lay the entirety of blame on Anna. Was she so terribly wicked? Mama did not think she had simply made a mistake. Did she carry some deeply rooted flaw her siblings did not? *She* was the one who rebelled, the one who went to the speakeasy. The one who drank and stumbled off to who knows where with some young man whose name she could not even remember. Who did such things? Shayna would never do that. If only Anna had thought it over more...or would it have made a difference?

But surely Anna was not the only woman in history to allow a moment of anger to affect her judgment? Had her mother never made a hasty, reckless decision she later regretted? Perhaps. But it was not Tovah Leibowicz lying sleepless in the dark now, unmarried and pregnant, facing censure, scorn, humiliation, and all manner of difficulties. Mama would never have gotten into such a situation in the first place. Mama would not have chosen the path that Anna had. Mama had compared her to Shayna, calling Anna skeptical and discontent, and in this, she was right. Anna had never possessed Shayna's ability to simply go along with whatever circumstances befell her and trust without question that things would all work out. Anna questioned everything—traditions, persecution, injustice. The misfortunes God had allowed...

The truth was becoming painfully clear. Mama said Anna was wicked and a curse to her family. Perhaps the time had come for Anna to admit that her mother was right.

On Wednesday morning, Mama finally spoke.

She took a dishtowel and began drying the dishes that Anna had washed.

"I have found something," Mama said, her tone flat. "The Campbell Home for Mothers and Children has rooms, a midwife, and an adoption agency all in one place." She stacked the plates so hard, Anna feared they would shatter. "It was not easy to find without arousing suspicion. This could be our salvation. *If* they accept you."

Our. Tears stung Anna's eyes. Mama was not leaving Anna to work this out alone.

"It is in north Manhattan. You will visit tomorrow and sign the papers."

Anna let out a slow breath and felt a glimmer of hope for the first time in days. "How much does it cost?"

Mama shoved the plates in the cupboard. "Girls do not pay if they cannot, but all are expected to work while they stay there. Everything is handled at the home. You go in before you are showing, give birth, then leave quietly. The infant is adopted by a good family who cannot have children. No one will ever know."

This was not entirely true—*Anna* would know. But what choice did she have? As Mama had pointed out, an unwed pregnant girl would face difficulty and shame at best, but an unwed, pregnant Jew? Her mother's plan was clearly the only option, and the best Anna could hope for.

But to say no one would ever know? For the rest of her life, Anna's heart would bear a permanent scar, a reminder that, for a few brief months, the life of a tiny person had been intimately and uniquely interwoven with hers.

Thursday morning, after her siblings left, Anna walked to the South Ferry, took a trolley north, and, several transfers later, reached the Campbell Home. She had not eaten that morning as she dared not take a chance on getting ill on the journey, and now her strength was sapped. She forced her wobbly legs to follow a nurse to the director's office, where she was left to wait for over an hour.

When Miss Campbell finally arrived, the middle-aged woman looked Anna up and down, made her turn around a few times, then scrutinized her face and features. "Yes," she said, finally. The discussion was brief, the information exactly as Mama had said. A date was set for Anna to be admitted the following Monday.

Relieved, Anna let out a pent-up breath. She had been accepted without question. In a few months, this would all be over, and she would be able to put the entire episode behind her.

Most of it, anyway.

Mama had said her life would never be the same, and Anna did not doubt this, even though public knowledge of her sin might now be prevented. In less than a year, she could return to her normal life. Outwardly, she would appear relatively unchanged. But inwardly, a stain would remain, invisible to all but herself and her mother. She knew this because she already felt as if she carried a permanent mark.

Anna asked Miss Campbell if she could see the facility, but the woman told Anna it was not open to visitors. The director had a pressing matter to attend to, so she placed a pen in front of Anna and told her to answer the questions and sign the release of rights before she returned.

As Anna filled out the form, some of the questions seemed strange. There was a lengthy list of detailed questions about ethnicity, social and economic background, the mother and father's lineage, eye and hair color-ing, known or suspected deformities or other defects, if the mother prone to promiscuity, and other intrusive questions.

One set seemed particularly odd, directed toward blonde, blue-eyed mothers. It asked for ages and detailed descriptions of all previous children born to these mothers. Where her other children lived. Of those mothers, the form required to sign over all rights not only to the current infant in question, but also all future children as property of the Campbell Home.

The hairs on the back of Anna's neck prickled. Something was not right.

Mama was confident in the orderly way the institution operated, in how tidy and uncomplicated it all was. Go in, deliver, and go out. Slick as a whistle.

A gasping, snuffling sound drew Anna's attention to the hallway just beyond the office, where a blonde-haired girl sat on a bench. She appeared to be crying.

Anna slipped out. No one was around, so she approached the girl, who could not have been much older than Shayna. The girl did not speak at first, but then, she looked around as if to make sure no one was listening.

"I brought my baby to this place for medical treatment, as I heard this is a safe, discreet place for single mothers to seek help. But a few hours later, they told me my baby girl was..." She broke out bawling and covered her mouth. "They said she died...and they buried her in private to spare me undue sadness. Without telling me! And with no chance to say goodbye!"

Anna gasped. "I am so sorry."

The girl's face twisted as she cried and fought to keep from making sounds. "I don't know what happened, she wasn't that sick."

Anna tried to console her, but the girl quickly excused herself. Her sto-ry not only made no sense, it added to the unnerving sensation Anna felt.

Cautiously, she explored a little more. After a few turns down dark, narrow corridors that all looked the same, she heard an awful sound. As she got closer, the sound became unmistakable. It was the sound of wailing infants. Not just one or two, but many.

Anna wanted to go no further, but she had to. She followed the dis-turbing sound until she reached a closed door. The anguished cries coming from inside tore at her. With hands that shook, she tried the handle, but the door was locked.

Was someone inside trying to comfort the babies? Or on their way to do so, perhaps?

A few feet away, a window revealed nothing but a sliver of darkness visible around an inner curtain. A dark chamber full of infants, choking on their unanswered cries.

She had never heard anything so disturbing. Anna turned and worked her way back the way she'd come until she saw a very expectant-looking young woman.

"Pardon me," Anna said, stopping her, "are you a patient here?"

"Yes," the woman said, "but not much longer." She winced, as if in pain.

Anna swallowed the dread in her throat. "Why are there babies crying in a room with a locked door?"

"I got to keep moving, I need to get this over with," she whispered.

"Can you please tell me?" Anna urged gently.

The woman shook her head and looked away. "You don't want to know."

"What do you mean?"

"Never mind. I have to go. I'm not packed, and she's fit to be tied."

Anna glanced over her shoulder, as if just speaking of the director might produce her. "How long have you been here?"

"Three months. I didn't want to come, but I got kicked out of my apartment when I couldn't hide it anymore."

"I am sorry," Anna said. She chose her words carefully. "But at least here, you know your baby will be adopted by a good family who cannot have children."

The other girl scoffed. "That's what they tell people."

"It is not true?"

She looked around. "Did you see Miss Campbell's jewelry? And her new car?"

Anna frowned. "The director is wealthy?"

The woman lowered her voice to a whisper. "She doesn't give a hoot about how nice the families are, as long as they're willing to pay. And I hear some babies go for top dollar, or even more, if she can get them bidding against each other—"

Miss Campbell appeared suddenly. "Susan!" She frowned at the two of them together. "What are you doing out of your room? Are you packed?"

"I'm almost finished," Susan said. Leaning closer, she looked Anna in

32

the eye and whispered, "Just keep your eyes open. Things here aren't what they seem."

The director slipped between them, grasped Susan's arm, then turned to Anna. "Go to my office. I'll be back for your paperwork." She took Susan by the elbow and escorted her away.

Anna's heart thumped as they disappeared around a corner. What did Susan mean about top dollar, and what was she not wanting to say about the babies in the locked room? The director would return soon for Anna's signed papers. Anna had no idea what she was going to do, but one thing she did know: she would not be checking into this facility, and she would not be placing herself or the unborn child into the hands of Miss Campbell.

She made her way back to the lobby. Near the front door, Anna saw a nurse speaking to the blonde-haired girl in hushed tones, but the girl's tearful voice continued to rise.

"No, I don't understand—she wasn't *that* sick."

The nurse glanced at Anna, then addressed the distraught girl. "You need to leave now. If you don't go quietly, you'll be escorted out."

Sobbing, the girl looked at Anna. There was something awful in her eyes, something deeper than defeat.

It was horror.

A terrible chill traveled down Anna's spine, and it was all she could do to keep from running out the door. Without another word, Anna hurried out and did not slow her pace until the Campbell Home was far behind her.

When Anna arrived at home, Mama wiped flour from her hands and faced her.

"Well? Did they accept you?"

Mama looked more hopeful than she had in days. Anna's heart sank. With a deep breath, she braced herself. "Mama, I know it seemed like a good solution, but there is something terribly wrong with that place. One girl was crying. She was very distraught."

"So there are unhappy girls there?" Mama scoffed. "Facing the consequences of one's mistakes is never pleasant."

"Another girl told me that Miss Campbell is not what she appears. I do not trust her."

Mama heaved an exasperated sigh. "Now you want a fairy tale? You should have thought of that before you got yourself into trouble. You will find no better solution than this." She folded her arms across her bosom and peered directly into Anna's eyes. "Tomorrow, you will pack a bag and check into the Campbell Home and stay until it is all over. I will tell everyone that you have gone to work in the Catskills for the summer."

Anna let her mother's words sink in. "You will lie?"

"What would you have me do—ruin your sisters' futures with the truth?"

Panic rose, along with her pulse. "Mama, I have a very bad feeling about that place. I heard babies crying in a dark, locked room. I am afraid something terrible is happening there."

Her mother shook her head. "See? Everything with you is to be debated, nothing is acceptable. There is nothing sinister about a dark nursery. Babies have to be trained to sleep. You *will* go. And you will leave tomorrow."

"But...could I not stay home and work a little while longer? I am not yet showing. Perhaps by that time, I will find another home. A better one."

"And still you choose your own foolish judgment over your mother's? No. I know what is best, Channah."

"But Mama, you did not hear what I heard. And those girls there, they told me—"

"I have decided." Mama's chin jutted higher. "You *will* go to the Campbell Home, or you will have no home with me."

Anna gasped. "You cannot mean that."

"We will discuss it no more." Mama turned her back to Anna and returned to her dough.

That evening, Anna went through the motions of preparing a tasteless stew, taking in little of what was said during the meal. She did not eat. She could not.

Shayna tried to get Anna to tell her what was wrong, and each time, Anna looked to her mother. How could Mama give Anna such an ultimatum? Why was Mama so unwilling to listen to Anna's observation of the place? Was she so ashamed of Anna that she did not care what happened to her and to the child?

Yes. This much was clear.

Long into the night, well after her siblings' breathing had turned to soft snores, Anna's mind continued to circle. Mama insisted that Anna pack and leave after everyone had left in the morning. Clearly, she wanted Anna out of the house and away from the family as soon as possible. She probably feared Anna's presence was drawing her wretched curse closer to the family with every minute she remained. Perhaps not so irrational a fear.

The haunting sound of babies crying and the face of the blonde girl pleading for answers kept Anna tossing throughout the night. She woke exhausted and with no solution. The more she thought about it, the more certain she was that she could never place a child into the hands of that director. And yet Mama had given her no choice. If she did not go to Campbell Home, Anna would be turned out. She would be denied the love of her family and forced to face the unknown alone. Where would she live? How would she survive? How would she manage outside her community pregnant and unmarried? How would she earn money to live?

She dressed quickly and went to the factory to collect her wages. The steady rain added to the weight of questions pressing on her, but one thing was very clear: she could not go back to that place, which meant she was no longer welcome in her mother's home. Where could she go? She knew no one outside of this neighborhood and had no other family in America, none besides—

Papa.

Were the rumors about him living in Chicago true? And what were the chances that Anna could find him? Less than slim, but what other choice did she have? At least it was a direction to head, something to try. Something was better than nothing.

What if she found him, but he turned her away too? After all, how could a man who had abandoned his entire family somehow welcome an unwed daughter in trouble?

This was a bridge she would have to cross when she came to it; she had too many other concerns now. Besides, her father may not have provided for his family, but he was not a heartless man. Perhaps he would have the decency to recognize his failure toward his family and help the daughter who had in many ways stepped in to fill his shoes. And if by some miracle she could find him and bring him home, the family could be whole again, and Anna might have a chance at being restored.

But whether or not she found her father in Chicago, she would first have to find a safe place to stay and give birth, and then, somehow, a good home for the child.

Chicago. It may as well have been Antarctica.

She clutched the money in her pocket as she walked. By the time she returned home, her siblings were gone, the apartment was quiet, and Mama was nowhere in sight.

Anna counted out her wages, kept out a few coins for her tin, and left the rest in the sugar bowl. The rent would soon be due, and in Anna's absence, Shayna would be forced to take up the wage-earning mantle that Anna had long carried. What would the weight of it do to such a tenderhearted girl? Would she have to forget about her beloved Isaak? What would become of Rivka? What of Anshel's studies?

Would her mother ever regret giving Anna such an ultimatum?

As she looked around the cramped apartment she shared with her family, tears spilled down her cheeks. But crying would get her nowhere. Wiping her face, she took a flour sack from the rag bag and stuffed her second brown gown and some undergarments into the bottom. The trip from New York to Illinois would take a couple of weeks, depending on her luck. She would have to camp along the road wherever she could find shelter.

She made a bedroll from a pillow and two blankets and tied it with string. She packed a tin cup, knife and spoon, matches, salt, a handful of carrots, and a half dozen potatoes. She added her sewing kit and extra spools of thread in hopes of earning mending money, then hunted through Anshel's things until she found his map of the United States and put that in her sack, silently asking his forgiveness. She counted the money in her tin: twenty-eight dollars and seventy-five cents. For more than two years, she had saved a quarter per week for college. How ironic that the money for her education would now be paying for a lesson she had never planned on needing to learn.

Spying a journal in the bureau, Anna took out a blank page and wrote a note for Mama saying that she would not be going to the place they had discussed—on the unlikely chance that her mother might try to visit her there. She placed the note in the sugar bowl with the rent money, then packed the journal and pencil in her bag so she could write to Shayna.

Shayna...

Anna's heart clenched. She took out the journal and tore out another page.

My Love,

By the time you get this, you will have heard that I am gone. I do not know exactly when, but I will see you again one day. Perhaps, if I am successful, I will learn what became of Papa, and if I am very successful, I will return with him.

Please do not despair but take each day one at a time and make the best of it. Marry that smart, quiet boy you love. And no matter what setbacks you face, get back up on your feet and keep going. You are a far better person than I can ever hope to be, and I have enormous faith in you. Make me proud.

I will write to you whenever I can. Remember you are forever in my heart and I love you more than life.

A.

Wiping her cheeks again, Anna tucked the note beneath Shayna's pillow. She hunted for her wool shawl and put it on, then slung her bedroll and sack over her shoulder. She took a lingering glance at the silent apartment and then stepped out the door.

Four

IGNORING THE RAIN, ANNA WAITED NEAR THE ENTRANCE TO the Holland Tunnel, dripping like a leaky faucet. One important piece of information that her little brother's map did *not* tell her was that pedestrians were not allowed to cross the tunnel on foot, so the only way she could cross into New Jersey was to hitch a ride. For some reason, on the wettest tenth of March she had ever seen, no one would stop. She must have looked like a drowned hobo standing at the curb with a knapsack over her shoulder and a thumb pointed west. Unfortunately, no one knew that the most dangerous thing Anna Leibowicz could do was vomit on the floorboard of their car.

Her only obstacle so far had been the "No Jews" and the "Gentiles Only" signs on the buses she had tried to board. Such things did not exist in her own neighborhood. If she had to, she would walk all the way to Chicago. But the journey was roughly six-hundred and sixty miles, and she still had six-hundred and fifty-eight to go. And only then would the search for her father begin. She would need to find work and a safe, temporary place to stay—a cheap boarding house, if she was lucky.

She was going to need all the luck she could get.

A car approaching the tunnel entrance slowed, and a hand waved her closer. Anna hurried to it, told the woman in the passenger seat that she was headed west, and then climbed into the back between two boys. The Clark family was headed to Pennsylvania to live with relatives and could take her as far as Harrisburg.

"Thank you for the lift," she said, trying to keep her dripping hair and soaked shawl from touching the boys seated on either side of her. After a half-minute of being stared at, Anna engaged the brothers in conversation and learned that Andrew was ten and Clive was twelve.

When the car stopped to pay the bridge toll, Mrs. Clark turned to Anna and said, "You don't mind splitting the toll, do you? Since you're getting a free ride and all."

"Of course not," Anna said. "How much is my share?"

"Half the toll is twenty-five cents," Mr. Clark said.

"Half?"

The man frowned at her in the rearview mirror.

Surely it was not fair for one person to pay half the toll for a carload of five?

"It's a small price to pay," Mrs. Clark said. "All things considered."

"What things?" Anna asked.

"Do you have any idea how dangerous it is out there for a young woman like you on the road, all alone? We're protecting you from God knows what."

Anna had not thought of that. And it was a free ride, so it would be best not to complain. She drew a quarter from her tin and gave it to the driver.

Andrew leaned close and peeked into her sack. "What else you got in there?"

"Just my traveling things," Anna said.

"You talk funny," Clive said.

Anna quirked a brow at him. "But you are not laughing."

"Not that kind of funny, but funny weird. Where you from?"

"Manhattan. Where are you from?"

"Queens. I meant you got a funny accent."

"You a foreigner?" Mr. Clark said over his shoulder.

Anna glanced at the boys. "My family is...from Poland."

In the mirror, the man's narrowed gaze met hers. "Are you a Jew?"

Her palms broke into a sweat. "Will my answer make any difference in your giving me a ride?"

Mrs. Clark laid a hand on her husband's arm. "Of course not. Right, dear?"

He glared over his shoulder at Anna, then at his wife.

"My family is Polish," she said quietly. It was not wise to give strangers needless information. Besides, her shoes would last longer the less she had to walk.

That evening, the Clarks and Anna camped alongside the road some-where in Pennsylvania. The family prepared their supper over a campfire and though Mrs. Clark was polite, neither she nor her family offered any to Anna. Odd, because no matter how hard times had been, Anna had always known her Jewish neighbors to share what they had. People looked out for one another. It had been the way of life for as long as she could remember. Not so outside her neighborhood, it seemed.

Anna crunched on a carrot, then tucked her blanket around her in the back seat and slept against the window.

In the morning, as the family shared breakfast around a small fire, Mrs. Clark came to Anna and offered her a flat biscuit with a smear of jam. For the first time in weeks, the thought of food first thing in the morning did not turn her stomach. The food was probably not Kosher, but Anna would not get far in her journey if she followed all the regulations of kashrut.

"Anna," Mrs. Clark said with a brief glance over her shoulder at her husband. "I'm afraid this is where we have to part company. You'll need to go on your own from here. You see, we...just don't have the room."

Anna paused, biscuit halfway to her mouth. "I wonder what would make a young woman traveling all alone suddenly take up more room?" She looked Mrs. Clark in the eye, but the woman would not hold her gaze.

"I'm sorry." She glanced over her shoulder at her husband. "Russell doesn't...well, he just doesn't trust...certain kinds of folks."

"Certain kinds meaning Jews?" She knew she should not say it but could not hold back.

"I'm sure it's nothing personal," Mrs. Clark said quietly.

Anna's cheeks burned. *Of course it is nothing personal,* Anna wanted to say. *He knows nothing about me but hates me enough to turn me out into the unknown. What could possibly be personal about that?*

With a sigh, she gathered her bag and her bedroll. She flung her things over her shoulder and started down the road. Her breath came out in puffs, the morning chill already numbing her legs and feet. She wrapped her shawl more tightly around her and trudged on.

After about a quarter mile, Anna stopped at a road sign and checked her map to be sure she was still headed west. As she studied the map, the Clarks' Ford passed her without slowing. She held out a thumb for each car that passed by, but it wasn't until late afternoon that she got another ride. She got as far as the junction in Woodville before her ride let her off and turned south. Night was coming, bringing with it the chill that came on as soon as the sun set.

Feeling shaky from her cold feet and even more from her gnawing belly, Anna sang as she walked. A half an hour later, she saw a diner on the outskirts of a small town. An OPEN sign hung in the window. She went inside and sat at the counter, ordered chicken soup with soda crackers and hot tea, and then used the facilities. When she returned to her seat, the waitress came over.

"Management wants to be sure you got money. We get a lot of drifters in here who eat and don't pay, and then we're out the check. You understand, don't you?"

"Yes, of course." Anna had taken a critical look at herself in the washroom mirror and was not surprised the woman thought she was a drifter. After all, she was.

She reached into her bag for her tin, felt around, then looked inside. She dug carefully, then dumped out a few of her belongings and searched frantically. Her tin of quarters was gone.

"No! Those boys must have stolen my money."

The waitress clucked her tongue. "Yeah. I guess Jimmy knows how to call 'em."

"I *do* have money. But when I took out my tin to pay the bridge toll, one of those boys must have seen it and taken it from my bag while I slept."

"Sure, they did." The woman did not look convinced.

Anna swallowed hard. "Might I please work in exchange for a cup of soup? I am very hungry."

"I'm afraid the boss don't—"

"I am...expecting." Too late, she realized her mistake. Her cheeks burned as soon as the words left her lips. "I have eaten very little, and I am feeling weak."

The waitress looked her over, then studied her ringless hand. She shook her head. "Ah. The dirty rat ran out on you, did he?"

It took a moment for Anna to understand what the woman was implying. "I am all alone." She swallowed hard. Those four words struck her heart like a truckload of bricks.

The woman heaved a sigh. "You can do the dishes after you eat. Step on it though, we're closing soon."

"Thank you," Anna said, trying to mask the sudden tightening in her throat. Neighborly care was a gift she would never again take for granted.

Over the next several days, Anna aimed west, walking and hitching rides every moment of daylight she could and camping either with those who were giving her a lift, or in the woods along the way. The green pasturelands and trickling creeks bordering the Pennsylvania roads were such a stark contrast to the grimy, trash-strewn streets back home. She had never seen such crystalline water nor tasted anything so refreshing. A few of the travelers who gave her a lift shared a little food with her when they had any to spare. Some were glad to help a fellow traveler, as many were relocating to stay with relatives due to the lack of work. Many had lost not only jobs in the lean years following the Crash, but also their homes.

One week on the road stretched into two. The road turned south to Greensburg, then took her west to Pittsburg, Cleveland, and then Toledo. Anshel's map was becoming soft from repeated unfolding and folding.

She was more than halfway to Chicago—a relief to her feet, now raw with blisters. Just as she mentally prepared herself for another day of possibly making all her progress on foot, a pickup stopped and offered a lift. Grateful for a truck bed with a layer of loose straw and the blessing of a sunny break from the clouds, Anna quickly dozed off, finally warm enough for the first time in weeks.

She awoke from a deep sleep only because her ride stopped to let her off—in the dark. Night had fallen. It took her some minutes to get her bearings. The pickup driver had said she was on the Zanesville road. She checked the map but didn't find a road by that name, so she walked on in hopes of finding a route sign. She waved down a Ford coupe passing the other direction and asked the driver if she was on the road to Chicago.

"No, ma'am, you're headed south. The road you're talking about is a hundred miles north," he said, pointing in the direction she had come. "But if you keep going, there's a junction that will get you going west again, and from there you should be able to get on the Indiana Falls highway. That'll point you toward Chicago."

"*Indiana?*" Anna said. "I thought I was in Ohio."

"No, ma'am."

Sleeping away the entire day in the back of that pickup had gotten Anna far off course. She thanked the man and continued on. Not finding a junction, she bundled herself in her blanket under the canopy of some trees for the night, too cold to do more than doze for a few minutes at a time, then set out again in the morning.

As she walked, she tried to remember when she had eaten last. The soda crackers from the diner had run out long ago. Why had she not packed more food? A handful of vegetables for two weeks was not the best plan. But then, neither was losing twenty-eight dollars to a young pickpocket. And of course, going out with Rosie and her friends had not turned out to be such a great plan, either.

Out of food and seeing no town where she might earn a meal, she resorted to eating dandelions. She pressed on, and after a while, heard water. Crossing a railroad track, she headed to the creek for a drink. Train tracks could be useful for many things, including a sure route to train stations and towns. She followed the tracks along the creek. If only she knew how to make a fishing pole. As she walked, she scoured the grass beside the tracks for anything edible or of value she could trade for food.

Cold nights, soaking rains, and limited food had taken a toll on Anna's strength. Though she needed to reach Chicago, right now, she needed food and warmth even more. She collected more dandelion leaves and flowers, even though by this time, she was sick of the taste and had to fight the urge to vomit. But perhaps a tea from the flowers might at least warm her.

She collected some rocks, found a stump on which to sit, made a fire pit, then hunted for twigs, dried grass, and bark. Once she got a small fire going, she filled her tin cup with creek water and then set it at the edge of the fire.

A rustle in the trees sounded odd, unnatural. She glanced over her shoulder. A slight movement in the woods startled her. A wild animal? Hobos?

Whispers followed.

She pushed her tin cup directly into the flame. Hot water would make a useful weapon, if needed.

The whispers sounded closer. Anna looked again. Three boys emerged slowly from the woods, one toting a fishing pole. She relaxed. They looked to be about Anshel's age, filling her with a crushing ache for home.

"When spying on someone," she said lightly, "it is usually polite to introduce yourself."

The boys shuffled closer. A smaller, shaggy-haired blond appraised her tiny fire while the other two studied her. They smelled of sweat and earth and ferns.

The blond one looked her in the eye. "I'm Albert." He pointed to the two dark-haired boys. "This here's Jack, and that's Pete. I ain't never seen a girl hobo before."

"I am pleased to meet you, Albert, Jack, and Pete. I am Anna." She stirred the water in her cup. "I am not a hobo. Hobos beg for food, but as you can see, I am making my own."

All three boys leaned closer and peered into her tin.

Pete snorted. "Shoot, that ain't nothin' but water."

On closer inspection, Anna spied a fat trout tied to Jack's fishing pole. She licked her lips. Stomach twisting at the thought of a fish supper, she formed an idea. "Actually, this is...Creek Stew," she said slowly. "It is a very old recipe. A favorite of sultans and tsars, in fact."

Pete snorted again, and the other two eyed her, clearly doubtful.

"I am happy to share, but there is one very important rule about Creek Stew. Only those who contribute something to it may eat it." Anna sprinkled in a little salt, stirred the water with her spoon, then took a taste. "Of course," she said slowly, "if we are to share, we will need a bigger pot and spoon."

Jack shrugged. "I can get 'em, but it still ain't nothin' but crick water."

"It will be good, trust me. Would you bring the pot, please?"

He set down his pole, and as he headed into the woods, Anna turned to Albert. "Do you think you can find a potato?"

"Sure." The boy grinned and ran off.

Pete crossed his arms. "This ain't gonna be good."

"You will see," Anna said. She took the knife from her sack.

Jack returned and set a pot of water on the ring of stones she had placed around the fire. Albert came back with three potatoes. Anna peeled and diced two of them into the pot. She stirred it with the wooden spoon Jack had provided, then sampled it. It was thoroughly tasteless. She smiled. "This is good," she lied. "But it would be even better with an onion. Do any of you have one?"

Frowning, the boys shook their heads, then Albert brightened and said, "The Tuckers have a root cellar. Bet they'd give us one."

"A good neighbor barters rather than asking for a handout," Anna said. "Albert, would you take this potato and ask Mrs. Tucker if she will trade it for an onion?"

Albert took it and ran along the tracks for several yards, then disappeared into the woods.

Pete sniffed the pot, then leaned closer with a narrowed a gaze at Anna. "I think you're pullin' our legs."

Anna shrugged. "The proof will be in the pot." She stirred it slowly. Anshel could start with nothing but charm and barter until he had a feast. "If only we had a carrot, or something we could trade for one."

Jack pulled out the linings of his pockets, producing a tiny shower of dirt.

Anna looked to the creek and sighed. "If only we could catch a fish."

"I got one." Jack gasped and grabbed his fishing pole. "Right here!"

"Jack, that is perfect," Anna said. "If you do not mind sharing."

As Jack went to clean his fish in the creek, Anna added bits of wood to the fire and repositioned the pot over the flames. Albert returned, out of breath and grinning. He handed Anna an onion. "Miz Tucker looked at me real funny when I said it was for Crick Stew, but she just smiled and gave me this onion."

Anna diced the onion into the pot, producing a growl from her stomach that could have chased away a herd of elephants.

Pete frowned. "I still got nothin'." He turned to Albert. "You got anything I could trade?"

Albert turned his pockets inside out. A tiny scrap of paper fell to the ground. He picked it up. "I found this in town the other day." He showed it to Pete.

Pete scoffed. "Three-cent stamp? You can't buy nothin' with that."

"You never know," Anna said. "It might be worth a carrot or two."

After Pete left, Jack presented his prized catch, now cleaned and headless. She added it, stirred the pot for several minutes, then tasted it. The broth bubbled, and the ingredients had now melded, putting off a savory scent.

"This is coming along nicely." She scooted closer to the fire, craving warmth almost as much as food. Her stomach bellowed. Surely the boys could hear that.

Albert sat cross-legged in the grass beside the fire, and Jack joined him.

"You are all brothers?" Anna asked, still stirring.

"No, ma'am," Albert said. "But we all live together. There's six of us, plus Mr. Tom."

"Six?" Anna looked around. "Where do you live?"

"Just over there, through them trees," Jack said, pointing beyond them. "It used to be a farm and workshop, but now it's a trade school."

Pete returned with three carrots and a broad grin.

"Well done, Pete." Anna quickly pared the carrots into small pieces. "And what trade do you study there?"

"Carpentry," Albert said. "We build things, fix furniture, stuff like that. We just made some radio cases."

"Do girls attend this school?"

Jack spluttered. "Heck, no."

"Girls can't be carpenters," Albert added.

Adding salt to the pot, Anna said, "Why not?"

Jack shrugged. "They just can't. Everyone knows that."

She stirred the soup. "What about doctors, lawyers, judges, and airplane pilots? Have you not heard of Amelia Earhart?" Anna scooped a small sample into her tin and blew on it.

"She's all right, I guess. But woodworking's a man's job."

Quirking a brow, Anna took a sip. Savory warmth radiated through her, sending a tingle down her spine.

"How is it?" Pete said, nodding at the cup.

She blew on it again and then quickly finished the entire contents of the cup. "See for yourself." She filled the cup and passed it to Jack, who tasted it and then handed it to Albert. Each boy took a taste and passed it on.

"It ain't bad," Pete said with a shrug. He handed back the cup. "Better'n regular stew."

"I am curious," Anna said as she refilled the tin again. "Why are you boys not in school on a school day?" She took three long swallows before passing the cup.

Albert glanced at the others, then turned to Anna. "Well, see, it's like this. The Sisters of Mercy School burnt down a couple weeks ago, so Mr.

Tom sent us to the public school, but that teacher told Sam he couldn't come. The ol' heifer."

"She stunk somethin' awful." Jack grimaced. "Like bootleg and dead possum, mostly."

Albert nodded. "So we all voted to ditch school till the sisters get theirs rebuilt. Us fellas all stick together." He lowered his voice. "We've been hidin' out at our fort every day."

Pete elbowed him. "Shouldn't have told her that, idiot. What if she's a truant officer?"

"I promise I am *not* a truant officer." She reached for the empty cup and refilled it. "But who is Sam?" She took another drink, her shaky insides finally beginning to calm.

"Sam Lewis. He lives with us," Jack said. "He don't talk."

She frowned. "A boy is not allowed to attend school because he does not speak?"

"No, he ain't allowed because that school don't let coloreds in." Albert reached for the cup. "Sam's mama couldn't keep him anymore, so she gave him to Mr. Tom. His daddy's white."

"You don't know that," Pete said.

"*Everybody* knows that," Albert said, tipping the cup with a loud slurp. He passed it back to Anna. "If Sam can't go to school, then neither will we. All for one and one for all. And no truant officer can catch us."

"True," a deep male voice said, "but he *can* turn you over to Sheriff Dooley, who can send you all to the orphanage."

Anna nearly dropped her cup as a grim-faced, white-haired old man in overalls emerged from the grove of trees.

Five

ANNA STILLED.

The man approached the campfire, followed by three more boys around the same age. On closer look, he was not old at all, perhaps in his late twenties or thirty at most. His light brown hair was coated with a film of white dust. His mustache did not conceal the stern set of his lips.

He frowned into the soup pot. "I hope these boys haven't exhausted your...generosity, miss." A pair of golden-brown eyes met hers. "I'm Thomas Chandler. And your junior chefs here are my apprentices."

Heat scalded her cheeks. How much of her meal-making scheme had he seen? "I am Anna," she said, hoping a first name was enough.

The three new boys inspected the soup, including a slender Negro boy that Anna guessed was Sam. He glanced over Anna's sack and bedroll, but when he saw her watching him, he quickly looked away.

"You fellas have put me in a real jam," Thomas said, his expression grave. "I just found out you've all been playing hooky."

In silence, six boys glanced at one another or the ground.

"Anyone want to tell me why?"

Albert glanced around at the others. "They won't let Sam go to their stupid school. We had to stick up for him."

"And if he can't go, we ain't going," Jack said, frowning.

"That's right," Pete said. "All for one and one for all."

Sam kept his head down but cast a furtive glance at each person as they spoke.

"We want to go back to the Mercy School," one of the new boys said. The others added their agreement.

"I'm sorry, but even if the sisters can rebuild, it won't be ready until next fall." Thomas heaved a sigh. "You still have eight weeks left to finish out this school year."

One boy shrugged. "We'll just ditch till summer."

Thomas shook his head. "That won't do, Jimmy. You boys have missed three weeks as it is. That's already costing me a fine I can't afford."

Silence. The two bigger boys cast a sheepish glance at each other.

"How'd you find out?" Albert asked.

"Sheriff Dooley just paid me a visit. Seems someone turned you in."

"Who snitched?" Pete said. "Bet it was that hag, Penny Withers. I caught her starin' at me yesterday."

Sam glanced over his shoulder, toward the creek.

"Doesn't matter," Thomas said, his look grave. "I wish you would've told me. Playing hooky is not the solution. Not only is it dishonest, but now you're all about to be turned over to the state orphan asylum."

"They can't take us," Pete said. "We didn't do nothin' wrong."

Thomas inhaled deeply as if drawing fresh patience, then turned to Anna. "Sorry, ma'am. I'm sure you don't want to hear about our troubles. Thanks for teaching the boys a valuable lesson on sharing. I saw the pot and spoon heading off through the woods, so I decided to investigate." He leaned down and gave the pot a few slow stirs. "These boys are clever, but I think they've just been outfoxed."

Anna said nothing. She was not sure how Thomas felt about her gaining a much-needed meal from the *lesson*.

"You oughta try the stew, Mr. Tom," Pete said. "It's real good."

"I'm sure it is," he said, studying Anna. "Are you and your family new here? I don't think I've seen you around town."

"I am on my way to Chicago. I only stopped here to rest."

Thomas frowned. "By yourself? Aren't you awfully young to be traveling alone?"

She lifted her chin. "I am twenty."

"Oh, sorry, I didn't mean to pry." He turned to the boys. The three new ones were now passing around the soup cup. "Let's go, fellas. We need to figure out a way to keep the authorities from taking you. We'll start by getting you back in school."

"We ain't going without Sam," a new, taller boy said. He looked to the others, who nodded.

Thomas sighed. "I'll talk to the teacher, Teddy, but there's not much I can do about it. I'll just have to find an alternative for Sam."

Sam glanced at Albert, his shoulders drooping.

Anna's mind raced. "I understand you operate a trade school. Does that not qualify?"

The man shook his head. "I don't teach academics, just carpentry and work skills after school. Or...after playing hooky, apparently." He leveled a stern look at the boys.

Her pulse sped. She could help them while earning food and shelter for herself. "What subjects are needed for them to catch up and finish the school year?" When Thomas listed the basics, Anna could not believe her good fortune. "I have tutored students in those subjects in order to pass several grades," Anna said. "I am willing to teach in exchange for room and board."

Thomas stroked his mustache, a hopeful spark mingling with the doubt in his eyes. "You can teach all six boys?"

She nodded, stifling her eagerness.

"What about Chicago?"

"I can delay my journey for a few weeks," Anna said. There was still plenty of time before her condition would be evident, and fortunately, her gowns were Mama's hand-me-downs, in the full-skirted, old world style. She could get the boys caught up and leave this place well before the pregnancy showed. She drew a deep breath. "You need a temporary teacher, and I need temporary food and shelter."

Sam's head was bowed again, but he seemed to be listening intently.

"Sounds like a swell deal to me," Albert said, grinning.

Thomas grunted. "I'm sure it does. What boy wouldn't like the idea of staying out of school?"

Albert frowned. "I meant I like the idea of Sam being able to go to school like the rest of us if he wants to."

The other boys murmured in agreement. The man shook his head, but his mouth held the hint of a smile. "Can't argue with that."

Sam stood rigid, as if holding his breath.

"It would sure help me out of a jam." Thomas stroked his mustache again as he looked at each of the boys, then turned to Anna. "I'm not in the habit of hiring strangers camped along the creek, but if that soup scheme of yours was any indication of your teaching skills, I guess I can make an exception."

"I will work very hard," Anna said. She glanced at the boys. "That is, *we* will work very hard."

Pete groaned.

"I have to warn you, they're a spirited bunch," Thomas said.

She could not help but smile at the warning. She had endured troubles far more daunting than six grimy boys. "Spirit does not frighten me. It can be a useful teaching tool. I accept."

Thomas studied her for a moment, the crease in his brow deepening. "There's a bedroom upstairs you can use. I'll move out to the workshop."

"Thank you." She looked over her new pupils. What good luck! And even if only temporary, a bed sounded magnificent after sleeping in slimy ditches. Anna could put aside her worries about the future for a few weeks. She could stay long enough to rest and gather food for her journey. Perhaps she could also earn a little mending money for herself and to send home to Shayna, since she was the one Mama depended on now.

A weather-beaten farmhouse emerged in the clearing just beyond the grove of trees, a strangely welcome sight. A few yards to the right was a workshop with a sign above it that read JOHANSEN WOODWORKS, and beyond that, a dirt road. Between the two buildings, a sagging wire fence encircled a forgotten garden full of weeds, and beyond that were the remnants of a chicken coop, collapsed in places and quite vacant.

A neglected garden and chicken coop would need to be remedied, and soon.

The boys led her up two steps onto the porch and then into the house. Anna caught a glimpse of a farm radio in the parlor to her left as they showed her around the main floor, then she and the boys followed Thomas upstairs to the bedrooms.

"This is where the boys sleep, two to a room," Thomas said, showing Anna three small bedrooms, each one containing two narrow beds. "And this," he said, opening the last door on the upper floor, "is your room. Or will be as soon as I move my stuff out." He frowned. "Sorry for the mess. We aren't the tidiest bunch."

Anna noted a bed, ancient bureau, chair, and kerosene lamp. "You are craftsmen, not chamber maids."

His dimpled half-smile made Thomas look, for the briefest moment, like one of the boys.

While Thomas gathered an armload of his things from the bedroom, Anna's new pupils took her back downstairs. They showed her the rest of the farm, beginning with a kitchen so filthy Anna had to bite her tongue hard to keep from exclaiming, and then the lean-to out back. It was stuffed with broken tools, empty jars, weathered crates, and assorted unrecognizable items. A sack of potatoes lay atop the heap.

"There's a root cellar in here too, but there ain't nothin in it," Jack said, pointing to a door behind the house. "Just some dried weeds and old jelly jars."

Another lean-to beside the workshop contained an ample supply of cut firewood, for which Teddy and Jimmy proudly claimed credit. For a little while, anyway, she would be warm and dry, and perhaps by the time she resumed her journey, the nights would be warmer.

Inside the workshop, the pungent smell of freshy shaved wood engulfed her. In the center of the room, amid piles of curly shavings and odd-sized wood scraps, stood three long tables. Some sort of treadle-driven, wood turning device was attached to the end of one. Various hand tools and project pieces littered the tables. A stove at the back of the room did not seem to be in use at the moment as the room was quite cold. Shelves on the walls and racks overhead stored lumber.

"This is where you study?"

"And work," Pete said. "We fix broken furniture for folks. But mostly, we make things to sell. I'm making this." He held up a three-legged stool and blew off a fine layer of dust.

"Very impressive," Anna said, stifling a cough.

Thomas entered the shop carrying a bundle of books. He glanced at Anna and the boys and then entered a door in the back.

"What is that room?" Anna asked.

"It used to be a supply room, but now it's Mr. Tom's office," Jimmy said.

The troupe led her back into the house through the kitchen, but there,

Anna stopped. Someone had carried the pot of stew from her campfire and placed it on the cookstove.

"Where do you store your food?" she asked.

"In here." Albert opened a cupboard. Two sacks in the lower section of the cupboard, marked as flour and dry beans, were nearly empty. A sack of cornmeal sat on the middle shelf, and assorted food cans and jars of jam were perched on top, along with a jug of molasses, peanut butter, canned sardines, and three tins of soda crackers.

"The ice box is over here," Pete said, opening the cabinet to reveal jugs of milk, a basket of eggs, a pot of jam, and a large tub of something solid and gray full of dark flecks.

"What is that?" she said, pointing to the tub.

"Bacon grease," Jimmy said. "We cook with it."

Anna stifled a shudder. This would also need to be remedied.

While the soup warmed, Anna gave the front sitting room and parlor a closer inspection. The table and chairs would make this room an excellent schoolroom. But when she looked over the bookshelves along the wall, she found no titles suitable for teaching.

"Surely you have textbooks of some kind?" Anna asked.

"Nope, not a one," Teddy said with a grin. As Thomas came through with another load of his things, Teddy added, "We don't use books."

She turned toward Thomas, suddenly uneasy. Without books, it would be difficult to know what lessons were needed for their grade levels.

He frowned. "I'll...round up some for you as soon as I can."

She breathed a sigh of relief. "Thank you. And when is washday?"

"What's that?" Teddy asked.

"It is the day you..." Anna studied six blank faces, and then turned to Thomas, who also appeared blank. "I see. Is there a washtub or something to wash clothing in?"

Thomas nodded. "There's a tub with a washboard and wringer in the lean-to. We use it, we just...don't have a special day for it."

"Water?"

"We all take turns at the well," Jack said. "I'm pump man today."

"Ah," Anna said. She raised a hopeful brow. "Soap?"

"Yes, ma'am, we got a big ol' hunk," Albert said. "We just whittle off a piece whenever we need some."

Anna nodded. "And the toilet is...?"

"Stinky and swarmin' with flies," Jimmy said.

"Out back," Thomas added quickly. "Farms around here don't have electricity or running water, like the city. Hope we're not too rustic for you."

She huffed out a laugh. "The city is no bed of roses." Anna had lived in far more rustic conditions than this. Frigid mountain villages, remote desert camps, noisy cities, cramped settlements. The Leibowicz family had been displaced so many times that Anna had long ago stopped putting down roots. But, until now, she and her family had always worked together to make do, no matter where the restless winds had blown them.

She forced down a suffocating wave of homesickness. "I am perfectly happy to haul water and swat flies. I am also happy to cook while I am here, if you wish," she added.

"Halle-LOO-jah!" Albert hooted. "No offense, Mr. Tom."

"None taken," Thomas said, his relief evident. "That would be much appreciated. Thank you, Miss Anna." He looked around at the boys. "And that's what you're all to call her."

Sam studied Anna with a cautious look. What kept the child from speaking? Had he ever spoken? What she would not give to find out.

"All right, fellas, time to get to work," Thomas said. As the boys headed toward the door, he turned to Anna. "When the sisters come tomorrow, we'll have more food supplies."

"Sisters?"

"A couple of nuns from the Order of the Sisters of Mercy," he said. "They deliver goods to the needy around here. Bread, milk, flour, kerosene, and other supplies. Sometimes clothes."

"So...your school is a charity home?" Anna had heard of welfare institutions, but nothing like this.

Thomas waited until the last boy had gone outside. "You could say that. Some of these boys are orphans, others have families too poor to keep them. If they weren't with me, they'd all be in an orphanage. Here they learn job skills, so at least they have a shot at a future."

Anna had noted their dwindling food supplies. "With seven of you living here, I imagine it is difficult to make ends meet."

"It's not easy. I get a monthly check from county welfare since some of the boys are wards of the state. But if not for the sisters, I wouldn't be able to keep them all fed and clothed."

She took another look around. This was more than a school; it was home, and to such an odd collection of fellows. "What a strange life you lead."

Thomas folded arms across his chest and stiffened. "I take it you don't approve."

"I only meant that your way of life is unusual," she said. "What you are doing is commendable."

He studied her with a piercing look. "I know it's unorthodox. But I don't believe in institutions, especially for kids. If I could, I'd tear down every orphanage in the country."

If Mama had gotten her wish, Anna's unborn child would now be the property of Miss Campbell and her dreadful institution.

A tingle shivered down her spine.

Afternoon soon gave way to evening. After a supper of biscuits and the remaining "Crick Stew," as the boys called it, Anna said goodnight and then retreated upstairs as Bing Crosby singing "I Found a Million Dollar Baby" drifted up from the radio.

The large bed, tucked beneath the sloped ceiling, had been hastily made with a thin coverlet. She stretched out her bedroll, hung her second gown, and climbed into bed. The mattress was a welcome relief. But even with the added layers, the bed was cold. She reached for her journal to write a letter to Shayna. As soon as she could buy a stamp, she would mail it.

23 March

My Love,

I have stopped to help a group of boys temporarily in need of a teacher. I hope to gather some food and perhaps earn a little money for the rest of my journey. You would like these boys; they are around Anshel's age and full of chutzpah (even the mute one, whose silence belies a highly inquisitive mind). They are an odd lot. The boys live in this home to avoid the orphan asylum and to learn work skills. Their headmaster is

Anna stared at the words she had written. She knew so little about these people who had taken her in, a starving stranger. Deciding to add to the letter once she got a little more acquainted, she put it away.

She snuggled down under the chilly covers, hugged herself into a ball, and closed her eyes. While she awaited the arrival of textbooks, she would test the boys in their abilities and try to determine what each one needed to pass to the next grade.

Anna tried to picture each boy's face, but her mind's eye drifted. She no longer saw six boys bound by a strange oath of loyalty. The faces filling her mind now as she lay shivering in the empty bed were those of Anshel, Rivka, Shayna, and Mama.

Tears left warm tracks on her cold cheeks.

ANNA WOKE TO AN ODD SMELL, LIKE BURNT TREE BARK. HER stomach lurched, and she froze.

Please, no...not now, not today...

She took a deep breath to steady herself, and after a few moments, the feeling passed. She chose the cleaner of her two dresses, washed her face, combed her hair, and went downstairs.

In the kitchen, Thomas—looking more presentable now, minus the layer of white dust—stirred a skillet of scorched potatoes on the cookstove, while Jimmy and Jack spread jam on what looked like corn cakes—also scorched. Sam stacked plates, and Pete held cups while Albert poured milk. Teddy came in the back door carrying a bucket of water, which he set in the sink.

Thomas looked up. "Good morning, Miss Anna."

"Good morning." She reached out to tousle Albert's hair, but quickly withdrew her hand. It would take conscious effort to remember that she had no little brother here. A lump formed in her throat.

"Did you sleep well?" Thomas asked.

"Yes, thank you," she managed to say. This was a lie—she had barely slept at all. In all her years of jostling with her younger siblings for space, Anna had never dreamed there was such a thing as too large a bed.

The boys filled their plates and took them into the adjoining dining room, but Thomas left. How odd. But then, she needed to get accustomed to differing ways of life, different cultures and customs. Perhaps where Thomas came from, adults did not eat with children.

Anna took a spoonful of potatoes from the skillet and a jelly-coated corn cake, poured a glass of milk, then carried her breakfast to the table and joined the boys. Sam stared at her, then glanced away. Teddy elbowed Jack and made him scoot over, then took his seat.

As Anna took a drink of milk, she realized no one had begun eating. She set her glass down.

Thomas appeared with another chair, which he squeezed in between Albert and Pete. Without a word, he got himself a plate and joined them at the table.

Anna's face warmed. He had not left the boys to eat alone. She had taken his seat.

Everyone bowed their heads and closed their eyes, but Albert squeezed his eyes shut so tight he looked as if he had sucked a lemon. Anna clamped her lips to keep from laughing.

Thomas said, "Blessed Father, we give You thanks for this new day. Thank You for sending Miss Anna, and thank You for sparing these boys the punishment their crime deserves."

As Albert's face curdled even more, Anna suppressed an incredulous laugh at the notion of being "sent" here. Washed ashore like sea foam might have been more accurate.

"Thank You for this food. We are grateful for every display of Your provision, large and small. As we offer a cup of water to a thirsty traveler, may You accept the offering as done unto You. In Christ's name we pray, Amen."

Anna could not help but stare at Thomas. In her experience, one did not speak in such a way to God. And in her understanding, the "Christ" Thomas named was the dead Jew depicted on the crosses that decorated Christian churches. Her mother had told her to steer clear of such places, as displaying such an unclean thing was morbid and irrational, and those who did so had to be completely mad.

As everyone began to eat, Anna studied her potatoes, which had very likely been cooked in pork fat. She turned to Thomas. "I see you have a chicken coop. Do you keep chickens?"

"We used to," Thomas said, chewing. "But something kept getting into the coop and tearing them up."

"Bet it was wolves," Jack said.

Albert nodded as he chewed, his mouth too full to speak.

"Ain't no wolves around here," Pete said. "It was old man Beckett's dogs. I've run 'em off a couple times."

"Did he not offer payment?" Anna asked. "Where I come from, when your animals destroy your neighbor's property, you compensate them for their loss."

Thomas wiped his mouth with a cloth and set it down. "And where is that, Miss Anna? Where you come from, I mean." He resumed eating without looking up.

She stared at him as she searched for a reply. How thoughtless of her to expose her personal life. "New York."

"You got a funny accent," Jimmy said, then suddenly bucked in his seat as if he had taken a boot to the shin. He glared at Teddy, seated across from him.

"She *could* say the same of you, although I doubt she ever would," Thomas said, drilling Jimmy with a sharp look. "You will apologize."

"Sorry, ma'am," Jimmy said, eyes downcast.

"All is forgiven, Jimmy." Anna took a bite of corn cake. The blackened potatoes were swimming in so much grease that she feared eating them would bring back the morning sickness that had mercifully passed. She ate the rest of her corn cake and washed it down with milk.

"I'm glad you're all going to school today," Thomas said, ignoring the groans that followed. "That is, if Miss Anna is prepared to begin?"

"Yes, I—"

"*Today?*" Jack's face wilted. "But it's Friday. Can't it wait till Monday?"

"You've had more than enough of a vacation," Thomas said. "No need to waste Miss Anna's valuable time. At least when you tell me you're going to school *now*, I'll know it's the truth." He stood and gathered his dishes. "I shouldn't have to remind you all to be on your best behavior and do exactly as Miss Anna says. I'll see you in the workshop after lunch."

As Thomas left, six pairs of eyes turned to Anna, their expressions mixed and unreadable. *Best* behavior? What thoughts and plans were forming in those six scruffy heads? She could only imagine.

She drew a deep breath. "And I will be waiting in the schoolroom when you are finished cleaning the dishes." She left to the sounds of sharp whispers.

In the parlor, heat from the fireplace had begun to soften the morning chill, easing away a bit of her trepidation. Pencils and paper had been placed on the table. Until textbooks arrived, school mornings would consist of spelling and vocabulary tests, followed by history, arithmetic, and geography drills until lunchtime.

As her pupils filed in, she greeted them with a smile she hoped looked more confident than she felt. "Good morning, students."

Despite some initial grumbling, her students applied themselves to her tests, and by lunchtime, all six boys had completed the work with only a little balking. She let herself exhale. So far, so good.

After a lunch of milk and soda crackers with peanut butter and jam, the boys headed out to the workshop. Everyone except Sam. He lingered in the kitchen and seemed to be waiting for Anna to do something.

"What do you need, Sam?" she asked.

The boy frowned at an empty plate on the drainboard, one she had not noticed before. Was he still hungry? This was no surprise. He was thin as a reed, and lunch had been meager.

Sam picked up the plate and pointed away, toward the yard.

She frowned. "I am sorry, I do not understand."

Sam took down a cracker tin, brought out the jam, and did his best to make three lopsided sandwiches. Then he filled a cup with milk, spilling some, and set it on the plate. Again, he pointed toward the yard.

Anna shook her head.

Sam hooked a finger above his lip like a mustache.

"Oy! Of course. Mr. Thomas needs lunch, too. Thank you for remembering him."

With a nod and a slight smile, Sam carefully carried the plate and cup outside.

Since it was Friday, and since she now had the means, Anna decided to make bread. Only after she had used nearly all the eggs did she realize she would need to replace them. She kneaded the dough, and while it raised, she looked more carefully through the kitchen and then ventured to the cellar out back. It was so dark inside that it took a few moments for her eyes to adjust. The "dried weeds" Jack had mentioned turned out to be herbs, which were actually usable. She gathered some dried leek, stopped at the lean-to and filled her skirt with potatoes, and returned to the kitchen to start a pot of soup.

As the soup simmered, she wove long ropes of dough into braids. She crimped the ends and tucked them under and then set the loaves to rise on the warming shelf. After she checked the fire in the cookstove, she gathered her students' tests and scored them while the bread raised.

That morning, she had learned that Albert and Sam were nine, Pete and Jack were ten, Jimmy was eleven, and Teddy was twelve. Knowing their ages only served as a starting point. She needed to somehow figure out how proficient they were for their respective grade levels. Textbooks would be very helpful, but in the meantime, she hoped her makeshift testing would give her a sufficient idea of how much work each boy needed to pass the year.

According to the test scores, Albert and Teddy appeared to be near grade level aptitude, while the others had some catching up to do. And while Sam could apparently read third grade level, his writing was barely legible. He would need plenty of extra help and practice to catch up.

As Anna gave the soup a stir, a vehicle pulled into the yard and the motor cut off. She went to the front room and looked out the window. A Model T pickup had parked near the workshop.

Just as she returned to the kitchen, Sam burst inside from the back door, his eyes alight with excitement.

"What is it?"

He pointed out back, then pressed his palms together. Anna cocked her head, not understanding, but grateful for his determination to communicate. She would love nothing more than to get to the bottom of his muteness and find a way to help him speak.

Two women wearing black habits came up the steps and into the kitchen, followed by Thomas. Anna had seen Catholic nuns in Manhattan but had never met any.

"Miss Anna," Thomas said, "I'd like you to meet Sister Mary Francis and Sister Mary Agnes."

Each woman nodded to Anna in turn. Mary Francis was a tall, slender, eagle-eyed woman, perhaps in her mid-forties. Mary Agnes was old enough to be her grandmother, with twinkling eyes the color of autumn sky and barely taller than Teddy.

"Sisters, this is Anna, the teacher I told you about."

"Welcome to Corbin," Mary Agnes said. She had a soft, melodic voice. "We understand you're living at Johansen Woodworks now."

"Temporarily," Thomas said quickly. "She is staying in the house with the boys. I've moved out to the workshop."

Mary Francis raised a dark brow at him. "And you believe this is a suitable arrangement?"

"Perfectly suitable," he said. There was a pronounced edge to his voice. "I have a cot and woodstove in the shop."

The door opened, and Pete came in with a basket full of eggs, followed by the others carrying bundles and sacks of food and a can of kerosene.

Anna addressed the sisters. "It is so good that you are able to help."

"We are the Lord's hands and are happy to serve as He provides," Mary Agnes said.

Under Thomas's direction, the boys put away the supplies. Thomas sniffed the soup and eyed the bread. A faint smile broadened his mustache.

"I understand you also operate a school," Anna said to the nuns.

"We did, until it burnt down." Mary Francis's mouth formed a grim line.

"I am so sorry," Anna said. "How did it happen?"

"It was an accident." Mary Agnes glanced at the other sister.

Mary Francis sniffed. "The empty kerosene can near the creek says otherwise."

"We are not judge and jury," Mary Agnes said lightly. She turned to Anna. "We brought clothing for the children, but there are some other things in the truck. You are welcome to see if we have anything you need. I believe there might be an apron."

"An apron would be wonderful." Anna sighed. An apron would not only be useful for cooking but would help cover signs of her expanding belly. She added wood to the stove and placed the raised loaf in the oven.

"I heard the St. Paul Catholic church over in Perryville was vandalized last week," Thomas said.

"It wouldn't be the first time," Mary Francis said. "And unless things change around here, it won't be the last."

Thomas nodded. "The boys and I will come by this weekend and get some more framing done."

"We're grateful for your help, but further repairs will have to wait until we have more lumber," Mary Agnes said. "The last shipment was...misdirected."

"Which we're also calling an *accident*," Mary Francis said, giving the older sister a look.

Mary Agnes ignored her. "A new shipment should arrive soon." She smiled at Anna. "We'll just go and see if we can find you that apron." She glanced at the other sister, then went out the door. Without another word, Mary Francis followed.

Anna turned to Thomas. "You are helping the sisters rebuild their school?"

He nodded. "It's good for the boys to keep honing their skills between paying jobs. But more than that, I want them to learn that no matter how hard times are, helping others is far more important than money."

Anna nodded. "An important lesson. Where I come from, neighbors always take care of each other."

Thomas looked her in the eye. "Sounds like a place I wouldn't want to leave."

Her heart raced. She had spoken without thinking again. "It is not the place as much as it is...a way of life," she said.

He studied her thoughtfully. A tingle raced across her nerves.

"If you don't mind my asking, what language do they speak, where you come from?"

The strain of the past few weeks must have made her accent more pronounced. This was unfortunate. She would have to work harder to lose every trace.

"Some speak Polish," she said, her cheeks warm. To include Yiddish could bring an immediate end to her employment and shelter.

"It's hard to tell, you know," Thomas said. "Your English is perfect."

"Thank you," she said, swallowing hard. "I hope to teach it well."

"I have a feeling you'll do great." He moved to leave but stopped and turned back. "I don't mean to pry, but there is one more thing I need to ask."

Anna stiffened. What else had he noticed about her? "What?"

"Your last name."

"Leibowicz," she said, and then froze. It was a name some people would know was Jewish. She drew a breath and braced herself.

Thomas nodded slowly. "Good. Now I can introduce you properly." He went out the back door.

With a deep exhale, Anna joined the sisters at their truck to sort through the clothing.

Seven

AS THOMAS PRAYED A BLESSING OVER THE MEAL, THE BOYS closed their eyes, but Sam stared at the bread in the center of the table. Anna had not covered the challah—what would be the point? Here, there would be no ushering in of Shabbat, no candles or wine, no wishing one another *Shabbat Shalom.*

Anna closed her eyes. Were her sisters and brother gathered around the candles and wine now? Was Mama saying the blessing? Were they passing the bread?

The clatter of bowls and spoons shook her from her thoughts. Anna ladled potato soup into wooden crocks while hands reached for the steaming bowls, fragrant from the dried leek.

Sam continued to stare at the bread.

She sliced the loaf and offered him a piece. Sam looked her in the eye but did not take it. Had the child never seen egg bread before? She sprinkled salt on her plate, dipped the slice of bread in the salt, and offered it again.

The child took it, then brought it to his nose.

She took a bite of soup and looked around. It seemed the other boys could not spoon up their supper fast enough.

"The soup is delicious," Thomas said between bites.

"So's the bread," Jimmy said, slurping soup from a slice he had dunked.

When Pete and Teddy offered their bowls for seconds, Anna glanced at Sam. He was still holding his bread.

She leaned close to him. "Is something wrong?"

He shook his head.

"You have not seen yellow bread before?"

Again, the headshake.

"Ah. Challah gets its color from egg yolks."

Sam cocked his head, then pointed at the loaf and questioned her with his eyes.

"Why the braid?"

He nodded.

Anna smiled. Curiosity was an excellent teacher. "Some say the braid is a symbol of unity. The strands are intertwined in the same way mankind is bound. It is a reminder that our survival is tied to the well-being of one another. Regardless of where we come from or what we do in life, we must value each other and remember how much we need one another to succeed."

Thomas paused and stared at her.

Slowly, Sam took a bite. Then he smiled and closed his eyes as he chewed, as if to deepen his sense of taste. As he took another bite, a faint sound came from his throat.

Anna suppressed a smile. Could something as simple as bread be the key to unlocking Sam's voice?

"Thank you for supper, Miss Anna," Thomas said. "It was the best meal we've had in a long time."

"Thanks," Albert said. Others echoed their thanks.

Sam slurped soup from his spoon, but his gaze remained fixed on the loaf.

"Would you like another piece?" Anna asked.

Sam nodded, accepted another slice, and smiled broadly.

Her heart did a small leap. She could not wait to add Sam's reaction to his first taste of challah to her letter to Shayna.

Saturday morning, over a breakfast of eggs and latkes, Anna waited for a break in conversation to bring up her thoughts on a garden.

Thomas put down his fork and wiped his mouth. "You're right. We have a garden spot just sitting there not being used. Great idea. The boys can help tend it over the summer."

"What can be planted now?" Anna asked.

"Potatoes, cabbage, onion, carrots. And maybe lettuce, once the last freeze is past."

That topic had gone better than expected, bolstering Anna's resolve. "And it is a shame that the chicken coop is run down. If it could be repaired, and you got a few laying hens, think of all the eggs you would have."

Thomas leveled a look at Anna, then sighed. "Right again. Since we can't work on the sisters' school until more supplies arrive, the boys and I will turn up the garden, and then we'll tackle the coop. Why don't you take Sam and Albert into town for vegetable seed? They can take you to the feed store and show you around town."

Sam shot an anxious glance at Albert, who nodded knowingly. "Sam don't much like going into town," Albert said.

With a frown, Thomas turned to Sam. "Is that true?"

The boy shrugged and averted his gaze.

Thomas studied the two boys thoughtfully. "It sure would be nice if you two could help Miss Anna find her way, since she's new here."

Albert turned to Sam and said quietly, "It'll be fine. It's daytime, and there's three of us."

Sam still looked at Anna with uncertainty.

Albert chugged his milk, stuffed his latke into his mouth, then stood and wiped his lips with his sleeve. "Come on, let's go."

Sam downed the rest of his milk and stood, wiping his mouth the same way.

"Well, apparently, I am also finished," Anna said with a chuckle.

A main road leading into town was visible through the trees a little to the north of the Johansen house, but Sam and Albert took Anna on a shortcut through the woods and along the railroad tracks that paralleled the creek where they had first met. They followed the tracks to a wooden bridge. Beyond the bridge, a small town churned with activity.

They crossed the bridge and followed Main Street, which passed through town and ribboned into the green and brown fields beyond. Two cross streets formed blocks that contained several businesses. In red lettering on the side wall, the Corbin General Store on the left promised everything from motor oil to an ice cream fountain. A service station and "Gertrude's Café" took up the block on the right. The feed store and library made up the next two blocks, and across the street sat a barber shop and bank.

Sam slipped a hand into hers. Anna smiled down at him, but he only looked solemn.

Albert led the way to the feed store. Inside, several people milled about, some toting goods, some making conversation with others. One clerk served a couple in the aisle.

Anna approached the counter and gave Thomas's seed list. While she waited for her supplies, a dark-haired young woman, who had been talking to a group of ladies, stopped and stared at her with steel blue eyes. Anna resisted the urge to smooth her hair, and instead, turned her attention to the boys. Albert was peering intently into the candy jars on the counter. Sam stood close to her side; his gaze fastened to the wooden planks beneath his feet.

"Here you go, miss," the clerk said. "You're in luck, we just got a new shipment of seed."

Anna put the purchases on Thomas's account, gave Sam a bundle, and then turned to give the other package to Albert, but he was not there. It took a moment to find him. He was near the door talking to a blonde woman with a small child on her hip and another one beside her.

Anna gently steered Sam toward the door. She offered a polite hello to the young woman and turned to Albert. "I am ready to go when you are."

"You must be the new teacher," the woman said. "Albert was just tellin' me. Hi, I'm Sarah." Smiling, she held out a hand.

Anna shook her hand and returned the smile. "I am Anna. These are your little ones?"

"Yes, ma'am." Sarah twisted to show Anna the toddler on her hip. "This here's Ivy, she's two. And the one tryin' to swing from my skirt like Tarzan is Violet—she's five. I guess we're neighbors. I'd introduce you to my Henry, but he's out back loadin' corn."

"Neighbors?" Anna handed her seed bundle to Albert. "Then you are Mrs. Tucker?"

Sarah laughed. "Yes, ma'am, but I don't reckon I ever been called that."

Beyond Sarah, Anna could see the dark-haired young woman saying something to her companions as she continued to stare at Anna. They all turned and looked at her.

Anna focused on Sarah. "So, it is *you* I must thank for the onion."

With a frown, Sarah shifted Ivy to the other hip. "Onion?"

"The other day," Albert said. "When you swapped me an onion for a potato."

Recognition dawned in Sarah's big, blue eyes. "Oh, yes, Creek Stew. My pleasure." She smiled. "So, where're you from?"

"New York."

The dark-haired woman took her purchases to the register but kept watching Sarah and Anna intently, as if trying to hear what they were saying.

Sam pressed himself closer to Anna's hip.

"I'm glad to hear you're stayin' at the Johansen place now," Sarah said. She tugged Violet close to let a customer pass through the door. "It sorely needs a woman's touch."

"It is only temporary. I must resume my journey soon. But for now, I am glad I can help the boys catch up their studies."

"Too bad you can't stay. Where you headed?"

"I am—"

"Who's your new friend, Sarah?" The dark-haired young woman joined them. "A mysterious newcomer to our quiet little town?" She glared at Sam, who slipped behind Anna's skirt.

"This is Anna," Sarah said. "She's the new teacher over at Johansen Woodworks."

"Teacher?" The woman frowned. "What on earth would a pack of thieving hooligans need with a teacher?"

"Well, it *is* a school, Penny," Sarah said quietly. "And the thievin's just a rumor. I'm sure Mr. Chandler knows what he's doin'."

Penny huffed a laugh, then shook her head. "Really, Sarah. Are you forgetting how poor his judgment is? Such a disservice you're doing your pretty new friend here. You ought to be warning her about the man's dealings and the trouble she's asking for by going anywhere near that place." Penny's gaze flitted over Anna's clothing. She heaved a sigh. "You'll have to forgive Sarah, she's very naïve. But she'll learn." Her heart-shaped face and pale blue eyes were framed by dark curls styled in the latest bob. "I'm Penny Withers. If you haven't heard, my daddy is Boyd Withers, local deputy, but he's going to be Alton County Sheriff one day. My mother, Alice, is on the school board. She's also a charter member of the Temperance Union, chairwoman of the Daughters of America, and president of a very exclusive women's society."

Sarah gave Penny a confused look. "Isn't that one supposed to be a secret?"

Penny shrugged. "Well, *officially*, but everyone knows about it, except maybe your friend here." Penny smiled at Anna. "She can join too, as long as she meets the criteria."

Sarah turned to Anna. "I do hope you'll join us, even if you're only here for a spell. We have tea parties and picnics and special speakers." With a side-long glance at Penny, she added, "and it's a good way to make friends."

"Of just the right sort," Penny added. She cocked her head at Anna, one brow raised. "What happened to your pickaninny?"

Confused, Anna looked from Penny to Sarah. "My what?"

"The colored boy," Sarah said beneath her breath.

Anna looked around the store, but Sam was nowhere in sight. "Albert, where is Sam?"

Albert spun away from the counter and looked around. "Shoot!" He bolted out the door.

"It's a shame the dummy didn't leave town when his mama did," Penny said. "So, Anna, where are you from? Because clearly you're not from around here."

But Anna could not get a sound past the stranglehold of anger in her throat.

"She's from New York," Sarah said, eyeing Anna cautiously.

"You don't say. Well, since you're answering for her, I have to wonder if deaf and dumb is contagious." Penny turned to Anna, nostrils flared in distaste. "Maybe you shouldn't have touched him."

Anna gasped. "Sam is neither deaf nor dumb, nor is his lack of speech contagious."

"Sarah," Penny said, ignoring Anna, "did you tell your husband that you're coming to the rally with me on Monday?"

"I—I'm not sure I'm goin'," Sarah said. "I still need to talk it over with him."

Penny shook her head. "See, this is exactly why you *need* to go. It's time for us women to band together. We have the vote now. No one—especially not a man of questionable intelligence—has the right to keep you from having a say in your own affairs."

Rosy blotches formed in Sarah's cheeks. Whatever Sarah saw in her friend Penny Withers, Anna would need help to see. *Much* help.

Sarah turned to Anna. "I gotta go, I need to help Henry see to our order. It was real nice meetin' you, Anna. Hope to see you around."

"Nice to meet you as well," Anna said.

Penny watched as Sarah collected Violet and left, then shook her head. "Sarah Tucker has a lot to learn." She turned and let her gaze roam over Anna's face and hair. "Maybe the girls and I will see you at the café sometime and you can tell us how you came to be Thomas Chandler's live-in teacher."

Anna felt herself stiffen. "Perhaps. If it is any of your business."

"Oh, it is." Penny's broad smile had all the warmth of glass. "But you'll find out. And I do hope we'll talk again."

"Perhaps," Anna said again, and she meant it. She would rather meet a snake face to face than be surprised from behind by its strike.

It was not until she was outside the store that Anna remembered to exhale. What had Penny meant about Thomas and his "dealings"?

Watching for Sam and Albert, she walked along Main Street toward the creek. As she reached the bridge, she could see both boys waiting for her on the other side. Sam and Albert led the way home, and as Anna followed, more questions formed in her mind. It seemed Sarah Tucker was not the only one who had much to learn.

Eight

IN THE DARKNESS BEFORE DAWN, ANNA STARED AT THE SLOPED ceiling, visible in the fading moonlight. The empty bed served as a needless reminder of the distance between her and those she loved.

Lying there was useless. She rose, dressed in the housecoat she had found in the clothing the sisters had brought, then gathered her own clothes in her knapsack and slipped downstairs as quietly as the creaky stairs would allow. She went outside and drew a bucket of water from the well. Thankful that the cook stove was still warm with embers, she stoked the fire and started a pot of water. If she worked quickly, she could bathe and wash her clothes before the boys awoke.

Her dresses would soon reveal her growing belly and would eventually no longer fit at all. She needed to gather enough fabric or flour sacks to sew a larger, looser gown.

She filled the washtub in the lean-to with water from the well, and when the pot came to a boil, she carried it out and added it to the tub, along with a sliver of soap. She bathed and washed her hair quickly in the tepid water. She had forgotten her laundry in the kitchen, but retrieving it would be a welcome errand since the kitchen was warmer than the lean-to.

Dripping and shivering, she put on the housecoat, then hurried out of the lean-to and crashed into someone. She gasped and nearly lost her balance, but Thomas caught her by the arms and steadied her.

"I didn't know you were..." With a befuddled look, Thomas released her and staggered back, blocking the doorway. He just stood there looking like a mustached fence post.

She wrapped arms around herself to halt the shivering. "I hope I did not wake you."

His hazel eyes flickered over her dripping hair and bare feet. "Shall I get you a—a—towel or—"

"I will be fine...once I am inside."

He looked as baffled as if she had spoken Chinese.

"In the kitchen, where it is warm."

"Oh. Yes. Sorry." He hopped clumsily aside, allowing her to pass.

She hurried into the house and to the stove. Through the window, she could see Thomas shaking his head as he stomped away from the house and into the woods.

Thomas did not return for breakfast, which Anna found odd. He had been dressed for outdoors in a thick coat and boots, so she assumed he had gone to work on something in town or on someone's property. But going without breakfast? How could a man work on an empty stomach?

While she and the boys ate, Sister Mary Agnes arrived bearing six thick, slightly singed textbooks.

"Miss Anna, I wonder if you and the boys might be able to use these. I'm sorry there aren't more. These are the only textbooks that weren't too damaged in the fire. I hope you don't mind the smell."

Anna took the books and gave the sister's arm a squeeze. "We are grateful to have them. Thank you for salvaging them for us." She turned to the boys. "We are thankful, are we not?"

A weak murmur of thanks came from the table.

"I also have a large crate of old sheets and clothing scraps you might find useful for making a quilt," Mary Agnes said. The twinkle in her eyes matched her gentle smile.

"Quilt?"

The older woman's smile faltered. "I assumed you sew?"

"Yes, I do."

"Ah, good. When we were here the other day, Thomas asked if we had any blankets in the load because he was one bed short."

Anna frowned. "But I got a blanket."

Mary Agnes nodded, still smiling gently.

"Then who—" Anna gasped. Thomas had given her *his* blanket? "But the workshop must be very cold at night." Anna frowned, distressed by the sudden image of him shivering in his cot. "Why did he not say I took his blanket? I would not have accepted it."

"Thomas has a motto, modeled from the words of Christ: Give to anyone who asks, and if anyone wants to borrow, do not turn them away." Mary Agnes met Anna's gaze. "You'll find Thomas Chandler has a soft spot for those in need—especially those who are alone in the world."

Anna opened her mouth to speak but did not trust her voice. Tears stung her eyes. "How kind," she managed to say.

There was a tenderness in the way the older woman looked into Anna's eyes. "Why don't you send one of the boys out to the truck for that crate? I'm sorry to say I have no thread."

"I have some in my sewing kit. And I will barter for more, if I have to."

Mary Agnes smiled. "You, my child, will do very well here."

By the time the sister left, breakfast was finished. Anna asked Pete and Jimmy to bring in more water and start big pots heating on the stove.

"But we already got water for the dishes," Pete said.

"That is a good start. But I am declaring today Wash Day."

"*Wash?*" Jimmy said, mouth agape. "Aw, nuts. You mean our *clothes?* Or *us?*"

"Both," Anna said.

A round of colorful complaints rose from the group.

"Believe it or not, water and soap will not hurt you in the least."

"Couldn't we do a spelling test instead?" Albert whined.

Anna chuckled. "Gather your clothes, gentlemen, and unless you like a chilly bath, I suggest you start Wash Day with yourselves."

Over the next hour and a half, Anna busied herself with trimming scraps and stitching them together, heating more water, and occasionally checking on the boys' progress. It had been hours since Thomas had headed into the woods, but the boys did not seem concerned. She sent Jack to find a long, thick stick to use as a paddle and Albert found some rocks for scrubbing out what dirt the washboard could not. Sam had the job of turning the wringer, and all six boys took turns hanging the clothes on the line. Their ability to work as a team was impressive.

As she worked in the kitchen, Anna made a point not to interfere with the laundering unless necessary, but remained within earshot just in case, smiling at some of the conversation. At one point, she heard Thomas's name and looked up to see if he had returned, but he had not.

"Maybe he found some squirrels to preach to," Jimmy said.

Snickers followed.

"How'd you figure out he was a preacher?" Pete asked.

Thomas? A preacher? Anna stopped stitching and focused on the voices.

"I heard him and Deputy Withers talking one day."

"Maybe Withers wanted to get religion," Teddy said. Everyone guffawed.

"Withers was razzin' Mr. Tom about something, but Mr. Tom got riled up and told him to mind his own business," Jimmy said.

"I'd give two nickels to see that," Pete said.

"What'd Withers say?" Jack asked.

"I don't remember all of it, something about how it'd be a real good idea for Mr. Tom to come to some meetin' and Mr. Tom sayin' he'd be busy that night and Withers sayin' he'd have to question anybody's morals who didn't go, and Mr. Tom sayin' he'd have to question anybody's morals who *did*. Then Withers said, 'My daughter may think you're the berries, but your brand of humor don't set well with me, Chandler, no wonder they took your pulpit away.'"

Silence.

"Holy smokes," Jack said. "Penny Withers likes Mr. Tom? I'd run for the hills like my britches was on fire."

"Aw, who cares if he was a preacher?" Albert blurted out. "He ain't one now."

"Yeah, but it don't sound like he wanted to quit," Jimmy said.

"Well, he ain't gonna find nobody to preach to out in them woods," Pete said. "Not unless he likes preachin' to ghosts."

"Ain't no such thing as ghosts," Jack said.

"Is too and I know it," Pete said. "I seen some once, and I heard other folks seen 'em too. They got pointy heads and carry fire on big sticks like—"

"Shut up, Pete," Albert said.

"Make me, runt."

"Sam! Come back!" Teddy yelled. "There he goes."

"Genius, Pete. Why'd you have to go and say that?" Albert said.

"We gotta go after him," Jack said.

Anna dropped her patchwork and hurried to the kitchen door.

"Now look what you done, idiot! He'll be gone for days, just like last time."

"Shut up!"

The sound of metal screeching on floorboards grew louder as Anna reached the lean-to. Pete and Albert had a grapple-hold on one another, knocking against the tub and slopping water all over the floor.

"Stop fighting," Anna said. She pulled the boys apart. "Where is Sam?"

"He ran off, Miss Anna," Jack said.

"Which way did he go?"

Teddy pointed toward the woods behind the house. Menacing clouds darkened the sky to the west.

"I will get my shawl. You boys go in pairs and holler if you see him. Albert, you will go with me."

When she returned downstairs, Albert led the way into the woods, hollering Sam's name. The others also called to the boy, their voices sounding from deeper in the woods. She followed Albert and called out, straining to see through the trees and brush. The foliage, thick and green, absorbed their voices, causing an eerie vacuum.

They trudged through the woods and followed a path to the north, looking for any sign of the child, still calling out to him. Rain began to fall, a drizzle at first, then a steady downpour. They kept going.

After a while, she and Albert came to a clearing where the other four boys had gathered.

No Sam.

"That's our fort," Albert said, pointing to an enclosure of evergreen limbs that formed a canopy between two trees. "I thought he might'a come here, but it don't look like he did."

Anna wiped rain from her face and addressed the group. "Why did he run away?"

Albert elbowed Pete, who shoved him back, knocking the smaller boy off balance.

"Fighting will not help. Does anyone know why he ran?"

"He's afraid of the ghosts," Jack said.

"They ain't ghosts," Teddy said. "They're men dressed in white, and they carry torches. They burn crosses and try to scare folks. I never seen it, but I heard they even hang people. Sometimes in the woods, sometimes right in front of their own house."

"Mostly colored folks," Jimmy said. "But others, too."

Nausea washed through Anna's belly. At the factory, she had heard of a secret society called the Ku Klux Klan, and stories that they terrorized Negroes and Jews and others, but she had never been certain if the rumors were true.

No one spoke. Jimmy nodded at Albert. "Tell her."

Albert turned to Anna. "I think Sam's seen things. Bad things."

"Here?" she asked. "In these woods?"

Albert shrugged. "I don't know, but I reckon it's why he don't talk."

Anna's heart dropped. She inhaled damp air and gave herself a moment to calm her apprehension, to think. "Okay. We must keep looking. Meet back here in one hour."

They spread out again in pairs and combed the woods, calling out to Sam, stopping to listen and look. Albert scanned the branches overhead. There were so many places to hide.

After nearly an hour with no luck, Anna and Albert headed back to the fort. Just as they reached the clearing, voices carried from the woods beyond. Four boys appeared, trailed by Thomas—and the missing boy.

"Sam!" Anna rushed to the child, knelt down, and gathered him into her arms. It was impossible to know whose heart was beating faster, his or hers. She held him out at arm's length and examined him, then glanced up.

Thomas watched her, his expression unreadable.

She met his gaze, wanting to ask, but not here, not in front of the child. Did Thomas know of the men in white, of the vicious things they did? Did he know anything about what Sam had seen or experienced?

Thomas rested a hand on Sam's head. "Come on, boys, we've had enough adventure for one day. Let's go home."

As they walked, Sam clutched the sleeve of Thomas's coat as if he would never let go.

Nine

ANNA GREETED HER STUDENTS MONDAY MORNING WITH A cheer she did not feel. She had fallen asleep the night before sewing by lamplight and woke much later in the dark with a stiff neck. And yet, after crawling into bed, she lay wide awake. Again. The blanket keeping her warm served as a reminder that Thomas was on a cot out in the workshop with no blanket.

This she planned to remedy as soon as possible.

The textbooks Sister Mary Agnes had brought made the morning's history assignments a little more interesting, even if one of them was a bit advanced for the younger boys. She gave them all a simple writing assignment meant to combine history, language, spelling, and vocabulary all in one: a report on someone in American history whom they looked up to. While the boys discussed possible subjects, Anna learned who fascinated her pupils most, including Daniel Boone, Lewis and Clark, and a few others, which gave her an idea.

"If you all complete your assignments, I will reward you with a special treat. But only if you complete it today."

Bribery did the trick. Each of the boys got right to work and did not whisper or dawdle, and they even took turns sharing the history book to glean facts. As they worked, she corrected the math quizzes she'd given them earlier, and by lunchtime, all six of them had completed their assignment, to the best of their ability. Sam's handwriting was still very difficult to read, but Anna was becoming more familiar with his attempts at lettering, which helped. She read their work while the boys ate lunch.

As she read, she overheard Thomas telling the boys that instead of working in the shop today, they would be helping him plant a new garden.

She marked a grade on Jimmy's paper and paused to listen as Thomas's announcement turned to a heated debate over which vegetable was the worst. She had purchased beet seeds, but she would be far away by the time any of the vegetables were ready to harvest. Anna heaved a sigh. She missed beets, especially in Shayna's borscht. The thought of Shayna going to market for the family and doing more of the cooking now, in addition to working at the factory, pressed at Anna's heart.

Jimmy, Sam, and Jack came to her as she finished grading the last paper.

"Miss Anna, do we get our treat now?" Jack asked.

"You must be patient."

Jimmy's eyebrows wiggled. "Betcha it's sugar cream pie," he said to Jack.

She chuckled. All of them had completed what she had asked. Now to see if the library in town carried what she had promised.

While Thomas and the boys worked on the garden, Anna walked to town hoping to trade a spool of thread for a few stamps, and to find some mending work. Trading away thread would be a sacrifice, as sewing was her only livelihood and she had little thread to spare. But a possible return letter from Shayna would be worth it.

She tried three businesses with no luck. If only Anshel were here. And in securing mending work, she had the same disappointing response. She asked everyone she met and left her name with two store clerks. Not to be defeated, she moved onto her next objective: the library. There, she found one of the books on her list. Whether the boys would find it a worthy prize remained to be seen.

As Anna came out of the library, she met Sarah Tucker going in.

"Anna! I'm so glad to see you. I was just goin' to the library. The ladies' temperance club is meetin' in there today. We're gettin' ready for tonight's rally."

"Is that the club your friend Penny was talking about?"

"One of 'em." Sarah glanced around, as if she feared being caught doing something wrong. "News sure travels fast. Word's goin' around you're a foreigner."

Anna's pulse sped. "People are talking about me?"

"Oh, my heavens, you're the talk of the town. Some say you're teachin' the boys voodoo spells." She giggled. "But I wouldn't worry. Folks around here got nothin' better to do than make up stuff just to give themselves somethin' to get excited about."

How disturbing. What kind of people made up things about a person they did not know?

"Whatcha got there?" Sarah asked, nodding at the book.

"I promised the boys a reward for finishing their lesson before I knew for certain that I could follow through. This book is a lifesaver."

Sarah sighed. "Gee, I wish my teacher back in Missouri had been half as interested in makin' school fun."

"I hope to make the most of the time I have." Anna smiled. "Sarah, do you know anyone in need of mending? I am looking for work, and I am quick and very proficient."

"Honey, I have heaps of mendin'." Then, she winced. "Thing is, I can't pay for it."

Anna studied her new friend, wondering if she could come up with a mutually beneficial arrangement. "I am willing to barter."

"Is that so? What sorta things would you trade for?"

Anna shrugged. "What do you have?"

Sarah laughed. "I live on a farm. I reckon I got *somethin'* laying around you need."

The greasy slab of bacon in Thomas's icebox appeared in her mind's eye. "We could always use eggs."

"I can do better than that. We are plumb overrun with layin' hens."

"You would trade chickens for mending?"

Sarah shrugged. "Sure. Why not?"

Hens would produce extra eggs that Anna could sell. She smiled. "I can pick up your mending tomorrow or Wednesday."

"Sugar, you got yourself a deal," Sarah said, smiling.

After supper, Anna made an announcement. "I have the reward for your history assignment, so after supper is cleaned up, I will share it with you in the parlor—unless you would rather wait until tomorrow."

"Now! Now!" Jack shouted.

"Come on, fellas, let's get at it and clean up," Pete said, heading to the sink.

Thomas smiled, then left the kitchen.

Anna took her library book to the parlor where she found Thomas adding wood to the fire. He retreated to an upholstered chair in the corner by the fireplace. Once the boys were all settled around the table, she held up the book.

Six faces fell.

"Aw, a book? *That's* the treat?" Teddy said.

Sam looked beneath the table, while Jimmy frowned. "You mean it ain't pie?"

"I think you will find this even better," Anna said.

In his corner, with a book of his own, even Thomas looked doubtful.

"Based on your biography choices," she went on, "I thought you might like this. It is *King of the Wild Frontier: An Autobiography* by Davy Crockett."

"You got a book on Davy Crockett?" Albert's astonishment was a good sign.

"Not only about him, but written *by* him. Shall I read it?"

Murmurs of agreement followed.

Anna smiled, then settled in and opened the book. It began a bit slow, but after a few pages, the adventures of a young Davy and the canoe that almost got away piqued the attention of all, including Thomas.

She read on. All six boys hung on every word, imaginations churning as the story unfolded. After an hour of reading, Anna marked the page and set the book down, drawing a collective complaint and requests for one more chapter.

"Perhaps we could resume tomorrow evening?"

"That's a swell idea," Thomas said. "Fellas, thank Miss Anna."

The boys thanked her, and as they trudged up the stairs, Thomas lit a lamp and brought it to the table. "The kerosene is all yours, Miss Anna. You've earned it." He turned to leave.

"No, please wait." She rose. "You need not leave the warmth of the fire. I will use the lamp in my room to work."

"Work?" He frowned. "On what?"

"On—" Anna froze. She wanted to keep the quilt a surprise. "I meant *write*. Letters." Her cheeks warmed.

"Letters." He studied her. "Telling Chicago about your delay? Or...preparing whoever is waiting for your upcoming arrival?"

Her mouth opened, but every reply that came to mind would reveal too much. Her only option now was diversion. "You are not only a carpenter, teacher, and farmer, but now, you are an investigator?"

He chuckled.

"And before that, I heard you were a preacher."

It was his turn to be silent. The muscles in his jaw tensed, rippling in the lamplight. He pushed a chair closer to the table. "If you need stamps," he said, his voice even, "I have some. You're welcome to them."

"Thank you," she said. How reserved he had become. She could almost hear Mama scolding her about the need to hold her tongue. Perhaps it would have been better to just tell him about the quilt.

Anna cleared her throat. "Sometimes," she said softly, "people have good reasons for keeping things to themselves."

Thomas stared at her for a moment. With a frown, his gaze fell to the book in his hand. Then he turned and headed toward the door. "You'll find stamps for your letters in the bureau," he said without turning. "Sleep well, Miss Anna."

"Thank you," she said to the door as it closed.

Ten

THE SOUND OF A CAR PULLING IN, FOLLOWED BY A KNOCK, brought Tuesday's spelling test to a stop. The sisters always came around back to the kitchen door. Before Anna could decide what to do, Teddy opened the front door.

A sandy-haired woman about Mama's age stood in the doorway. She took a quick look around the room. "Where is Thomas Chandler?" she said.

"He is working in his shop," Anna said. "Perhaps I can help you."

The woman's visual sweep came to a stop on Anna. "You're the new teacher?"

"Yes."

Whispers erupted from behind Anna.

The woman stepped into the parlor. "I'm Alice Withers, and I'm here on behalf of the Alton County Board of Education and the Corbin Public School Board. I'm here to inspect your curriculum."

Curriculum? Anna glanced over her shoulder. Six boys sat in awkward silence, their spelling test thoroughly forgotten.

Alice went to the table. "What curriculum are you using?" She looked over the tests.

Anna stared at her. "I am not—"

"Is it State approved? I'll also need to see your credentials." She turned to Anna. "When did you receive your State of Indiana teaching certification?"

Anna moistened her suddenly dry lips. "I do not have—" Aware of how young she sounded, she cleared her throat. "That is, I have been hired as a tutor."

"Tutor...?" Frowning, Alice slowly scrutinized Anna's gown from the bottom up. "I don't know how things work where you come from—wherever that is—but around here, we abide by the law." She picked up Jimmy's spelling test, then scanned the list of words. "*Assimilate*?" She tilted her head at Anna, eyes narrowing. "I have a mind to turn you in to the Board of Education. What do you hope to accomplish by coming here without credentials posing as a teacher and undermining—"

"That's enough," Thomas growled from the kitchen doorway. He wore a film of sawdust and a look of fury that would have made Stalin quake. "Miss Anna is a highly experienced teacher. There's no call for any of this."

Alice's chin jutted out. "It's my duty to inspect the curriculum of every school in the county."

Thomas came into the parlor and stood, arms crossed. "For your information, I've assumed responsibility for these boys' academic studies for the rest of this school year."

"You can't do that. It's unorthodox."

Thomas shrugged. "I can, and there's nothing unorthodox about it. And when the rest of our curriculum arrives, you're free to look at it."

Alice tossed Jimmy's paper aside. "What about her accent? Clearly she's—"

"Fluent? Yes, I've noticed." His crossed forearms tightened, sending ripples along his skin. "Miss Anna's English is better than most people I know."

"Well, considering the company you keep, that means very little," she said, matching his crossed-arm posture. "You're already drawing disapproval in town for your involvement with undesirable influences. If I were you, I'd be eager to steer clear of anything questionable."

Thomas took a step closer to the woman. "The only *undesirable influence* I've come across is the self-righteous hogwash coming from the committees you lead. The company I keep is none of your business. Which reminds me—thanks for the charity."

With a frown, Alice fingered the string of pearls at her throat. "What charity?"

"Exactly." Thomas scoffed. "The food and clothes your club collects for the needy never seem to go to anyone truly in need."

The woman stared at him. "We can only do so much. Unfortunately, in times as hard as these, there will always be some who go without." She appraised Anna's second-hand gown again. "All the more proof that there isn't room for everyone here."

"That's not for you to say."

Alice answered with a flat smile. "I don't have to. Plenty of others are saying it." She dismissed Thomas by turning to Anna. "When I return, your lessons had better meet state standards and you had better produce some kind of credentials. And you can be sure I *will* be reporting this to the board." She left without closing the door.

Anna watched the woman get into her car, feeling as if she had just been through an earthquake.

Pete jumped up and slammed the door, then spun around. "Attaboy, Mr. Tom! You really let the ol' buzzard have it."

"And you *better* produce some kind of *credentials*," Albert mocked, his shrill voice breaking. The others roared with laughter.

"That's enough, fellas."

As the hoots and chatter continued, Anna looked Thomas in the eye. "I am sorry, but I do not have an Indiana teaching certificate."

Thomas shook his head. "Don't worry. She thinks that just because her husband is a deputy sheriff, she can stick her nose into everyone's business. Her visit isn't worth the breath we're wasting on it, trust me."

Anna nodded, but she did not share Thomas's indifference. Based on her dealings with the Withers family so far, she would bet one of Pete's nickels that she had not seen the last of them.

The chicken coop repairs were nearly finished, so on Tuesday afternoon, Anna and Sam borrowed Jack's red wagon and set off for the Tucker farm to collect Sarah's mending. Sam towed the wagon ahead of Anna, leading the way. He checked over his shoulder several times as if to make sure Anna was still following.

She smiled.

After crossing a stretch of woods and a lane, the Tucker farm came into view. The house sat surrounded by plowed fields. A few cows lowed in the small pasture beyond the house.

Sarah put Ivy down for a nap, offered Sam a snack, and then presented

Anna a pile of mending that would take several days to finish. Sam sat on the edge of the porch with a sweet pickle and glass of milk while Sarah and Anna carried the mending out to the wagon.

"That's quite a pile, Anna. You sure a coupla hens is all I can give you for it?" Sarah said. But before Anna could reply, Sarah added, "Wait, I'll be right back." She put down her armload and disappeared around the side of the house.

Anna folded items and stacked them in the wagon. A small "Hi" from the house made her turn.

Violet flattened her face against the screen door. "Whatcha doin'?"

Anna smiled at the fair-haired girl. "I am taking these clothes home to mend for your mama."

"We got a dog." Violet opened the screen door and watched Sam drink his milk. "You got a dog?"

Sam shook his head, wiped his mouth, and took another bite of pickle.

"What is your dog's name?" Anna asked.

"Owen. He stinks. Pa calls him the Great *Gas*by." She picked at a splinter in the doorframe. "He's smart as a whip, though. He chases rabbits and catches mice better'n our cat. Sometimes, he sleeps under my bed. Till Pa gets wind and runs him out."

A golden-haired lab must have known he was being discussed and lumbered out to the porch. He looked more inclined to chase a long nap than a rodent. Sam scratched the dog's ears, and Violet went to Sam and joined him.

Sarah returned out of breath with a basket full of eggs. "Here you go. Consider it a down payment for the mendin'."

"But Sarah, a down payment is not necessary."

"Honey, I got eggs comin' out my ears. If you don't take 'em, they'll just go to waste. Cook 'em up for supper."

"Well then, if you insist," Anna said with a smile. "Thank you. Perhaps we will have crepes for supper."

"Crepes? Now you're making me hungry."

Anna laughed.

"Gee, you got a pretty laugh." Sarah smiled. "Pretty everything, in fact. Those boys are real lucky to have you there. Not just to help with their schoolin', but, you know. A woman's touch around the house and all. Must make for a nice change."

When Sam looked up, Sarah saw him and answered with a laugh. "What—don't you think so?"

Sam glanced away and nodded.

The visit from Alice Withers still nagged at Anna. The children were occupied with the dog, so she spoke lightly. "Sarah, do you know Mrs. Withers?"

"Alice? Oh, everybody in Alton County knows her." Sarah lowered herself to sit on the porch. "She likes to have a say in everything from politics to prohibition. She's a real fireball. I reckon she'd fix all the evils in the country if she could. Why do you ask?"

"She came by this morning. I just wondered how well you knew her." Anna hesitated. "Since...you and her daughter are good friends."

The light in Sarah's eyes flickered. Her gaze dropped to her feet. "Penny's not bad. You just have to get to know her." Sarah plucked at a piece of grass growing up between the porch boards. "Farm life gets real lonely sometimes, Anna. I take whatever friends I can get."

Shayna's face came to mind. Anna had been blessed with not only a devoted sister, but a faithful friend. One who believed only the best, was quick to forgive, and was unflinching in her support. Sarah deserved a friend like Shayna.

Anna met Sarah's gaze. "I hope you will come to consider me your friend."

Sarah chuckled and the light in her eyes returned. "Aw, sugar, I already do."

Eleven

THE NEXT SEVERAL DAYS PROVED TO BE ESPECIALLY FRUITFUL, as if the mere thought of seeds sprouting and chickens laying gave Anna an added burst of energy. Perhaps it was the sunshine and sweet April breezes. Or the new supply of potatoes, milk, and kerosene delivered by the sisters. Or perhaps Anna's renewed energy was a sign that she had entered the second trimester of pregnancy. Whatever the reason, Anna spent the week tending the new garden, finishing Sarah's mending in exchange for six fat hens, and acquiring, surprisingly, some mending work from Sister Mary Francis.

She had also mailed Shayna's letter, using *General Delivery, Corbin, Indiana* as the return address, on the whisper of a chance that Shayna might send a reply before Anna moved on. She tried to suppress her hopes of a return letter, but this was becoming more difficult with each passing day.

Her greatest accomplishment of the week, however, was finishing Thomas's quilt. Since she had to make do with what scraps she had been given, the quilt was quite ridiculous—a chaotic mishmash of color and shape. It had no design or pattern, no symmetry. And, in addition to being the strangest looking thing she had ever made, it had been the most challenging. She had to find ways to connect the varying sizes and shapes like puzzle pieces. There was no order to it. But thanks to sheer determination, those odd scraps had become something new and sturdy, and though nothing about it matched, it would serve its purpose well, and that was what mattered.

Friday afternoon, Thomas and the boys went to work at the Mercy School, leaving Anna alone to prepare supper. The kneading of dough took Anna back home, back to Mama's kitchen, to Shabbat preparations, to Rivka, Anshel, and Shayna. Somehow, the distance from home did not feel as great as it had when she first arrived. Had it only been nine days? For now, this peculiar family of six boys and their mentor, along with her newfound friend, had become the entirety of Anna's community. Finally, being part of something bigger than herself brought a small measure of peace that she had not felt in weeks.

After setting loaves of challah to rise, Anna made sure no one was around, then took the quilt out to the workshop, peeked inside Thomas's office, and ventured in.

She had never been in the room where Thomas conducted business and now slept. Various books and ledgers rested on shelves above the desk. The cot was nothing more than a low platform topped by a thin, stained mattress, with no pillow or bedding. How did the man sleep? Surely it was difficult. She spread out the quilt on the cot. As she turned to go, she saw two framed photographs on a shelf above the bed, along with a worn Bible, which she took down. Inside the cover was written the name *Gabriel Johansen.*

A twinge of guilt arose. She should not be touching his personal things, spying on his private life. She put the Bible back, but her gaze landed on the two photographs on the shelf. A young woman in one photo had eyes which somehow looked directly into Anna's. A small child in breeches sat on her lap, his light-colored hair a sharp contrast against the woman's dark frock. There was something in the woman's eyes that reminded her of Thomas. It was an old photograph, so it was possible that the child would be his age now.

The other photograph was an older man with a thick shock of blond or white hair—it was difficult to tell—and eyes that crinkled at the edges as though creased from a lifelong, ready smile. He wore a toolbelt and a thick leather apron, and he seemed to be covered in the same pale coating of dust that Anna often saw on Thomas and the boys. The man stood beside a horse-drawn wagon loaded down with lumber.

Anna looked closer. On the side of the wagon, a sign read: Johansen Woodwoorks.

Did the Bible bearing the Johansen name belong to the man in the photograph?

A crash of shattering glass and the sound of a revving engine shook Anna from her ponderings. She rushed outside in time to see a pickup truck heading away. Cautiously, she looked around the property but saw no one and nothing to account for the sound. As she approached the front of the house, she stopped. The front room window was broken, with glass fragments glittering all over the porch, and the pane hanging in shards.

Pulse quickening, Anna turned and scanned the road and area for the return of the pickup, but it had disappeared.

Avoiding the glass, Anna went inside. There, in the center of the front room, was a brick wrapped with a slip of paper and tied with string.

Her heart thumped. The window had been deliberately broken.

Anna wrapped her arms around herself, suddenly cold. Who had done this? And why?

The brick held the answer. Stepping carefully, Anna retrieved it. With shaking hands, she untied the string and removed the paper. The brick was blackened on one side with soot. As she suspected, the paper contained a note, which read:

> *only a devil worshipper would take up with the devils wives.*
> *if you keep dealing with the devil its only a matter of time*
> *before you and your dirty little mongrels get whats coming*

Anna read the note twice before realizing that she was trembling. It was clearly a threat, but what was "coming," and what did the note mean?

By the time Thomas and the boys returned, Anna had cleaned up the glass and tucked the brick and note out of sight. Luckily, the troupe came in through the kitchen, so she suggested everyone stop right there and wash up for supper. Meanwhile, she took Thomas aside and told him what had happened.

He strode to the front room and looked over the damaged window, hands on his hips. She gave him the note, which he read, and then crumpled.

"The note was meant for you?" Anna asked.

"Probably." He raised his arm as if to throw it into the fireplace, then stopped. "I guess Sheriff Dooley might want to see it."

"Do you know who did this?"

Thomas's lips pressed into a line. "I have my suspicions."

"Will they come back?" Anna tried to remain calm but could hear the tremor in her voice.

He shook his head. "I doubt it. Anybody who'd wait until I'm gone to throw a brick through a window and run away is a coward. Certainly not man enough to threaten me to my face. Besides, it's pure nonsense. They don't know what they're talking about."

"What do they mean by 'devils wives'?"

"They mean the help we get from the sisters."

She tried but could not understand the accusation. "This makes no sense."

"You're right about that," Thomas said. "There are a number of folks in this area who believe that certain people are a poison to our society. They use bully tactics like this to scare off or force out those they think are polluting their 'pure' community."

Anna could still hear Papa promising his wife and children that America would welcome them because it welcomed all people. But very little of what Papa promised had been true, after all. "What kind of people do they want to force out?"

Thomas blasted a sigh. "They have a list. Mainly Catholics, Jews, Negroes, and most immigrants."

Anna belonged to not one but two of those groups and was certainly no stranger to such treatment. Throughout history, her people had been rounded up and caged, or forced to pull up stakes and flee. They had been brutalized. Harassed. Enslaved. Scattered. Herded. Blamed. Loathed. She herself had been threatened and oppressed and uprooted too many times to count. Why these things took place, she never fully understood. Neither Mama nor Papa had ever been able to explain the reason for such deep-seated bigotry, such vigorous exclusion. All she knew was you could be tormented for a heritage you did not choose. You could inherit a life of constant upheaval and uncertainty whether you wanted it or not. You could be despised for the odious crime of simply being born.

She also knew with increasing certainty that there was no such thing as a golden country. There was no place free of hate, no place where the Jewish people could settle and breathe freely. No place where Anna would ever truly belong.

"It's muleheaded ignorance," Thomas said quietly. "These people are like sheep, believing rumors without question, despising others based on broad, blind assumptions."

Anna frowned. "Can they not see they are wrong? Realize the rumors are not true?"

"The sad irony is that many bigots have never even *met* an actual person belonging to the groups they hate."

She stared at the man. This was no *irony*; it was appalling. And it was wrong.

With a sigh, Thomas went to the broken window and studied the frame.

Anna's thoughts circled around the Sisters of Mercy. Mary Francis had hinted that the fire that destroyed their school had been deliberately set. And now, the boys who once attended that school were helping the sisters rebuild it.

"So, they have added to their list," Anna said slowly, picturing the note in her mind. "Whoever hates the Sisters of Mercy enough to burn down their school has now turned their hatred toward you and six young boys for being their friend."

Thomas continued to examine the window. "I don't know."

Anna listened to the sound of chatter and horseplay in the kitchen. "I think you do."

He turned and met her gaze for a long moment before turning away again. "Probably."

"What about the boys? Are you not concerned for their safety?"

Thomas shook his head. "No. Like I said, whoever did this is a coward. And these boys are a lot more resilient than you think. They've been through a heck of a lot worse than a brick through a window."

But would resilience be enough if the promised threat was carried out? Anna had not forgotten what the boys told her about the ghostly, torch-wielding men cloaked in white.

Thomas faced her. "If I ever have reason to think these boys are in any danger, I'll do whatever it takes to protect them. And everyone who knows me knows that."

Later that evening, when the boys gathered around the radio to listen to *The Shadow*, Anna took her basket of fabric into the kitchen to work near the stove. Between mending jobs, she planned to make more quilts to sell. With any luck, she might even earn enough to send a little money to Shayna.

She had stitched together a large block when Thomas stepped into the kitchen.

"I want to show you something." He handed her a crumpled, folded paper. "About two months ago, a starving boy turned up on my front porch, wet from the rain, silent, and shaking like a leaf. He was all alone, and this was pinned to him."

Anna opened the paper, held it closer to the lamp, and read,

> *I done give up prayin but I heard about you so I got one last prayer. I pray to Jesus that you can give my Sam a better life than I can. —hopeless*

Tears stung her eyes. "Sam's mother?" she asked.

Thomas nodded.

Anna read the note again. A woman giving up a child she could not care for, one she hoped might have a better life with a total stranger. A child whom she clearly loved and wanted, but was, for whatever reason, unable to keep. As she handed it back, a twisting sensation in Anna's chest made it impossible to breathe.

"I was once angry, alone, and headed down a dangerous path," Thomas said. "But someone cared enough to take me in and straighten me out, teach me a trade, give me a reason to hope." He folded the note and returned it to his shirt pocket. "I'm here to do the same for these boys, and no one's going to stop me." He met her eyes with a look that burned through Anna, stole her breath. "I'm not going anywhere. Sam's mother knew that, and so does everyone else in this town."

Anna studied the man, the one who now dedicated his life to the care and guidance of others. His determination to look out for the boys was admirable. But if protecting them meant taking a stand against such hateful and hostile people, Anna hoped he had something more than determination to fight with.

Sunday afternoon, the sisters arrived with a truckload of new supplies, including a large assortment of cast-off clothing and shoes. Anna hunted through the pile and found, to her delight, a full-length apron, which would be especially useful. Then she spied a large gown, and on further inspection, saw that it was Mama's old-fashioned, full-skirted style. She seized it, folded it quickly, then added it to her pile.

Mary Agnes watched Anna, her look confused. "Surely that dress is much too large for you?"

"Yes, but I...need something large enough to wear over extra clothing, for warmth," she said. Lying was becoming too easy. "For when I resume my travels. The nights will be cold."

Mary Agnes eyed her curiously but said nothing.

"I almost forgot about your journey," Thomas said as he hefted down a large bag from the truck. "You still haven't told us your story."

Anna tried to dispel the sudden panic that his comment caused her with a laugh. "Sorry to disappoint, but I have no story."

"*Everyone* has a story." Thomas hoisted the bag onto his shoulder.

This was true. But even a snippet of her story could lead to questions that would become too revealing.

As Thomas headed for the house, Anna said quietly, "Some stories are not as happy as others."

"I guess you're dead set on keeping yours to yourself."

Anna froze. Would Thomas suspect she could not be trusted since she was not more candid? If he insisted on knowing more, she would have no choice but to leave.

He looked over his shoulder, then stopped and set his bag down. "Sorry, didn't mean to pry. Forget I asked. By the way, I've been meaning to thank you for the quilt. Working on it must have kept you up late many a night."

"It was no trouble. It is a very small price in exchange for a roof, a warm bed, and food."

He shook his head. "You already earn those things by teaching. Many times over. The quilt was an added labor of kindness, and I just want you to know how much I appreciate it."

She swallowed hard. "You are welcome."

He stood quietly for a moment with a faraway look, as if the woods beyond the small farm invited him to come and explore deeper questions, away from prying eyes and shallow conversations.

"Anna, I didn't mean to be nosy," he said finally. "I don't question your character. Your actions tell me all I need to know. Your story is your own business."

"Thank you," she said, breathing a deep sigh of relief. Somehow, he had read her mind.

"Some stories can take unwanted, unexpected turns," he said. "So many that a person can wind up lost." With a sigh, Thomas hoisted the bag to his shoulder and headed toward the house.

"So, you are lost, too," Anna whispered.

Twelve

THE FIRST MONDAY OF APRIL BROUGHT A STEADY, GRAY RAIN that battered the windows without ceasing, like a cranky child who awoke in a mood and wanted everyone to know. But the fire crackling in the parlor defied the gloom and reminded Anna again of how fortunate she was to have a roof over her head. It also reminded her that time was marching on and she still had much to accomplish.

A firm knock at the front door interrupted the morning's arithmetic lesson.

"I'll get it," Jimmy said as he leapt from his seat. "My turn to give that ol' battle-axe the kiss off."

Anna shook her head. "*I* will deal with this, Jimmy." But even as she said the words, her shoulders tensed. Thomas had said nothing about expecting visitors before he left on a delivery. She had no wish to be interrogated again, and without Thomas. But then, if she could not stand up to Alice Withers on her own, how would she manage in a world full of Alices?

Anna steeled herself and opened the door.

An older man wearing a drenched raincoat over a beige police uniform stood on the porch.

"It's the sheriff," someone hissed.

The man removed his dripping hat, revealing thinning gray hair. "Morning, ma'am," he said. "Is Chandler at home?"

"I am sorry, he is not." Anna shot a look over her shoulder. Pete was addressing the others in a vigorous whisper. Jack motioned to her with his head until Pete caught on and clammed up. They all went still.

She turned back to the sheriff. "We expect him to return after lunch. Perhaps you can come back then?"

"I *would* like to talk with him about the investigation I'm conducting," the officer said. "But that's not the only reason I'm here." He glanced beyond her. "I'm Colin Dooley, Alton County Sheriff. Mind if I come in?"

Anna wished Thomas was home. "I am Miss Anna, the boys' teacher," she said as she opened the door for him. "May I ask why you are here?"

The sheriff shook the rain from his hat and stepped inside. He peered at the boys. "I need to speak to Sam."

A chair screeched, and Anna turned to see Albert pressing a hand to Sam's shoulder, pinning him to his seat.

"Perhaps the three of us can speak in the kitchen," Anna said. "Sam, will you come with us, please?"

Sam did not budge.

"It is okay, Sam, I will be there." Anna did not wait for him but turned and led the way. She felt a surge of relief when Sam rose and followed the adults to the kitchen.

More heated whispers erupted from the other room. Meanwhile, Sam stopped near the cookstove and waited, eyes never leaving his feet.

"Did you say you are conducting an investigation?" Anna asked.

"Yes, ma'am, the Sisters of Mercy have reported a series of thefts," Sheriff Dooley said. "Building materials, kerosene, and other supplies keep turning up missing."

That the sisters reported the theft surprised her. Perhaps Mary Frances had finally convinced Mary Agnes to acknowledge the attacks as crimes. But what about the fire?

Albert peeked around the doorway, but Anna gave him the look she gave Anshel when he needed help remembering his manners, and the boy ducked out of sight.

"And I'm not getting a lick of cooperation from anyone in town," Dooley added.

A cold dread crept over Anna. Did the sheriff think Sam had something to do with the missing supplies? She glanced at the boy, but Sam did not look up, not even to steal a glance.

The sheriff spied the braided loaf cooling on the counter. "Never seen bread like that. Did you make it?"

"Yes."

"It looks too fancy to eat."

Anna frowned. What was the sense in making food one could only look at? "Would you like a slice?"

"It's tempting, but I'd best get to doing what I came for." With a sigh, he turned to Sam. "Now then, I've had a report that you were seen down by the creek carrying a pie. When you were questioned about it, you took off running. Is that true?"

Sam stiffened but did not respond or look up.

"Did you steal that pie?" the sheriff asked.

The child shook his head vigorously.

The sheriff folded arms across his chest. "Miz Beckett is a long-time member of this community, and she says she saw you running off with someone's pie." He eyed Sam carefully. "Now, son, are you going to tell me what you were doing with a whole pie, or am I going to have to take Miz Beckett's word for it?"

Sam's gaze traveled from the officer's badge to his gun belt.

Panic flooded Anna's nerves, numbing her. There was no telling what punishment a colored boy would receive for such a crime, but she could only imagine, and the possibilities turned her blood cold.

"Pardon me," she said, heart racing, "but has someone reported a pie missing?"

Sheriff Dooley rubbed his chin. "Well, now, that I don't know."

God forgive her for what she was about to do. "Because it seems Mrs. Beckett has not considered the possibility that Sam was...delivering the pie for me."

Sam stole a sharp glance at her. Anna fought a powerful urge to fan her blazing cheeks.

"Is that so?" Dooley tilted his head and studied her for a dreadfully long moment, scrutinizing her carefully, as if reading something written on her face. "Then why'd he run?"

"If you or I were in Sam's shoes, would we not react the same way?"

As the sheriff turned to appraise the boy, Anna longed to reel back her words, her tone. Surely her defiance would get her into trouble sooner or later, and she feared sooner.

The officer was taking far too long to respond.

Sweat beaded on her lip. Surely God would punish her for the lie.

He studied Anna again, then glanced around the kitchen until his gaze rested on the cooling loaves of bread. "Chandler pays you well to work here?"

Such an odd question. "I teach in exchange for room and board."

Dooley wore a puzzled frown. "So you don't earn any money at all?"

"I am paid for mending and sewing, when I can find work." Why did the sheriff want to know of her earnings?

"Mending," he repeated, his look thoughtful. "You don't say." He looked her in the eye, and then nodded slowly. "On second thought, I believe I *will* take you up on that slice of bread, if you don't mind."

"Yes...of course."

Anna prepared two slices of bread with butter and jam, baffled by the change of topic, but glad for it all the same. Sheriff Dooley took his with thanks, and Anna offered the other one to Sam. Both ate their bread together in silence, which only added to the strain on her nerves. She searched for a diversion. "Do you have any ideas about who is responsible for the trouble at the Mercy School?"

Dooley nodded. "Oh, I'm plumb full of ideas. The heck of it is, I have no evidence."

Two scruffy heads peeked around the doorway. Anna gave them her sternest look, and they quickly vanished.

"Best bread I've had in a long time. Don't tell my wife, though. Dorothy has a hard time baking and such these days, though she tries, bless her heart." The sheriff grimaced. "It's too painful for her hands, with the arthritis and all." He took another bite and chewed, slowly, thoughtfully. "We'd gladly pay you to get our mending caught up, if you could."

"Yes," Anna said, surprised. "Thank you."

He finished off the last bite and brushed crumbs from his hands. "I'd appreciate it if you'd tell Chandler I'll catch him next time around."

"Yes, I will."

He returned the parlor, and Anna followed him to the front door. He took his hat from the hook, then turned to her. "Ma'am, if you tell me Sam was carrying that pie for you, I'm obliged to take your word for it."

She let go the breath she did not realize she had been holding. She avoided Sam's gaze.

"Thank you for the bread. I'll be back in a day or two to drop off that mending."

"That will be fine," Anna said.

After the sheriff left, the boys flocked around Sam, all clamoring with questions and comments at once, but Sam covered his ears and shook his head.

"Leave him be," Anna said quietly. "He has endured enough questioning for one day."

By Tuesday afternoon, the skies cleared, and steam rose from the rain-soaked earth. Thomas sent the boys to do a simple porch repair for an elderly widow in town while he delivered a cabinet with an ancient flatbed pickup, so Anna collected the quilt she was making to sell, along with her supplies, and headed into town.

The grocery store seemed the best place to offer her mending services. She sat out front and worked deftly, piecing the colorful squares together with quick, even, stitches. After a while, several comments and compliments on her work turned into two mending jobs. Both customers went home and promised to return shortly with their items.

Pleased with her success, Anna took a break from sitting and went inside the grocery store to stretch and browse the aisles. Glass jars on the counter displayed a tempting assortment of colorful sweets. Anna smiled lightly. Little had she known a month ago she would come to miss Anshel's badgering for a penny candy. If her little brother were here now, Anna suspected she might even indulge him.

Life on her own had certainly changed her.

Of course, she now had *six* little brothers she could indulge, but her pennies were too precious to spare. Future work was uncertain. There was no telling how long she would be able to stay at Johansen Woodworks working and saving for the rest of her journey. With luck, as long as the boys were progressing, and as long as she met no further opposition, and as long as no one asked her too many questions, she would stay through the end of May, when the school year and assessment tests were complete.

"Did you tell Chandler about the rally?" a woman said in the next aisle.

Anna froze. Tall shelves of boxed and canned goods blocked her view, but she knew to whom the voice belonged. As little as she wanted to eavesdrop, she wanted to run into Alice Withers even less.

A male voice replied in tones too low for Anna to understand.

"Well, what did he say to that?"

"Dug in like a mule, same as always."

"Doesn't he know what'll happen if he doesn't join?"

The man grunted. "He's either too stupid to know, or too stupid to care. I told him if he thinks he can keep making his own rules, he's got another think coming."

"It's no wonder the church defrocked him and ran him off," Alice said. "Heaven only knows what depravity he espouses now. I wouldn't be surprised if those bead-rattlers put a hex on him." The woman's voice was much closer. "Boyd, he'd better not be teaching their filthy lies, because if he is, he'll wish he'd never—"

Alice and a man in a beige deputy's uniform appeared in the aisle and paused when they saw Anna.

Numb, Anna stared back.

"That's her," Alice said. "The *teacher*."

The dark-haired, beige-uniformed officer, who Anna assumed was Deputy Withers, crossed arms over his chest and eyed Anna from head to toe.

"But then," Alice said coolly, "I suppose there are far worse things those boys could be learning."

"Such as geography and penmanship?" Anna said. Every one of her nerves crackled.

The woman's chin lifted. "Since I have yet to see any curriculum, for all I know, you could be teaching spells and incantations."

"I am not acquainted with those subjects. Perhaps you can come and teach them yourself."

Deputy Withers sputtered and coughed, while Alice turned the color of a beet.

If Anna had her sister's moral decency, her reply *might* have been a little more diplomatic. She strode past them and left the store. She braced herself for more, but she saw neither Alice nor her husband come out as she collected her mending work and headed home.

By the time the boys returned, Anna had nearly succeeded at putting her encounter with the Withers couple behind her. This teaching job was temporary. She would focus on completing her task as best she could and ignore anything beyond that which did not concern her.

She was collecting eggs at the chicken coop when Sam joined her.

"You have finished the repair job for the elderly woman?"

Sam nodded and then crouched at the coop, tilting his head to look at the chickens.

"I hope these hens lay many eggs for us."

Sam turned to her, a question in his eyes.

"What?" she asked.

The boy made a sawing motion across his hand and pretended to take a bite.

"Yes, the eggs from these chickens will allow me to make plenty more challah," Anna said, shaking her head. Just like Anshel. Boys could be so single-minded when it came to food.

She carried her basket of eggs toward the house, and Sam followed. In the back yard, the rest of the boys were playing kick the can, and Sam took off at a run to join them.

Thomas appeared from his shop and joined her, spying the basket. "I never would have guessed a pile of mending could turn into a steady supply of food. Well done."

"Thank you." Seeing him brought back the exchange between Boyd and Alice Withers. "I overheard something about you in town today."

He huffed. "What's new."

Anna hesitated. While she had sense enough to mind her own business, this was difficult to ignore. "I heard the word 'defrocked.' I am unfamiliar with this term."

He came to a stop but said nothing.

She also stopped. "I also heard that your church kicked you out. Is this true?"

With a sigh, he planted hands on his hips. "The best gossip usually has a nugget of truth to it." He turned to the boys. "Did you fellas finish fixing Mrs. Poole's steps?"

"Yes, sir," Teddy said. "Once we anchored the new frame, the steps slipped right in and we nailed 'em down tight, just like you showed us."

"So which part is untrue?" Anna was unable to let the topic pass, even if he seemed determined to.

Something crossed his face, a grim shadow. "The church didn't kick me out, I left. Once in a while, I attend the Methodist church over in Perryville. But mostly, I worship right there." He pointed to the woods.

"And what about 'defrocked'?"

His jaw muscles twitched. "You must have bumped into Boyd Withers. He's chock full of hot air...among other things." He turned to Anna, catching her in his steady gaze. "That part's true. It means I was relieved of my duties and credentials. In a word, dismissed."

"Dismissed?" Anna frowned. "On what grounds?"

The can skidded toward them, and Thomas kicked it deftly back into play. "I broke a rule."

She studied the man, her thoughts swimming. She knew nothing of what Christians practiced in their religious gatherings and could not imagine what he could do that would warrant a dismissal. What rule had Thomas broken? Was he guilty of misconduct? A crime? Dishonesty? No. Though she knew very little about him, she was certain that Thomas Chandler was not a wicked man.

"What, now you're suddenly done prying?" He shook his head. "This is a first."

"I do not pry." She frowned. "I am not nosy."

Thomas watched the game with a light chuckle. "You could've fooled me."

Anna's jaw dropped. Perhaps it was his sarcasm that had gotten him dismissed. But it suddenly struck her that *she* was the one who had not only brought up the topic but insisted on pursuing it. "Fine. I am very curious about what kind of rule you broke."

He kept his eyes on the game. "I got a divorce."

Her jaw threatened to drop again. Thomas, married *and* divorced? This, she had not expected. "Why would they dismiss a minister for this?"

With a frown, Thomas smacked wood shavings from his trouser leg. "The leaders felt that if a man can't even manage his own home, then he doesn't have what it takes to manage a congregation. He is *'clearly disqualified to teach scripture.'*" He turned to the boys. "How much did Mrs. Poole pay for the repair?"

Teddy and Jimmy eyed each other, and everyone stopped the game in mid-run.

"She didn't," Jack said.

"She'll pay later?" Thomas asked.

"See, I *knew* he'd be sore," Pete said to Albert. "*You* tell him."

Albert took a deep breath. "We told her she didn't owe us nothin'."

"Is that so?" Thomas said. He stroked his mustache. "Why did you tell her that?"

A long, awkward pause.

"She was making tea from a used teabag," Teddy said. "We think that was her lunch."

"We hope you ain't sore, Mr. Tom," Jimmy said. "We talked it over and figured she needs her money a lot more than we do." All six boys waited for his reaction.

"Where I come from," Anna offered, "it is said that 'he who is gracious to the poor lends to the Lord.'"

"Proverbs nineteen-seventeen," Thomas added.

She stared at him. Did he know the Torah?

Teddy looked from Thomas to Anna with a confused frown. "So... you're not sore?"

Thomas moved across the lawn and rested a hand on Teddy's shoulder. "No. That was a real good decision. Shows you fellas have been listening. Well done."

Albert nudged Pete and held out his hand. "Pay up, toad."

Thomas shot a glance at Anna, a faint smile visible beneath his mustache.

As he headed up the steps to the house, Anna followed. "I am no expert, but it seems your leaders were wrong."

One brow arched as Thomas held the door open for her.

She stopped in the doorway and faced him. "Clearly, you are still qualified to teach scripture." She went inside the house, but when he did not follow, she glanced over her shoulder.

Thomas was still staring at the spot where she had stood.

Thirteen

9 April

Dearest,

Much has happened in the two weeks since I stopped at this unusual place. Johansen Woodworks is a business, an apprenticeship school, and a charity home, all in one. I am the only female amongst a pack of boys. I have learned a few new words, some inventive ways to avoid bathing, and new uses for a pocketknife. Mumbley Peg is a game I must teach you all one day.

The garden is in—although the rows look more like meandering rivers, but they will do. The repaired coop is now home to six laying hens. Thanks to the sisters (two nuns) and their generous gifts of scraps, I make quilts to sell. And I have acquired mending work, which explains the enclosed money. It is to help with rent. Put it in the sugar bowl with your own earnings and do not tell Mama where it came from.

After school and on weekends, the boys work to rebuild the Sisters of Mercy School. The Sisters Mary (I must ask why they are all Mary?) are important to Thomas's work. It seems that neither the nuns nor Thomas could succeed without the other. The Marys and Thomas do not practice their faith the same way, which confuses me, as I think they worship the same G-d, yet they seem to be willing to overlook their differences. If only everyone else could.

Besides Thomas, the Sisters of Mercy are the only ones

in this town willing to educate a Negro. Because of this, and some of their Catholic customs, they are despised by a certain group of people. The sisters are mistreated and harassed (the source of the fire that destroyed their school remains a mystery even though the local sheriff seems to know who harasses them, but for some reason, he is unable to arrest anyone). But even though they are maligned and harassed, the sisters continue to help those in need. Their commitment to serve comes from a deep sense of duty or godly principle, which I find strangely comforting. It reminds me of home, of our neighbors' collective efforts to care for one another, even during our most unsettled of times.

This bigoted group has threatened Thomas for helping and receiving help from the sisters. And yet, the man is unconcerned. I find this odd. In fact, I find many things odd about Thomas Chandler. I just discovered he was divorced, which cost him his job as a minister. He says it was "a different time, a different life." He still worships his G-d, but he does this alone now, out in the woods. The woods! Is this not odd? Would Reb Yosef have to give up his duties if divorced? This, I do not know. And though I have already asked Thomas many "prying" questions that are clearly not my business, you should be proud of me for not prying about his failed marriage. I do have <u>some</u> restraint. But just between me and you, the wondering is maddening.

I have learned so much these past two weeks. I have learned that bigotry thrives in the shadows of ignorance, that intolerance can make people do ugly things, and that the truly righteous may not always earn the favor of man, but will always find joy in humble devotion to G-d.

Please give my love to Rivka, Anshel, and Mama. And write soon if you can. I miss your disarming laugh, your tireless hope, and most of all, your forgiving smile.

All my love,

A.

Monday afternoon, while Thomas and the boys worked with Henry to repair something in the Tuckers' barn, Anna took Jack's red wagon to town to deliver mending. Word had spread that she was a good and fast seamstress, and she was delighted to find new requests waiting at the Corbin General Store.

"Anna?"

Penny Withers hurried over and caught up with Anna at the cash register. "I was just asking Sarah whatever happened to you. The girls and I are meeting at Gertrude's. You should join us."

Anna hesitated but remembered Mama's adage that the best way to conquer an enemy was to befriend them. Perhaps Anna could spare a nickel for a Coke, just this once.

"Perhaps I will stop by the café for a few minutes, after I am finished here."

Penny's face lit up. "We are *sorely* in need of a fresh face. About the only thing to do around here is count flies on the old coots asleep in front of the barber shop." She promised to save Anna a seat, then left.

Anna marveled at the odd invitation. Sarah Tucker had said Penny was "not bad." What harm was there in getting to know her and some of the other girls in town? After all, if Anna wanted to prove that knowing people better could help combat blind prejudice, then should not the initiative begin with herself?

After she finished her business, she crossed the street and entered the café.

Penny waved to her from a booth full of young women, then she shooed out a red-haired girl and pointed. "Sit here. Everyone, this is Anna, the one I told you about."

"Hi," Anna said, taking the seat next to Sarah Tucker.

Sarah beamed and squeezed her arm. "I'm so glad you came."

"You already know Sarah, and that's Leota Beckett there," Penny said with a nod at the red-haired one who did not look at all pleased about having to drag over another chair for herself. "And next to me here is Dot."

The freckled girl across from Anna wore a weak smile that did not match the confused look in her blue eyes. "Nice to meet you," Dot said with a puzzled frown. "Are you...here to join up?"

Penny made an exasperated sound. "Dot, we're not doing that now, remember?"

"Oh, right," Dot said, her cheeks flushing. "Sorry, Penny."

Penny rolled her eyes. "Don't worry, Anna, we're not recruiting you. We just want to get better acquainted. Maybe you can come play cards at our next social."

Sarah threw Penny a wide-eyed look.

"Sarah Tucker, don't look at me like that. I know Anna's not planning on staying in Corbin long. Isn't that right, Anna?"

"Yes," she said. "I am only staying until school ends in May."

"Since you brought *that* up...people are in a tizzy about what you're teaching those boys," Penny said, "but just so you know, *I* don't hold to any of that nonsense."

Anna was not sure if she should believe Penny. Was it not her own mother who had started the rumors?

"But just so we know, what exactly are you teaching them?"

Anna bit back the urge to answer *spells and incantations* and instead, said, "Nothing worthy of a *tizzy*, I am afraid. Reading, writing, and arithmetic. My goal is to help them to pass their grade levels."

"No parochial subjects?"

"What is that?"

Penny smiled knowingly at the other three. "It's a kind of indoctrination that we don't want here. We only want teaching that's a hundred percent American."

"American?"

"Yes, we're very patriotic," Dot chimed in.

Penny ignored Dot. "As the next generation of wives and mothers, it's our duty to protect the purity of the American home. Part of that duty is ensuring the right sort of education in our schools."

"That is very noble of you," Anna said slowly, still uncertain what to think of Penny Withers, and especially now, when she sounded like she was reciting from some kind of pamphlet. "So you want to help shape America's future through education."

"Exactly." Penny smiled. "In the shape of native-born Americans and upstanding communities."

"Native-born?" Anna frowned, uncertain she had heard correctly. "But America is made up of people who came from many countries over hundreds of years."

Dot shot an alarmed look at Penny.

Sarah spoke up quickly. "I think what Anna means is the pioneers, like my grandparents. They came from Sweden to provide a better future for their families."

"But that makes them immigrants, not pioneers," Leota said.

"Sarah's folks were the right sort of people," Penny said. "But many who came here were not. And there are still too many here who are not *real* Americans."

Anna looked at the others. "So some immigrants are real Americans, but others are not?"

"Let me put it this way," Penny said. "Before the immigration quotas, low-class people came bringing all kinds of depravity and corruption that threaten our nation's moral fiber. Others came planning to infiltrate our schools and overthrow our government. That's why we all need to work together. We have to keep the bad influences out of our community. By rallying the local citizens, we can protect our nation from foreign threats and uphold true Americanism."

Penny seemed to be waiting for her to respond, but Anna held her tongue because what she wanted to say would likely get her thrown out of the café. Jews were among those whose entry into America had been limited by quotas. The only reason her family was able to bypass the quota was because they had a sponsor in the country who could vouch for the fact that their father was already here, and a citizen.

Pulse racing, Anna drew a calming breath and glanced at the others. Sarah stirred her soda, a crease in her brow. Dot and Leota seemed to be waiting for Penny to do something glorious, like burst into song.

"For some people," Anna said quietly, keeping her tone even, "coming to America is a last and desperate hope. A hope that comes at a great price and often with great loss. They must pass citizenship tests and complete a lengthy naturalization process. It is difficult, but they do all that is required, learn the language, and adapt to the culture, because they love this country and want to put down permanent roots. A country they can defend and be proud of. A place—" she swallowed an unexpected lump in her throat— "where they can belong."

With a snicker, Penny clapped. "Fabulous speech."

Dot and Leota gaped at Penny as if she had sprouted horns.

Penny leaned closer to Anna. "You weren't born here, were you?"

"What difference does that make?" Sarah said, her voice low.

Penny shrugged. "Maybe it does, maybe it doesn't."

"You can't be serious, Penny," Leota hissed. "What would your mother say?"

"Ah, Mother." Penny gazed into her soda. "Mother would want to know *exactly* what Anna's background is." She stirred circles in the drink with her straw, watching the bubbles spin. For a moment, it seemed as if Penny had tired of the topic. Then she glanced up at Anna. "So what are you?"

Silence settled over the table.

Anna was unsure how to respond. Thomas knew that her family had come from Poland and had not run her off for it. But then, Thomas did not keep a list of the *right sort* of people. Anna was not ready to leave town, not until she had fulfilled her commitment and earned a little more travel money.

"I came from Poland." Anna held her breath and then hated herself for it, hated that she could not just answer boldly, hated that she felt as if she were on trial before a jury of girls no more grown up than herself, and certainly not superior to her.

"I knew you were a foreigner," Penny said, eyeing her thoughtfully. "I just didn't know what kind. But Polish folks are white, right?"

Anna resisted the urge to glance at the color of her hands and instead lifted her chin. There were so many things she could say to Penny. So many things Anna had seen in the world outside these city limits, things about life, about the magic of human touch, about honor and grief and survival and courage, about humankind in its vast array of colors and shapes and textures, the giant, crazy patchwork quilt of human interconnectedness that existed beyond Penny Withers and her tiny empire in Corbin, Indiana.

"I've decided." Penny smiled at Anna. "You can join us."

Dot shot a glance at Leota.

"I don't care what Mother says." Penny sniffed. "I can add whomever I want."

It suddenly occurred to Anna that she had become sufficiently acquainted with Penny Withers. She scooted out of the booth and stood. "I must go. Thank you for including me in your discussion. It was...educational."

"I'll walk with you to the bridge," Sarah said, sliding out to join her.

Sarah followed Anna out of the café, and they headed down Main Street. Clouds covered the sun, casting filmy shadows across their path.

The sudden ah-ooo-ga of a car horn startled Anna. The car plowed through a puddle, dousing their feet in muddy water.

"Anna, I'm sure once you meet some of the other—"

"Wait...just a minute," Penny's voice called out.

Anna looked over her shoulder. Penny was heading toward her, the other two girls trailing behind. Anna and Sarah stopped and waited.

"You said, 'I *came* from Poland,'" Penny said as she came near.

Anna stiffened.

"You didn't say, 'I'm Polish.'" Penny faced Anna now, nostrils flaring. "You didn't say it because you're not, are you?"

Dot and Leota now flanked Penny.

Sarah looked anxious. "Come on, Penny. We all talked to her. She's one of us."

As Sarah spoke, an oddly detached feeling came over Anna, as if she was suddenly watching the scene from above, like a spectator at a play.

"You're a *Jew*, aren't you?" Penny hissed. "A *filthy Jew*."

Anna's belly shuddered, followed by a sudden kick.

Fourteen

IT WAS ONLY WHEN SHE REACHED THE FRONT PORCH AT THE JO-
hansen place that Anna realized she was shaking. The sound of Penny's
voice shouting, "And just keep on going because you're not welcome here!"
continued to echo in her head.

It would be best to pack her bag now, before Thomas heard the news.
Would he immediately throw her out? Despise her for being Jewish?

He was not like them, but what did she know? And even if he did not
share their views, he had to live among these people, these tyrants who
made their own rules and dictated who was allowed to live in this town and
who was not. He had to go along with the majority, did he not?

Anna closed her eyes. The kicking in her belly resumed, this time a
persistent series of flutters. "You are not the only one," she whispered. "I
am angry, too."

By the time Thomas and the boys returned, Anna had her bag and
bedroll packed and supper warming on the stove. She waited in the parlor,
nerves humming like too-tight violin strings.

Thomas came into the kitchen, his face stern. "Henry Tucker told me
what happened."

She braced herself.

"Are you all right?"

A lump formed in her throat. This was not the response she had expected. "It is nothing I have not heard before."

Thomas heaved a sigh. Then he spied her bundle in the corner and
frowned. "What's that? You're not leaving? Just because of Penny Withers?"

"I am leaving because I am Jewish, and it is better for you and the boys if I am not here."

"Penny and her family are full of hot air. They don't make the rules, and they don't get to decide what I do or who stays on my property. The Withers and their kind will just have to get used to it."

She exhaled, but it did not loosen the tension in her gut.

"You are exactly what these boys need now."

"But my being here will bring more trouble to you. If they disliked you before, I cannot imagine what they will think of you with a Jew under your roof."

"I couldn't care less what they think." He picked up her bag and placed it in her hands. "This belongs upstairs. Don't give Penny—or any other Withers—another thought."

On her way to gather eggs the next afternoon, Anna stopped to check the garden's progress. A faint line of green seedlings had sprouted, and recent rains had done the job of watering. There was little to do but wait and hope for a good crop—a crop she would not be here to see.

But she was dawdling. It was the time for Passover, and being in the kitchen only served as a reminder that she was far from home, and among strangers.

This time of year had always been one of preparation, a time of bustling alongside her siblings, of endless directions and inspections from Mama. For the past few years, Anna had silently resented the holiday, but now, all she could think about was her family removing every crumb of bread and cleaning every crack in the house, combing the cupboards to remove all traces of leaven. Mashing horseradish. Shaping matzo. She had long resented the arduous preparations for the Seder celebrations, but even more, she had grown to resent the birthright forced upon her.

And yet now, far from loved ones and exiled from all the busyness, the holiday only made her feel disconnected, as if she traveled on a current above the earth like a seed in the wind, driven carelessly, without place or purpose.

"The garden is coming along," Thomas said from behind her. "Thanks to you."

"Its gardeners are doing a good job caring for it."

"They're learning. It helps that they're excited about harvesting their first crop."

"I know," Anna said with a chuckle. "Jack and Albert nearly fell over each other bringing me their first yield. I did not have the heart to tell them they had picked a handful of weeds. I am only thankful they did not ask me to cook it."

Thomas belted out a laugh, hearty and infectious.

Anna burst out laughing.

He studied her, a broad smile lingering on his face. "That's a first," he said. "I think Indiana is good for you, Anna. Maybe you ought to stick around."

Her smile collapsed. "That is not possible," she said lightly.

"Right, Chicago. I keep forgetting," he said, his face sobering.

"I am going there to look for my Papa," she blurted without thinking. She swallowed the sudden dryness in her throat. "My family has not heard from him in six years."

"Why Chicago?"

"That is where he was last believed to be."

Thomas nodded. "Do you have any leads on his whereabouts?"

She hesitated. No, she had no leads, so her venture would seem quite foolish to others. It was desperation alone that drove her into such a blind search, a groping in the dark. But the reason for her desperation was something she could never divulge.

"I am hoping for very good luck."

He opened his mouth to speak, then closed it, as if he thought better of it.

With no warning, she was struck by how very attractive a man he was. But although he was strong and quite pleasing to look at, it was actually his kindness and character that made him so. He would make some lucky woman a wonderful husband one day.

Her cheeks burned.

He smiled. "Thank you," he said, looking into her eyes.

"For what?"

"For trusting me enough to share part of your story."

Friday's visit to the post office yielded not one but two letters: one for Thomas, and one for Anna. She could not stop smiling.

She pocketed the one for Thomas, but not before noting its return address, marked simply *Concerned Citizens for True America*. She took a seat on the bench in front of the store and tore open the envelope from Shayna, her hands quaking so badly that she nearly dropped the letter.

7 April

Dearest Anna,

When I received your letter, I cried for half an hour. I am so glad to know you are safe and well. I miss you and worry about you every day. Please write again soon and tell me more. What does Mr. Thomas look like? Shame on you for not including this detail. I am glad you have a friend in Sam and all it took was sharing a little challah.

Everyone misses you, too. Especially Anshel. He kvetches because you took his map. Not because you did not ask, but because you did not take him with you on your adventure. Sometimes I wish you had taken me, too, but then I would miss Isaak.

Oh, Anna, why did you have to go? Mama says that it is for the best now, but I must confess that sometimes what others say is best is difficult for me to accept. However, if you tell me it is truly for the best, then I will say no more. I trust your judgment.

Yes, we are eating and making do, so you can stop worrying. Isaak comes by a few times a week and helps Mama, and she is slowly warming to him. Is he not wonderful? Still, I must say that the role of eldest is not as easy as you have made it look. But I shall do my best to make you proud and help take care of our family in your absence. I hope you find Papa and can bring him home. Then we will be together, and ALL will be right again.

I love you, Anna. Please come home soon.
S.

P.S. This week, Rivka is in love with Gary Cooper. Last week,
it was Cary Grant.
P.P.S. Anshel got an "A" on his geography exam and he says
you owe him a penny candy.

Anna could hear her sister's voice in every word. Tears flowing, she pressed the letter to her chest, then read it again. But as much as she treasured this glimpse of home, Shayna's letter was also a painful reminder of what she was missing. The hugs, the touches, her siblings' teasing. And no greeting from Mama, which did not surprise Anna.

It was so like Shayna to praise her, and yet, Anna did not deserve it. Shayna's innocence was a stark reminder of Anna's guilt. Her recklessness and resulting pregnancy would completely ruin her family if it were ever publicly known. The letter and the distance it had traveled to reach her was a blatant reminder that she was untouchable. Forever spoilt. For Shayna's sake, no one could ever know the truth.

After supper, Thomas invited Anna to work on her quilt by the fire in the parlor, instead of retreating to her room upstairs, and while she hesitated, the temptation to be nearer the fire—and adult conversation—won out. While she laid out pieces to create a larger square, Thomas drew a chair to the fire.

"You saw who this was from?" he asked, pulling out the letter she had brought to him.

Anna eyed him.

He held up palms. "I forgot. You're not nosy." He tamped down a smile.

She focused on her stitching. "I *might* have noticed." Noticed and also steeled herself for its contents. The letter surely had to be a complaint about a Jew living there. "What do the 'concerned citizens' have to say?"

"They want me to join them, as usual. The trouble is, I don't share their 'concerns.'"

"That is all? No reprimand about the Jew under your roof?"

"No, sorry, they didn't even mention you at all. I'll read it."

"To Thomas Chandler

From the Concerned Citizens for True America

You don't need papist handouts. If charity is the only way you can operate your school, wouldn't you be better off getting the support you need from the upstanding members of your own community?

We want to help you. And in exchange, you can help us. The Pope wants control of our country. He wants to dictate what is being taught in our schools and infiltrate our country with poisonous lies. The papists are trying to gain a foothold, but we will maintain our ground to protect true America against the Catholic menace which is spreading like a disease in politics, the business world, the newspapers, and in our schools.

They practice bizarre, secret rituals. They store up weapons and munitions in secret armories beneath their churches, as part of their plot to overthrow our government. They aim to influence our country through our children and to dominate America with a Roman papist government.

We will not allow that. You must stand with us against this threat to our country. If you join us, your business will receive exclusive patronage of store owners, teachers, farmers, and countless businessmen all across Alton County. We can guarantee your trade will multiply and you will have more income than you have ever known, more than you will ever need. Join us today and we promise you will be financially set for life."

"*Your Concerned Neighbors,* blah blah blah." Thomas folded the letter.

Anna finished a block and began a new one. "They are eager to give you money."

"Yes, ungodly amounts, by the sound of it." He went to the fireplace and held the corner of the letter to the flame. "Wouldn't be the first time."

She watched the paper catch fire. "Is it not tempting to accept?"

"Nope," he said without hesitation. "I'd rather starve."

"Why are they so insistent?" Anna asked.

Thomas tossed the burning paper into the fire with a shrug. "Either they don't understand the word 'no,' or maybe because misery loves company." He stared into the flames.

"Are any of those things true? About the Catholics?"

He shook his head.

Anna frowned. "Why do these concerned neighbors have such a distorted view?"

"I think people often misunderstand anyone who is different. Some simply don't know any better, others thrive on hate and slander. No one's perfect, of course. Every nation and religion has its blemishes and troublemakers. I imagine every group has a few mistakes in the history books they'd like to blot out."

"This could apply to people as well," Anna murmured.

"Sure. But people aren't usually banished for making one mistake."

They are if they have a mother like mine. Anna faced two blocks and began stitching them. "Is it because Christians and Catholics worship the same God that you continue to work with the Sisters of Mercy?"

"I'm just helping a neighbor, and that neighbor is kind enough to help me. If you really want to complicate things, Christians also worship the same God that Jews do."

Anna's brows rose.

He chuckled. "But *that* topic would take more than one quilt to discuss. Several quilts, I think." He took a seat near Anna, watching the fire.

"So you are born Christian, as one is born Jewish?" she asked.

"No. It's a choice—a decision you make. A confession of faith. I was fifteen when I gave my life to Christ." Thomas leaned back, closed his eyes, and let out a long sigh. "It was life-changing."

A *choice*? To belong to a religion? How strange. Being a Jew was not a choice. In all its complexity—that it was a nationality and an ethnicity and a religion—it was certainly not hers by choice. If given a choice, Anna was not certain that she *would* choose it, as difficult as her life had been because of it.

Anna waited for him to continue, but he seemed to have no more to say. "What led you to make this choice?"

"Gabriel Johansen."

"The man in the photograph?"

He turned one eye on her. "Photograph?"

Anna's cheeks ignited. "In your office. There are two photographs on the shelf."

Thomas nodded. "That's him. The other is me and my mother, when I was about three."

She suspected so. She took up another square of assorted colors, matched the edges, and began stitching.

"You've been in my office?" he asked.

"Only once. To deliver the quilt."

"Ah." He leaned back and closed his eyes again. "I was ten when my mother died, and I had no father, so I was sent to an orphanage." He hissed out a slow, even breath. "It was horrific. No child should ever have to suffer that."

A locked room with infants wailing in the dark immediately came to mind, haunting her again. Anna forced the terrible sound out of her mind.

"So when I was twelve, I ran away."

"Twelve? So young. Where did you live?"

"For a few years, I lived on the streets."

She could picture Teddy or Jimmy all alone, without family or home. Touched by his candor, Anna studied him. Though her mind raced with many more questions, she waited.

"When Prohibition went into effect, bootlegging became highly profitable. I got on with a gang of rum-runners in Ohio, but when I barely missed a bullet in a shootout—"

Anna gasped, eyes wide. "You were a *gangster*?"

"Like you said, everyone has a mistake or two in their history books."

Yes, this was true. And she was glad that Thomas was being candid about his past. But if Thomas thought Anna would also reveal *her* past transgressions, he thought wrong.

"So, I ditched the gang and went looking for sawmill work in Indiana, but they weren't hiring fifteen-year-olds. About that time, Gabriel Johansen was picking up a load of lumber. He saw me starving and trying to get mill work. He had pity and took me in. He made me his apprentice, but over time, he was more than a boss and a mentor. He became a father to me."

"And then you took over his business?"

Thomas rose and pushed his chair close to the table. "He died when

I was twenty-five and left me this place. About a year later, I started the carpentry school, to carry on what he began with me. Or to try, anyway."

"He sounds like a mensch—a very good man. He was an inspiration to you."

"Yes. Gabriel's love and faith were constant, even in the end when he was slipping away. It was his solid faith in Christ that led me to want what he had—mercy, forgiveness, and a real, personal relationship with God. Knowing Gabriel and his love for Jesus made *me* want to know Him, too. That led me to faith and my own relationship with God. I only wish I'd met Gabriel sooner, known him longer."

Anna examined the expression of the man standing before her. Whatever Thomas's faith, he certainly seemed to value it. "What good fortune that you had Gabriel in your life, even if only for a short time."

He studied her with a tilt of his head. "I guess that's a good way of looking at it."

She smiled. "Thank you."

"For what?"

"For trusting me with a piece of *your* story."

Thomas seemed surprised. He studied her for a lengthy, quiet moment, as if he had suddenly found something he had forgotten, something lost. Then he shook his head. "I haven't told anyone that story in a long, long time."

"All the more reason I am grateful."

Fifteen

WHEN THOMAS ANNOUNCED THAT HE WANTED THE BOYS TO attend an Easter Sunday service, Albert said the only way he was going to set foot in a church was if Sam came, too. The nearest church they could all attend was the Negro Baptist church in Fort Wayne, twenty miles away.

Since the old delivery truck would not start, it took nearly every drop of gasoline in Henry Tucker's pickup truck to get Thomas and all six boys to the service and back. Sarah said that Henry had grumbled about the gasoline at first, but she told her husband she was proud of him for doing the Christian thing. Henry muttered that he owed Thomas anyway, and decided to call it an even trade. Anna suspected that Henry had not come to the same "decision of faith" that Sarah and Thomas had, but she kept this to herself.

The Sisters Mary spent "Holy Week" at a town several miles away. St. Aloysius had a parish school where the sisters were promised truckloads of materials, curriculum which they would make available to Anna and her pupils, and supplies for their soon to be reopened school.

For Anna, the week marked her own dates of significance. Not only was the 18th of April the last day of Passover, it also marked the end of her fifth month of pregnancy. Until now, Anna had avoided thinking about the baby, but her thickening middle was an unmistakable protrusion, and tiny kicks were becoming a regular occurrence. Though her gown still hid her shape, she worried that others might somehow see the lump, the movement. There was no telling how long she would be able to keep the baby concealed. This uncertainty hung fixed in her mind, like a full moon on a clear night.

Not knowing where she would deliver was another source of anxiety.

But even more unnerving was having no experienced woman to talk to or confide in. How should she prepare herself for birth? What could she expect to happen when labor began? Where would she be? Who would attend her?

And how should she prepare herself for the immediate removal of the child? She had no delusions about keeping it, but would she be allowed to see it at all? Touch it? Hold it?

If only she could talk to Shayna...but of course, she could share none of these concerns with her sister. Anna was again forced to hold back what troubled her most when she wrote to her dearest confidante.

20 April

My Love,

Your letter is water to my soul! I read it many times each day. Your words give me a precious glimpse of home.

You are so strong, and yet I fear you are working too hard. When one is swallowed up by work and always being the strong one others depend on, it becomes easy to forget to dream. Promise you will keep dreaming. If not for yourself, then for me. I have such high hopes for you.

After 4 weeks, my pupils are doing well, but there is still much work to do and only 4 weeks left. Thomas asked if I could stay through the end of the school year, and he went out of his way to find more textbooks, and the sisters have given us curriculum. I agreed to stay until the end of May, but then I must resume my journey to find Papa.

Our neighbor, Sarah Tucker, is a kind Christian. I will miss her when I leave Corbin. She longs for friends, but the women she spends time with share a strange bond and all answer to one named Penny. Sarah's husband Henry calls these women a "horde of hornets" and does not approve of Sarah spending time with them. And now, thanks to Penny, everyone in town knows I am a Jew, and Jews are not welcome here. Thomas says I should ignore such talk, but the requests for mending have suddenly stopped, and the people in town who used to greet me are now cold and avoid me like street muck.

Please write again soon and tell me if you hear from Papa. I have no solid plan for finding him, only hope. Wish me luck.

    A.

On Tuesday, a steady rain dampened Anna's cloak as she hurried home from the Tucker farm. But the rain could not dampen her joy. Sarah did not mind that Anna was Jewish and had invited her over to teach her how to make pancake syrup from sugar, water, and maple flavoring. She had also accepted Anna's invitation to come on Friday to learn to make challah.

Anna shook rain from her cloak and entered through the kitchen but heard a commotion at the front of the house. She hurried to the parlor and saw the boys clustered on the porch.

As she went outside to join them, Albert's hand clasped Sam's shoulder. "It's already dead, Sam. Ain't gonna hurt nobody."

Anna took a closer look. The creature tied to the post stared at her with empty, beady eyes. She gasped and stepped back. "What is that?"

"Dead coon," Teddy said.

Jack turned to her. "Did you see who put it there?"

Blood had dried to a crust in the animal's fur. "No," Anna said, cringing. "I just returned from the Tucker farm."

"It's fully dead," Pete said. "I checked."

A piece of paper was attached to the string that held the animal to the post.

Anna grimaced. "Untie it, please. And carefully, it may be diseased."

Jimmy took a pocketknife to the twine and released the creature. Anna picked up the paper by a corner. She looked around at the boys. "Where is Mr. Tom?"

"He went to Huntington. Won't be back till nightfall."

She nodded. "Can someone please dispose of the animal?"

Jimmy, holding the raccoon by the tail, took off toward the woodshed for a shovel, with Teddy and Jack following. Pete stayed with Albert and Sam.

"What's it say?" Pete said with a nod at the note.

Anna shook her head. "Clearly not a friendly note, and therefore, nothing you need to see." She gave instructions for the three of them to clean up the mess, then went inside.

The note was scrawled in the same handwriting as the note that had come wrapped around the brick.

> *dirty jews spread their filth to everyone they touch*
> *you'll catch it if you didn't already*
> *a tar and feather party is coming if she don't leave*
> *lying, scheming jews don't belong here*
> *dirty coloreds don't either*

Anna already knew what Thomas would do about this note, the same as he had done with the others. And she was not opposed to burning it. But this one hinted about Sam, so Thomas needed to see it.

The week dragged on so slowly that Anna began to fear Friday would never come. The longer the rain persisted, the more fidgety her pupils became. But finally, Friday arrived and with it came a blessed break in the clouds. Thomas and his young workmen left at noon to work at the Sisters of Mercy School. Albert had been talking about this day all week, as this was the day they would raise a new wall, which they had built.

Sarah arrived, wearing one of the dresses that Anna had mended for her. The robin's egg blue and yellow daisy fabric had come from flour sacks, reminding Anna to save the fabric from the sacks as they emptied. She hoped to collect enough of one pattern to make herself a dress.

Ivy and Violet played in the dining room while Sarah and Anna kneaded dough.

"Folks at the café are all abuzz about Sheriff Dooley takin' down the sign outside of Perryville," Sarah said.

"What sign?" Anna asked.

"The sign at the edge of town, same as the one in Corbin." She sprinkled more flour on her dough. "You know, the one that warns coloreds about leavin' before sundown. Haven't you seen it down by the railroad tracks?"

"No," Anna said. "What does it say?" Perhaps this sign was the reason Sam did not like going into town.

"Most towns in Alton County have signs that say things like 'whites only in city limits after dark,' that kinda thing. Folks are spittin' mad at Dooley."

Anna frowned. "People in Corbin are mad about some other town's sign?"

Sarah nodded, then divided her dough into three sections the way Anna had done.

"Why do these towns warn Negroes to leave by sundown?"

Sarah shrugged. "It ain't safe for coloreds to be in town after dark. It's been like that for ages, far as I know."

Anna needed no help picturing the kind of "not safe" that a Negro might encounter, especially if the fire-wielding men cloaked in white were behind such warnings.

"The government passed a law a while back saying towns can't put those signs up no more, but they never ordered anyone to take them down. The law ain't never really been enforced."

"Then why does the sheriff enforce it now?"

Sarah pushed hair off her forehead, leaving a flour streak. "Folks at the café got all sorts of theories, but I don't know. If you ask me—though nobody ever does—he's just doin' his job."

Anna tucked her braid under at each end of the loaf and started another braid. "I have met the sheriff, and he seems to be a fair man."

"Maybe so, but Alice Withers is fit to be tied. She said before we know it, Dooley's gonna invite colored folks to move in here and mix with whites, just like over in Clyde County. I didn't tell her, but I don't think that'll ever happen here—even if ol' Dooley *was* fixin' to do that, which he ain't. The reason I know is because every colored family that ever tried to move in since I've lived here was either froze out, burnt out, or run off."

Anna finished her braid in silence, pondering this news. How disturbing that an entire town was somehow able to act as judge and jury and circumvent the law. And if this was the way they treated Negroes, Jews probably received the same treatment.

"What do you think?" Anna asked. "About Negroes living in Corbin, I mean."

Sarah shrugged. "I don't know. I mean, *I* got nothing against folks just because they're different than me." She frowned. "But the Women of Virtue Society has special speakers that come. I heard some shockin' stories, mostly about Negroes and Catholics." She shook her head slowly. "Anna,

I never heard such revoltin' things in all my life. But they get lots of new ladies joinin' up whenever those speakers come."

This did not surprise Anna. "And you believe these stories?"

Sarah frowned at her dough. "You think they might not be true?"

Anna tilted her head. "I think any story that makes blind assumptions or blanket accusations about an entire group of people could not possibly be true."

Her friend seemed to be considering this. "That makes sense. I just always figured those ladies *must* know. They're a whole lot smarter than me."

"You are much smarter than you think, Sarah Tucker."

"You think so?"

"Oh, yes. And I think this is why you have not officially joined the society."

With a sigh, Sarah stopped braiding. "I just thought I was too Missouri muleheaded. I have to see somethin' myself before I *really* believe it."

Anna smiled. "Well, if it is muleheaded to not believe everything you hear, then count me muleheaded as well."

Sarah chuckled, then sobered. "Alice keeps pressin' me to join. Anna, the truth is, I *want* to belong. I believe in preservin' morals and doin' good in the community, but I'm just not sure. I can't see myself goin' around convincin' other folks to run off people we don't even know."

Anna wanted to ask her what she would do if she were ever asked to run off Anna, or Sam, but since Sarah had not yet pledged her allegiance to this group, such a question might be pointless.

And besides, the answer was obvious: Sarah was here, in her kitchen, kneading dough with a Jew. What more did Anna need to know?

Sixteen

AFTER SUPPER ON SUNDAY, ALL SIX BOYS CROWDED AROUND THE radio in the parlor to hear *The Lone Ranger*. Anna joined them at the table with her latest quilt and was quickly caught up in the adventure. What intrigued Anna most about the Lone Ranger was his views on friendship, equality, and fighting for what was right. Since the boys were so fascinated by the masked hero, she decided his mottos would be perfect for the next essay assignment.

When the show concluded, the boys shuffled upstairs to prepare for bed, leaving Anna alone. Her quilt was nearly complete; she needed only to tie down the corners of each square. This quilt, like the others before it, was decidedly ugly, which was mildly aggravating. It was difficult to settle for producing something with so little aesthetic appeal, but limited time and materials did not allow for indulging her creativity. She had to accept these quickly produced wares as something to meet an immediate and practical need, and nothing more.

As she knotted a new length of thread, Sam returned to the parlor with a book. On closer look, she realized it was the Bible. He sat near her, placing the open book on the table.

"What are you reading?" she asked.

Pointing to the chapter heading, his finger rested on the word *Samuel.*

Anna studied the child, awash with homesickness. Though Anshel was very intelligent, he had to be prodded to read. But to Sam, books were a treat, which Anna understood. They were a doorway into worlds without limits, unrestricted by things like nationality or skin color.

The boy kept his finger on the word and aimed a determined look at Anna.

"Samuel. The long version of Sam. Your name is short for Samuel?"

He nodded.

Anna smiled. "In Hebrew, this name is *Shemu'el.*"

Sam studied her.

"Do you know what Shemu'el means in Hebrew?"

The boy shook his head.

"It means, 'the Lord has heard.' Samuel's mother, *Channah,* gave him this name because she asked the Lord for a child, and after many prayers, He heard her. Then his mother sent the boy to live at the temple to learn priestly duties for the Lord. He was a very special boy who heard the Lord speak to him. He grew up to become a very important prophet to his people."

Sam's mouth gaped in silent wonder. He drew in a breath that stretched his small frame straighter, taller. He studied the word for a moment or two, then pointed to the name again. Then he turned to Anna and pointed to himself.

"Yes, this is your name."

With a sigh, he again pointed to the word and then to himself. He looked intently into her eyes, as if asking her to try harder to understand what he was trying to say.

Anna pondered what he meant, then it occurred to her. "You wish to be *called* Samuel?"

The boy nodded vigorously, his eyes alight with the joy of being understood.

"Ah! Well, of course you must be called by your true name. Samuel it is." She smiled, then took his hand and shook it. "*Shalom Aleichem, Shemu'el.* This means, 'Peace upon you.'"

A look of pure satisfaction set his smile aglow.

Monday morning marked the first of May. Her pupils must have sensed that they were in the final weeks of school now, and it showed. Jack could not stop elbowing Teddy who shoved him off with bursts of "cut it out!" while Pete squirmed as if his trousers were on fire. As soon as the spelling and math quizzes were completed, Anna gave them all a combined vocabulary, grammar, and penmanship assignment that she hoped would focus them long enough to give her time to score their previous work. Each boy was to choose one of the Lone Ranger's codes of conduct, and, while employing vocabulary words from her list, to write an essay describing something practical he might do to exemplify it.

With this, the room soon fell silent. Anna smiled.

When she had finished grading their quizzes, the boys were still at work. She rose and went from chair to chair, taking a peek at the topics the boys had selected.

Jimmy had chosen *Being prepared physically, mentally, and morally to fight when necessary for what is right.*

She moved along to Albert, Jack, and then to Samuel. He had chosen *That all men are created equal and that everyone has within himself the power to make this a better world.* Tears stung her eyes, but she quickly blinked them away. She moved on to Teddy and Pete.

Pete turned in his seat and accidentally elbowed Anna.

"Gee, Miss Anna, you sure are gettin' fat."

With a gasp, Anna recoiled out of reach.

Teddy slugged Pete. "Blockhead! Did they drop you on your head when you were born?"

Frowning, Pete rubbed his arm. "What? I didn't mean nothin' bad. I just meant she's not skin and bones like when she got here. She's fillin' out, that's all."

Anna stiffened, her mind racing. "Yes, this is what you get for turning over your kitchen to a starving stranger." Fire spread through her face. She would need to do better at keeping her distance from now on.

Keep distant. Avoid contact. Avoid closeness.

The thought brought a sudden ache. But it struck Anna that she faced a future of keeping her distance, so she must get used to the feeling. She needed to prevent involvement, attachment, closeness. No one could ever get close enough to know her shame, to know what she truly was.

To Anna's relief, the school week passed without further mention of her growing "fat." She hoped it had been forgotten. Not only had she feared the boys' further discussion and scrutiny, but she also worried about Thomas hearing it. The boys seemed satisfied with her reply, but an adult might speculate, begin taking notice, and grow suspicious. She would not be staying much longer, but even so, she had grown to care for these boys and the thought of them discovering her moral failure was too painful to contemplate. She was instructing them on codes of moral conduct. If these boys ever learned of her shame, it would not only ruin what she had tried to instill in them, but they would be disgusted with her and disillusioned.

They could never, ever find out.

After school on Friday, Anna took two new quilts into town. As a group of women passed her on Main Street, one of them muttered, "There she goes, can you beat that? Mr. Pitts is going to send her packing."

She turned and watched them as they continued on their way. Were they discussing her? She went into the store and waited at the counter for the grocer to finish helping a customer. When Mr. Pitts turned to her, he shook his head.

"I can't buy or sell any homemade wares."

"But last week you said—"

"No, I can't do it. You need to take those somewhere else."

Anna stared at the man, then glanced around her. People in the store were staring at her. What had happened? She stepped outside, heat rising in her cheeks. Had Penny told people she was Jewish and interfered with her business?

"You won't be selling any more of your things around here," a middle-aged woman said as she came up the steps. She reached the top and narrowed her gaze at Anna. "You best take those and be off."

"How do you know I will not sell them?" Anna asked.

"Because selling takes customers, and nobody around here does business with Jews."

Anna's face felt hot.

"And you better tell that little colored boy he's lucky it was me that saw him running off with a pie, and not my husband or some of the other men in town. They would've tied him to the flag pole all night for stealing. Or worse—the train tracks."

"Train tracks? He is just a child!" Anna swallowed the bile rising in her throat. "You would allow this? Over a pie?"

"All I'm saying is he got lucky. This time. Make sure he knows if he even touches so much as a cookie crumb, he might not be so lucky next time."

The woman went into the store, leaving Anna with her mouth ajar.

This had to be Mrs. Beckett, the woman who reported Sam to Sheriff Dooley. Did Samuel know of the danger he was in? Anna feared he did not.

She hurried to the post office and found that she had received a new letter from Shayna. But as much as she wanted to read it on the spot, the thought of running into Mrs. Beckett again set her teeth on edge. She stuffed the letter in her pocket and hurried home.

While the boys finished cleaning up from supper, Anna made a decision about Samuel's accuser. She called Samuel into the parlor, away from the hearing of others.

"I need to talk to you."

His eyes turned instantly wary.

"The woman who saw you with the pie, Mrs. Beckett? I saw her today, and I think it would be best if you do not go near her. At all. You must promise me you will be very careful to avoid her."

Samuel held her gaze steady, but he did not reply. His nostrils flared.

"Do you understand what I am saying?"

The child's lips tightened, and his chest moved with quickened breaths, but he gave no answer.

Thomas stepped into the doorway, frowning. Too late, Anna wondered if she should have left this to Thomas. He might have preferred that she not interfere in the matter.

"I...p-paid."

"What?" Stunned by the strange, husky voice, Anna lowered herself onto a chair and met Samuel eye-to-eye. "What did you say?"

Thomas burst into the room. "Sam?"

The child frowned at Anna and drew a deep breath. "T-t-twelve cents."

Still reeling from hearing the unfamiliar voice, Anna threw her arms around the boy and hugged him tight.

Stiffening, he pulled back with a grave look. "I...d-d-didn't s-s-steal it."

"Oh, Samuel." Tears filled her eyes, blinding her. "I am so sorry."

Thomas crouched to the boy's level. "What's this?"

Samuel only stared at Anna, nostrils still flaring.

Swallowing hard, Anna turned to Thomas. "The sheriff stopped by and said Mrs. Beckett saw him—"

"You d-didn't even blink," Samuel said. "You tol' the sh-sheriff you sent me to f-f-fetch it."

Anna's breath caught. He was right. That lie had come so easily. Heat crawled up her neck and across her face. "Samuel, you are right to be angry with me for making such an assumption, and for not asking you what happened. I am sorry."

Thomas studied her. "What happened?"

Her face had to be the color of a tomato. "I told him that Samuel was carrying the pie for *me*. I was afraid...I could only imagine what they would do to him..." She turned to Samuel. "But you are right, it was wrong of me to assume, and even worse to lie about it. My only thought was to protect you."

Samuel cocked his head at her, then his face relaxed. "It's okay, Miss Anna. All f-for one and one for all."

Relief flooded her.

Thomas stood. "Don't you worry about Mrs. Beckett, Sam," he said. "I'll straighten her out."

Samuel nodded, then headed back to the kitchen.

Watching him go, Thomas shook his head. "That voice! It's like music to my ears."

Anna laughed, her heart nearly bursting. "Yes! Beautiful, glorious music."

Thomas turned to her and stilled, staring at her face. Then he reached out and touched her hand, his golden eyes aglow. "Anna, you're a miracle worker," he said softly. "Thank you."

Anna withdrew her hand, murmured goodnight, and hurried to her room.

That could not happen again.

She undressed quickly and slipped beneath the covers, and then remembered Shayna's letter. How could she have forgotten? She had heard that pregnancy made women scatterbrained. Shivering, she searched her pockets for the letter, already planning her reply. Samuel spoke! Though Shayna had never met him, Anna knew her sister would be thrilled to hear the news.

Eagerly, she pored over Shayna's letter, noting the lack of greeting from Mama, as usual. Shayna sounded tired, confirming Anna's suspicions that her sister was working too hard and beginning to weaken beneath the burden. Tears stung Anna's eyes for the second time that day.

Reading on, her heart sank. Isaak had not come by to check on them nor had he spoken to her for over a week, and Shayna now feared he might be wanting to see someone else.

Then Anna read the closing lines:

> *Oh, Anna, why did you leave us? Nothing is the same, and the more time that passes without you, the more certain I am that nothing will ever be right again. I cannot bear it. Please come home.*

This despair was so unlike Shayna, and this troubled her. Anna penned an immediate reply, wishing a postman could somehow magically dispatch the message to her sister tonight. She closed her burning eyes. Shayna had always been the one Anna could count on to bear up gracefully under distress, the one to speak sense and calm over everyone else's emotional upheavals. And now, it was Shayna who was falling apart, Shayna who needed bearing up. And Anna was too far away to do anything about it.

The threats to Samuel, the need for distance and avoiding the simplest touch, and now miles from a beloved sister who needed her—it was too much. Alone in the dark, Anna wept long into the night.

Seventeen

ON SUNDAY, JACK BURST INTO THE KITCHEN FROM OUTSIDE, HIS load of firewood forgotten. "We been ransacked!"

"What do you mean? What happened?" Anna asked. With Thomas away as was usual on Sundays, overseeing breakfast had been left to Anna.

"Somebody raided the chicken coop. There's feathers scattered all over the garden."

"One of our hens?" Anna moved the skillet of potatoes off the heat.

"You sure it wasn't wolves?" Albert asked.

"The roof on the coop has been smashed in. Wolves wouldn't do that. Come on!"

The other boys raced out the kitchen door. Anna reached for the coat that Thomas kept on a hook near the door and joined them.

Jack was right, nearly half the roof of the chicken coop looked smashed, and chicken feathers were strewn all over the yard and garden.

Heart racing, she joined the boys in searching through the mess. Two of the six hens were missing. On further inspection of the woodshed, Jimmy discovered that three new cans of kerosene were also missing.

"Who did it?" Teddy asked

Anna glanced around the property but saw no sign of intruders. She exhaled, which did not alleviate her frustration. This was clearly intentional.

"Who'd smash our chicken coop and steal our kerosene?" Pete asked.

Anna shook her head. What would Thomas do about this? The damage was more than a window this time. Assuming the culprit was the same as before.

She looked around the yard again for a sign, a note, a clue.

Albert and Samuel copied her, also looking, though they probably did not know what they were looking for. The others scoured the area as well, looking for clues.

After a minute, Samuel yelled out, and Albert ran to him. Anna and the others followed.

Near the well pump, the two missing hens lay dead in a mess of blood and feathers. Both had a crude wooden stake driven through them, pinning them to the grass. Beside them, at the base of the water pump, a single phrase had been scrawled in blood:

BEAT IT OR YOUR NEXT

Heat raced through Anna, set her nostrils flaring. Though the idea of someone coming onto the property and doing damage was disturbing, the idea of someone coming to anonymously threaten Anna and Samuel—she assumed the chicken message was aimed at them both—angered her. Thomas was right, sneaking around in secret to leave such messages was cowardly. Why not show themselves in the light of day and say this, face to face?

A touch at Anna's elbow gave her a jolt.

Teddy studied her with a solemn look. "You look kinda pale, Miss Anna. Why don't you go back inside? We'll clean this up. Come on, fellas."

He directed Albert and Samuel to clean up the mess, and then he and the other three went to get tools and materials to fix the coop.

Anna went inside and finished making breakfast. By the time Thomas returned, the damaged part of the coop had been shored up and patched, and Jimmy and Pete were adding new shingles. She could see him through the window in the kitchen door, talking to the boys and nodding. Then he came in, grabbed his hat, and headed back out.

"I'm going to see the sheriff," he said, the set of his jaw grim.

Later that evening, Anna went to her room to collect her sewing supplies. Shayna's letter still lay on the bureau. Being the weekend, she had not mailed her reply yet, and for that, she was glad. Since she had time to think it through, Anna decided she needed to add a calming, positive note of encouragement to her letter. Which she would do—just as soon as she felt calm and positive.

She grabbed her sewing kit and picked through her basket of scraps but then stopped. Who would buy her quilts now? Penny Withers had turned the entire town against doing business with Anna. But Penny could not influence the rest of the country. There would be other customers, somewhere along the way. If Anna could not sell them here, she would just take them with her when she left Corbin.

Heart heavy, she took her supplies downstairs to the parlor.

Thomas sat near the fire, staring into the dying flames, his book abandoned.

Anna stilled. The damage to his property was due to her being here.

"Dooley will look into the vandalism," Thomas said, still staring at the fire.

Anna wanted to believe this would do some good, but she held little hope. "Thomas, I should leave. If not for me being here—"

"No." He rose and faced her. "These acts are purely childish. I'm not caving in to that."

She studied him, frowning. "There would be nothing to 'cave in to' if I were not here."

He shook his head. "They'd have it in for me either way. And besides..." He went to the fireplace, took up an iron poker, and stirred the coals. "No matter what they do or don't do, we're all far better off *with* you than we are without."

Warmth raced through Anna's veins. She swallowed hard. To be part of a family, to be a vital part—how her heart ached for this.

Thomas watched her. She inhaled, lifted her chin, and nodded. "Very well. If *you* are not going to throw me out, then I am certainly not going to let childish cowards run me off."

With a chuckle, he shook his head, then grabbed his coat and headed for the door. "That's the spirit. Good night, Anna."

The latest quizzes showed Anna that her pupils still had much work to do if they were to pass their grades, so she spent the next several school-days drilling them, and working extra with Pete and Samuel after everyone else was finished for the day. By Wednesday, she was ready for a break, so she walked to town for a spool of thread.

On a whim, she stopped at the post office, and to her surprise, found another letter from Shayna. Her sister must have sent it immediately on the heels of the last one.

> *Anna,*
>
> *I am sorry about my last letter. <u>You</u> would never be so dramatic. Things are not so bad, and I suspect you have enough problems of your own. I will try not to be such a baby. I think of you often, especially how you always face difficulties head on and do not back down. You have far more chutzpah than I will ever have.*
>
> *I confess that sometimes I ask myself, "What would Anna do?" and I am instantly ashamed of my weakness. So instead of fretting that you are not here, I will make use of your absence as an opportunity to grow up.*
>
> *So please disregard my letter and write soon about your clever pupils. I expect to hear that they have all passed with straight A's as soon as you have finished tormenting them with your impossible vocabulary challenges. For which I am eternally grateful, of course.*
>
> *With Love,*
>
> *S.*

As Anna warmed a pot of soup for supper, Sarah Tucker dropped by with another basket of mending. Anna managed a grateful smile. Sarah, the Sisters Mary, and the sheriff were the only people in town willing to do business with her now. She thanked Sarah and promised to have it finished soon.

Sarah glanced around the kitchen, sniffed the soup, and made small talk, but to Anna, she seemed preoccupied, as if she had something weighing on her mind.

"Have you planted your corn?" Anna asked.

"It goes in next week. But Henry's got the ground tilled and ready," Sarah said. "Sounds like Thomas plans to lend a hand."

"Ah, good."

Sarah gave the pot an absent-minded stir, then inhaled deeply. "There's gonna be another rally next week. Several of the ladies from the Society have invited me to be an officer for the chapter. Me! Can you beat that?"

An officer. A leader in an organization that decides who could live and do business in their town. Anna could think of nothing helpful to say, so she just listened.

"It's a real honor, Anna. They look for women who uphold decency and family ideals. Not just anyone can be an officer. Penny and some of the others said I'm a 'model citizen.' Ha!" Sarah chuckled half-heartedly, then glanced at Anna.

Anna nodded. "This is clear to anyone who knows you," she said slowly, still deciding how to respond. "What do *you* think about the invitation?"

"It's a real honor," she said again. "To be an officer in the Women of Virtue Society would mean bein' connected, bein' known. To finally fit in somewhere," she added softly.

It had never before occurred to Anna that a sense of belonging might be no easier for those born in America than it was for the foreign-born. "What would being an officer require of you?" Anna asked.

Sarah frowned. "I guess I was so busy soakin' up their praise I plumb forgot to ask. I suppose I'd have to attend the rallies, keep records, stuff like that."

And encourage your neighbors to do dreadful things to prevent certain people from moving or living here... Anna kept the interjection to herself. Too many times lately, she had spoken without considering the outcome. And besides, Sarah was not asking Anna for advice.

Sarah looked to her. "What? You got somethin' on your mind, I can tell."

"What does your husband think of you being an officer?" Anna managed to say.

Giving Anna's soup another stir, Sarah frowned. "Henry ain't wild about me goin' to the rallies, so I doubt he'd be thrilled about me bein' even more involved."

Anna wanted to ask if Sarah's position in this Society would impact their friendship, but there was no point. Anna would soon be leaving, so any impact on her would not matter. If this was what Sarah really wanted, then it was not Anna's place to influence or interfere.

"Well, if it is your wish to serve in this way, perhaps he will warm up to the idea."

"Maybe." Sarah glanced around the kitchen again, then straightened a tea towel. And another. Now it was Sarah who held back.

Anna waited.

Sarah heaved a sigh. "The other day, I...told some of the ladies at the chapter meetin' what a good job you're doing with these boys. How you find clever ways to trick 'em into studyin' and all. Well, *I* always thought it was clever, anyway." Frowning, she took a tea towel down and picked at a loose string. "Well, anyway, I was just tryin' to shed some helpful light on the debate over you bein' a teacher here." She looked up from the towel but did not quite meet Anna's gaze. "But somehow, it came out all wrong. I tried to fix it, but Alice just lit up like a torch and said how disturbed she is about you trickin' children into doin' things, and...Well, she flat out don't approve of you."

Heat rose up Anna's neck. "Alice Withers will have to learn to live with disappointment, because her approval or disapproval has no bearing on me and the job I am doing."

Sarah came to Anna, her eyes teary. "Oh, Anna. You're angry. I didn't mean to sic Alice on you like that. I was tryin' to do just the opposite. I'm sorry."

"I know, and I appreciate what you were trying to do."

What Anna really wanted to know was how long would it take her friend, if she accepted the invitation, to turn into another Penny Withers? Would she turn on Anna and tell her she was not welcome in Corbin?

A thought ignited in Anna's mind. Was *Anna* the reason they wanted Sarah to serve on their committee?

She kept her ponderings to herself. Sarah was clearly flattered that they had asked her. And at least for now, Anna was not going to take that away from her friend.

Eighteen

THE KNOCK ANNA HAD BEEN DREADING CAME FIRST THING FRI-
day morning, while the boys were settling into the schoolroom. Alice
Withers appeared at the door, and this time, she brought reinforcements.
Mrs. Beckett and another middle-aged woman stood behind Alice.

Anna ignored the sudden squeak and scrape of chair legs behind her.
"Yes?"

"I am here to inspect your curriculum." Alice tried to step inside, but
Anna did not move out of her way. Alice folded arms across her trench
coat and assessed Anna's full-length apron. "You can't keep me out. You're
nothing but a vagrant. You have no claim on this property, nor any authority here. Now stand aside."

Anna held her ground. "I do not believe you have the right to come in
uninvited. Do you have papers? A judge's order?"

One brow arched. "A judge's order? How absurd." Alice inched closer,
the blackness of her small eyes intense. "I don't need anything of the kind,
and furthermore, I don't need to see the curriculum to make my determination, after all." She glanced at the two women behind her, who nodded. She
turned to Anna. "I hereby determine the curriculum *and* the teacher in this
establishment to be grossly deficient and unqualified. I will be giving my
findings to the School Board today, along with my recommendation that
you be removed from teaching here. The children will attend the Corbin
public school, or they will be taken into custody for truancy."

"Fat chance!" Pete's voice.

Anna did not move, but her body shook, her mind raced. Could Alice
do this? Did she have the right to make such a determination, the authority
to have her removed?

Alice narrowed a gaze at Anna. "And if you don't step aside, we can just stand here until the deputy arrives. *Then* you'll move."

Someone clung to Anna's skirt. She glanced down. Samuel had a fistful of her dress, and Albert, Jack, and Teddy had crowded around her. "Why would the deputy come here?"

"To place you under arrest."

"For what?"

"For being a con artist and a swindler."

"This is a lie." Her heart raced. "There is no basis for such an accusation, and certainly no proof."

Alice's narrowed gaze fell to the boys surrounding her and settled on Samuel. "Forget the public school. I'll have them all sent to an orphan asylum, where they belong."

"You'll do nothing of the kind," Thomas's voice thundered. He shouldered past Anna and the boys, nearly knocking them over, and faced Alice.

Alarm widened the woman's eyes.

Thomas leaned toward her, anger pulsing from him in waves. "If you were a man, I'd take a crack at you."

Anna gasped.

Fists balled at his sides, he added, "I have half a mind to do it anyway. Now take your freak show and get off my property."

One of Alice's eyelids twitched. "There *is* a 'freak show' as you've so elegantly put it, but it's not out *here*. Penny tried to convince me you were something special, but you're nothing but a common low life."

Thomas stepped out onto the porch, forcing Alice to take a step back. "I couldn't care less what you think of me. I'm not looking to impress you or anyone else in this town."

"Well, congratulations, you've succeeded." She started to leave, then turned back to add, "And you're in luck, because if it's enemies you want, that's exactly what you'll get."

She headed for the steps, and her companions trailed her without a backwards glance.

"For two cents, I'd bust her nose," Pete muttered.

"Pete!" Anna scolded.

Thomas came inside and slammed the door. He headed for the kitchen, then stopped in the hallway, hesitated, and turned back to face them all.

Samuel still clung to Anna's skirt. She rested an arm across his shoulders, watching Thomas. "This is getting worse."

"Can she do that?" Jack asked. "Send us to the orphan asylum?"

"I don't think so," Thomas said. "And even if she *can* get the state involved, I doubt she can do anything before the end of the school year. And by then..." He eyed each of the boys. "We can put a stop to her nonsense with six passing achievement tests."

Silence filled the room.

Six?

Anna held her breath. If all six boys did not pass and were sent away, it would be her fault. Her legs felt shaky. She reached for a chair to hold onto.

"Y'all go on ahead to the public s-school," Samuel said to the others. "Then she can't d-do nothin' to you."

Albert shook his head. "We leave no man behind. We're not goin' without you, Sam. Right, fellas?" The others nodded in agreement. Albert looked at Thomas. "We'll just work real hard and make sure we pass."

Jimmy moaned. "But I still can't figure out fractions. What if some pass and others don't?"

Six pairs of eyes turned to Anna. The longer she stayed, the worse things could become for her. But leaving the boys before they passed would mean their certain removal.

"We have to make sure you pass, that's all there is to it." Thomas turned to Anna in earnest. "Three more weeks, Miss Anna. That's all we ask. Sure, she's a pain in the neck, but if I stick close by and keep her from pestering you, will you stay?"

"You have to help us not get sent away," Pete said.

Anna opened her mouth, but the tiny acrobat in her belly arrested her words.

"Only three more weeks," Teddy said. "We'll try our hardest *and* we'll be on our best behavior."

Samuel came close and looked up at Anna. "Please," he said, his eyes imploring. "Mr. Tom won't let n-nobody get you, he promised."

Could Alice have Anna arrested? She did not think it possible, but how could she be certain? And could the boys all pass? If it were up to her, and they applied themselves diligently, perhaps it was possible.

"We will need longer days, and I will need everyone's help," she said, finally.

"We'll work extra hard," Jack shouted.

Anna met Thomas's steady gaze. "Then I will do the best I can," she said.

Thomas nodded. "That's all we ask."

13 May

Dearest,

It is now of utmost importance that all six of the boys pass the school year, and the weight of this falls heavily on me. If they do not pass, they could be sent to an orphan asylum. According to Thomas (and I agree), this is something a child should never face. He personally knows the horrors of institution life. I think he sees himself in these boys, sees in them his own lostness. Not only when he was an orphan, but I suspect he is still lost in some respects now.

In a way, I know how he feels. To be among people and yet to feel utterly alone, to be on a path in life and suddenly have no idea what direction you are going. The worst kind of lostness is looking into the mirror and realizing you are no longer the person you thought you were, and do not recognize the person you see. I think this is how Thomas feels. It is a kind of lost that can make a devout man question himself so deeply that he must seek solitude in the woods, week after week, hoping to find direction from G-d.

So, as passing grades are of utmost importance, Jimmy is spending extra hours in the school room. He spent all day Saturday studying because it turns out he found a way to understand fractions. It involves sugar cream pie, which my friend Sarah taught me to make. Jimmy informed me that he will need several more pies if he is to really master the addition, subtraction, and multiplication of fractions. While I suspect an insatiable sweet tooth inspires Jimmy's willingness to work so hard, I will use this. I have no time to worry about rotten teeth. If it is sugar cream pie that helps Jimmy pass sixth grade, then pie it is.

Samuel and I saw a dove this morning—one I have seen before. Today, she was on top of the chicken coop. I think she is hungry, but she never goes down into the pen for food. Perhaps she is afraid of the chickens. Perhaps it is because they are different. But perhaps they think it is <u>she</u> who is different. Who decides what is 'different'? What if there is no such thing? If you removed their feathers, then they are all just birds, are they not? I do not know if she has a nest, perhaps she has young. Samuel wants to leave a few kernels outside the chicken pen for her. If she comes back, I will give her a name. She is not beautiful, but she is serene. I think she comes to bring peace. I will call her Salome.

I miss you and our family very much. Please give an extra hug to everyone, and as always, do not tell Mama it is from me.

Much love,

A.

By the middle of May, the extra hours in the school room made Anna feel as if she had been cooped up all week with the chickens. On Sunday, after putting a stew on to simmer, she gave her pupils a well-deserved break and then slipped outside for a stroll.

Sunlight glowed like long, probing fingers through the trees, warming the damp undergrowth. She followed the footpath along an evergreen corridor, breathing in the pungent, pine scented woods. Where the trail split, she chose the left fork. The right fork led to the Tucker farm, but the left one she had never taken.

After five minutes of walking, her belly muscles tightened, forcing her to slow her steps. This surface cramping was a new development, and was a reminder that the longer she lingered, the more evident her condition would be. As soon as the boys took their achievement tests, her next step would be to get to Chicago and find a safe place to stay. Then the search would begin, both for Papa and for someone she could trust to deliver her baby.

The baby she would never know.

She paused on the trail and looked down, assessing the fullness of her large gown. It still looked normal, and still hid the protrusion beneath it. But how much longer? The muscles hardened again, and without thinking, Anna cupped her hands around the pineapple-sized bulge. A tiny heel thumped her hand. With a gasp, Anna jerked her hands away.

Mama had experienced this four times. No, five—there was a pregnancy between Rivka and Anshel that miscarried in the fourth month. Papa had said that he believed it was a son, and for him, this made the loss all the more crushing. But Mama had spoken very little of the death of her fourth child. She said that part of her heart had also died that day, and then she never spoke of it again.

It struck Anna that after Mama's child died, she wanted no more reminders of it. Perhaps the silence from Mama in Shayna's letters was a sign that Anna was *also* dead to her.

She turned back and headed toward home. Samuel's mother had known him for nine years. How difficult had it been for her to give him away after all that time? What an odd coincidence that this Samuel had been given away by his mother, similar to the way the young prophet, Shemu'el, had been given to the temple priest by his mother, Channah, *and* that both were sent away to be trained in their life's work. Shemu'el was the child his mother had desperately longed for, and yet after the Lord granted her plea, she gave him up. Gave him up! That this mother could let go of her beloved miracle child was something Anna could not grasp.

Anna longed to know what had happened to Samuel's mother, what had caused her to lose hope to the point of giving him up, what gave her such certainty that his future would be better without her. Had she been bullied and forced to leave? Had the frightful things Samuel had witnessed befallen her? One thing Anna was certain of: Samuel's mother had valued his life and his future more than her own. Had loved him more than herself.

Perhaps this was a love only a mother could truly understand.

Was it possible that Samuel knew why his mother felt so hopeless? Anna could never bring herself to ask him. His ability to speak had returned so unexpectedly. She would not risk reminding him of his loss and abandonment, or the terrors that had likely caused his muteness.

"Running away?"

Anna jumped. While she had been lost in her musings, Thomas had joined her on the trail.

"Mind if I walk with you? You can't be too careful, I hear there are hobos in these woods."

Anna offered a light chuckle. "Yes. Hobos who trick children into making stew."

His smile revealed both dimples as he fell into step beside her.

"Spending Sundays in the woods is good medicine for you," she said.

He glanced at her. "Why do you say that?"

"You seem calm. More so than you have been in a while."

His steps slowed and he heaved a sigh. "I'm not proud of my encounter with Alice the other day. I'm afraid that lately, I've been...letting people get under my skin."

Anna studied him. His face was relaxed, his expression unreadable.

"So you come out to the woods where there is no one to get under your skin."

He eyed her.

"But at some point, you *do* have to go back to where people are."

He let out a laugh. "No, coming out here is the only way I know how to clear my head." He stared at the path. "There are a lot of things I don't understand, things that get to me, but when I get alone with the Lord, He restores my perspective."

"How?"

"I'm reminded that when God doesn't answer my questions or prayers, He has a good reason, and I just need to trust Him. All I need to know is that He is faithful, and He's good. He'll never leave me, and His love..." He stopped and turned to her.

She stopped also.

"'The steadfast love of the Lord never ceases, His mercies never come to an end.'"

"This comes to you in the woods?"

He shrugged. "Well, *that* was Lamentations, but yes, He reminds me who He is when I pray and study the Bible and spend time with Him. It comes from having a relationship with Him."

Anna pondered this. "I always thought Christians gathered in churches to practice their religion. Is church not a good way to 'restore perspective'?"

"It is a good way. And I *do* attend, sometimes. It's just...difficult for me right now."

They both continued along the trail at a slow, steady pace.

"Well, I do not know about relationships found in the woods, but there is one thing I *do* know," Anna said. "Being with people will always bring us pain at some time or another, but there is even more pain in being alone and disconnected. As humans, we are meant to be connected."

As the last word left her lips, a dull ache pressed on her heart. In one reckless moment, Anna had destroyed her chances of being connected with anyone ever again.

Thomas eyed her thoughtfully. "Are you preaching at me, Anna?"

She winced. "I am sorry. That was not my intention."

"No, that's okay, you're right. But just for the record, you're not exactly in *your* usual place of worship, either."

Anna drew a long breath, then let it out slowly. "I have allowed things to get 'under my skin,' as you say. And I, too, have lost perspective. But I am afraid that an entire lifetime in the woods cannot bring it back."

He stopped and faced her, his eyes alight with something cautious, yet hopeful. "Maybe we can help each other."

Anna studied him, the sincerity of his expression, the patient way he waited, the strong, pleasing angles of his face. "How?"

"You can help me work on being more connected, and...I can help you search for what you've lost."

He was no longer jovial, but suddenly very attentive, the hope in his eyes entreating, tender. Tempting.

It was not difficult to see herself spending time with Thomas. It was quite easy. So easy, in fact, that she suddenly saw the two of them, in her mind's eye, making a home, working together and sharing a life, loving these boys, loving...

A small gasp escaped her.

"Anna?" His voice was breathless with wonder. He dipped his head closer and peered into her eyes, studying her carefully.

As clearly as if in a waking dream, she saw herself married to him, saw herself loving him with all of her heart and soul. Which, of course, was impossible. Painfully so.

Quickly, she dropped her gaze, blocking his scrutiny. Surely her eyes would give away both her foolish feelings *and* her dirtiness.

He reached up with his fingertips and gently tilted her chin upward, forcing her to look him in the eye. "Forgive me, but...I need to see if that was just my imagination."

She swallowed hard. *Look away, Anna...*

But she could not. The bronze glow in his beautiful eyes captured her, held her fast, as if she were trapped beneath a giant, crashing wave.

Shouts and sounds of thrashing underbrush shattered the grip of his gaze. Albert and Teddy came running toward them as fast as they could.

"Mr. Tom!" Albert gasped.

"What is it?" Thomas said, turning quickly. "Is someone hurt?"

Teddy reached him first, panting. "No...dead!"

Nineteen

THOMAS STARTED TO BOLT, BUT TEDDY CAUGHT HIS SLEEVE.

"It's none of us fellas, it's Sheriff Dooley."

"Wait.... The sheriff is dead?" Thomas paused, his look distressed and confused. It took a moment for his initial alarm to subside. "What happened? How do you know?"

"We were down at the creek and heard a commotion over by the bridge," Albert said. "So we dropped our poles and ran to see. A crowd of folks were all talking about how Sheriff Dooley's wife found him dead in his bed."

Thomas winced. "When?"

"Today," Albert said. "They said he laid down for a Sunday nap and didn't wake up."

Shocked, Anna covered her mouth. The sheriff was perhaps in his late sixties at most. Poor man. And for his beloved wife to find him that way—such a terrible shock.

"I'm sorry to hear that. Colin Dooley was a good man." Thomas frowned. "Died in his sleep—I never would've thought. He always looked well."

All four headed back to the house in silence.

Anna, still digesting the news, tried to recall how the sheriff had looked the last time she saw him, when he came by the house to pick up his wife's mending. He had seemed well then. Even hinted for another helping of her "fancy bread" with butter and extra jam.

When they reached the house, the two boys went to find the others, since they had split up to find Thomas and Anna. They all returned moments later.

"Mr. Tom, did you hear?" Jack burst into the kitchen, breathless. "The whole town is talking about how the sheriff up and died."

Jimmy came in with a fishing pole. "Arguing, more like."

"Arguing about what?" Anna asked.

"What he died from," Jimmy said. "The librarian said he must've caught a deadly disease. The old coots from the barber shop said he probably sampled a bad batch of bootleg. And the barber said Dooley was way too old to be playing Sherlock Holmes and gave himself a heart attack."

"Then Mr. Pitts came out of the store," Pete added. "He said Dooley had it comin'."

Frowning, Thomas said, "Are you sure you heard that right?"

"Yes, sir. Then Henry Tucker said what the Sam Hill does that mean, and Mr. Pitts said somethin' about consequences, but I couldn't make it out because everybody was yakkin' all at once."

"Deputy Withers was standing at the top of the bank steps," Jack said. "He didn't say nothin'. Just stood there lookin' like a bulldog."

Anna felt an odd sense that something was off balance. She examined each face as the conversation ping-ponged around the kitchen.

Then it struck her. "Where is Samuel?"

Albert shot a look at Jack. "Wasn't he with you?"

Jack nodded. "But last time I saw him was when we were fishin', before all the racket."

Teddy jerked his head toward the kitchen door. "Come on, we gotta go find him."

As the boys left, Thomas came to Anna. "Will you stay here in case he comes back? I doubt he's gone far. I need to go into town and see what I can find out."

"Yes, I will wait here."

Anna willed herself not to worry, and to trust that the boys knew where to find him.

But when they came back twenty minutes later without Samuel, Anna's heart lurched.

"The only place we didn't check was the crick," Pete said. "Maybe he drowned."

Albert swung and punched Pete square in the face, knocking him back three feet, then the two boys lunged for one another, fists flying.

Anna yelled for them to stop, while Teddy and Jimmy grasped at flailing arms and clothing until they could pull the two boys apart.

Pete shrugged off Jimmy's clutches, then wiped blood from his mouth and glared at Albert. "You busted my lip!"

"Take it back!" Albert fumed. "That was a stupid thing to say."

"Okay, okay! I take it back," Pete said, wiping his mouth with his sleeve. "I sure didn't see *you* coming up with any brilliant—"

"I think I found what y'all are lookin' for," Sarah Tucker said as she entered the kitchen. Samuel stepped in behind her, followed by little Ivy.

Sarah gasped at Pete. "Oh, my heavens, what happened to you?"

Albert pushed through everyone to get to Samuel. "You okay?"

Samuel nodded, then reached into the pocket of his trousers and showed Albert a small pocketknife.

Sarah smiled at Samuel. "I heard somethin' rustlin' around in that little old wood hut where our pasture meets the woods, and I figured I better see if we had some uninvited critters. I can't have raccoons packin' off our new barn kittens, Violet would *never* get over it." She patted Samuel's shoulder. "But instead of a raccoon, I found Samuel. I think he's found himself a quiet place to think." She glanced up at Anna.

Anna met her friend's gaze. "Thank you for bringing him home."

Shrugging, she said, "That's what neighbors are for." She plopped Ivy on her hip and turned to leave, but Thomas met her in the doorway.

"Evening, Sarah," he said. "I just spoke to Henry."

Sarah's smile faded. "I guess he filled you in?"

"On the facts *and* the speculation," Thomas said. He turned to Samuel. "Say, we were starting to wonder where you'd gone off to."

"S-sorry," he said, his voice low. "I was playin' like I was on an ex... exa..." His brow furrowed in concentration. "Expedition."

"Like Matthew Henson, the explorer?" Anna asked.

The boy nodded. "Yes, ma'am."

Anna felt a rush of surprise mingled with delight. The Negro explorer was the subject Samuel had selected for his book report.

"Sorry, Mr. Tom," he went on. "I lost t-t-track of time."

"That's all right," Thomas said. "Just next time you go exploring, take someone with you, okay?"

Samuel nodded again.

"Well, I best be gettin' home to fix supper," Sarah said.

Anna walked her to the door, and Sarah paused, shaking her head. "It still don't seem real," she said quietly. "One day someone's here, next day, they're gone, just like that."

After Sarah left, Thomas headed out to the woodshed, and Pete approached Samuel. "I'm glad you didn't drown," he said with a pointed look at Albert. "Anytime you need an expedition leader, count me in."

"And me," Albert added. "We could be Lewis and Clark."

Anna checked the stew while the boys washed up for supper.

Thomas returned carrying an armload of firewood. "Henry told me that Boyd Withers has assumed the role of acting sheriff," he said as he headed for the parlor.

Anna followed him to the fireplace, confused. "So soon? Is this typical?"

Arranging wood on the grate, he shrugged. "I don't know about that, but the last sheriff's been dead less than five hours." He brushed dirt from his hands. "That has to be a record."

Like a shroud, a hush had settled over Corbin. By Monday afternoon, the crowd Anna had heard about the day before had vanished, and the town was quiet.

Anna stayed close to Samuel as they hurried along Main Street. She would not have spared precious time for such an errand, but the other boys were still working on book reports, and she needed the money. Sister Mary Francis had promised to pay Anna for her mending, and Mary Agnes had suggested she bring a wagon to the presbytery to take back supplies. The sisters' ability to deliver supplies was becoming limited by a number of shortages, including fuel.

The empty wagon rattled over the rough ground as they passed the café. Anna glanced in the windows at the same time Penny Withers looked out.

Anna quickened her steps, wishing she and Samuel had chosen the other side of the street. Penny did not frighten her, but she needed no reminder of their last encounter.

"See how Jews and coloreds collude? Disgusting." Penny's voice. Clearly, she had wasted no time exiting the café when she saw Anna pass by.

"That's right, just keep walking," Penny shouted. "That road will take you right on out of town."

Samuel ducked his head and walked faster.

Anna's blood boiled, but she did not look back. *Don't stop, for Samuel's sake. Don't give her the satisfaction...*

"Look at them, the thieves. Probably planning what else they can steal with that wagon, in broad daylight, even."

She did not stop, but called over her shoulder, "We have stolen nothing. You have no basis for such a charge."

"*All* you Jews are thieves. Everyone knows it."

The murmuring behind her now made Anna suspect Penny had been joined by the rest of her entourage.

Don't do it...

But she could not stop herself. She looked over her shoulder. Penny was surrounded by five or six other young women, including Dot and Leota. Sarah was not among them, to Anna's relief.

Samuel shot Anna a glance, a distinct plea of *Just keep walking*, then resumed his focus on the ground.

"We will ignore them," Anna said. The words tasted bitter, of forfeit.

The boy kept his gaze fastened on the road.

"We've been hearing all about how pushy you Jews are." This was a voice Anna did not recognize. "How you weasel your way into banks and businesses, always scheming and cheating decent folks out of their hard-earned money."

Anna seethed but kept silent for Samuel's sake. How quick people were to spread lies. If only they knew of the tyranny and persecution she and her people had suffered, the oppression she had faced.

"Swindler," another voice shouted.

"I can guarantee you won't be getting away with any of your scheming around here," Penny hollered.

Anna focused her sights on the corner ahead where they would turn off toward the sisters' parish house, but not before a cry of, "Jew witch!" hit her like a shot in the back.

Later that night, Anna retired to her room early, her back and feet aching from taking turns helping Samuel tow the wagon loaded down with beans, flour, and kerosene. She leaned against pillows as she added finishing stitches on what would probably be the last quilt she would have time to make.

At the sound of men's voices, Anna froze, listening. It was too late for a social call. She could not make out what was being said, so she stepped into the hall and crept quietly to the top of the stairs, staying hidden on the landing.

"You sure don't waste time," Thomas was saying.

"Figured I'd make my rounds, check on all the citizens, make sure folks feel safe."

"That's mighty big of you, Deputy." Thomas's voice sounded flat.

"*Sheriff*, and think nothing of it. Just doing my job."

The voice belonged to Boyd Withers. As the tinny radio sounds of the song "Stormy Weather" drifted up the stairwell, Anna leaned over the railing to hear better.

"I'm glad you're making rounds," Thomas said. "There are a lot of rumors going around. Hopefully you can put a stop to them."

"Exactly what kind of rumors are you hearing?"

A slight pause followed. "I don't think the particulars matter," Thomas said.

"Why don't you let me be the judge of that?"

Something about the man's voice sent an icy shiver down Anna's spine.

"He was a dirty old Jew lover and caught a disease," Withers added.

Anna covered a gasp.

"What did you say?" Thomas asked.

"The rumors," Withers said. "Was that one of them?"

The tiny corridor suddenly began to tilt. Anna steadied herself against the railing to keep from staggering. Was Sheriff Dooley despised for doing business with *her*?

"He was a good man," Thomas said. "He doesn't deserve to be spoken of that way."

"I'll see what I can do, but I can't influence the way people think."

"I have a hard time believing that, Deputy."

Anna's skin prickled at the tension in the air.

After a weighty pause, the hinges of the front door creaked, followed by another pause.

"The old man just didn't wake up one day," Withers said. "Sobering, ain't it? If it could happen to him, I guess it could happen to anyone."

Anna crept back to her room and closed the door. A confusing tangle of emotion washed over her, and she wept in silence.

Twenty

BY THE THIRD WEEK OF MAY, HER PUPILS' QUIZ SCORES WERE BE-ginning to fill Anna with a cautious hope. But with the hope came the reminder that she would soon be saying goodbye.

She had known all along that this job, this community, was temporary. She had not been so foolish to think she would not develop an emotional attachment to these boys during her stay. To bond wherever she landed was in her nomadic blood, always had been. But the connections she had made here, in this home, felt vascular, as if the relationships were interconnected by arteries, and to sever such ties could be fatal.

This had not been part her plan.

By Thursday, her hopes for ending the week strong sank. Over supper, Thomas announced that the boys would be taking Friday off from schoolwork, and instead, they would all be helping Henry Tucker plant his corn.

Stunned, Anna said nothing at first, knowing Thomas would not wish to do anything to jeopardize the boys' success, but silently wondered if he understood what he was doing. Only two weeks remained in the school year, and if she was to succeed *and* stop Alice Withers, she needed every bit of that time.

After supper, while the boys listened to Amos and Andy, Anna went out to the wood shop to see Thomas, saying she admired his desire to help the Tuckers, and in any other circumstances she would gladly do the same, but she did not think the boys could afford to miss an entire school day *now*, when there was still much to do in preparation for testing.

"The Tuckers are in a real bind, Anna," he replied. He took sandpaper to what appeared to be a table leg on a lathe. "He needs to get his crop in the ground this week, but his tractor's shot, so he and Sarah have to plant it by hand. They can't do it alone."

Anna frowned. This was unfortunate, but so was the boys' situation. She did not know how capable Alice was of carrying out her threat, but she preferred not to find out.

"Aren't you the one always saying neighbors need to take care of each other?" he asked.

"Yes, but—"

"Wouldn't you grab a chance like this to teach an important principle to *your* child?"

Your child...? Stunned, she could only stare at him, cheeks roasting. Yes, she would seize such an opportunity—*if* she had not ruined her chances of having a child she could keep, to love and nurture and prepare for life. *If* she had not forever dirtied herself and jeopardized everyone she loved with her shame.

"Yes, of course," she said, finally, "but can the planting at least wait until the weekend?"

Thomas shook his head. "We'll be paying our respects to Sheriff Dooley on Saturday. The funeral is at one o'clock." He removed the piece of wood from the lathe and gently wiped off the powdery, yellow dust. "Look, Anna, I know we're putting a lot of pressure on you, and I hate to add to it. You've been busting nails to teach them, and I appreciate it. But this is too important to ignore."

So was keeping the boys from being sent to the orphan asylum, and Thomas knew this. But *he* was not the one facing a rapidly approaching due date. He did not share her desperation to complete the task as soon as possible.

"Anna, we'll always have important work to do, and there'll be plenty of times we'll have to buckle down, avoid distractions, and work hard. But if we're always working so hard that we work right past a chance to help a neighbor in need..." He stepped closer, his gold-brown eyes earnest. "Then we'll be missing the entire point of our God-given reason for being here."

Her mouth gaped, but she had no reply. The passion in his voice gripped her.

"When the Lord shows me someone in need, He always provides a way for me to help meet it. He always has. That's what this place is all about, Anna. It's the reason I'm here. And the only reason I'm *still* here. If helping people costs all I have or brings me up short, it's okay. He takes up the slack. He's come through too many times for me to stop trusting Him now, to take my eyes off those in need."

Tears blurred Anna's vision.

He studied her, waiting.

"You are right."

His brows rose. He cupped a hand around one ear and leaned closer. "Sorry, could you say that again?"

She narrowed her gaze at him. How could a man be so aggravating and so charming at the same time?

Thomas heaved a sigh. "I sure do appreciate you, Anna. More than you know."

More tears gathered. The man needed to stop speaking. "You are surprisingly wise—for a gangster," she said.

"*Former* gangster," he said, amusement tucked into a hint of a smile. "So, you'll let me take your students to help the Tuckers?"

"Who would dare not to?"

He chuckled. "Thank you," he said, eyes twinkling.

After breakfast Friday morning, Anna insisted on cleaning up so that Thomas and the boys could get an early start at the Tucker farm. Once she had everything tidied and put away, she went over to the farm also. While the men planted, Anna helped Sarah with her household chores and to fix lunch for the *menfolk*, as Sarah called them.

Anna was amazed at Sarah's endless stream of words as she pinned wash to the clothesline, untangled the giant knot in Violet's bootlaces, and scooped a kitten off Ivy's highchair and deposited it outside. Sarah did not miss a beat and barely drew a breath between topics.

Anna blinked away the sting in her eyes. There would soon be a very large hole in her heart where Sarah had been.

"What? Why're you lookin' at me like that?" Sarah asked.

"I was just...listening."

"Yeah, I'll bet. And thinkin' what a blabbermouth I am." Sarah snickered and took the empty laundry basket to the porch, then came back to the kitchen. "Sorry, I run off at the mouth sometimes." With a frown, she hunted in a drawer and pulled out two paring knives.

Anna took one and began peeling pie apples. "Do you think they will finish the planting today?" Anna asked.

"I don't know, but they'll get far more done than we ever coulda without 'em. We sure appreciate Thomas for bringin' the boys to help." Shaking her head, she dumped flour into a mixing bowl. "I don't know what we woulda done. Probably go into debt, because we'd have to pay back the government subsidy, and we already spent half of it tryin' to fix the dadgum tractor, which *still* ain't workin'."

"I heard about President Roosevelt's new plan to pay farmers to *not* plant all their fields," Anna said. "But this..."

"Don't make a lick of sense? Oh, I agree." Sarah squeezed the pie dough ingredients with her hands. "You know what makes even less sense? Plowin' cotton under and lettin' beautiful crops rot. Ruinin' perfectly good food, meanwhile folks are starvin'. But that's government for you." She placed a ball of dough onto the table and smashed it flat. "I bet Franklin D. Roosevelt never even *saw* a farm plow in his entire, old-money, Harvard-schooled life. He's got no business tellin' farmers how to run a farm or make a profit. But he's got a plan, yes, ma'am, he's gonna drive up market prices so farmers'll earn more. Ha! How the folks who were already flat broke are supposed to pay even higher prices for food beats me." She smacked the defenseless dough with her rolling pin. "Sorry. Guess I shoulda warned you you'd find me on a soapbox today."

Anna smiled. They worked in silence for a while, mixing sugar, flour, cinnamon, and bits of butter into the apples Anna had sliced, and then added the filling to the pie shells.

"Will you and Henry be at the funeral tomorrow?" Anna asked.

"Yes, ma'am. I 'spect it's gonna be a big one, too. Colin Dooley had a lot of friends in this county. He was always tryin' to keep the peace." She pinched the edges of a crust, shaping the rim into little points. "He was firm, mind you, but he also had a kind heart. Too bad, because in the end, it was probably his kind nature that—" Her hands froze in mid-pinch.

"That what?" Anna said.

Frowning, Sarah shrugged and centered a rolled-out dough on top of another filled pie. Her hands trembled slightly.

"What do you know, Sarah?"

She wiped her glistening brow with a wrist. "He had some...concerns."

"Concerns? About what? How do you know?"

Hands shaking now, Sarah pinched the crust, then turned the plate. After a few more pinches and turns, she glanced at Anna. "I heard he had a feelin' somethin' bad *might* happen to him, but you didn't hear that from me."

"Who told you?"

Focused on her crust points, she shook her head slowly. "Can't say."

"But we must tell the police."

"Police?" Sarah's face paled, her blue eyes wide. "Oh, no, Anna. You can't tell *anyone*."

"But...if he was afraid for his life, then the police need to know this."

"Then they'll know it was me for sure. You gotta promise not to breathe a word of this. Not to Thomas. Not to anyone."

Anna stared at her friend, mouth agape.

They would know? Who were *they*? Surely, *they* could not circumvent the law.

"But the police can arrest them, and then—"

"Anna, if the sheriff himself didn't even want to involve the police, what good are they? How are they gonna protect me?"

Anna gasped. "Oh, Sarah!"

"You have to promise me, Anna. If you care about me even the slightest bit..."

Her mind circled. Had Sheriff Dooley reported his concerns to the authorities? Anna could see Boyd Withers in uniform, could hear his voice just as clearly as if he were here.

He was a dirty old Jew lover and caught a disease...

Anna shuddered.

"Promise me, Anna."

Anna searched the pleading eyes of her friend. This secret was wrong, so desperately wrong. But she could not take even the slightest chance of inviting harm to Sarah.

"I promise I will not say a word to anyone."

"Not even to Thomas?"

"Not even to Thomas."

The sky beyond the cemetery looked ashen, like the face of a voyager too long at sea, and the air smelled old and stale, like it needed forced out by a good, stiff wind.

Mrs. Dooley wept quietly, concealing her shock and grief behind a handkerchief. The reverend read the twenty-third Psalm in solemn tones over the gaping hole in the earth where the late sheriff lay. He said things like *We are but sojourners breaking our journey in this place. The body is transient, but the soul is everlasting. Our loss is Heaven's gain.*

Dorothy Dooley wept louder.

A deputy from Perryville stepped up and spoke of the sheriff's dedication to public service. A long pause was followed by a tearful tribute by a waitress from Gertrude's, followed by another painfully long silence.

How odd that so few people wanted to speak. The family was understandably too overcome with grief to say anything. But apparently, so were the many friends that Sarah said the sheriff had made in Alton County.

Anna strained to hear the service from the outer edge of the black-clad throng. Thomas, along with Jimmy, Teddy, Pete, and Jack, stood in the middle with the Tuckers, while Albert and Samuel remained in the back with Anna, one on either side. She felt a keen sense of gratitude for their presence—the *all-for-one-and-one-for-all* loyalty of two nine-year-old boys. Loyalty to a woman who, two months ago, was no more than a hobo to them, to whom they had no lasting ties, who was hated by members of their community for the crime of being a Jew. Loyalty to a woman who had shown disdain for her own people, a woman they did not even truly know.

Because if they *truly* knew her, Anna felt certain they would not be standing beside her.

We are but sojourners breaking our journey in this place...

God only knew where Anna's journey would lead from here, what difficulties and obstacles she would encounter along the way, and what lonely desert she would come to, in the end. Only God knew how far her exile would take her. Was there a place far enough, though, a journey long enough to atone for her insolence? Her immorality? A sufficient sacrifice for turning her back on Him and her family, for throwing away her chastity, her future?

Was her journey to be a long, one-way road, or could it eventually circle back? Would God one day accept her *teshuvah*—her atonement—and allow her to return?

Was returning even possible?

No, this was a useless question. Her rebellion and immorality were unforgiveable. There would be no going back.

From where she watched the funeral, Anna could see Alice Withers seated beside Dorothy Dooley, with Penny on her other side. Boyd and the other deputies remained standing, but when the reverend invited an officer of the law to give the closing word, Boyd stepped up to the grave.

When Boyd Withers spoke, Samuel went instantly rigid.

27 May

My Love,

In answer to your question, I think it is unlikely that Thomas would marry again, devoted as he is to people in need—unless he can find a lovely, selfless woman who is equally driven to live and serve in such a way. Too bad you are already spoken for. (Ha!)

Yes, I have heard of the World's Fair, and no, I am not close enough to Chicago to attend today's opening. One hundred years of progress! Perhaps the next century will bring other advancements this world desperately needs. When I get to Chicago, I will try to find the Fair and send you a postcard.

This week began with a funeral on Saturday, which was not only sad, but caused a brief relapse in Samuel. He did not speak all day, and when he finally did, it was only in whispers and stutters. But the rest of the week was uneventful and busy with writing, quizzes, and study, study, study. I am proud of my pupils. They have developed a deeper level of fortitude—when they are not slugging one another or packed around the radio like sardines listening to The Shadow, *who claims to know what evil lurks in the hearts of men. (I do not know the extent of the evil or where it lurks, but I think wherever apathy, superiority, or injustice rule, evil is not far.)*

I have faith the boys will pass their grade levels. The sisters have arranged to administer the achievement tests provided by their order, even though their school is not yet finished. They have gone to great lengths to assist us. Their servanthood inspires me.

Yes, I have thought about what might lie ahead—more than you know—but as the time draws nearer, all I can think about is what I am leaving behind. Who will make challah for Samuel? Who will mend trousers and make sure they all wash behind their ears—with soap? Who will see that this home is a warm and peaceful refuge? Who will encourage them not to allow their pride, their mistakes, or the thoughtless ignorance of others determine who they are and what they can and cannot be?

As they grow into men, will they remember the nurturing touch and compassionate heart of a woman, and prize these things in a woman far more than her appearance?

Shayna, will they remember me?

Twenty-One

ANNA'S RESTLESSNESS ON SUNDAY, HEIGHTENED BY THE BABY'S latest fascination with bouncing up and down on her bladder, sent her on a walk in the woods, the only place she could go to spend her pent-up energy while avoiding townsfolk. In the past week, she had not seen Alice nor Penny and her flock. And his new duties as sheriff took Boyd Withers to the outlying precincts of Alton County. Anna could think of no better place for him to be.

When her swollen feet complained that she had gone far enough, she turned back, and nearing the fork, she spotted Thomas.

"Spying on me again?" he said.

"I am sorry, but you are not very interesting to spy on."

He chuckled.

They walked toward the house together, strolling at an unhurried pace. For the moment, all Anna wanted to do was to drink in the clean forest air and breathe in the quiet. And, if she were being honest, to soak up the calming presence of the man beside her.

"You should be proud of your boys, they have worked very hard."

"I am."

In all her experience, Anna had never known anyone like Thomas, or his unique family. "No stranger would guess you are not their father."

He eyed her. "In spite of the fact that none of them resemble me or one another in any way, I'm sure that is *exactly* what people think who see us together." He chuckled.

"But still you are a good father. A natural."

"That's kind of you to say, but the truth is, I never knew my father, and only had a mother until I was ten. Parenting is not in my nature. I grew up with a whole lot of puzzle pieces missing."

"But Gabriel, the man who took you in, was he not like a father to you?"

Thomas slowed his pace. "Yes, he was. And I try hard to follow in his footsteps the best I can, try to mentor the boys the way he did with me. But his shoes were enormous. The more I try, the more I realize how impossible they are to fill."

She chuckled. "He sounds like a myth, or a legend. Not human."

Thomas smiled. "I don't mean to say he was perfect. He was just a simple, hard-working man. But he was rarely ever impatient, always generous, never spoke an unkind word. He prayed morning and night without fail, always read his Bible, never missed church if he could help it. I was grateful that he took me in, but to a numbskull kid like me, he just seemed like a kind, ordinary fella. He lived a fairly unremarkable life. But now that I'm grown, and I know how challenging it is to raise boys into good, decent men, while staying steadfast in faith and grace and humility, I realize how extraordinary he actually was." He shook his head. "I just wish I'd seen it sooner, told him how much I appreciated him."

"Perhaps he knew."

"I hope so."

"But I think he would have been too humble to accept such praise."

Thomas eyed her. "You're right. Praise always embarrassed him."

She forced a smile, hoping he could not see on her face that the baby's bouncing was suddenly making a visit to the outhouse her very next order of business.

"He never thought about himself, only others."

The sincerity of love in Thomas's voice warmed her, made her wish he had someone special in his life. Some girl lucky enough to be the object of that caring, devoted heart.

"You miss him," she said softly.

"I sure do. Especially now," he said with a sigh. "I could really use his advice."

"What would you ask him, if you could?"

With a frown, Thomas turned his attention to the trail beneath him, as if suddenly needing to watch where he was going. "Oh...there are a few things I'd like his opinion on."

"I will bet a nickel that you already know what he would say."

His slow smile turned to a laugh. "You're assuming I won't cheat."

Smiling, they walked on until the house, garden, and chicken coop came into view. At the coop, Samuel stood very still, looking at something on top of the coop.

"If Gabriel was the mensch that you say he was," Anna went on, "then I believe he is watching you from heaven and saying, 'You are doing an excellent job, my son. Well done.'"

Thomas's gaze remained on Samuel, but his eyes glistened. He swallowed hard.

Samuel saw them and pressed a finger to his lips, eyes alight with excitement. The dove was perched atop the coop, watching the boy. Samuel made a throaty sound, and the bird answered with a soft coo. The boy lifted his hand slowly, and the bird took a step toward him, eyeing him, then took another.

Samuel turned to Anna and Thomas, awestruck. "She's not s-scared of me," he whispered.

"That's good, Samuel," Thomas said. "Maybe you can find a way to persuade her to stay."

But Thomas was no longer looking at Samuel. He was looking at Anna.

Her heart leapt, but she said nothing. For her, staying was not an option.

The next three days passed in a blur of reading and grading the boys' assignments and giving final quizzes. Anna hoped these would give her an accurate idea of their readiness for the test, which they would take on Friday, administered by Sister Mary Agnes.

On Wednesday, the last day of May, the boys completed their work by lunchtime, and Anna felt a twinge of sorrow as she dismissed her class for the last time. Amid whoops and hollers, the boys scattered, leaving her alone to grade and go over their work.

By the time she was finished, Thomas had supper on the table and the boys were eating. She went to the dining room to deliver the results.

Thomas saw her first. "Well?"

Forks stilled, all conversation ceased.

Anna smiled. "No matter what happens when you take your achievement tests on Friday, I want you to know that you have all made remarkable improvements. You have worked very hard, and I believe you are all capable of passing your grade level tests."

Samuel frowned. "Even me?"

"Yes, Samuel. You have worked hard and have done very well."

Albert grinned and elbowed him. "See, told you."

Thomas cleared his throat. "Boys, is there something you want to say?"

"Thank you, Miss Anna," Teddy said quietly. "For teaching us and helping make sure we don't get sent away." The others echoed him.

The boys resumed talking, but Thomas met her gaze and held it.

The baby kicked, as if on cue. As if to say, *I am still here, do not forget about me.*

How can I forget? she wanted to scream. The child inside her was a constant reminder and proof of her recklessness. She turned and headed for the parlor.

Jack hollered, "Hey! Miss Anna? You're not leaving *now*, are you?"

Stopping, she turned around. Seven pairs of eyes were fastened on her. "Not...at the moment."

Pete frowned. "Wait—you're *leaving*? You don't care about us anymore?"

"You're not gonna stay?" Jack said.

Teddy and Jimmy watched her, waiting.

She drew a deep breath. "I wish I could. But—"

"Why can't you?" Albert asked.

Samuel's face sagged.

"It is...complicated," she stammered. "I must go to Illinois and find my father." *This* was the best she could do?

"Well, if that's all, why don't you just come back after you find him?" Albert said.

"Good idea," Thomas added quickly. "You could come back...if you want."

Jimmy's face lit up. "Hey, since we're almost out for summer, we can *all* come help you."

"No!" Anna yelled without thinking.

They all stared at her, stunned.

"Thank you, but...I am sorry, you cannot..."

A wall of wounded faces stared at her until the room began to swirl, and she feared she would be sick.

"Excuse me," she whispered as she rushed out.

She headed straight for the woods, the trail still visible in the waning light, with no real destination, just a need to get away and think. Perhaps she could drop in and call on Sarah. Perhaps she could—

"Anna?"

With a groan, she stopped. At six and a half months pregnant, she had no hope of outrunning Thomas.

He caught up with her. "Say, what Jimmy said isn't a bad idea. With school out, we *could* come and help you. I mean, after all you've done for us..." His voice trailed off and he looked into her eyes.

Anna winced. She avoided his gaze.

"I mean...I'd really like to help you," he said softly.

She closed her eyes, searching frantically for a reply that would both satisfy him *and* put an end to this persistent line of questioning, something... But nothing came. She should have known this would happen. What a fool she had been.

She opened her eyes and found him watching her in earnest. "That is extremely kind of you, Thomas. But this is something I must do. Alone."

His expression was desperate, as if he had lost something of great worth and needed to find it. "I sure wish you'd let me help. If I could just..." he trailed off again, looking forlorn.

Heart sinking, she shook her head. He could not help her, he could do nothing for her. He could never get close, never know what she really was.

No one could. Ever.

"Anna, please. If you would just let me—"

"No!" The strain was too much, and she burst out sobbing, which was new and absolutely mortifying, and probably another traitorous side effect of pregnancy. She felt herself careening toward an emotional breakdown, and that would be disastrous.

She fought for control. "Thomas, please just accept that I must go alone." Tears streamed down her cheeks. "Please?"

"Okay..." he said, palms up, a quiet uncertainty filling his eyes. "I'm sorry I upset you, Anna," he said gently. He swallowed hard. "Hurting you is the very last thing I want to do."

No, no, no... You should be angry with me, not kind, not persistent, not compassionate...

Perhaps she should be horrid to him, *make* him angry. *Any* response from him at that moment would have been better than the tenderness pouring off of him in waves, the tenderness that threatened to make her go mad.

Twenty-Two

SINCE THE BOYS WANTED TO SHOW ANNA THE WORK THEY HAD done on the Mercy School, she accompanied them on Friday for their testing. Sister Mary Agnes set up a table at the small, sparsely furnished parish home she shared with Mary Francis.

The school building was shaping up nicely, the walls secured, the roof nearly finished. Albert and Samuel showed her the windows they had framed with little assistance.

"Speaking of windows," Mary Agnes said to Anna, "I have a proposition for you. I know you are preparing to leave soon, but if you can spare a few more days, I believe we can make it worth your while."

Anna waited, cautious but curious.

"We need curtains, and the school would pay you very well. We had hoped to take advantage of your excellent skills and the fact that you might welcome the extra funds for your journey."

The baby took that opportunity to hiccup, as if Anna needed a reminder that it was already the second of June and she really needed to move on.

Mary Agnes, perhaps sensing her hesitancy, named an astonishing price and then smiled, brows raised. "Take a moment to think it over, if you like."

"I will do it," Anna said. Prolonging her departure and her goodbyes was not wise, but it would be far more foolish to turn down such a sum.

It was decided. While the boys settled in to take their tests, Mary Agnes provided Anna with a measuring tape and showed her the fabric that Mary Francis had selected. The austere gray of it reminded her of winters in Poland.

For the next several days, Anna worked many hours at the sisters' residence, alone, since they served a large parish and had duties that kept them away most every day. She could not believe her good fortune. She mentioned it to Sister Mary Francis on Monday afternoon when the nun returned for more delivery supplies.

"Why would you wonder at Providence?" Mary Francis asked, frowning. As if everyone could expect God to drop blessings on a person simply because they needed it.

Anna only smiled and kept working, hemming a panel with long, hidden stitches.

"If you don't mind my asking, where are you going next?"

Anna told her of her father, whom the family had not heard from in six years, who had come to America ahead of them and had later vanished.

"Where are you planning to stay?" Mary Francis asked.

Anna dreaded thinking about the answer, much less saying it aloud. "I hope to find something when I arrive."

The woman frowned. "Where do you think your father is?"

"I do not know."

"And what makes you think he's in Chicago?"

Tying off a thread, Anna shook her head. "Very little. A rumor, nothing more."

Mary Francis hoisted a box and headed toward the door. Anna followed and opened it for her. The sister paused and turned to her. "I've spent some time in Chicago, and I may know of a cheap boarding house. You can start with that, see if they have a room for rent."

"Thank you, I would very much appreciate the referral."

"I can't promise anything."

"Of course," Anna said. She followed the woman as she carried the box out to the bed of the pickup truck.

Mary Francis closed the tailgate, wiped her hands, then turned to her. "Do you think he's still alive?"

The bluntness of the question stunned Anna for a moment. "I do not know."

"Well, if he is, and your family hasn't heard from him in that long, he probably doesn't want to be found."

Anna could not imagine why this would be true. What would make a man go into hiding? Mary Francis did not know her Papa.

"What's his name?"

"Hershel Leibowicz."

With a sigh, the sister opened the driver's door. "I am sorry to be the one to tell you this, but if your father is still alive, it's highly unlikely he's using a Jewish name."

Anna's heart sunk. If this was true, then she had no hope of finding him at all.

By Tuesday afternoon, Anna had the curtains completed, and a good bit of money to last her a little while. She arrived back at the Johansen place just before supper. She found Pete and Jack in the kitchen, making something on the cookstove.

"Where is everyone?" she asked.

"In the shop," Pete said, opening a can of green beans. "Mr. Tom got a contract for more radio cases." Pete dumped the beans into the pot Jack was stirring.

She peeked into the pot. "What is that?"

"Spaghetti," Jack said proudly.

Anna bit her lip to keep from making a face. It did not look like any spaghetti she had ever seen.

Pete brought over a jar of ketchup.

"What is that for?" Anna asked.

"We didn't have no—I mean, *any* tomato sauce. Figured this is close enough."

Before Anna could comment, the others came in, all talking at once. Samuel came to her, smiling.

Thomas came in last and looked surprised to see her. "You're back early."

"I finished the curtains."

He said nothing, just nodded and glanced away.

"We've been taking turns making dinner all week," Albert said.

"We can do it ourselves now," Jimmy said.

"Yeah, since you've been over at the sisters' every day, we've been getting used to what it'll be like after you're gone." Pete dumped ketchup into the pot.

Anna's heart twisted.

Thomas turned and left the room.

"What the heck is *that*?" Teddy said, frowning into the pot.

"Spaghetti, what does it look like?" Pete said.

WINGS LIKE A DOVE

"Pig slop," Teddy said.

"We didn't want to wash any more pots than we have to, so we just mixed it all together. All goes to the same place anyhow."

"Yeah, to the front porch, when I puke it out," Teddy said, his upper lip curled in disgust.

Anna bit both lips to suppress a chuckle.

The sound of voices carried from the parlor, then Thomas came into the kitchen with Sister Mary Agnes.

The older woman smiled. "Something smells wonderful."

"Gee, thanks," Jack said, jutting his chin at Teddy.

"Fellas," Thomas said, "Sister Mary Agnes is here with some news."

"I was on my way back from Yoder," she said, "and thought I would stop here first. I received your test results."

No one said a word.

"I have given Mr. Thomas your assessment reports, which list areas of strengths and weakness, but overall, each of you have met the minimum criteria. You have all passed your respective grades. Congratulations."

"Halle-LOO-jah!" Pete shouted.

Above the hooting and hollering, Anna thanked Mary Agnes for her help and for the report. Then Thomas escorted the sister to the door.

Albert smacked Samuel on the back while the others continued to revel in their success.

"You did it, Miss Anna," Jack said.

She tousled his hair with a laugh. "Oh, no. *You* did it." She smiled, then bent and kissed his head.

As everyone scattered to wash up, Anna turned around, collided with Thomas, and nearly lost her balance. He grasped her arms to steady her. Terrified that she might brush against him, she tried to step back, but he did not release her.

She met his eyes and found a quiet desperation there that captured her breath, made her heart shudder.

He shook his head, his gaze fastened on hers. "Look, Anna, I'm not very good at this—"

"Thomas, whatever you have to say—"

"Please, I promise I'm not going to keep pestering you," he said. "But I just have to say this one thing. I don't think you know how much you mean to us." He frowned as if inwardly scolding himself, then cleared his throat. "I mean, to *me*."

Tears blurred her vision. "You are not making this any easier for me," she whispered.

"Good. That was my plan."

She felt her eyes widen. He had a plan?

"Chandler?" The deep male voice outside sounded like Henry Tucker. A pickup door slammed.

Ignoring the summons, Thomas reached up and gently cupped Anna's cheek in his hand. The warmth of his touch made her skin tingle. His gaze fell to her mouth and lingered, as if all that mattered in the world was right there, in the palm of his hand. Then, with a sigh, he turned and left.

Stunned, Anna reached up and touched the still-tingling place where his hand had been. Remembered to breathe. Despite her best effort to stop it, her heart sang.

But she was only tormenting herself. The time to leave had come. She gave herself a mental shake and went to the parlor.

Henry Tucker stood inside the front door, overalls smudged with dirt. "And you're not going to believe this, but Beckett tells me it was a 'private' election." He winced at his muddy boots and added, "Sorry, ma'am."

"He can't do that," Thomas said, frowning. "There are laws. Procedures."

"Well, that don't seem to stop anyone in this county. Especially the law."

"What happened?" Anna said.

Thomas turned to her. "Somehow, even though it's not election time, Boyd Withers got himself *officially* elected as the new Alton County Sheriff."

Now that it was June, the sun rose much too early. As the glow of dawn spread across the ceiling, dispelling the darkness, Anna finally gave up hope of falling asleep. Throughout the night, her mind had been too full of questions, her heart full of too many powerful and warring emotions. Fears. Hopes. Deeply rooted, silent longings she felt certain were useless to explore...and yet her certainty was beginning to crack.

Thomas clearly wanted her to stay, and perhaps in some permanent way. Which of course was impossible. But the way he looked at her, the way he touched her and told her she meant something to him...his endearing offer to help her find her papa. Was his offer born of special feelings, or his benevolent desire to help all people in need?

Thomas was a compassionate man. What if she told him about her quarrel with Mama the night she went out? What would he say if she explained her momentary lapse of judgment, how she had foolishly put herself in the wrong place? Would he understand that she had made an awful mistake and not hold it against her? Could he be that understanding? If he cared about her at all, was there a chance that he could forgive her?

Surely such hopes were ludicrous—even her own *mother* could not forgive her. But Thomas Chandler was nothing like Mama. If he could forgive her for that, and perhaps *then* if she told him about the child...

What was the worst that could happen?

This was the question that had kept her awake all night long.

Anna awoke suddenly. Bright sunlight spilled glowing warmth over her and had heated the room like an oven. She had finally fallen asleep, and now, the morning had turned to afternoon. Why had no one bothered to wake her?

No one was around the kitchen or anywhere downstairs, so Anna fried herself an egg, then took the apron she had sewn as a gift for Sarah and headed to the Tucker farm.

Sarah met her on the porch, joined by Ivy and the dog. Violet was out in the field helping her daddy.

"So, I guess this is it, then," Sarah said, sniffling. She looked at the apron and hugged it to herself, but didn't seem to see it. "I knew you weren't stayin', but, I always hoped in the back of my mind that you'd...I don't know, find somethin' here worth stayin' for."

Owen padded over and sniffed Anna's feet, wagging.

Anna had no reply. If Sarah only knew how firmly and deeply Anna's heart had become lodged in this place, about the questions that nagged at the back of her mind. If only Sarah could see that Anna was a prisoner of circumstances outside her control and was not free to pursue her heart's longings and desires. Whatever Anna found precious in Corbin, Indiana did not matter.

"I will never forget you, Sarah. You are a truly good person, inside and out. I will always treasure your friendship."

"You had to go and make me blubber," Sarah said, dabbing at her eyes with the apron. Ivy tugged at her mother's skirt, and Sarah hoisted her up. "I feel the same way about you, too, Anna. You've opened my eyes, got me thinking. I hope to be like you someday—when I grow up." She attempted to chuckle, but it fell flat. "You leavin' right away?"

"Tomorrow morning, when I have a whole day ahead of me. I accidentally slept half the day away today."

Sarah's brow rose. "Say, I could get the boys to hog-tie you, then you'd have no choice."

Anna smiled. "Goodbye, Sarah."

"You take care, Anna. And I mean that."

When Anna returned to the house, she took down her traveling bag. Anshel's map was still there, in the bottom, untouched since her arrival here. Ten and a half weeks ago. It seemed a lifetime.

She went downstairs to the parlor and found Thomas at the picture window, staring across the yard. He held a paper in his hand, and on closer inspection, he was trembling with rage.

Twenty-Three

ANNA WAITED, UNCERTAIN WHAT TO MAKE OF HIS POSTURE, then spotted the envelope at his feet. She could not see who it was from.

"Thomas?"

He spun around. The dark look on his face arrested her words. "The sheer nerve," he hissed. He crumpled the paper in his hand and threw it with enough force to send it across the room to hit the wall and land near the fireplace. His eyes glistened, his jaw clenched.

Stunned, Anna stood frozen. "What—"

"She's gloating. *Gloating*, Anna. Of all the things to brag about."

"Who?"

"Josephine." Resentment edged the word. "My ex-wife."

She waited, resisting the urge to go to him. What had his ex-wife written, and why? What could she have said to make him so upset?

Absently, he wandered to the fireplace, kicked the wadded paper, then turned to Anna, fists on his hips. "She just *had* to tell me that she's rolling in the dough now, and *all* her dreams are finally coming true. Why she thinks I'd care..." He scowled.

Clearly he *did*, but Anna was not about to say so.

"A year after we married, the Crash changed everything, including our lives. Church donations went down too, and I took a voluntary pay cut. I did my best to make ends meet, but she hated being poor, and worse, she despised my helping folks who were even more down and out. I should have seen it long before we married, should have known. But I was a dumb kid, too infatuated. And too dumb to figure out when she started seeing someone else." Disgust twisted his lips.

Her heart broke for him. After a lonely childhood and losing the only people who had cared about him, Thomas had been rejected by his wife and dismissed as a minister all at one time.

"I guess now she has what she always wanted."

She hated to ask. "What is that?"

"A rich guy she can dangle like a puppet on a string, money she can spend like water. Furs and jewels. Pretending she's high class, wasting money that could help a lot of needy folks."

Anna watched him, suddenly aware that she had been holding her breath.

He was still fuming, nostrils flaring with every breath. He stomped over to the balled-up letter and scooped it up but didn't look at it. He just shook his head, forearm muscles twitching.

"So let her gloat," Anna offered. "If she is so shallow that she would marry for money, then perhaps it is best—"

"*Marry*? Ha! If only she were married to him, that might make this a little easier to swallow." He held up the letter in his fist.

So Josephine was a rich man's mistress.

"Not only is she not married to him, but he's already got a wife." His mouth pressed into a grim line. "And not only is she reveling in her illicit affair with a married man, she's having his—" He twisted away, his body quivering.

Dread flooded every inch of her.

"She's having his child. And not only is she having her lover's illegitimate child, she's bragging about it. She knows me, knows what I believe. She knows it's immoral. Knows how much she's already hurt me. Why would she throw this in my face, flaunt her behavior to me? Why?"

Barely able to breathe, Anna watched Thomas rake a hand through his hair. He looked as if he would vomit.

The baby kicked, hard. Three times.

Anna held herself as rigid as stone, terrified that the baby's movement could somehow be suddenly visible.

"What kind of woman does this? And brags about it? Was I that much of a disappointment? Well, that's a dumb question."

A tear slipped down Anna's face.

He turned and looked at Anna, his glistening eyes red. He looked so wounded.

She shook her head. "Some people strike at others as a way to divert attention away from their own disgrace. It is she who is flawed, not you."

He strode to her and took hold of her arms. "Oh, Anna. You're so good. So kind and selfless, so different from her."

She felt dizzy and fought a sudden desire to flee, to run as far and as fast as she could.

"She's nothing like you. She's—no, there's no comparison. If only I'd met—" He spun around and shook his head. "What kind of woman would flaunt her illicit child with such brazen conceit?"

Swallowing the painful knot in her throat, Anna slowly took a step back. He could *not* get near her. The look of pain, sickened disgust, and betrayal in his face made her own stomach turn.

Voices sounded in the kitchen.

Thomas snatched up the envelope and turned to her. "I'm sorry, Anna. I never thought I'd hear from her again. And when I do, it's this..." He shook his head, his face still sick with disbelief. "I'm going to take a walk. I just need some time alone."

Anna watched him leave and then let out a shaky breath, willing herself not to be ill.

What a pure fool she had been, an utter and absolute fool. There would be no more wondering about him understanding her mistake, her condition. No more hesitation. She would leave at dawn's first light.

Anna realized she needed to tell Shayna she was leaving Corbin and not to send any more letters until Anna reached Chicago and could give her new address. She jotted a brief letter, then hurried to town to mail it.

On Main Street, a group of young mothers had apparently taken their children for ice cream, as the children were now eating cones and chasing each other around in front of the café. Anna crossed to the other side of the street. One of the women, a friend of Penny's, saw her and jabbed another. They passed knowing glances amongst themselves.

Anna shivered. Thankfully, these looks were only evidence of their hatred of her as a Jew, but after hearing about the letter from Josephine, Anna felt conspicuous and on edge.

She mailed her letter, then crossed the bridge and hurried toward the house.

An unusually loud splash in the creek drew her attention, but when she looked around, she saw no reason for it. It was probably a fish, or perhaps a bird. She kept walking along the creek, curious about the source of the sound, wondering if the fish in the creek had grown larger now, large enough to—

She saw a child in the water then, a toddler in blue, bobbing up to the surface, flailing an arm, then going under again.

"Help!" Anna screamed. "A child is drowning! Help!" She screamed as loudly as she could and looked around for help. No one was near enough to hear; the mothers were still across the bridge.

The child's head bobbed again but did not break the surface.

In a panic, Anna sprang into the creek and waded toward the child, groping in the current, fanning her arms out from side to side, until she spotted a white collar. She lunged and caught hold of the gown, pulled the girl to her, and then carried her, stumbling, to the bank.

She laid the child on the grass. The girl coughed several times, blinked, and then burst out crying.

Screams and shouts grew louder as people, children, mothers rushed to the spot.

One woman screamed, "My baby! My baby! What happened? She was there just a minute ago—" The woman snatched up the sobbing child, then stared at Anna.

Others came, crowding around with murmurs of *what happened, did she drown, is she all right* while the child's mother continued to gape at Anna.

Anna's drenched gown clung perfectly to her belly, molded to her like a second skin, revealing her very round shape. She tugged at the wet fabric, but it was too late. Hissing whispers grew into a swarm of accusation.

"Pregnant!"

"Shameless!"

"Harlot!"

The only thought in her mind was to push past the mob and get back to a dry change of clothing, quickly, before—

But it was too late. Thomas was sprinting toward the creek like someone was on fire.

"Anna, are you all right? I heard—"

He stopped as if he had been clobbered in the face with a cast iron skillet.

Anna could not move. Though the water was not cold, she went completely numb. The shock on his face was nothing like the icy current racing through her, fastening her to the spot.

"She's pregnant!"

"The vulgar, dirty Jew!"

"See? They *are* immoral, this proves it."

Oddly, the only reaction that had any impact on her was the look on Thomas's face as he continued to stare, horrified, at the obvious melon-shape of her belly. His expression ranged from mortified to stunned to wounded—deeply wounded—to repulsed.

He spun away.

Anna held her emotions in the tightest grasp to keep from sobbing, but she could not stop the rush of tears.

"Chandler! You've got some explaining to do," someone in the crowd shouted.

"I always knew there was something fishy about her living there..." said another.

"That's a tidy little tutoring arrangement you two have going on," Penny said to Anna, her lips pursed. "You can't hide your depravity now. You disgust me. Both of you."

Anna watched Thomas pacing the bank, shaking his head slowly as if to clear a fog. A weird, muddy feeling stole over her, as if she were watching the scene unfold from under water.

From higher on the bank, Alice Withers glared at Anna, pure loathing in her eyes. But instead of questioning Anna, Alice spun around and marched straight to Thomas.

"Thomas Chandler, explain yourself. What kind of depravity has been taking place here? This is appalling, and with all those boys... Just what kind of a business are you running? How long have you two been carrying on? This is outrageous! I *will* be speaking with Sheriff Withers."

Suddenly feeling like a wilted reed, Anna staggered, her legs buckling. Shaking, she tried to take a few steps, but the pressing crowd would not part, would not allow her to escape. She was trapped within a circle of hateful accusers, her prison walls closing in around her.

"Let her pass," a quiet but firm voice said.

Anna looked up. Sarah was pushing her way through the crowd and coming down the bank toward her.

"Well, despite your claims of ignorance," Alice was shouting at Thomas, who was now walking swiftly toward his house, "the Jew harlot must leave your home at once."

Sarah reached Anna's side, took her elbow, and steered her up the bank. "You need to get out of those wet clothes and warm yourself." She did not look at Anna.

Whispers trailed them.

Look at that Sarah Tucker—she's touching that whoring Jew...

Nodding, Anna went with her, shaking violently, unable to speak, unable to look her friend in the eye.

Twenty-Four

WITH SARAH STILL FOLLOWING, ANNA STOPPED AT THE FOOT OF the stairs but did not turn. The names they had called her, the sharp cries of *shameless* and *filthy* and *whoring,* echoed still, hitting her heart like flaming arrows.

"Please, do not trouble yourself any further," Anna whispered.

"Let me at least...help you out of those wet things," Sarah said quietly.

Anna shook her head. "Thank you, but I will manage." She trudged up the stairs alone, suddenly feeling so enormous, her shame so blatant, her depravity so fully exposed.

Alone in her room, she shoved back the sobs that threatened to burst and began removing her drenched clothing, a difficult task as her hands shook violently. After she changed, she stuffed the dripping wet gown into her bag.

Stairs creaked, then a knock on her door sent her heart pounding.

She froze. She could not see him. She could not bear to see the look on his face again. Not ever.

"Anna?" It was Mary Agnes. She came in, followed by Mary Francis and Sarah.

Her teary eyes drifted closed. Perfect. Another audience to witness her shame and humiliation.

"Anna, the accusations out there could bring serious trouble to Thomas and the boys," Mary Agnes said. "And the mood in town is..."

"Volatile," Mary Francis finished. "For the boys' sake as well as yours, you'd best leave town as soon as possible."

Anna nodded, unable to trust her voice.

"Do you have somewhere to go?" Mary Agnes asked.

"She was on her way to Chicago to find her father," Mary Francis said.

Mary Agnes frowned. "Do you have friends or family there, someone to take you in?"

She shook her head.

"What about...your beau? The...baby's father?" Sarah asked quietly.

"There is no beau," she whispered. "No father. There is no one."

"You won't be safe," Mary Agnes said. "Especially as a Jew, and pregnant, and unwed."

"I understand," Anna said.

"I'm not sure you do," Mary Francis said. "You're in danger. As an unmarried woman, pregnant, homeless, and alone, you'll be considered a vagrant. You could be put into jail." Her expression darkened. "Or...worse."

"Let us help," Mary Agnes said. "There are homes for unwed mothers where you can stay until your child is delivered and turned over to the state."

"I have seen such a home, and I would rather be in jail."

"I don't think you realize what awaits you out there, Anna." Mary Francis looked stern. "Let us arrange for you to go to a home."

Dark, shadowy images of infants wailing in the dark, unanswered, unfed, uncomforted, assailed Anna's mind. She shook her head again.

"I...know of an option that won't mean goin' to one of them homes," Sarah said slowly. "And, if you want, it'll also allow you to keep your child."

Anna stole a glance at her friend. Sarah's face was red, either from mortification or from weeping. Whatever the cause, Sarah's discomfort sent fresh tears spilling down Anna's face.

"I was not planning on being allowed to keep the child," Anna whispered. She had avoided referring to it as *her* child. She suspected that the immediate removal of *the* child would be painful enough.

With a glance at the sisters, Sarah went on. "I know a widowed farmer desperate for someone to care for his five little ones. He's my Mama's cousin, lives in Ohio. She was just tellin' me the other day he's goin' plumb outta his mind, poor man. He'll take anybody willin' to come. You could marry him and be a mother to his children, and I reckon he won't mind that you're...with child."

"Marry? A complete stranger?"

"It's not ideal by any means, but this'd protect you from danger and jail, and...this way, if you were wantin' to keep your baby, you can."

More shouts and raised voices rose from outside, from the lane at the edge of the property. A crowd must have gathered in the time Anna had been upstairs.

The situation was suddenly painfully real: She was Jewish, an immigrant, pregnant out of wedlock, homeless, and alone. She had no choice. At that moment, the only thing there was to think about was her safety, and the safety of the unborn child.

But her mind could focus on nothing but the betrayal and shock on Thomas's face. His bitter disgust.

"Anna, I hate to be the one to say it," Sarah said quietly, "but you have no income, no family, and no other options."

Slowly, Anna lifted her gaze and met Sarah's for the first time since the creek. Something like hurt and confusion mingled there.

As the three women waited, watching her, Anna knew they were right. She could not venture out alone, not now.

"But are you certain the farmer will agree?"

"I'm sure he will, he's so desperate he's beside himself," Sarah said. "I'll telephone right away and start makin' the arrangements."

It was agreed that Mary Francis would come before dawn and take Anna to the train station in Huntington. The sisters offered her train fare, but Anna declined, saying she had a little money now. But there was something else they could do. They could speak to Thomas for her and tell him she would be leaving before dawn. Before anyone had to see her.

None of them would ever have to set eyes on her again.

In the pre-dawn hours on Thursday, the sky still black and bottomless as the sea, Anna waited for the headlights of the sisters' pickup truck, then gathered her bag, crept down the stairs, and slipped out the door. Her eyes, dry from crying, were sore and swollen.

As Mary Francis shifted the truck into reverse, Anna took one last look at the house. No one stirred. She thought she saw a flicker of light in Thomas's office window, but it was just her imagination.

For the next several hours, the rocking of the eastbound train alternated between making her nauseous and lulling her into a fitful sleep, haunted by wretched images of standing on the creek bank, the angry mob, the shouting. Penny, Alice, and the townsfolk accusing Thomas of immorality, condemning him. His mortification. The letter from Josephine, and then the look on Thomas's face when he saw her at the creek, as if the cruelest joke ever conceived had just been played on him.

And what about the progress Anna had made with the boys? All that she had worked so hard to achieve was now ruined. Forever smeared with the stain of shame. *Her* shame. There was no question the boys would remember Anna now. Just not the way she had hoped.

You bring a curse on them all. They will all share in your shame.

Her layover at the train station in Marion was a long wait on a hard bench amongst strangers. She never knew a time would come when being unknown would bring such relief.

While she waited for the next train, she forced herself to think about the future, to prepare herself for the new life that lay ahead. As a farmer's wife.

What did Farmer Parker think of Anna coming into his home already with child? Sarah had assured Anna that he said he did not mind, as long as she could take care of the others. He had asked no questions about Anna. So what sort of a man was he? Was he kind? What would he expect of her? Would he love her child? Would she grow to love him, his children?

Could she?

Perhaps he would allow her to resume her search for Papa, once she was settled in. Perhaps he would even offer to help her, as Thomas had.

She willed herself to put Thomas and the boys out of her mind, once and for all, then focused on her next stop. She was scheduled to arrive at the station at Prospect, Ohio, very late, and as Farmer Parker was a very early riser, the arrangement was for him to collect her at the station early Friday morning. She would first spend Thursday night in the train station, alone. Then, in the morning, they would be married at a local church on the way to his farm. She would be married before she even set foot in her new home.

Married. She was to be a bride, after all.

Using her damp bag as a pillow, she laid her head down awkwardly and slept on the hard bench.

In the early hours of Friday morning, before Anna was awake enough to remember where she was, the farmer arrived. Their meeting was brief and businesslike. The tall, lanky man carried her bag to his wagon, and they set off without delay from the train station, instantly surrounded by dirt brown fields striped with green. The dusty, bumpy wagon ride was not unpleasant, just unnervingly silent.

The quiet gave Anna time to observe Frank Parker. That he was overworked, overtired, and underfed was apparent. What she could *not* see was what kind of man he was. What manner of man would agree to marry a pregnant Jew whom he had never met?

As she studied him, he appeared to be a decent, hard-working man. So why was Anna suddenly having intense qualms about the arrangement? It was foolish to question her good fortune, this gift of Providence. She would be safe and provided for. No questions would be asked, no unknown dangers would lurk around every corner. She would be able to love and raise her child—something she had not allowed herself to even consider, a hope she had refused to give wings. So what more could she ask for?

Nothing. She could ask for nothing more. She did not even deserve *this* much.

Anna was childish and ungrateful to want anything more. Purely foolish. These misgivings were simply a sign that she had not changed, that she was as determined as ever to be obstinate, ungrateful, and skeptical.

She glanced at Frank again, trying to picture five miniature versions of himself scuffling around the farm, wondering if they, too, looked gaunt, worn, and weary.

How long would it take for the seven faces she had left behind in Indiana to fade from her memory?

They reached the church where a minister and his wife were waiting, prepared to marry Frank Parker and Anna on the spot. Five hastily scrubbed children, ages ranging from one to seven, shuffled down the church steps to meet her.

"This is Betty, Robbie, Donny, Willie, and Daisy," the minister's wife said, pointing to each child in turn. All five children stared at Anna, including baby Daisy, attached to what appeared to be a fixed spot on seven-year-old Betty's hip.

Anna smiled, but it felt false, deceptive. Perhaps, in time, she could come to love this man and his sullen children.

The woman shooed the Parker children up the steps and into the church, and then told Frank that the minister and witnesses were ready and waiting inside.

The farmer removed his hat and trudged up the steps.

Anna tried to follow but found she could not. Her feet refused to move.

When the man reached the church door, he stopped and looked over his shoulder.

Until that moment, Anna had never known that love could be so consuming, so tenacious. That it could take root and burrow down so deeply, even in ground that rejected it, even when there was no hope of it ever being cultivated.

How unkind it would be for her to marry this man when her heart ached so deeply for another.

"I am so sorry," Anna said to the man in low, contrite tones. "But I have made a mistake. I am afraid I will not be staying, after all."

With a weary sigh, Frank Parker put his hat back on, then went to his wagon and hauled out Anna's sack.

"Train station's thataway," he said, depositing the sack at her feet. Then he turned and headed for the church.

"Will you not give me a ride back?" Anna asked.

"Day's a wastin'. I got loads of work and I'm already far behind."

As the farmer and his wagonload of children disappeared in a cloud of dust, Anna stood alone in the middle of the road, in the middle of Nowhere, Ohio, having made another reckless decision that had, once again, altered the course of her life.

The midday sun beat down on her as she walked, sapping her already vanishing strength. Her swollen feet screamed, but there was nowhere to stop and rest, nothing but a dirt road cutting a path down the middle of green-striped fields stretching out of sight on either side.

Not only was there nowhere to rest, but thanks to the obstinate streak that clearly still ran deep in her, she now had nowhere to go.

Hours later and hoping she was still headed in the right direction, Anna shifted her bag to the other shoulder and longed for a sip of water. What now? She had just thrown away her only chance at safety and provision. What future had she just chosen for herself and her child?

Could she even find Papa? What if it were true that he did not wish to be found? What would a man in hiding want with a pregnant, unwed daughter?

Finally, in the late afternoon, when the Prospect train station came into view, Anna cried in relief.

Once inside the station, she found an empty seat to rest her aching back and feet, and to face her pressing dilemma. Where to go? Chicago? Manhattan? Was there any hope of persuading her mother to change her mind? No, that would be as unlikely as bumping into her papa the minute she set foot in Union Station. Going home came with conditions—*if* Mama would even take Anna back now. But Anna could never sign her child over to the Campbell woman. On this, she would not relent.

Although Anna did not know what awaited her or where she or her child would eventually end up, one thing she did know, with a new and growing certainty: the child she carried would have at least one champion in this world—its mother.

She stood slowly, parched, stiff, and aching all over, and then shuffled to the ticket window. "When is the next train to Chicago?" she asked the clerk.

"Twenty minutes."

"*Anna?*"

Her mind was playing a very cruel joke. She turned around.

It was no joke—it was Thomas.

Twenty-Five

ANNA STARED AT HIM, BOTH CONFUSED AND OVERCOME BY AN absurd joy that was immediately doused by his demeanor. He looked even more cold and stiff than he had two days earlier.

"I didn't expect to find you here," he said.

Anna saw that he carried no bag. "Why are you here?"

"I was on my way to the Parker farm to talk to you. But it seems you've been delayed."

Her face burned. "Not delayed. There has been a change of plans."

His gaze dipped briefly to her abdomen, then recoiled. The scowl on his face had not lessened since the last time she saw him.

"Why do you wish to speak to me?"

"I came to ask you to wait, if it wasn't too late." He still would not look her in the eye.

Anna resisted the urge to tuck in her protruding belly. There was no sense trying to hide it from him now. "Why?"

"It's Sam. He's in a terrible state. We don't know what's come—"

"Samuel? What happened?"

"He disappeared yesterday, and it took us all day and half the night to find him. When we did, he was…" His eyes misted. "I don't know what you call it, but he's in some sort of shock. He's withdrawn, he won't talk. He won't eat. He barely moves."

Samuel? Her legs shook and felt as if they would buckle. She lowered herself onto a nearby bench.

"The boys have all tried. Sarah and the sisters even came and tried to get him to respond, but he won't. He's shut everyone out. Sarah thinks…

She said he was at the creek when…" He turned away again, his lips twisting. "She thinks all the shouting scared him, reminded him of something terrible."

Anna wiped the tears slipping down her cheeks. "Poor Samuel" was all she could say.

Thomas frowned. "Since you got him to speak, I was…hoping you could help. I was hoping…you would return. Just long enough to get Sam back to his old self."

"Return?" Anna spluttered, then lowered her voice. "How can you suggest this? Everyone knows my—" she glanced at the other travelers "—situation. I would do anything for Samuel, but returning is not possible."

His eyes, hard as stone, met hers for the briefest moment. Then he turned his attention to the window, the muscles of his cheek rippling as he clenched and unclenched his jaw. "You'd have to return married."

"Married?" Anna studied him, unable to grasp his meaning. "To whom?"

"Me." He all but spat the word.

Her mouth hung open in disbelief.

Bitterness radiated from him. He stared out the window and spoke in low, even tones. "With the protection of my name in marriage, you'll be relatively safe in Corbin and…wherever else you go after that. Traveling safety for both you and—" he almost choked on the words "—your *child*."

Stunned, Anna tried, but could not guess what might have come over him. He clearly despised her, so this proposition was puzzling. *He* was puzzling.

He cleared his throat. "You don't have to stay any longer than necessary. Just until Sam is better."

"How do you know my returning will help him?"

"I don't." Frowning, he met her gaze. "But I have to do something."

His concern for Samuel wrenched Anna's heart.

"I don't know what he's been through, what still haunts him," he went on, "but I'm afraid of what might happen to him if he doesn't snap out of this soon. Someone might take him, lock him away. The things they do to orphans—the experiments…"

Anna rose, went to the window overlooking the loading platform, and watched the porters scurrying around, preparing for the next batch of passengers. There were no guarantees she could help Samuel. What if she could not? And what about returning to the boys for a little while, only to leave them again? Leaving the first time was as painful for Anna as leaving home had been. More so, in some ways. Painful in ways she was trying very hard to forget.

And what about returning under such terms? Married? To *Thomas*?

Thomas spoke from behind her. "And of course there would be no... marital obligations or expectations," he said, his voice as brittle as dead leaves. "Of any kind."

Of course not—she repulsed him. She was immoral and unclean. A disgrace. No better than Josephine. And what he thought of such a woman had been made so painfully clear.

Something cold and heavy pressed against her heart, crushed it, squeezed the lifeblood from it. To live with his repulsion, day after day, and to return to his home, now that the town knew about her—

"What about you?" she said, turning, suddenly aware of the impact this would have on him. "You are already a target for your sympathies. Marrying a Jew—and in my situation, which everyone knows now—will make it far worse."

"Bricks and dead rodents don't concern me. All I care about is getting Sam better."

"But if the previous sheriff was afraid, then you ought to be even more so."

Thomas frowned. "Dooley? Afraid? How do you know that?"

Anna froze. Sarah had begged her not to say, made her promise. Anna could not betray a promise. "I cannot say."

"What do you know, Anna?"

"I am sorry, I...cannot tell you."

His gaze flickered to her belly again, then he stiffened, his deep scowl returning. "Keep your secrets. Your affairs are none of my business."

Her cheeks blazed. Unkind as it was, she deserved that.

A train whistle blew, and the porter was calling for passengers to Chicago.

She could go back with Thomas, despised by him and his community, and hope that despite all of that, she could somehow help Samuel, or head out into the unknown, alone and destitute.

"I thought you had a bond with Sam," he said, his voice grim. "Will you do it for him?"

I will return for Samuel and the boys and I will marry you in name only for both your protection and mine, and I will not trouble you with my grieving heart...

"I will. For Samuel."

He nodded, then went to the ticket clerk. He spoke for a few minutes, bought tickets, and then returned. "There's a Justice of the Peace two blocks from the train station in Marion. We can stop there and be married on the way home."

Stop and marry on the way. Like picking up a bag of chicken feed.

"Fine."

They traveled in silence, speaking only when they had to respond to the Justice of the Peace. They were married at the jail a few blocks from the Marion train station, with a pair of bootleggers locked in a cell as witnesses.

The only other time they spoke was when Thomas asked Anna why her plans to marry the farmer had changed.

It turns out I cannot promise to love one man when my heart belongs to another, she could say, but this would only sicken him.

"I thought you were not interested in my affairs," she had said finally, and then instantly regretted it.

Not another word passed his bloodless lips the rest of the way home.

They arrived home at nearly midnight on Friday, so it was not until Saturday morning that Anna saw the boys. She went straight to the room Samuel shared with Albert. Samuel was still in bed asleep, or so it seemed. When she sat on the edge of his bed, he did not stir. But when she said his name, he opened his eyes, then reached out and clung to her, as if he were drowning and she was the only raft in sight.

"I am back," she said. *For a little while, anyway.*

He did not move, only gripped her more tightly.

"Are you coming down for breakfast?"

No response.

Anna sighed. "You will turn into a stick of kindling if you do not eat."

Samuel released her, laid back down, and curled up beneath the covers again, eyes closed. She talked to him for a while and told him of her train ride, but with still no response. She finally decided to let him rest and try again in a little while.

The boys were finishing their breakfast by the time she came down. There was no sign of Thomas, but this did not surprise her.

"Do we have to call you Mrs. Tom now?" Jimmy asked.

She had not thought of this. She put a corn cake on a plate. "Of course not, I am Miss Anna, just as before."

"We heard about what happened at the creek."

Anna stiffened.

"I heard you saved Miz Martin's baby from drowning," Albert said. "Except folks forgot about *that* part."

"Mr. Pitts said dirty rotten things about you and Mr. Tom," Teddy said. "I told him he didn't know what he was talking about. I said you're not a witch, 'cause if you were, we'd be the first to know it. And you aren't dirty, because you're always pesterin' us to take baths."

Anna huffed lightly. It was the closest thing to a laugh she had heard from herself in a while. A lifetime, it seemed.

"We don't much care what people say you did," Teddy added. "Because we know you, and you're one of us."

Tears stung Anna's eyes.

"That day, down at the creek...that's when Sam curled up inside himself," Albert said.

Anna cringed. She could still hear the hateful, clamoring mob.

Pete nodded, adding, "When the townsfolk started shouting and saying nasty things about you, Sam took off running, straight into the woods. We still don't know what got into him."

"Where did you finally find him?" Anna asked.

"He was curled up tight as a ball, up in a tree," Jack said. "Took us forever to find him. Albert ran up and down the creek for over an hour, scared he'd drowned."

"Well, at least he is safe now," Anna said. "We must be patient and give him time."

"I bet he'll come around, now that you're back," Teddy said. "Good thing we sent Mr. Tom after you when we did, or he mighta got there too late."

Anna's brows rose. "*You* sent him?"

Teddy nodded, then downed the last of his milk.

"We made him tell us where you went," Jimmy said. "He told us you had to go take care of a family problem, but we told him we ain't stupid, we heard about the baby."

Anna did not know what to say to this.

"We asked him where your husband is, and he said you didn't have one, and that you were on your way to marry some corn farmer you never even met. And then Albert said why don't *you* marry her? If Miss Anna would agree to some total stranger, she'd probably agree to you."

She gasped and covered her mouth. The boys had no idea how hurtful this would have been to Thomas, especially on the heels of Josephine's letter. She could only imagine the look on Thomas's face when Albert told him *that*.

"Then I said it was Miss Anna who got Sam talking in the first place," Pete added, "and he needs her even more now, so if you don't go bring her back, we're all leaving."

"Liar." Teddy shook his head. "You told him if he didn't go bring her back, we'd never take a bath ever again."

"Never!" Jack echoed. "All for one, and one for all!"

"And...what did Mr. Tom say to that?" Anna wondered.

"He muttered a bunch and kicked a chair, and then he stormed out," Albert said. "Didn't come back for over an hour."

"Yeah, and that was only to get his hat and billfold," Teddy said. He turned to Pete. "Your extortion idea worked. You're a regular little Al Capone."

Pete nodded and then snatched up a piece of bacon and pretended it was a cigar.

Thomas might as well have been invisible. Between a new radio case order, the Sisters of Mercy School, and the boys' apprenticeship, Thomas stayed extraordinarily busy. When Anna did see him, he barely said a word to her, and when he did, he was still as stiff as ever.

On Sunday, four days after the incident at the creek, Anna was finally able to get Samuel to eat a slice of warm challah. But he still slept most of the time, would not speak, would not play, and rarely got out of bed. His withdrawal puzzled Anna, but as long as he was eating and responsive, she would continue to coax him.

Monday morning, Anna was in the kitchen putting on a pot of stew and overheard the boys out in the lean-to.

"I think it's a boy." This sounded like Albert.

"Yeah. We'll name him Daniel, after Daniel Boone," Pete said.

"What makes you think *you* get to name it, numbskull?" Teddy said.

"What if it's a girl?" Jimmy said.

Silence.

Anna stilled. Were they speculating about *her* baby? She stepped out back on the pretense of needing herbs. All five boys looked startled to see her, but Pete stood and took a critical look at her middle.

"Yep, it's a boy."

She wondered how long it would be before word got around town that she was back, and married to Thomas. Perhaps it was already known, but she had no desire to go to town and find out. She had yet to see the sisters and could not bring herself to call on Sarah.

Anna was torn between gratitude for Sarah's kindness to Anna that exposed her friend to criticism, and guilt for changing her mind and turning down the help Sarah had gone out of her way to arrange. And though Sarah had come to her aid, she was clearly troubled by Anna's pregnancy.

Later that afternoon, Anna took food upstairs, and this time, she got Samuel to take not only bread but also milk, to her relief.

"Albert tells me that *The Shadow* is on at six-thirty," she said, "and I understand it is a very mysterious case involving a creepy, mad scientist."

No response.

"Pete is taking bets that no one will be able to solve it."

Samuel nodded.

Anna breathed a tiny sigh of relief. A nod was better than nothing.

Since Anna's return, Thomas never joined the others for meals. That evening, after she and the boys had eaten supper, she left a bowl of stew out for him, then went to the parlor with the boys. Teddy was tuning in to the radio station, in preparation for their program.

Samuel came down the stairs.

While Albert and the others greeted him, Anna held her breath and resisted the impulse to hug him or show too much excitement. She smiled instead. "Are you going to help solve the case?" she asked.

He shook his head but joined the others around the radio.

A flash of orange outside caught Anna's attention and she looked out the front window. Flames leapt from something in the yard. She hurried outside and discovered a burning sack, the stench coming from it stinging her nose.

Jimmy and Teddy came out also, followed by everyone but Samuel. Pete ran to get a bucket from the pump, while Jimmy took an old rug from the porch and whacked the fire with it. Pete came running with a bucket of water and tossed it onto the smoking pile, now a steaming mess.

Anna noticed another brick tied with a string not far from the sack. She took the note.

"What's in the sack?" Jack asked.

Teddy inspected what was left of the smoking burlap, then turned away, gagging.

"What is it?" Pete poked it with a stick.

"Dead cat," Teddy groaned. "Or part of one, anyway. I wouldn't look, if I were you."

Pete immediately opened the sack, then turned away, gagging.

With dread, Anna read the note, then covered a gasp.

"What's it say?" Albert asked.

Nostrils flaring, she tore the paper to shreds.

There are names for girls like you, her mother had said, and apparently, Mama was right. Anna was now thoroughly acquainted with a long list of them.

Twenty-Six

A WEEK AFTER HER RETURN, ANNA FINALLY VENTURED INTO town to buy a bag of salt, but Mr. Pitts told her he had none for sale. She did not believe him. The only other market in town was small and did not carry much, but at least Mr. Jarvis was willing to sell to anyone who could pay up front.

Everyone Anna passed on the street seemed to know who she was. Or, more specifically, *what* she was. And it seemed that being married to Thomas Chandler made no difference. The looks, the disdain, the insults were everywhere now, and bold—no longer covered with a hand or sent by surreptitious glance.

The only way Anna would be able to earn money now was to sew things that the boys could sell door to door. When there were any extra eggs, she had the boys sell those as well.

16 June

My Love,

I am back in Corbin, as you can see by the return address. Much has happened in the past ten days, and I am sorry, but you will have to wait for the full story, it would take more postage than I can afford. So for now, know that I am back, and hoping to solve Samuel's mysterious withdrawal. There are rumors that he saw horrors before he came to live here, things that haunt him. I suspect my leaving triggered this re-gression, and I am determined to help him regain his courage as well as his voice. Meanwhile, he found a pocketknife and has begun to whittle. I think he is making Noah's ark. He is quite talented, especially for a nine-year-old.

My friend Sarah has not been by since I returned. Perhaps she is too busy helping her husband with the farm. I have not seen the sisters either. I am not sure they know that I am back. They have been finding it more difficult to serve the needy, as they are now experiencing shortages themselves.

Dearest, when you go to shul, I hope you will think of me, and perhaps remember me in your prayers. If there are any prayers the L-rd would bend down to hear, they would be yours.

I am not one you should look up to. It is I who look up to you. I am nothing but a seed blowing in the wind. Though peace was rare when our family was uprooted and scattered about, there was still a measure of stability between us. Now, I feel disconnected, adrift. And the fault is entirely my own. I cannot explain now, but perhaps one day, when I am toothless and gray, if you will let me, I will tell you more. Perhaps.

Be careful not to make the mistakes I have made. Do not be hasty to assume or judge anything or anyone, as ignorance is a great and terrible deceiver.

A.

Nine days after Anna returned, Thomas finally spoke to her. He came into the dining room just as the boys sat down to supper and pulled out an envelope.

Anna held her breath, hoping with all her might that it was not another letter from Josephine.

"I have bad news," he said. "The Welfare Children's Aid Society has cut off our funding."

Several of the boys looked puzzled. "Why?" Jimmy asked.

"The letter is vague, but I think Alice Withers is behind it."

"How can the old battle-axe do that?" Albert scowled.

"Apparently, she can pull strings. The point is, I have to bring in more money now, a lot more than what we make from the woodworks. If I don't, we can't keep this place going."

Teddy dropped his fork. "You mean you'll have to send us away?"

Thomas shook his head. "I'm going to do everything in my power not to let that happen."

"We don't need their money," Albert said. "Miss Anna has been making stuff to sell. We'll go door to door. We'll make more stools and chairs. We'll—"

"I appreciate that, Albert," Thomas said. "But I have another idea. I heard the President's Public Works Administration is creating some new jobs, and they pay real well."

"You're going to get a *job*?" Jack asked.

"I'm going to try."

No one spoke, and the sudden silence pressed heavily on Anna. The loss of funding was due to her being there—this, she knew without a doubt. What had begun as a temporary rest from her journey had become the systematic ruination of seven other lives.

For the next week, Thomas spent every day job hunting, and no one saw him except a few late evenings. Each time Anna saw him, he looked more discouraged than the last.

Meanwhile, the boys followed through on their promise to go door to door, and they did manage to sell a few items. They also spent hours in the shop, making things to sell, mysterious things that Anna was not allowed to see.

Samuel's appetite continued to improve, and he now spent most of his days whittling. Albert commented on a frog Samuel had just finished, told him it was real good and that folks might even buy something like that. Samuel handed it to him.

"You want me to sell this?"

Samuel nodded, then started on something new.

Finally, on the twenty-third of June, Thomas got a Public Works job ten miles away in Huntington, one that was scheduled to last several weeks.

Anna had grown accustomed to Thomas's long absences. Since her return, he had been away more than he had been home. She almost wished she could trade places, because at times, she felt like a prisoner. With the mood in town as it was, venturing off the property meant hearing a steady stream of insults and accusations. The latest came from Penny Withers, who made a point to cross Main Street just to tell Anna that she and her nasty little mongrel were not welcome here, and never would be, and that since Thomas Chandler seemed to prefer women who "whored around," he was also nothing but a vulgar, low-life.

Anna had no reply. Her shame was now evident to everyone, and to Anna most of all. There was no escape from her now rapidly growing abdomen. And since being sole guardian of six boys tested Anna's limits, and the rising heat sapped her strength, it became easier to stay close to home and send the boys on errands.

The sisters stopped in one day when they heard she was back, and Anna was grateful that they did not question her return or her change of plans. Mary Francis only said that she hoped Thomas knew what he was doing.

Sarah, on the other hand, still had not been by.

Anna continued to work with Samuel, reading to him, talking with him even though he still did not speak. He showed no interest in reading, except for the story in his Bible about the young prophet, Samuel. He brought it to Anna to read one day, and when she had finished, he quickly replaced the ribbon that he had been using to mark the page. Anna smiled. There were several ribbons in the book.

"May I?" she asked, curious about what other stories interested Samuel.

He nodded.

Anna opened to another one, but instead of a story, this was Psalms, chapter 55. Interestingly, this passage read very similar to the Tehillim she had heard at shul. She read a few verses aloud, uncertain why he had marked this page.

Samuel put his finger on the line: *If only I had wings like a dove! I would fly away and be at rest...*

She studied the boy. "You wish to be like a dove?"

He shook his head.

"Ah, you wish to fly away."

Frowning, he shook his head again.

"Then...you wish to rest?"

Samuel heaved a sigh, then his gaze fell to her rounded abdomen. On impulse, she recoiled, even though by now, this was pointless.

The boy reached beneath his pillow and took out his knife and a block of wood and continued his whittling.

"What are you working on now?" she asked.

He held up the block with a few curved edges and several chunks missing.

"What is it going to be?" she asked.

With a slow smile, he shook his head.

A smile! This was new. She smiled back, noting it as a sign of progress, then, with a sigh, she reached an arm around him and gave his shoulders a squeeze.

On Sunday, Jimmy came rushing in from the back yard. "The chickens are gone, every one of them."

"My hens? *All* of them?" Anna fumed.

"And all the eggs are smashed."

Heat scalded the back of her neck. This menacing had to stop. But what would Sheriff Withers do if she brought the complaint to him? The reaction she pictured was not at all encouraging. Thomas would probably have better results if he were the one to deal with it.

"We need someone keeping watch at night," Jack said.

"*I'll* do it," Pete said.

"Whatcha gonna do if you catch someone in the act?"

Pete frowned. "Shoot 'em."

Anna gasped.

"Got my sling shot right here." He patted his back pocket.

Nerves frayed, Anna sent Albert and Teddy out to the coop to assess the damage, and while they straightened up the mess, Sister Mary Agnes pulled into the drive.

Anna went out to meet her. "Your timing is excellent," she said with a sigh. She fanned herself. "We are out of milk, and now our chickens and eggs are gone."

Mary Agnes looked grave. "I'm so sorry, but I don't have any supplies for you today. I came to say that we've been vandalized, again. We've lost all our kerosene, along with crates of food, and our tires were cut. Praise the Lord for Sister Mary Francis and her handiness with a lug wrench." She shook her head. "I'm trying to understand why someone would be so opposed to our helping the poor, but I confess, I really can't."

"I am sorry. What will you do?" Anna said.

"Keep praying for providence," the sister said. "As long as the Lord has us here serving, He will have to provide."

Anna nodded, but she was not very confident that the Lord knew what was happening in Corbin. Those who did not want Anna here also did not want the sisters, and vandals were very persistent about sending this message.

"Will you report it to the police?" Anna asked.

"I already have. Sheriff Withers assures me that the police are going to 'look into it very soon.'" She gave Anna a knowing look. "Meanwhile, we decided that a few large, well-placed rat traps might help deter some of the mischief."

"Rat traps? Sister Mary Francis certainly *is* handy."

"That was *my* idea," Mary Agnes whispered with a wink.

As the sister turned to go, Anna asked her to wait and hurried inside to get one of the quilts she had made to sell. She brought it out handed it to her.

"What's this?"

"Providence." Anna smiled.

"Thank you, my child." The old woman stepped closer and looked Anna in the eye. "Forgive my bluntness, but...what happened to your baby's father?"

Anna considered several possible answers, but each one made her cringe. "The baby has no father," she said, finally.

The sister quirked a brow. "Imagine that. I know of only one other such case."

Anna flushed.

"I guess all I really need to know is when does the baby arrive?"

At least this question was easier to answer. There was no doubt about when the baby was conceived, so there was only one possible due date.

"The middle of August."

Twenty-Seven

THOMAS LEFT FOR HUNTINGTON ON MONDAY, PROMISING TO RE-
turn late Friday night. He asked Henry Tucker to check on his place in case
Anna or the boys needed anything. Anna was more than a little uneasy
about Thomas being gone for a whole week, but there was no other option.
All she could do was focus on Samuel. He was making steady improvements, and was interacting with the other boys more now, much like he did
when she first met him. He was still not speaking, but Anna was patient.

By the end of June, the temperatures had changed from very warm to
very hot, and Anna could stand her prison no longer. She summoned the
courage to go call on Sarah. The boys, all but Samuel, were at the Mercy
School working on things they could do in Thomas's absence, armed with
a list and his instructions.

Anna prepared a loaf of challah—a peace offering of sorts—and also
brought money in hopes that Sarah might sell her and Samuel a few more
laying hens.

Sarah met Anna on the porch, drying her hands with a dishtowel.
When Violet saw Samuel, she invited him to help make mud pies.

Anna took a deep breath and offered Sarah the bread. "All of our laying
hens were stolen. I wonder if you have any more you could sell us."

Sarah took the bread, confusion on her face. "Thank you, Anna. Sure, I
think we can spare a coupla hens. Come inside."

In the kitchen, Sarah offered Anna a chair and some lemonade. As she
handed her a glass, she eyed Anna's belly, then looked quickly away.

"I...know what you must think of me," Anna said. "And I do not blame
you." Her throat constricted. As she said the words, it struck her just how

much she had missed her friend. That there was now a gulf between them stung.

Sarah took a knife from the drawer. "And what exactly is it that you're *not* blamin' me for?"

Anna wetted her suddenly dry lips. "You must think I am...immoral." *Dirty. Untouchable.* "And you are right."

Sarah shook her head. "No, I don't think that, Anna. I *thought* I knew you pretty well, and I never saw you that way." She frowned as she sliced the bread. "But I did have one thing figured all wrong."

Anna held her breath.

Still frowning, Sarah said, "I thought you was my friend." She turned away abruptly and fumbled with the butter crock.

Tears filled Anna's eyes.

"If I was your friend, you would have confided in me. Findin' out you were with child like that, along with everybody else—that hurt."

"I am sorry, Sarah," Anna said softly. "I did wish to be your friend. And I still do."

Sarah buttered two slices of bread, and then looked Anna in the eye. "Why didn't you tell me?"

Anna's mouth fell. "How could I? And what could you have done?"

"I could...I don't know, I could help."

Anna's brow raised. "Help?"

"I could tell you how miserable you're gonna be in a coupla months when it's hot as blazes and you're big as a barn."

"Oy! It gets worse?"

"Ohhh, sugar." Sarah shook her head, then chuckled.

Anna exhaled her relief and smiled.

Violet and Samuel ran in, followed by Ivy and the dog, whose tail wagged in joy at being included.

"Uh-uh, take yourselves back outside and wipe off that mud," Sarah said. "Owen! I thought you knew better'n to let 'em in here like that."

The dog's wagging slowed, and he turned and went back outside with the children.

Sarah sighed. "Things are heatin' up, and I don't just mean the weather." She offered Anna a slice of bread, then sat down and took a bite of hers. "There was a rally at the town hall last week. And while I was there, I...I went and signed up."

Anna drew a deep breath. Would Sarah become another Penny? Could she?

"I don't hold to all their ideas. But there are some things they focus on that are real important to me. The society fights for temperance and morality. I'm all for gettin' rid of liquor and vices. They do nothin' but ruin families." Her lips pursed.

"Not your family, I hope? Not...Henry?"

"No, not Henry." She met Anna's gaze, nostrils flaring. "My daddy was a drunk, Anna. A mean one. Liquor and gamblin' kept our family dirt poor. About destroyed me and my brothers. Nearly killed my momma."

"I am so sorry, Sarah."

"I'm all for helpin' rid our town of things that destroy the family. We can't keep up when stuff like that's flowin' so freely. It's like an epidemic."

"I am glad you are trying to do something about it," Anna said.

"The Women of Virtue do a lot of good. They work hard to make sure things don't destroy morality in our community." Her gaze drifted to Anna's belly again. "Anna, it's none of my business, but I been wonderin' what happened. I mean, how you wound up pregnant and alone. Knowin' you, I figured there's a good explanation. Like maybe you were engaged or somethin' and the fella got you in a family way and then abandoned you."

It was not a question, but it hung in the air all the same.

If only it had been a case of someone Anna had loved and lost. That might sound better than the scandalous truth, that it was nothing more than a night on the town with a blind date. As awful as the truth was, Anna did want to confide in her friend. But how much of her tale would end up as the topic of discussion at one of her society meetings?

"I promise not to tell anyone," Sarah added.

Anna sighed. With a deep breath, she began by explaining the fight with her mother and how Rosie changed plans and took her to a speakeasy. Then she winced, remembering Sarah's father and how much Sarah despised liquor, and realized that the rest of the story would only add salt to Sarah's wound.

"The details are not important," Anna said. "Liquor was involved. I let a moment of anger make me reckless, and I let flattery ruin my judgment. It was a very stupid mistake I will regret for the rest of my life." She wiped a tear.

Sarah shook her head. "See? That's why we have to abolish liquor. It ruins lives."

"Yes, but the main reason this happened is because I am..." She could hardly bring herself to say the incriminating word aloud, even to Sarah. "Immoral."

Sarah studied her, a slight pucker in her brow. "I guess I just don't understand. I mean, I don't personally know any loose women, but you don't strike me as one. And you don't strike me as a reckless gal bent on makin' a habit out of immoral behavior."

A *habit.* How Anna wished she could explain to Sarah that a depraved character—as her mother had made so *very* clear—was far worse than a bad habit, and was, Anna suspected, much harder to change. Perhaps she could not change her nature, but she could do her very best to avoid repeating past mistakes.

"The only habit I want is one of making nothing but wise choices from now on."

Sarah smiled. "Honey, we could *all* use a habit like that."

While Sarah went on to describe a rally she had attended, Violet and Ivy came inside with Samuel. He had his block of wood and pocketknife, and whittled away while the girls watched, being careful to stuff the loose shavings in his pockets. Owen lumbered in and stretched out to sleep by the screen door.

"The rally was long, and I confess, after a while, I got lost in all the numbers they were throwin' around. Statistics about what Americans think on this or that. Mainly, they want women to rally together to protect our interests and protect our schools from the Catholic menace."

Anna frowned. This sounded like the notes and letters that Thomas had received.

"They also want us to vote for political candidates who want to get rid of liquor, prostitution, and gamblin'. They say Catholics, Jews, and coloreds bring the vice and corruption that ruins families and our nation. They say Catholics and immigrants come from other countries to do the Pope's biddin' and take over the country one town at a time. They want us women to make sure that don't happen here."

Anna stared at her. "Immigrants taking over?" She glanced at the children and lowered her voice. "Jews and Negroes bring corruption? Sarah... this is what you believe?"

Sarah blinked, as if she suddenly remembered who she was talking to. "Oh, heavens, no, I don't believe that about *you*, Anna. Or sweet little Sam there. Maybe I don't understand or believe it *all*, but there is still a lot of good the society is trying to do." She shrugged and took a bite of her bread. "I admit it all confuses me sometimes. They give so many facts I can't keep it all straight. But mainly, it's about women takin' a stand against things that undermine our homes and our families. We can't just sit by and watch corruption destroy our loved ones."

Anna saw a lightness about Sarah that reminded her of a feather, as if a good, strong wind could blow her along, with no preference as to where, landing wherever the wind took her.

"Sarah, do you think that certain races or groups of people can be all good, or all corrupt, or all immoral?"

"I don't know." Sarah frowned. "I guess I wouldn't be thinkin' that at all, if it weren't for the statistics, and all those dreadful stories they tell us."

Anna fumed. It sounded as if the people telling these dreadful stories were intent on influencing people, and for some sort of gain she did not understand. Or trust.

Thomas returned very late Friday, so Anna did not see him until Saturday morning, and then only for a moment. He checked on Samuel and the others, and then asked Anna if anything was needed.

"Yes. We need whoever stole our hens to bring them back or replace them," Anna said. "Or at least get someone to investigate the theft and the vandalism."

He drew a deep breath. "I don't know if I can do anything about that on a weekend, but I'll see if there's anyone at the sheriff's office and file a report. Anything else?"

"We have had no milk in two weeks. The sisters are only delivering every other week now. They are getting fewer supplies."

He nodded. "I'm going to the Mercy School now, so I'll see what's happening. And I'll stop in town for milk."

She nodded. He had grown much thinner, and yet, despite that, he had somehow managed to become even more handsome. Her heart thumped, which was most inconvenient. She lowered her voice. "What about you?"

Thomas frowned. "What do you mean?"

"How are you? Do *you* need anything?"

He stared at her, as if trying to decipher some dark, hidden meaning in her question. His scrutiny was unnerving. "As a matter of fact, I need a job."

"But you have one. Do you not?"

"Not anymore. They laid me off yesterday, after only a week. Everyone else that was hired with me is still working."

Anna frowned. "Why would they only lay *you* off?"

He turned toward the door, took down his hat. "That's what I'd like to know. But there's an even better job in Illinois. The Public Works is building a dam near Ottawa. I'm going Monday to apply, and if I'm lucky, I'll start right away."

He went out without a backwards glance.

Anna's heart sank.

Later that afternoon, Thomas returned with three quarts of milk. With six growing boys, three quarts would last less than an hour, unless they rationed it, which she would have to do.

"This is all I could get," Thomas said. "Jarvis is going out of business."

"The little store at the north end of town?" The only store where Anna could still shop?

He nodded. "His business has completely dried up. He has no choice but to close."

Sunday afternoon, Henry Tucker came by to call on Thomas, who came out of the shop at the sound of the pickup.

Anna sewed on the porch while she waited for her bread to rise and could not help but overhear their conversation.

"Did you hear?" Henry said. "The General Store is the only grocer left in Corbin now."

"It's too bad about Jarvis," Thomas said. "He said his customers suddenly disappeared."

"You know why?" Henry asked. "Pitts dropped his prices dirt cheap."

"How can he afford to do that and still stay in business?"

"That's the question. Do you think it's any coincidence that Pitts recently became an official card-carrying member of the Klan?"

Thomas shook his head slowly. "What are you thinking?"

"I think the Klan is backing him, funding the difference. Shuttin' down anyone who opposes them. Getting rid of non-supporters and people who do business with outsiders." Henry glanced in Anna's direction. "Sarah says Pitts won't sell to us on credit anymore. Cash only. She went and joined that busybody ladies' society, and they *still* want to blackball us."

"It's not right," Thomas said.

"I lost a calf last week. I thought it might've slipped out when the gate was open, but I found some signs of tampering and now I'm sure it was stolen. I reported it to Withers."

Thomas's hands went to his hips. "Let me guess. He said he'd file the report and add it to his pile?"

"Yep. I need your help, Chandler. We need to force Withers to do something."

Slowly, Thomas shook his head. "We'll never get him to do the right thing. We need to go over his head."

"How? He's the sheriff now."

Thomas shrugged. "We have to go far enough over his head to find law that isn't intimidated or backed by the Klan."

Twenty-Eight

ON MONDAY, THOMAS LEFT BEFORE DAWN TO CATCH A TRAIN for Illinois. He had told Anna the night before that he could return Tuesday, unless he was hired on the spot, which was his hope.

If he *was* hired, Anna felt more than a little uneasy about what the coming days and weeks would hold.

Late Monday afternoon, Sarah arrived at the back door, just as Anna was taking bread from the oven. "Thomas telephoned from Illinois," Sarah said. "He asked if I'd come give you a message. He got on with the PWA at the Lock and Dam, near Ottawa. He said it pays real good." Sarah offered Anna a thin version of her usual smile. "*Real* good," she repeated.

"What are you not telling me?" Anna closed the oven door.

Sarah winced. "He won't be home for six weeks, Anna. He said to tell you he's real sorry, but he just can't pass up the money. In fact, he said he can earn more in six weeks than he usually brings in all year. He's concerned about leavin' you and the boys alone that long. So Henry promised him he'd look out for you. You need anything at all, you just holler."

Anna nodded, trying to keep from showing her disappointment. The boys were not difficult, but parenting six energetic children in the heat, day after day, all alone, was beginning to wear on Anna's nerves, and she was afraid that at some point, they would simply snap.

"You want to bring the boys over for a picnic after the parade tomorrow?"

Anna frowned. "There is a parade?"

"You bet. Every Fourth of July. The kids get balloons and popsicles and penny candy. The 4-H club shows their prize-winnin' horses and lambs. We always watch from the bank steps. Y'all can join us if you want."

"All of the people in Corbin will be there?"

"I reckon so."

Anna looked her friend in the eye. "Thank you, but I had better not watch with your family, Sarah. I would not want your daughters to hear the things I will be called."

The light in Sarah's eyes faded.

"And what will your society friends say if they see you with the immoral Jew?"

Sarah's mouth opened, but she had no reply.

"Thank you for inviting me, but it would be best if I did not come to the parade. But if you would not mind keeping an eye on the boys so they can watch, I would be very grateful."

"Sure, Anna. And the picnic offer is still open, if you want to come."

Anna smiled. "Yes, I would love to come. Thank you."

Swatting at flies and sweating, Anna was working on peeling boiled potatoes to make salad for the Tucker's picnic when the kitchen door burst open.

Samuel looked as if he had been running at full speed, his chest heaving. His eyes had a wild, terrified look.

"What is wrong? What happened?" Anna dropped what she was doing and went to him, her shuffling steps lumbering from her swollen feet. She guided him to sit on a chair and looked him over for injury but saw none. His body trembled, so she sat beside him, wrapped her arms around him, and shushed him, making soothing sounds like she had with Anshel when he was an infant and she all of ten years old.

Anna had felt like a little mother even then, or so she had thought, having cared for her siblings from the time she was four, when Mama had first placed her newborn sister into her arms. To Anna, Shayna was beautiful, already living up to her name. Anna was six when Rivka came, and had prided herself on being the only one who could make little Riv go to sleep. By the time Anshel joined them, Anna knew every baby bouncing, burping, shushing trick there was.

Wiping sweat from her brow, Anna ignored the added heat from the child she held.

Samuel relaxed, finally.

"What happened?" Anna said.

"G-ghosts," he whispered.

Anna's breath caught, both at the fact that he spoke and what he said. He pulled back and looked her in the eye.

"Where?" Anna asked.

Samuel looked out the kitchen window. "P-p-parade."

"They came out to watch the parade?" If so, how brazen the Klan had become, to appear in town, in broad daylight, wearing their white robes and pointed hats.

Samuel shook his head, then fixed his eyes on hers. "*In* the parade. M-marching at the end."

Anna gasped. The Klan was marching in a community parade?

Their collective presence, until now, had been mostly the stuff of rumors, reported glimpses of them in the night, but it seemed they were coming out now, bolder, more visible. Suddenly empowered. If they were coming out in such a public way, what did that mean for Negros, immigrants, Jews, and Catholics? What did they hope to accomplish?

And who would stop them?

In the shade of the Tucker's front porch, the boys ate fried chicken and potato salad as if they would never see food again. Anna's heart sank. Food supplies were running low, and she had been forced to make things stretch even farther than usual. Thinner soups, eggless bread. Even if Thomas sent money, buying food in Corbin was becoming a challenge. Teddy and Jimmy could only buy things at the General Store when Mr. Pitts was not running the counter.

Samuel had brought his latest whittling project and was again fascinating Violet and Ivy with his work. The other boys played Mumbley Peg with Henry.

Sarah brought a glass of lemonade to Anna and frowned. "Anna, you're red as a tomato. You need to get out of the sun." She towed Anna over to sit in the shade of an old poplar. Anna was only too happy to comply.

"Did you get anything to eat? I didn't see you."

Anna shook her head. "It is too hot, and everything gives me heartburn."

Sarah sighed. "Oh, honey, I'm sorry, but that's only gonna get worse. You figure out yet what foods rile up the little one?"

Anna's brows rose.

"I couldn't eat beans with either of my girls, they'd get to flippin' around somethin' fierce."

"I have not noticed." Anna watched the girls giggling over Samuel's carvings. "Samuel spoke today."

"That's wonderful, Anna."

She looked Sarah in the eye. "It was to tell me he saw Klan members marching in the parade." She watched her friend. "Is that true?"

Sarah nodded. "He shot off like a bullet when they came along. Teddy followed and said he went straight home, so I didn't think to mention it."

Owen stood up from his spot on the porch and woofed twice, then lay back down. Sarah shaded her eyes and looked toward the road, studied the dust from a passing car.

"Just the neighbors, Owen." She snickered and turned to Anna. "Guess he thinks we need to know about all the Becketts' comin's and goin's." She sobered. "Why'd you wanna know about the parade?"

"I am surprised they would be marching in their robes, for everyone to see."

"Guess they like to dress up and parade themselves."

"Do they?" Anna stared at her. "Have they always appeared so boldly in broad daylight?"

Sarah shook her head. "I don't think so. But I don't really know. They aren't as active as they were years back. I think they're mostly just a club for big-mouthed old fellas now."

"*Big-mouthed old fellas,*" Anna repeated, half to herself. Her cheeks burned. "Are they not the same Klan who lynch people and burn crosses and terrify people out of their homes and cities?"

"I don't know. I haven't heard much of that happenin' around here. Not since I been here, and I came in '27."

"But the Klan *is* still the Klan, is it not?"

Sarah glanced at her with a shrug. "I reckon so."

"Why do they march now?" Anna asked. The baby kicked hard.

"How should I know? *I'm* not a Klan member." She got up abruptly and went into the house.

With a sigh, Anna hoisted herself up from the ground, which took some extra effort, and gathered the boys. Violet balked, as Samuel was in the middle of showing her how to whittle a canoe.

Sarah came back outside with a plate of cookies. "You ain't leavin', are you?" She offered cookies to the children.

"I am afraid I have worn out my welcome," Anna said lightly.

"It's just the heat gettin' to us, that's all," Sarah said. "I'm sorry I snapped at you, Anna. That was rude of me."

Anna sighed. "I cannot ask you to answer for other people. It is I who owe you the apology."

Sarah smiled, then reached an arm around Anna and gave her a hug. "I just wish folks could learn how to get along."

Anna looked into Sarah's eyes. "Perhaps they can, if people's blindness toward others was from compassion instead of ignorance."

Sarah frowned. "What do you mean?"

"I think people dislike those they do not know because they cannot see the good in others. What if we choose instead to be blind to people's flaws and shortcomings, and the differences we do not understand?"

Sarah studied Anna as if pondering this. "Like...closing our eyes to the things we don't like about folks?"

"Yes. And opening our hearts to make room for those who are different. Showing mercy to those we do not understand. Having compassion for people who seem strange to us."

"That might do the trick," Sarah said slowly. "*If* everybody would do it."

The day after the parade, Anna received a letter from Shayna.

26 June

Anna,

I am so sorry. I wish you were not feeling detached from

all those you have come to love so dearly. Which I am now convinced includes Thomas, since you did not mention him once. You have a way of saying much when you say nothing.

But wishing will not help, so I will offer hope. I hope that Samuel will soon learn to draw on his courage, because he clearly possesses it, deep inside. I hope your friend will soon welcome you back with open arms, and I hope the sisters will not be interrupted in their good work. And I hope that Thomas will one day see you the way I do. Not the way you do, because I know you better than anyone, including yourself. In all of your striving to do your very best, you are sometimes—no, often—your very own worst enemy. You are so hard, Anna. On yourself, and on G-d.

You say you are adrift like a seed driven on the wind, but sometimes I wonder if you are exactly where G-d wants you?

Anna, you sound weary, and this breaks my heart. You are the bold one, the brave one, the one who does not sit back and wait for life to push you along its currents like flotsam on the river.

I will always look up to you, because you are the only one who challenges me to believe in what I can be and not to let anyone tell me I cannot succeed. It is because of YOU that I have enrolled in business school and am asking Isaak to wait for me to finish my degree. It is because of you that I now stand up to those who tell me no, little Jew, you cannot ride this bus, or no, little girl, business is only for clever, important men.

Please do not give up, because I am counting on you to overcome every obstacle in your path. Your tenacity gives me hope. If you, the bold one, cannot press on, then how can I?

Your very favorite sister,

S.

P.S. I only wrote that because Riv was spying over my shoulder.

Twenty-Nine

BY THE END OF THE FIRST WEEK OF JULY, ANNA HAD MENDED every hole in every sock, shirt, and trouser knee that the boys owned. None of her quilts were selling, which was no wonder, as hot as it was. She would have better luck selling ice at the North Pole.

Sarah, Violet, and Ivy came to the back door on Friday, bearing a gift. A wrapped gift, tied with ribbon.

Anna frowned. "What is this? It is not my birthday," she said.

Violet grinned, eagerness shining in her blue eyes.

"Sorry, but it's not for you, Anna," Sarah said. She smiled down at her daughter. "Violet wanted to bring this over...for the little one."

Anna gasped. In all of the turmoil of leaving and returning, it had not occurred to her to think about things the baby would need. She smiled at Violet and unwrapped the parcel. Inside was a pretty little newborn gown in yellow with white dots, and a matching bonnet.

"Violet, this is lovely. But it is too much." She glanced at Sarah, confused.

"It was Vi's first, then Ivy got it, but she got chunky so fast she only wore it once. Violet found it the other day and said she wanted to give it to Miss Anna and Mr. Tom's baby."

Anna's breath caught. *Just Miss Anna's baby,* she wanted to say. Unfortunately, people in town considered Thomas responsible for her pregnancy—people who either had no idea how long she had been there, or who assumed he had known her before she came to town. This had to be a constant source of mortification and anger for him.

She stared at the tiny gown, tears blurring her vision. She started to speak, but all that came out was a sob. She covered her mouth. "Violet, I do not know what to say," she whispered. "It is beautiful. The baby will be honored to wear it. Thank you."

"You're welcome." Violet smiled, her pink cheeks glowing.

"I got a p-present for Violet, too," a small voice said.

Anna turned. Samuel stood in the kitchen doorway holding a bread-sized parcel wrapped in paper and string. He came in and handed it to Violet.

Sarah shot a confused smile at Anna.

"Open it," Samuel urged. He drew a breath and held it.

Ivy stuck a finger in her mouth and watched while Violet untied the string and unwrapped the paper. Inside was a wooden ark, and on the deck were a dozen or so tiny animals. There was even a little Noah.

Violet laughed. "I *knew* that's what you was makin'! It's my favorite. I'm gonna take it right home and play with it."

Samuel smiled at his feet.

"Violet...?" Sarah said, eyeing her daughter.

"Thank you, Sam," Violet said, already arranging the animals on the deck. She handed an elephant to Ivy and showed her where to put it.

"Samuel, it's simply exquisite," Sarah said, her voice soft with wonder. "What amazin' talent you have." She crouched lower to meet him at eye level. "My girls are real lucky to have a friend like you."

His head lowered a bit more, but Anna could see his smile.

After Sarah and her girls left, Anna turned to Samuel. "That took a lot of work," she said. "You are a very kind and generous friend."

He eyed her. "Wait," he said, then he left. He came back a few moments later with another, smaller bundle, also wrapped. He held it out to Anna. "This one's f-for you."

She looked into his eyes, which met hers briefly, before casting down.

"Samuel, it is okay to look people in the eye. It is polite, even."

He nodded, still looking down. "Open it." He fidgeted.

With a laugh, Anna opened the package and then gasped. In the center of the paper sat a pale, wooden dove, about the size of an egg. It had been sanded and polished silky smooth. Her lidded eyes gave her a serene, knowing look.

"Samuel!"

He looked up.

Tears blurred her vision again. "This is absolutely stunning. You *made* this?"

He nodded.

"It is just like her," Anna said, stroking the soft, smooth curves. "The dove that comes to the coop."

The boy shook his head slowly.

"No?" Anna studied it more closely.

Samuel disappeared into the parlor, leaving Anna confused, then returned after a moment with his ribbon-marked Bible. He opened it to the first ribbon, scanned a few lines, then turned the book around for Anna to see.

She read from the eighth chapter of Genesis,

> *"But the dove found no rest for the sole of her foot, and she returned unto him into the ark, for the waters were on the face of the whole earth: Then he put forth his hand, and took her, and pulled her in unto him into the ark."*

"Ah. So this is the dove from the ark," she said, admiring it in the palm of her hand.

He shook his head again, then tapped the first line.

Anna read aloud, *"But the dove found no rest for the sole of her foot, and she returned unto him..."*

His talent for whittling was stunning, and especially for a child. But it was his desire to communicate deeper thoughts that truly astounded Anna. Suddenly, she got the feeling that Samuel was a young man who would leave a lasting mark on the world, somewhere, some day.

"It's just like *you*," he said. "You f-flew away, but you came back."

She smiled but hoped her smile did not look as sorrowful as she felt. Yes, sadly, she *was* much like Noah's dove. Did Samuel not know the rest of the story?

She looked at that passage again. There it was, a few lines down, similar to the way it read in the Torah. Noah sent the dove out again later, and this time, she did not come back. Just like Anna, who would also leave again one day soon, and this time, she would not be coming back.

But she was not going to tell him this. Not now.

9 July

Dearest Shayna,

I am always proud of you, no matter what you do. But I am excited about your decision to enter the business world. I hope Mama is as proud of you as I am.

Sarah and I have reconnected, which lightens my heart, and yet, our views continue to grow apart, and this worries me. How long will we be able to remain friends?

The sisters no longer bring food and supplies, as their shipments have dwindled. So we make things stretch, make things last, make do. And the heat! I sometimes fantasize of lying in the creek. This is not a bad idea, now that I think of it...

Samuel is returning to his old self. I do not think it is only because I am here, but what if it is? When I go, will he relapse? I had returned only to help him, but since Thomas must work far away for several weeks, I must now stay with the boys until he returns. When he does, then I will move on. An enormous part of me will stay behind. But I suspect it is a part I will have no more use for, anyway.

The boys are secretive about what they are making to sell. Just between us, I am afraid it is not wares they hide, but a tobacco pipe. I overheard Pete saying he can swipe tobacco undetected from the old men who doze in front of the barber shop. Perhaps a surprise visit while they are "working" is in order. Would you, if you were me?

I am sorry, but you are wrong. Thomas is hundreds of miles away, but even if he were standing beside me, there would be nothing between us. Whatever connection might have been forming is gone. I have destroyed it beyond hope. If there was anything I could do to fix this, if ripping out my organs or giving up my last breath could heal his wounded heart, I would not hesitate to give them up.

Do you remember the story of Noah? While he waited

for the flood waters to recede, he sent out a dove to learn what he could of the earth. Did you know that she came back with nothing, and yet he invited her to come back inside? She came back with no news, no information, nothing. Only herself.

Do you think that G-d would allow me to return, empty-handed, stained, with a long list of sins I cannot atone for? Would He reach out like Noah and invite me to return to Him, only as I am?

By Friday, the tenth of July, her mid-August delivery loomed, and it occurred to Anna that she needed clothing for the baby. With school long over and the boys spending their time either fishing at the creek or working at the Mercy School, Anna had more time to sew. And she had plenty of scraps, but no pattern, so she did her best to copy the tiny gown that Violet Tucker had given her. She worked all day Monday, and by suppertime, she had finished two gowns and had begun another. Energized by her accomplishment, she took a basket of leftover scraps out to the back porch where it was cooler and began a tiny blanket.

Inhaling the scents of evening, she savored the mild breeze cooling her skin. Thomas had been in Illinois for a week and would be gone many more still. She figured he would be finished with the job and back on his feet—as he had put it—about the time she was due to give birth. She would therefore have no choice but to deliver here in Corbin, then prepare herself to travel.

She had not told anyone of her plan to move on. The sisters probably assumed the marriage was typical in nature. Anna did not know where to begin in her explanation of their temporary, in-name-only arrangement, so she decided to let Thomas report the dissolve of their arrangement once she had gone, in whatever way he saw fit. Unlike him, she had no reputation here to protect, and she was fully prepared to take all of the blame.

That Thomas would be an abandoned husband, not once, but twice, struck Anna with a heart-wrenching sorrow. And yet, he had willingly placed himself in this position the second time. What an enormous sacrifice, and all for the love of a child, despite the abhorrence that the idea of marriage and nearness to Anna must have caused him, the disgust it *still* brought him. Perhaps Illinois truly was the closest work he could find. But even so, Anna suspected Thomas was relieved to put so much distance between himself and her.

Since Sister Mary Francis had mentioned the possibility of finding a boarding house, Anna was eager to find out more about this. She hoped something could be arranged *before* she delivered, because once Thomas was back and Anna was free to go, she wanted to linger no longer than necessary.

Shouts and sounds of a revving engine startled Anna. She looked out across the yard, then hauled herself to standing and went around to the front of the house. Dusk cast shadows over the front drive and the road beyond. All she could see was a car and the silhouettes of some young males, who now hurled foul names for Samuel and herself. She did not understand why anyone felt the need to shout their hate. What did it accomplish? What had she or Samuel ever done to them? She hoped the boy could not hear the names they called him.

As for the words meant for her, she was becoming impervious.

The shouts faded away as the vehicle swerved and disappeared down the road, so Anna shook off the insult and headed back to her work.

Something smelled terrible, an acrid smell, like burnt twine.

"Fire!" someone shouted.

Heart pounding, Anna hurried around to the front of the house as quickly as she could. The boys were emerging from the shop as smoke wafted from the porch. As she got closer, she could hear the crackle of flames.

"Get back!" she yelled. "We need water! Hurry!"

The boys scrambled to move, and Anna followed.

God, if You are listening, please. You must send help, You must save us...

Nearing the pump, Anna croaked, "Be careful—" but the older boys were already thrusting buckets at the younger boys and taking turns pumping the handle as fast as they could.

Anna grabbed a pail and joined the procession.

When she reached the front of the house, her heart nearly stopped. Flames climbed up the corner post. Smoke rolled out from the porch, surrounding her and the frantic boys like a black fog. Coughing, she went back for more water.

A vehicle screeched to a stop, stirring up clouds of dust, followed by shouts. Anna hurried to the porch. Henry Tucker grabbed Jack and Albert's buckets and sprinted to the pump.

Anna tossed water and went for more, did it again, and again, eventually losing count of the number of trips she made.

Henry and Teddy grabbed the rug by the door and beat the dwindling flames while the others kept the water coming. The fire finally fizzled to a smoldering hiss with the last dousing of water. The scorched corner post still smoked. Henry beat the smoking places, then tossed one last bucket on the charred wood.

Anna wiped her face. Her hands came away smeared with soot. Albert and Jack coughed, and Anna looked around for Samuel. He was with Teddy, staring at the charred, smoking mess along with everyone else.

She turned to Henry. "If you had not happened by..."

"It was pure luck. I was heading home and then remembered I'd promised Thomas I'd drop by and check on y'all," he said.

Anna stilled. She had silently called out to God to send someone. Surely this was a coincidence. Surely He would not listen to *her*.

Henry stood with hands on his hips, shaking his head. "What happened?"

She told him of the young men shouting insults, and that the fire had begun when they left.

Henry spat and swore. He went onto the porch and poked around with his boot. "Here it is," he said. "Bundle of burlap soaked in kerosene. Most of the flames were from the gas, not the porch itself. I don't think it went deep, mostly just charred on the surface. I'll come back tomorrow morning, see what needs replaced. But I think we got to it quick enough."

"Thank you," Anna said. "If you could get a message to Thomas, I think he needs to know."

"I'll see if Sarah can telephone his foreman, maybe get a message to him," Henry said.

"Thank you."

Thirty

SISTER MARY AGNES CAME ON WEDNESDAY WITH A BUNDLE OF baby clothes. Humbled by the gift, Anna thanked her, too overcome to speak. Kindness had become a priceless gift.

"Dreadful what happened in town last night, isn't it?" the sister said. "Poor Henry. And now Sarah having to do all that extra work, with him laid up. What's happening in this town is just appalling."

"Laid up? What is this?" She had heard nothing. The boys had been out in the shop, so they must have also missed whatever it was.

"You didn't hear? Last night, Henry Tucker called a town meeting about all the mischief to his place, yours, and ours, and it turned into a brawl. Henry ended up taking a pipe to his skull. Didn't knock him out, saints be praised—Henry's got the head of a bull—but he got a nasty gash, a giant knot, and he can't stand up straight without getting dizzy."

Anna gasped. "That is terrible."

"Sarah is going to need some help, since she's got the babies, tending to him, and now all the farm chores."

"We will help," Anna said. Not only would she not hesitate to help her friend, but she knew it was what Thomas would do, if he were here.

Anna rounded up the boys, and within the hour, they were at the Tucker farm. Violet hollered when she saw Anna and the boys and then ran inside, still shouting for her mama.

Sarah thanked them for coming and gave the boys a list of chores she needed done in the barn. Then she took a basket of wash to the clothesline. Anna followed. Sarah seemed a little subdued, but this was understandable, given what had happened to her husband.

"What can I help with?" Anna asked.

223

Sarah finished pinning a dress, then paused. "Thank you, Anna, and I mean that, but...I don't really know if it's such a good idea for y'all to be here."

This, Anna had not expected to hear.

"I knew things have been heatin' up in town," she went on, "but now everyone's takin' sides. It's worse than the Civil War. Henry near got his head busted open."

"Taking sides? Over what?"

Frowning, Sarah shook out a pair of overalls. "A bunch of things. The Catholics and their school, who gets to have a say in what happens in our town. Who has to go, and what needs to go back to bein' the way it was." Her eyes glinted with tears. She pulled out a skirt, then turned to Anna. "And now, me and Henry got ourselves caught in the middle. I can't buy nothin' at the grocery because Pitts cut off our credit and we don't have cash till harvest. We've lost two calves. Somebody in a pickup truck turned one of our fields into a racetrack, and we found a sack of feed soaked in kerosene."

Anna gaped. "Who would do this? And why?"

"I don't know, but I sure don't want no more of it."

"Did you tell the sheriff?"

"Withers?" Sarah scoffed. "Henry says he's purely good for nothin'."

"But...why do they bother you and Henry?"

With a terse shrug, Sarah pinned the skirt.

Anna pondered this, stunned that the bullies would target Sarah's family. If Sarah and Henry were *not* the acceptable folks, the "right sort" of people that the bigots wanted here, then who *did* they want?

No. This was not about the sort of people that Sarah and Henry were. It was about the sort of friends they kept.

She met Sarah's gaze. "They are tormenting you because of me. Punishing you because you are friend to a dirty Jew."

Sarah shook her head but said nothing, just kept pinning her wash. She looked tense.

"I am sorry, Sarah. I will leave and will stay away from you and your family."

Sarah turned. A frown pinched her brow. "Oh, Anna, I wish..." She just shook her head.

"I know," Anna said quietly.

Anna left Sarah and gathered the boys, then said goodbye to Violet and Ivy.

As they headed down the lane, Sarah came running and stopped them. She looked into Anna's eyes. "I'm sure someday soon, this'll all blow over. Folks'll eventually forget and go back about their own lives."

Anna tried to smile but found she could not. "I wish I could believe that."

"Things can change. Why, you've come back, in spite of all the hostility, and now you and Thomas are together..."

Shaking her head, Anna glanced down at her bulge, no longer masked by the fullness of her gown. "We are married in name only. And it is only a temporary arrangement, nothing more. There is nothing *together* about us, Sarah, nothing..." Shrugging, she said simply, "There is nothing."

Sarah blinked at Anna. "I'm no mind-reader, but the way you look when you tell me there's *nothin'* tells me there's *somethin'*."

Anna shook her head. "Not as far as Thomas is concerned." She lifted her chin to keep her lips from trembling. "He despises me."

Sarah studied Anna with a confused frown. "Before he left on the train, he came by and asked Henry to go by and check on y'all as often as he could." Sarah leaned into Anna's gaze. "For a fella that despises you, he sure looked torn up about leavin'."

"Thomas is a good man," Anna said quietly. "He is devoted to the boys in his care and feels deeply responsible for them."

"I'm sure he does," Sarah said. "But I know what I heard. He said, 'Henry, if you'd watch over Anna, I'd be especially grateful.'"

Anna finished two tiny blankets, four newborn gowns, and two larger ones. At this rate, she would need a steamer trunk to take it all with her.

When she told the boys over breakfast that the ice box no longer had ice, and there was no more meat, they decided to go fishing and promised to bring back a "mess" of fish for supper.

Longing to dip her swollen feet in the cool water, Anna joined them.

At the edge of the creek, Anna stopped, immobilized by the memory of the day her pregnancy had been exposed in that same spot, as if it were yesterday and not several weeks ago. The vile insults and hatred seemed to hang in the air even now, like a bitter aftertaste.

She took off her shoes and sat at the edge of the bank, dipped her feet in, and watched the young fishermen. Samuel brought a bucket to take home their catch. Such a man of faith.

Anna smiled, leaned back, and closed her eyes.

"Guess you just can't get enough of that creek," a drawling male voice said.

Startled, Anna opened her eyes and sat up, blinking. She had fallen fast asleep. She turned and looked behind her.

Sheriff Withers stood between her and the trail back to the house, with fists on his hips.

Prompted by a rush of adrenaline, she glanced around. Most of the boys had moved downstream, but Samuel was nowhere in sight.

She remembered Henry saying he wanted to force Withers to do something about the grocer's business, and Thomas saying they needed to go over the sheriff's head, to find law that was not intimidated or backed by the Klan.

Was he intimidated? Backed? Something else?

He came toward her.

Anna would not allow him to tower over her. Clumsily, she got to her feet, hating the fact that her pregnancy was so awkwardly obvious, and especially in that moment.

His gaze crawled over her body as he approached. "You don't belong here."

I do not belong anywhere, she corrected in silence. Her chin jutted. "I am married to a citizen of this town and therefore I have every right to be here."

He took a step closer. "Maybe you didn't hear me." His dark eyes had the look of a man who was not fond of argument. "I'd watch myself if I were you."

She took a step back. "You must be here to investigate the theft and property damage happening in the neighborhood." She chided herself inwardly. Goading Withers might make things more difficult for Thomas once he returned.

He shook his head. "I'm afraid that kind of thing happens when tempers flare. It's impossible to nail down a suspect, with the mood in town and all." His nostrils flared. "It's like being downwind of a pig farm. It's a foul stench you just can't get away from."

Several of the boys came along with their catches, chattering at once. Albert saw the sheriff and stopped, the pail slopping water. When the others saw Withers, they stopped, too.

Anna could not understand how the sheriff could stand by and do nothing when people were being attacked. Upholding the law was his job, was it not? Were there not superiors he had to answer to?

"I thought protecting the citizens was your job. You are the law."

He nodded. "That's right. I am. And don't you forget it."

Thirty-One

INDIANA IN JULY WAS NO PLACE FOR BAKING BREAD, ESPECIALLY for a woman eight months pregnant. Anna found the heat from the cookstove unbearable, so she baked in the late evenings, which only made the days seem suddenly longer, hotter, and more tedious. She found she needed to invent new ways to occupy herself, ways to keep her mind off of things she preferred not to think about. Like how quarrelsome the boys had become in the stifling heat, or how constantly her back ached, or how aggravating her itchy, distended belly had become. How clumsy she felt. How desperate she was for adult conversation.

How lonely she was.

Since there would be no more visiting with Sarah, Anna busied herself with making diapers from the flour sacks she had collected and harvesting the first of the produce from the garden. She picked a large bowl of green beans, three cucumbers, and seven ripe tomatoes, and served it all with fried fish. Jimmy voted it the best supper he had ever tasted, almost as good as sugar cream pie, and everyone agreed.

The boys continued to spend hours each day working in the shop and still forbade Anna to come inside. She decided to give them the benefit of the doubt, but she did not hesitate to give them a sniff when they came in for supper—especially Pete. She was uncertain what pipe tobacco smelled like, but Pete only smelled of sawdust and sweat.

On a Saturday in mid-July, Anna sat on a bench under the shade of a tree hemming a stack of diapers while the boys painted the new plywood that Henry had replaced on the porch. Henry said that Sarah had telephoned the PWA, but she had received no reply from Thomas yet, or any indication that he had gotten the message about the fire. The job site was miles from the main office in Ottawa. In the meantime, Anna would simply have to wait.

The sound of a car approaching drew Anna's attention. A newer Model T Ford was coming down the lane, but as it drew closer, it slowed to a crawl.

Anna peered into the car to see if she knew who it was and then stiffened. She could think of no good reason Penny Withers would have to call at Johansen Woodworks.

The shiny, black car came to a stop, blocking the driveway, the engine still running.

"I heard Thomas walked out on you," Penny hollered, a smug tilt to her chin. She wore a white cloche hat and matching pearls and looked the part of a fashionable young woman of means out for a mid-summer drive. "Left you with his mangy pack of hooligans, I see."

Stiffening, Samuel put his brush down. He did not look directly at Penny, but he seemed to be watching her out of the corner of his eye. Waiting. Ready to disappear, probably.

Anna glared at her but said nothing. She would not give Penny the satisfaction of a response.

"Serves you right," Penny said. She narrowed a gaze at the stack of diapers that Anna had finished. "He doesn't love you. He'll *never* love you. Or your little brat." She spat out a few more choice words for her baby that prickled Anna's skin.

Why Penny felt the need to come here and taunt Anna was a mystery, yet one she did not have the energy or desire to solve. She would one day soon be gone from here. She had nothing, no family, no possessions, no comforts. Penny had no reason to take Anna's lowly condition and push it down her throat. What possible gain could she derive from rubbing Anna's nose in her poverty and loneliness? Was it pure hatred that drove Penny Withers to be so unkind? Or something else?

With a sigh, Anna said, "I cannot help but feel sorry for you, Penny."

Penny scoffed. "*You* feel sorry for *me*?" She laughed loudly. "Oh, *this* ought to be rich."

Albert and Jack came close to Anna and stood beside her, glowering at Penny.

"I may be lonely and unloved," Anna said calmly, "but at least I am not surrounded by people simply because of what I can do for them, or because they are afraid of me. Unlike you, I will never have to wonder if I am liked for who I am."

Penny's smugness vanished. Her face reddened. "You're pathetic," she said, grinding the gears as the engine revved.

"No, *you* are," Jack hollered.

The car lurched a few times and then roared away in a cloud of dust.

Anna let out a breath, then rubbed the sharp twinge in her side. That family had a way of turning every one of Anna's muscles into a solid knot.

"I don't know what you just said, Miss Anna, but you sure got her goat," Albert said, snickering.

Anna had to admit she had certainly not expected to *get* anything of Penny's, including her goat. Anna's unkind reply had bubbled out with the same effortless ease as had her lie about Samuel and his pie.

Lies and insults. At the root of it all, it seemed that Anna was no different than Penny.

Late Sunday evening, just as Anna set two loaves of bread to cool, Samuel appeared in the kitchen, as if on cue. If there was ever a day that fresh bread did *not* make him appear, Anna would have to check him for a fever and see if he was ill.

"Would you like a snack?" she asked.

He looked appreciatively at the loaves. "Yes, ma'am." He sat at the table in the corner with his Bible, now marked with more ribbons than before.

She hunted for a bread knife and then cut a slice, watching Samuel. He had opened the book to one of the marked pages and was reading. Anna spread a thin smear of jam on the bread. They had run out of fresh butter some time ago.

"You really like that Bible." She could not imagine Anshel carrying around the Torah—or any book, for that matter. Her heart lurched at the thought of her brother. Had he grown many inches? Would he become the man Anna hoped he could without his own father to model after, as Thomas had?

"It's my mama's," he said.

Instantly curious, Anna took a seat beside him. "She gave it to you?"

He stared at it. "I found it. It's the only thing I got left of her."

Tears stung Anna's eyes. She focused on the page. "What are you reading?"

"Psalm of David. He was a k-king."

Anna smiled. "Yes, I have heard of King David."

Samuel returned her smile, then his face turned solemn. "I gotta t-t-tell you somethin'." He drew a deep breath and looked down at the page. "But first, read this." He pointed to a spot.

Anna leaned closer and read aloud, "Deliver me not over unto the will of mine enemies: for false witnesses are risen up against me, and such as breathe out cruelty. I had fainted, unless I had believed to see the goodness of the Lord in the land of the living. Wait on the Lord: be of good courage, and he shall strengthen thine heart: wait, I say, on the Lord."

Trembling, Samuel looked out the screen door, although there was little to see but dusky woods and darkening sky. Turning back, he closed his eyes. "Lord, I been f-faint," he whispered, "but I will be of good courage. Thank You, Lord, 'cause You s-strengthen my heart, Lord. In Jesus' name, Amen."

He opened his eyes, took a deep breath, and looked at Anna. "I reckon I know who s-set fire to the s-sister's school."

She gasped. "Who?"

He glanced out the door and lowered his voice to a whisper. "Pointy-headed ghosts."

Anna nodded. She had suspected as much. "How do you know?"

"Late one night, I acted like I was goin' to the outhouse, but really, I snuck off to Mama's cabin, to see if she left anything else behind." His eyes widened. "Then I saw flames across the creek. So I slipped over the b-bridge and hid in the b-bushes." He shivered. "Then I saw 'em. They was all dressed in white and one carried a gas can. They went right p-past me. I was real quiet. They d-didn't even know I was there."

Anna huffed. "Oh, yes, they are so brave. They torment others, yet they do not show their faces. I think they do not show themselves because they *know* their actions are evil."

Samuel swallowed hard. "I been faint, but the Lord tells me be of good courage, so I...I had to tell s-someone."

"You are far braver than they are, Samuel. Unfortunately, no one saw their faces, so no one will be punished for that fire."

"I didn't s-see their faces, but I heard 'em talkin'. I know who they are."

Anna stared at him. "You do?"

He nodded. "I didn't know whose voice it was till we was at the f-funeral. I heard that very same voice when he talked at the end."

She stilled. Boyd Withers had spoken at the end.

"Then I heard it again the other day. When you f-fell asleep down by the creek."

Anna gasped. Boyd Withers, local sheriff and top enforcer of the law, had committed arson, had deliberately set fire to the Mercy School?

Heart pounding, Anna got up and went to the screen door. She needed air.

"It was Miss Penny's d-d-d-daddy," he whispered. "The new sheriff."

She nodded. She did not doubt what Samuel had told her, or that he was correct about what he heard and saw. The trouble was, would anyone else believe him? Would anyone even listen?

Thirty-Two

ON HER WAY TO THE SISTERS OF MERCY ON MONDAY, ANNA TRIED to figure out what to do with Samuel's story. She had to do something but was not certain what, and what effect it would have. Would it do any good? Would anyone listen?

And was it wise to stir up trouble while Thomas was away? Or would it only make things worse for everyone here? Would it bring trouble for Samuel?

Perhaps Anna was the best person to call out the sheriff for his destructive behavior. After all, she would be leaving, eventually. If *she* were the one to report it, perhaps no trouble would come to anyone else.

The day before, Anna had mimicked Thomas's Sunday tradition and had taken a walk in the woods, an experiment of sorts. She needed time to think, but she was also curious to see if a calming perspective would also come to *her* as it seemed to for Thomas. But all she had gained from her walk was a hitch in her back and a muscle spasm in her side. And a dreadful longing for Thomas to return and relieve her. She longed for rest.

How much longer would she have the strength to continue?

By the time she reached the parish house, she was out of breath, aching all over, and drained. The day she would have full use of her lungs again would be a welcome relief.

Sister Mary Francis met her at the door and invited her in for a rest and a cup of water. Mary Agnes was out.

Anna related to Mary Francis what Samuel had seen and heard the night of the fire.

The sister looked grim. "I knew it was arson. I just didn't know the

233

crime had been committed by the very ones who are supposed to enforce the law." She rose and paced the kitchen. "We need to report this."

"Yes, but to whom? He is the law over all of Alton County."

Mary Francis frowned. "I don't know. And I don't know if the testimony of one young boy is enough to launch an investigation. Assuming they even find the child credible."

Anna held very little hope that a child's word would be enough to begin an investigation of a sheriff, especially the word of a nine-year-old Negro boy.

"We will never know unless we try," Anna said. "We must begin somewhere, even if it is the next county over."

The sister went to the telephone on the wall and tapped the switch hook, waited a few moments, and then spoke. "Yes, Operator, please connect me to the sheriff's office in Fort Wayne."

Even though the sheriff's office had given Mary Francis and Anna little more than the standard promise to "look into it," Anna felt that she had at least started the wheel of justice turning. If they did not see action at the local level, they would try the state police, and if that did not work, they could contact someone in Washington. Surely there would be a law enforcement official *somewhere* who would listen to their claims and look into the sheriff's unlawful behavior. Of course, Samuel's story offered no solid proof, only the testimony of what he heard, and while Anna believed him without a doubt, she feared a young colored boy would be dismissed as an unreliable witness, at best. More likely, he would be interrogated for his tale, or even worse.

Anna suspected that for an investigation to even begin, some sort of solid proof or evidence would be needed. But since Boyd was himself the law, would he have ways of hiding evidence and avoiding scrutiny?

Tuesday morning, Anna took the basket and headed out back to gather eggs, grateful that Sarah had sold her some hens to replace the missing ones. What would Sarah say if she heard Samuel's story about Boyd? What would the rest of the townsfolk say? Would this be one of the things that split the town into opposing sides? Anna could not be certain how many townsfolk shared the same mindset as the Withers, the Becketts, Mr. Pitts, and the angry crowd that had accused her at the creek that day. Were they a small portion, or the majority?

Did the sheriff have the power to do as he pleased?

Anna feared she already knew the answer to that.

Nearing the coop, Anna looked for Salome. But there was no sign of the dove. In fact, there was no trace of any birds.

Anna looked around, instantly on guard. But there were no feathers, nothing broken. She opened the door, preparing to find that the birds had again been stolen.

Dead. All four hens lay lifeless on their nests or on the floor. With no sign of a predator, no blood, no feathers—just stiff, dead birds.

Anna slammed the door and stormed back to the house.

Over a breakfast of dry cereal and old potatoes, Anna's blood boiled. Someone had killed those chickens, but how? This was clearly the same people who had committed all the other acts of destruction.

The boys each had their own theories.

Though it was probably not a good idea, Anna headed to the Tucker farm, armed with an empty basket and some money, and a desperate hope that Sarah would set aside her worries about being seen with Anna long enough to sell her some eggs.

Henry came out of the house before Anna reached the porch.

"I am sorry," she said, "I know—"

"Sarah can't talk to you now, Anna," he said, his face grim.

Sounds of sobbing came from inside the house, and not just one person, but several.

Her heart hammered. "What is wrong? Has something happened to Sarah?"

Sarah came out of the house and down the steps to Anna, her face blotchy, eyes swollen and wet. Violet trailed her, bawling.

"They killed Owen, Anna. Someone came onto our property—"

"Or lured him with food," Henry said, jaw set like stone. "We found him layin' by the front door, and at first, we thought he was asleep. Looks like they poisoned him."

"Poisoned?" Anna's mind raced. "Our chickens are also dead in the coop. All of them. And no sign of harm."

Henry scowled. "Guess they called on you, too."

"Owen wouldn't hurt a flea," Violet sobbed. "Big ol' dummy. He probably walked right up to 'em and let 'em do it."

Anna's mind raced. Why would someone want to harm the Tuckers' gentle dog?

Sarah wiped her face with her apron, then shook her head. "I'm sorry, Anna, but we have to think of our children."

"What do you mean?"

"I hate to do it," Henry said. "But I have to look out for my own family now. I have to think about my livelihood. If that means choosing a side, then I guess that's what I have to do."

Disturbed and confused, Anna stared from one adult to the other.

Henry shook his head. "We can't have you comin' around no more, Anna."

For the rest of that day, and the several that followed, Anna felt as if a dark, scornful cloud had covered the sun. Sorrow cinched every muscle in her body. Even the baby seemed tense; it barely moved. She could not eat, her appetite alternated between nausea and indigestion, and she could not sleep. If not for her frequent need to visit the outhouse, Anna would have stayed in bed all day with the curtains drawn.

If only I had wings like a dove, I would fly away and be at rest...

Were they winning? The hateful horde, the slanderous women, the fire-wielding, masquerading men? The Klan?

But as Anna lay pondering the ceiling, she wondered if these people really were the enemy, or if the real enemy was much bigger than women who gathered with their purification agenda and men who terrorized in disguise. Perhaps it was not just the lingering presence of a brutal old brotherhood, or even a bigoted general public that felt justified posting signs at their city limits warning coloreds to stay away. It was not just a Romanov czar or bands of raiding Cossacks or the bellowing German chancellor who had recently enforced a ban on all his political opponents.

Anna was beginning to think that the enemy was much deeper, wider, and farther-reaching than any one group of bigots or bullies or rebels or radicals. It was not limited to a color or creed or religion or nationality. The enemy was a disease; a ravaging, spreading epidemic, its symptoms: cold, hard indifference, smallness, and intolerance. Deliberate blindness. Fear.

The enemy's creed: *I* am the center of the universe. *I* am the apex of all that matters.

So what was the enemy? The Egocentricity of Man? And how was such an enemy to be vanquished?

Anna could allow and even forgive naïveté and ignorance, the kind that came from simply being raised in a place and among a people who knew no better, like Sarah or Henry. Those whose lives had been largely untouched by outsiders, those who had not chosen to live in an all-white, all-American town or county but had simply been born there, unaware that the reason their town appeared so uniform in color and nationality was because someone, long before them, had systematically driven out, frozen out, burned out, or lynched out most every person of every other kind. Ignorance of this type, while troubling, did not make one guilty. These people simply did not know better.

No, the guilt belonged to those who knew better and still chose to be small, closed, afraid, and blind. And to Anna, all alone now, the enemy certainly seemed to be winning.

On Thursday, Albert and Teddy went into town for milk and beans and returned with a letter from Shayna, which Anna pressed to her chest as if it were a letter of parole.

14 July

Dearest Anna,

I have not stopped crying since I read your letter. Mama is certain I am dying and insists on telephoning the doctor. I cannot stop thinking about you and the people in your life. (I know there is more you are not telling me, and this, I confess, hurts almost as much as knowing you are lonely and hurting.) My heart breaks and I feel so helpless. I have no useful words to offer. I long to be there with you now. If I could shield you from your pain or take it from you or suffer in your place, I would gladly do it.

Forgive me, but I must ask since you are always so cryptic: Must you leave Thomas and the boys? And are you so certain that Thomas's wounds are irreparable? Since you would give up your very life to see him whole and happy, will you not fight for this?

You have changed, Anna. What has happened? I know you face oppression, but this is nothing new. You were once a woman who planned to harness the wind and make it take you wherever you wished to go. Now you sound defeated, like a woman who has decided that the wind cannot be tamed and can cast you aside like a rag.

The winds may blow, dearest, but you <u>do</u> have a choice. You can give up and be cast aside, or you can choose to live with purpose every moment you are alive. You can choose to pour out your heart wherever you are, no matter your circumstances. Anna, you do not see it, but your compassion and ability to love are powerful and precious gifts.

And yes, I believe that G-d welcomes our return. The question is, do you wish to return? Do you wish for atonement?

All My Love,
S.

P.S. As much as I wish you home, I truly hope you find Papa first. Mama has changed. She no longer speaks as if he is due to arrive any day now. In fact, she rarely mentions him at all. She often just sits, staring. Not even Anshel's clever jokes cheer her anymore. I fear something has crept in and stolen her hope.

20 July

My Love,

You are right, I have changed. I am a coward. And I am tired. Tired of fighting, tired of the heat. Tired of hatred and this business of having to choose sides. Why must there be sides?

We are all guilty, and we are all victims. Of ignorance.

Of smallness. Smallness in our ability to see and trust. Of indifference. Of wanting to be the center of our world, of wanting only our own way without giving up a single speck of our will or way of thinking.

Shayna, do you think there is any hope? Will we always create racial and societal barriers where none need exist? Can man ever get along as one family? Did G-d not know this would happen when He created so many races of man, so multi-colored a family?

We will never have unity as long as people demand sameness. Unity is not sameness, but oneness of purpose. But whose purpose? Who gets to decide? If only everyone would stop shouting and hating and burning down and forcing out, perhaps we would hear the voice of wisdom. Perhaps.

(I look at young Shemu'el with his whittling knife, and sometimes, I wonder if the voice of wisdom may be closer than I think. And if hope may be found in the unlikeliest places.)

Yes, I hope there is atonement because I have much to atone for. My ability to be unkind (whether justified or not, because I suspect it never truly is) has reached a record high. Perhaps I am no better than the women who shout at me and call me filthy names. Who decides what bitterness is acceptable and what is not?

I am sorry to hear about Mama. She has suffered much sorrow. I can only imagine how broken her heart must be. I will do my best to find Papa, but if I do not, please do not let Mama give up. She has a wealth of hope right in front of her. She still has you, Riv, and Anshel, the most priceless treasure anyone could ask for.

It is lucky that we planted the garden, as we are facing even more food shortage. If only the beets were ready! I have been craving your borscht like a raving madwoman.

All My Love,

A.

Thirty-Three

THE BOYS SPENT THE WEEKEND FISHING, AND WITH GREAT SUC-
cess. They brought home enough fish each day to make a filling supper for
everyone. Anna rounded out the meals with eggless bread. Samuel noticed
that the bread was not yellow, and there was no braided challah, but he
said nothing.

Yet food scarcity was not the only problem. Jack and Pete were especially cranky and could not stop bickering. Anna became so weary of them
that she dreamed of putting them on a train to Illinois so Thomas could
settle their disputes.

She had heard nothing from Thomas. She hoped this meant he was
busy, and not that he was ignoring her and the message about the porch
fire. Surely he would not be indifferent to such a threat to his home and the
boys, regardless of his feelings about Anna. No. She had to assume he was
too busy or unable to respond.

She was beginning to sound like Mama.

On Sunday, over yet another supper of fish and bread, Jimmy lifted his
plate. "You know what this reminds me of?"

The others shook their heads.

"The story about Jesus using the boy's bread and fish to feed five-thou-
sand."

Pete looked at his plate. "Wonder if *they* got sick of eating only fish
and bread."

Anna sighed. "So now you are sick of having this lucky streak of plentiful food?"

Pete eyed her, then shook his head. "No, ma'am." He went back to eating in silence.

Samuel chuckled. Albert frowned and then elbowed him. "What's so funny?" Samuel shrugged and kept eating but snickered again and stole a look at Anna.

"What?" she said, frowning.

"Reminds me of the day we found you." He tore off a hunk of bread.

Anna smiled. "Ah yes, fish stew."

"*Crick* Stew," Albert snickered. "Or did you already forget what it's called?"

"Yeah, that was some trick," Pete said. "Bet you made that recipe up, didn't you?"

"Wasn't a trick," Teddy said. "It was just an...ingenious way to get us to share a meal."

Anna smiled at Teddy's use of a "big" word.

Pete shrugged. "It *was* pretty clever."

After supper, some of the boys went out to the workshop, and Samuel whittled on the porch. Anna and Albert joined him. Anna worked on diaper covers, an idea she got from a ladies' magazine Sarah had given her, using scraps of woolen clothing.

Samuel loaned his pocketknife to Albert while he sanded his latest piece. On closer inspection, Anna saw that it was a cross.

She said nothing but was curious about his choice.

"Why did Jesus let those soldiers put Him up on that cross?" Albert asked Samuel. "Seems like if He was really God's Son, He could've stopped 'em."

Samuel shrugged and kept sanding the wood.

"If it was me, *I* wouldn't have let 'em put *me* up there." Albert turned to Anna. "Wouldn't you save yourself, if you could?"

Anna nodded. "I am sure I would, if I could."

Albert grunted. "I bet He couldn't, that's why He didn't."

Samuel stopped and looked at Albert. "He coulda saved Hisself." He blew off the dust and held the cross up to the sunlight, inspecting the edges.

"Well, then, why didn't He?"

"He wanted to save us more."

"Us?" Albert rose to his feet. "So Jesus is like us fellas, all for one and one for all?"

Samuel shook his head. "No, One for all. And One for one."

Anna listened without comment. What an unusual boy, this young

Samuel. She wondered if his mother had instilled the stories and ideas in her son's head before she left him. Or if he had concluded these things on his own from reading his Bible.

The boys headed to the creek for a quick swim, and Anna finished her diaper cover. She would have to find something to make it fasten over the diaper, but this could wait until she had relocated to a town where the stores had no reason to refuse to sell her diaper pins and thread. Sister Mary Francis had told her that there was a good possibility of securing a cheap room to rent in Chicago, and they would find out more soon. This was one less thing for Anna to worry about. Now, she could focus on keeping the boys from turning to skin and bone until Thomas returned.

Monday morning, Jack and Pete came to Anna in a sweaty rush. Their faces and teeth were smeared with purple.

"We found blackberries, over in the woods, across the lane. We came to get buckets and get y'all to come help us pick more."

Excited, Anna helped them find as many buckets and jars as they could carry, then rounded up the others and followed the pair.

Down the lane toward the Tucker place, at the edge of the woods, a mass of blackberry vines grew like a long, tangled hedgerow. Anna was already thinking about pie and trying to remember if she had enough sugar, flour, and lard.

She and the boys picked for quite a while, sampling the berries along the way. Some sampled more than they picked, but she did not stop them. This was such an unexpected treat. Or perhaps it was Providence, as Sister Mary Agnes would say.

Anna stopped to stretch and looked back over the vines they had picked. She and Samuel had picked farther than the rest of the boys. Samuel's bucket was only half full, but his face explained where his harvest had gone. She laughed.

A rustling in the trees behind them made Anna stiffen. She pulled Samuel close to her side, her belly twinging from the burst of adrenaline.

"Shh..." a voice whispered. "It's just me."

Sarah Tucker stepped cautiously through the trees bearing a covered basket. She looked around quickly. "I can't stick around, but...I saw y'all crossin' the road from my window and wanted to..." She looked around again. "These are for y'all." She set the basket down, turned, and hurried away.

242

Frowning, Anna went to the basket and lifted the cloth. The basket was full of eggs. At least a dozen, maybe more. She looked up again, but Sarah was gone.

Later that evening, Anna and the boys gathered around the table in the parlor and listened to the radio while the boys made themselves sick on blackberry pie. Anna passed on the pie, as she had been feeling ill all afternoon from the heat, both from picking berries, and from the cookstove, which she willingly suffered in order to bake the rare treat.

President Roosevelt was giving one of his "Fireside Chats" about something called the National Recovery Administration and the plan for Americans to work together to attack unemployment.

Anna thought the president had already *attacked* Thomas's unemployment by creating the dam-building job and others like it. Perhaps President Roosevelt could also get people to band together and *attack* the bigotry in the land. The president ended his chat with the call to seek "God or Providence" and urged listeners to face the difficulties ahead with faith, patience, courage, and understanding.

After the president signed off, Pete and Teddy took their turn washing the dishes while the others tidied up the kitchen. Anna pondered the president's final words. His speech was a good one, positive and reasonable even. Anna wanted to take encouragement from it. She wanted to hope that the joblessness and economy would improve soon. She wanted to hope that people could choose to be compassionate toward those they did not understand. She also wanted to see justice served. For Boyd Withers to be removed from his position of power, for Alice Withers to lose her ability to "pull strings," and for Thomas to regain the state support he had been receiving so that he would never again have to go so far away to earn enough money to tide him and the boys over. If the government was really interested in helping people get ahead, perhaps the government could listen to the oppressed.

Anna trudged up the stairs, suddenly overwhelmed with fatigue. Instead of encouraging Anna, the president's radio address only left her feeling bone-weary.

Oh, to have wings like a dove, to fly away, and be at rest. Was this too much to ask?

Sister Mary Agnes came by on Tuesday morning with a burlap sack full of potatoes and several quarts of milk, apologizing that it was all that she could manage to get for them. Anna thanked her, grateful for the help. There was still no ice for the icebox, so she made a large batch of potato soup for the boys, adding onions and carrots from the garden. She could not bring herself to eat it though, as the idea of warm milk turned her already nauseated stomach.

Still feeling unwell after lunch, Anna napped in the shade on a blanket, the only place to sleep that did not feel like an oven, and awoke much later to shouts. The sun was already setting. She did not realize she had slept so long, and yet, the rest had done little to ease the illness she had been feeling.

Teddy came running to her, eyes wide. "Miss Anna, you gotta come quick!"

"What is it?" Anna worked to get herself up and on her feet. The sudden movement made her back and belly cramp sharply.

"Sam took the little Owen dog that he whittled over to the Tuckers for Violet, and now he's gone."

Anna tried to shake the fog from her sleepy head. "Gone?"

"That ain't all. There's a burning cross, and there's something bad hanging on the Tucker's tree." Teddy swallowed hard. "It's a...it's a lynched little colored boy."

Anna gasped. "A *what?*"

"I mean, it's a dummy made to look like a little boy, and..." His eyes widened even more. "And there's another dummy in a brown dress. With dark hair like yours."

She stared at him. "What...?"

"Pete thinks Sam saw them hanging by a noose when he went to the Tuckers."

Anna went suddenly numb. Why images of Samuel and Anna, and why on the Tucker's property? Had someone seen Sarah giving food to them? Someone hateful enough to send such a sickening message?

"We need to go to the Tuckers, see if he is inside with them or if they have seen him," she said, swallowing back fear.

Teddy hurried ahead of her on the path through the woods, now dim from the growing dusk. Before she reached the Tuckers' lane, Anna could see a fiery, orange glow through the trees. Panic raced through her.

Teddy ran faster, and Anna tried to follow as best she could, but she was halted by a dreadful ache from her pelvis to her back. When they came out of the trees, Anna's breath caught.

A large cross planted in front of the Tuckers' house was on fire, shooting flames up at the night sky.

"Sarah? Henry?" Anna shouted. "Teddy, please go see if you can find them."

He flew up the steps and banged on the door, with no answer. Then he went around the house and disappeared.

Anna looked for Samuel, the Tucker family, the tormentors. There was no one.

Then she saw them—the "dummies" hanging from the poplar tree, each one dangling from a noose.

She retched and bent over, holding her hard, cramping stomach.

Teddy returned. "I don't see anybody, not outside," he said.

"Please look inside the house," Anna whispered. She could not bring herself to do it. The dog had been killed—poisoned, probably, and now this...

The brutes who had done this might have no qualms about harming Sarah and her family.

She looked over her shoulder, half expecting to see the villains at any moment.

Albert, Jimmy, and Jack came running, then stopped when they saw the figures dangling from their nooses.

Teddy came back and said no one was inside.

"Miss Anna, we gotta find Sam," Albert said. "If he saw that little boy hangin'..."

She nodded, heart pounding. "Please go look for him, and hurry."

Horrible images came to mind, of Samuel running, being chased, hunted even. Tied to a train track. Someone wanted him and Anna and the Tuckers to know they were as good as dead.

Shaking, Anna tried to keep from collapsing. The dark closed around her, intensifying even more the glow from the burning cross. She waited for another deep, painful cramp to pass, gave the Tuckers' house one last look, then headed into the woods to look for the child.

Where were the Tuckers? Was Samuel with them? Was he frightened and hiding, or had he been caught by those who set the fire? She could not think about this possibility, so she forced herself to keep looking. She heard the shouts of Samuel's name in the distance and kept going.

A powerfully hard cramp stopped her in her tracks. She waited for it to pass, then kept going. A sudden flow of watery liquid showered her legs and feet.

No, baby. No, not yet...too early...

She needed to think.

The little cabin—Sarah had found him there once. And Samuel had said something about his mother's cabin, that he had gone there to look for something of hers. Anna did not know exactly where it was, but she knew it was at the edge of one of the Tuckers' corn fields.

She tried to walk in that direction but had to stop several times and wait for hard pains to pass. It felt like someone had dropped a large, wooden ball into her pelvis and was pushing it down hard.

Not now, not now, not now, baby...

She yelped in pain and then saw the small hut thirty feet away. She made her way to it and flung open the door.

Samuel was crouched inside, balled up in the corner on a straw mat.

Anna moaned in relief, then buckled at the knee.

The boy jumped up, a terrified look on his face.

"Samuel..." Anna swallowed the dry panic in her throat. "Please go get me help." She winced and held her breath through another sharp contraction. "Go find..." She bit her lower lip to keep from crying out. "Go get Sister Mary Agnes. Run!"

Samuel only stared at her, frozen, the same look of shock she had seen in him before.

"Samuel," she breathed. She cradled his face in both hands. "I am having the baby now and I need help. I am counting on you—" She tensed all over again as another wave came.

Samuel quaked.

"It is very important that you...go get Sister Mary. Do not go near...the Tucker farm.... You must...hurry. Run!"

Dazed, Samuel backed away from Anna, then turned and vanished.

Anna sank to the floor of the tiny, one room hut, panting, then pulled herself over to the straw mat in the corner. Vaguely, in the fading light, she saw on the wall a wooden cross, a dead sunflower, and a row of tiny wooden figurines standing on a brace between two posts.

She had no idea if Samuel had gone to get help or to go hide. He was clearly in shock. Anna could not think about that, could only focus on quelling the rising panic, the wave of fear threatening to crash as the next contraction came. She held her breath.

Darkness overtook the tiny hut. But she could no longer see the walls, her mind beginning to swim, to play tricks on her. She saw Mama's face, her sisters, Anshel. Her papa, dressed in his one good suit and hat, boarding the ship to America, promising to make a better life for them, promising to send for them soon. His promises dissolving in the ship's horn blast...

Then she was younger, hiding beneath the floorboards as the horses thundered past, rocking the tiny one-room house. Baby Rivka's eyes wide with fear, three-year-old Shayna tearful and whimpering. Anna shushed them and then told them to pretend it was a game to see who could be the quietest. Just focus on breathing silently. One breath at a time. Breathe in. Breathe out. In. Out. In. Out.

Focus.

Survive.

Pain, sharp, rising, peaking...

One breath at a time. One heartbeat at a time. Focus. Breathe.

She listened. Were the Cossacks still out there? She could not tell. Had it been hours? Days?

"Mama..." Anna whimpered. "Where are you? Why are you not back yet?"

"I'm here, shhh..." a voice said.

Anna's moan grew louder with the rising wave of pain. She gripped at the mat on either side of her and cried out.

"Help is on the way, just...just try to hold on," the voice said.

It was not Mama...or Mary Agnes. It was a man's voice.

"Papa...?"

"Samuel, go see if she's coming. Hurry!"

Anna gulped air and opened her eyes. Light outlined the silhouette of a man in the doorway, hands gripping his hair.

Thomas.

Thirty-Four

SISTER MARY FRANCIS WAS SUDDENLY AT HER SIDE, AND ANNA realized she had been drifting in and out of consciousness. Mary Francis worked quickly, removing garments, checking Anna, barking orders for boiled water, a sharp knife, a sheet.

"We have to get her to the house," Thomas said, sheer panic in his voice.

"It's far too late for that," the sister snapped.

Anna felt a powerful urge to push but Mary Francis gripped Anna's face and said, "Not yet, Anna. Not this time. Hold back, you can do it..."

Other voices clamored outside the thin walls. Anna panted and yelled out, trying to do as she was told, trying to breathe instead of holding her breath, afraid of losing consciousness again.

"What can I do?" Thomas hollered. "Give me something to do!"

"Get a blanket, or something to wrap it in," Mary Francis said.

Thomas tore off his shirt.

The urge to push swelled again. Anna moaned and the low, guttural sound in her throat rose from a moan to a wail to a scream.

Thomas spun and bolted out the door.

"Okay, Anna. Time to push. Give it all you've got. You can do it."

Anna pushed with all her might, her moans constant now and turning to gut-wrenching screams. Mary Francis told her to rest for a count of ten, and as the next wave came, she told her to push again.

Yelling, Anna reached inside and summoned every bit of strength she had and pushed, suddenly bolstered by a burst of vigor, of life, of an inexplicable, unnamable knowing.

She was delivered quite suddenly of her burden, instantly relieved of all pressure and pain, then exhaled and listened. Nothing.

"Where is that knife?" Mary Francis muttered. Then she worked hurriedly, her movements muffled sounding. Moments passed.

Not a sound.

Tearful, Anna held her breath, dreading the silence. It would serve her right, of course. She deserved nothing, no pardon, no mercy—

Squalling cries pierced the night.

Anna exhaled and sobbed, joining the infant in relief, in breath. In life.

Mary Francis placed the messy, mewling newborn, wrapped in a shirt, into Anna's arms. She was vaguely aware that there was no one else around but Mary Francis.

"He's all there, but you can check," the sister said.

Anna sobbed. "He is beautiful," she whispered. "And impatient. He was not supposed to come for a few more weeks."

"It's the baby that decides when labor begins, you know." She wiped her gleaming brow with her wrist. "I guess he just wanted to see what all the fuss was about."

Fuss... Anna remembered what had been taking place when she went into labor. "The fire...there was a cross burning at the Tuckers..."

Mary Francis shook her head. "I don't know about that. I came as soon as I could after little Samuel came pounding on my door."

So Samuel *had* made it to the Sisters of Mercy. Such a brave boy. "And...Thomas?" Her mind suddenly whirled with questions. Why was he suddenly home? And where was he now?

"I sent him to get water and some help," Mary Francis said.

Anna inspected her son.

Her *son.*

Mary Francis was preparing Anna for the post birth process when Sarah entered the hut, covered in soot and carrying little Ivy.

"Anna! Oh, my heavens, you did it."

Anna burst into tears. "Sarah, your house...?"

Sarah shook her head. "Henry got that fire put out. It didn't catch the house, thank the Lord, dry as everything is. I came to help, brought water and supplies."

"Thank you," Anna said, confused. "Did the boys tell you I was in labor?"

"No, Thomas came and found me at the café. Poor man was in a pure panic, hoppin' around like he had ants in his pants. He told me you needed help, the baby was comin' and you was out in the woods. He was so shook up he could hardly tell me where. He about drug me outta the cafe." Sarah tilted her head. "What a handsome little fella," she said, smiling at the baby. "Well now, that swaddlin' blanket certainly explains why Mr. Chandler wasn't wearin' no shirt." She grinned, then her face sobered. "Okay, Mama, let's get you taken care of."

By the time Anna was able to stand and walk, Sister Mary Agnes arrived with a change of clothing for Anna, and together, they all helped her into the sisters' pickup truck and took her home.

Anna spent the next hours and days getting accustomed to her baby, to feeding him, learning what his signals meant, but the dark shadow of what had happened the night he was born lingered. She still did not know what happened after the Tuckers found their property had been targeted. If Henry wanted his wife and family to avoid Anna before, the burning cross and lynched figures on his property would certainly solidify that decision.

And while Thomas was back, Anna had not seen him more than a moment or two. He had fully resumed his role as mentor and guardian, and appeared to be staying home, at least for now. Anna wondered if his job at the dam had been completed early, or if he had been laid off, the way he had with the first job. Was he finished and back for good? Or only home until he could find more work?

One thing she *did* know was that the boys seemed to be under the impression that Anna was starving, based on the amount of food they brought to her, and they also seemed to fear she would shatter like china if they made a sound. She chuckled to herself when Pete tiptoed into her bedroom with yet another glass of milk.

The way the boys cared for her brought tears to her eyes. She had not expected to be treated with such kindness and dignity. Not that the boys could ever be truly unkind. But that she, the immoral woman with an illegitimate child, was being shown compassion, was being allowed the time and space to recover and learn how to feed and care for her newborn, overwhelmed her already fragile emotions.

On Friday morning, when her son was three days old, Anna took him down to the kitchen to bathe him. On the eighth day of life, a Jewish boy would be circumcised and given his name. But Anna could not hold a bris, not here, not now. She was uncertain what to do. But the more she thought about it, the more she wondered if her half-Jewish son would even grow up as a Jew. She was just not certain. But either way, he still needed a name.

She was still pondering what to do when she heard a knock at the kitchen door.

Sarah was there, surprising Anna not only that she was coming to visit her in broad daylight, but that she had brought a casserole, and two other women bearing gifts. Anna had seen them in town. The taller of the two was one of Penny's followers.

"Rose and Helen are my friends from the Society," Sarah said. "They have something for you." Sarah scooped up the baby and walked around the kitchen, cooing at him.

Had she heard correctly? The *Women of Virtue* Society?

The two women looked at each other, and Helen, the taller one, came forward. "It's just a few of my little boy's things, but still in fair shape." She laid a bundle on the table next to Anna.

Rose added, "And I brought diapers and pins and some other things, if you need 'em."

"Thank you. I do need them... I was not expecting him to arrive yet."

"What's his name?" Rose asked.

Anna glanced at the baby in Sarah's arms, who started to fuss. Sarah handed him back to Anna. "I have not named him yet. My people—" She remembered who these women were and what made her very different from them. "My *family* observes a tradition of naming a baby boy in a ceremony when he is eight days old." She tried to get him to nurse, but he pulled away and fussed. Anna frowned, wishing she knew what else to try.

"Anna, we won't stay long and wear you out, but there's one other reason we're here." Sarah looked at the other two again.

Anna shushed and bounced the baby, waiting.

Helen's face paled. She swallowed hard. "Sarah says I ought to tell you what I know about the sheriff that died."

"Sheriff Dooley?"

Helen nodded, glancing at Sarah. "I never said anything before, because..."

"Because of Alice," Rose finished. "But Sarah's been talking to us, and we're ready to stand up to Alice. To all of them."

Anna frowned. "What do you know?"

Helen looked around again. "I overheard Boyd Withers tell my husband...that he poisoned Old Sheriff Dooley."

Anna gasped. "He *murdered* him?"

Helen and Sarah nodded.

"And I heard other folks saying they wanted to get rid of Dooley," Rose added. "Because he was trying to break up the Klan. He told me he wanted to turn them all in before they got to him, but first, he was planning to send his wife to stay with her sister, just in case."

"Will you report this to the authorities?" Anna asked.

"We already called the Indianapolis police," Helen said. "It was Sarah here who talked us into it."

Sarah met Anna's gaze. "A real, bona-fide investigation is underway, Anna. They're gonna exhume Dooley and do an autopsy. But even if they can't determine it was poison, there are several folks who said they'd testify. So now we're waitin' to hear if they have enough to arrest Withers."

"This is excellent news." Anna beamed. "I am proud of you all for coming forward." She smiled at Rose and Helen, then turned to Sarah. "And you, my friend, are a very brave and remarkable woman."

Sarah shook her head. "If I was a *true* friend, I woulda listened to you and done this a long time ago. I woulda stood up to them instead of turnin' my back on you."

"Only a true friend would come to the aid of a woman giving birth in the woods," Anna said.

Sarah smiled. "Aw, sugar, it's what any neighbor would do." She winked. "I just hope I'm invited to the ceremony when you decide what to name him."

Anna smiled. If there would even *be* a ceremony. How she would manage that was still uncertain. But for now, Sarah was no longer afraid to stand up to the enemy, and was no longer afraid to call Anna friend. *This* was a day to celebrate.

Thomas entered the kitchen.

Sarah tapped Rose and nodded to Helen. "C'mon, girls. We best let Anna get her rest," she said, then she and her friends left.

Thomas stared at the door that the ladies had just closed, as if he wished it would open and bring them back in.

Anna felt a strain in the air, a silent tension. She waited for him to get whatever he had come for and leave again, as he usually did.

But he did not go.

She continued to wait. Perhaps he had decided that since he was home, and Samuel was well, and the baby had been born, it was time for Anna to leave. Perhaps he was working up a way to say it.

When he still did not speak, Anna spoke up. "Did you finish the job in Illinois?"

He turned to her, frowning. "What?"

"You came back sooner than you planned."

"Oh, sorry. No, the job's not finished. I just got the message about the fire set to the front porch. I asked for a leave of absence and came straight home. When I got here, Sam told me about you...in the cabin..." He winced. "He'd gone to fetch Sister Mary and came back here looking for more help, but the other boys were still out looking for him. I got to the cabin just before Mary Francis did, but... Well, I was completely useless."

Anna shook her head. "No, not useless. I needed not to be alone."

He stiffened and turned away, rigid as a fencepost.

Clearly, he would have preferred someone else be the one to wait until help arrived. She waited for him to speak, but again, he was silent.

"So when are you returning to Illinois?" she said.

He turned to her, his frown awash with confusion. He looked at the baby, then shook his head. "I don't know. This changes things." He let out a long, heavy sigh. "I'll wire the boss on Monday. I'll know more then."

Thirty-Five

INSTEAD OF HIS USUAL WALK IN THE WOODS ON SUNDAY, THO-mas went into town. All Anna knew was that Henry Tucker had called for another town meeting, and that Sarah was also planning to attend. Perhaps to make sure Henry did not get caught up in another brawl. She did not know what Henry intended to do or what he hoped to accomplish. Anna was still recovering from childbirth and was still sickened by the image of her likeness swinging from a noose, so she stayed home. She had no interest in running into any of those responsible for that, not today.

Anna sat in the parlor while the baby slept in her lap. Samuel sat close by and watched the infant sleep.

He looked up at Anna. "Does he have a name yet?"

"I will name him when he is eight days old."

Samuel counted on his fingers. "Three more days?"

She nodded.

"Then you'll tell us our brother's name?"

Anna's mouth opened, but she could not answer.

Jimmy and Teddy came in from the kitchen. Something knocked against the wall in the hallway, and someone else whispered sharply.

"Miss Anna, we need you to close your eyes," Jimmy said.

She closed her eyes, hoping it wasn't another dead thing.

More knocking and scraping sounds and a "Watch it, blockhead!" followed by shushing.

"Okay, you can look now."

Anna opened her eyes. Before her sat a beautiful wooden rocking chair and a matching cradle. Brand new and recently finished, judging by the wood smell and the pride beaming from all six faces before her.

She let out a sob and covered her mouth. "Oh! You did that?"

Teddy and Pete nodded, grinning to their ears.

Jimmy brought the cradle closer. "See, it rocks." He demonstrated.

Albert came close to Anna. "If you wanna try out the rocker, I can hold the little fella."

Anna laughed and cried at the same time. As she handed the baby over, she tried not to think about the fact that she could not take these beautiful things with her. She instead basked in the joy of seeing these boys so proud of their excellent workmanship.

She sat in the chair and began to rock. It was beautiful, rocked perfectly, and fit her just right. Albert handed the baby back and she rested on the arm of the chair and rocked him.

"This is beautiful, and so well made. So sturdy. You boys did this?" she asked again.

"We been working on it day and night," Jack said.

"Yeah, for weeks," Pete said.

Samuel stood next to the cradle. "When you give him his name, I can carve it here." He pointed to a place at the foot of the cradle.

Teary-eyed, Anna beckoned them closer and gave them all a wide, mother hen hug.

Thomas came in the front door and froze, eyes instantly glistening.

"Sorry, Mr. Tom, we couldn't wait," Teddy said.

Anna took a closer look at Thomas and gasped at the bloody gash on his forehead. "What happened to you?"

"There was a...little scuffle at the town meeting." Thomas smiled, then came closer and appraised Anna in her rocking chair. "Well?"

"I love it," she said, frowning. "What do you mean, *scuffle?*"

Thomas looked around with a gleam in his eye. "Do you guys want the serial version, or the full blow-by-blow?"

"Blow-by-blow!" Albert and Pete both shouted.

Thomas smiled. "Henry Tucker assembled a town meeting at the Methodist church calling for an end to all the vandalism and harassment, and he called out some of the men by name as cowards and bigots. Most everyone in town was there." He glanced at Anna. "Some people made accusations at Sarah and Henry for befriending you and Sam."

Anna fumed. She suspected as much.

"Sarah told everyone they all needed to start opening their hearts and to stop turning a blind eye to the bigotry happening right under our noses. Then your gutsy little friend took a big sign, the one that Sheriff Dooley took down that says, 'Whites Only in City Limits After Dark' and she smashed it to pieces, and said, 'And this nonsense ends right here, right now.'"

Samuel glanced at Anna, a hopeful look in his eyes.

Thomas drew a deep breath. "A bunch of folks stood with Alice Withers and they were shouting at Sarah. But the more they shouted, the more undecided folks went over to stand with the Tuckers. People said they'd never seen anyone take a stand like Sarah just did, and they felt the same way but were too afraid to do it themselves. The sisters were there, too, but they didn't take a side. Then Henry said, 'Anyone else who feels it ain't right to bully people, come on over.' Then more people went and stood beside them."

Anna shook her head, stunned.

"Then Boyd Withers showed up in uniform acting like he was there to keep the peace. He stood in the center of the room and told Henry to shut his wife up."

"Ohhh, no," Jimmy said, shaking his head.

"Boyd spouted off some rotten things about Sarah, then he and Henry exchanged words that I'm pretty sure have never been uttered in that sanctuary."

"Holy smokes!" Jack said.

Thomas's mouth curled up on one side. "Now for the best part."

"The part where you ended up hurt?" Anna said, brows raised.

"It's just a scratch."

Anna eyed the "scratch"—which looked deep enough to need a stitch or two.

He leaned forward. "Sarah stood up on a pew and hollered, 'Just so y'all know, Boyd Withers is currently under investigation for the murder of Sheriff Colin Dooley.'"

Anna gasped. "*Sarah* did that?"

Thomas nodded. "Everyone was in an uproar then. Boyd lunged for Sarah and nearly knocked her off the pew, then someone tackled Boyd and took him down, and a bunch of folks held him there. They placed him under citizen's arrest until the Fort Wayne deputy arrived—on orders from the U.S. Marshall's office—and they took him away in handcuffs. He's under arrest for murder, arson, and multiple counts of menacing, vandalism, and the list was growing still when I left because others were still coming forward."

Sweet relief flooded Anna, but she continued to eye him. "And why are you bleeding?"

"I was the someone who tackled Boyd." Thomas reached up and swiped at his forehead, then chuckled. "It was worth every drop."

Anna shook her head. "I still cannot believe it." She could hear the wonder in her own voice. "To think that there might actually be justice in Corbin."

"Thanks to you, Anna," Thomas said quietly.

Anna frowned. "Me? I was not even there."

"If not for you, the Tuckers might have kept on as they were, going along with the crowd, following the loudest voices, too afraid of persecution to speak against it."

Anna shook her head. Sarah was a strong, intelligent woman. She would have decided to do the right thing on her own without Anna. In fact, this was exactly what she had done.

Shouts clamored outside on the lawn.

Thomas hurried out the door, and the boys scrambled to follow.

Anna rose with her son and went to the window.

"You won't get away with this," a female voice shouted. "My daddy and my granddaddy were both Grand Dragons."

Anna could not see what was happening, so she placed the baby in the cradle and went outside.

Smoke drifted across the lawn. Crackling sounds and smoke poured out of the woodworks shop, then flames burst from the roof.

Anna coughed and tried to see who was out there, but the smoke was growing thicker by the second.

Thomas and Teddy ran toward the shop with buckets of water and tossed them on the burning building. Flames shot out the windows now, curling up and over the roof, engulfing it in orange tongues and giant billows of black smoke.

"The lacquer!" Teddy shouted. "It'll blow!" He took off toward the pump again.

Jimmy and Jack arrived with more water. Voices and shouts became louder as neighbors and townsfolk came running from the road.

"*You're* the ones who should be rotting in jail," a woman yelled.

Anna knew that voice, and she could see her now. Alice Withers stood near the far end of the shop with a can of kerosene.

Anna held her breath, heart racing. The woman had fuel near flames.

"You don't get to stay here all safe and snug while my husband, the Alton County Sheriff, rots in a jail cell. You're getting what's coming to you."

More people came running.

Penny Withers pulled into the driveway, skidded to a stop, then jumped out and ran to her mother.

Thomas tossed water at the burning building, while others ran to get more. The boys took turns dousing the fire, but the shop was now completely engulfed in flames.

Alice saw Anna and stormed toward the porch, her eyes full of loathing. "You have no business walking around free. If you won't leave, then you'll burn."

Anna gasped and took a step back.

"Mother!" Penny shouted, following Alice. "What are you doing?"

"They're getting exactly what they deserve!" Alice shouted, coughing. She looked around her as if searching for something, then saw a stick of firewood and picked it up. "They can't get away with this."

"No, Mother, stop! You can't do that!"

Alice turned to her. "They had your father—the sheriff—*arrested*. And the filthy animals have to nerve to walk around free?" She ran past the shop toward her gas can, but part of the burning roof fell away and struck her.

Alice was on fire.

Without thinking, Anna ran to her and knocked her to the ground. Penny was right behind her. She tried to pull Anna off at first, but Anna continued to slap at the flames on Alice's clothing. Penny stopped tugging, as if suddenly realizing what Anna was doing, and joined her, and together they slapped out the flames. Then they turned Alice over.

She was unconscious.

Thomas came quickly, scooped up the woman, carried her away from the fire, and set her on the lawn in front of the house. He felt her neck, put an ear to her nose and listened, then opened her mouth and blew breath into her. He pressed her chest, then blew in her mouth again.

"Press her chest in the middle, like this," he croaked.

Penny stared, eyes wide, frozen.

Anna pumped the woman's chest as Thomas had done.

More people came to try to put out the fire and others gathered around, all shouting at once. A fire engine's siren sounded in the distance, growing louder as it approached.

Thomas kept blowing breath into Alice until finally, she coughed. "Give her room," he shouted. Alice coughed again, and her eyes fluttered open.

"Alice Withers is going to jail, just like her husband," someone shouted. "We saw her do it. Someone hold her until the deputy comes. And grab the daughter, too."

The crowd closed in on Penny.

"Penny did not set the fire," Anna hollered above the noise. "She had nothing to do with it. Let her go."

"She's just like her folks," one man shouted. "*All* the Withers are evil. Lock 'em *all* up."

"No!" Anna shouted. "No more blanket accusations. No more blind assumptions. No more! Just...stop!"

The people surrounding Penny stepped back, while the fire engine pulled in, siren blaring. Firemen and others jumped into action, battling the fire.

Penny turned to Anna, angry tears filling her eyes. "This is great. *Both* of my parents are going to jail."

"Do you think this is unjust?" Anna asked. "They have both committed serious crimes."

Penny watched as a police car approached. "I didn't know my daddy killed that sheriff." Her voice was raw. "I didn't know they would go this far..."

"Maybe you did not want to know."

Penny turned, tears brimming, and met Anna's eyes. "Why did you do that? She hated you and tried to hurt you. Why did you try to save her?"

Anna frowned. "She was fighting for her life. Would you not do the same?"

"Are you asking if I'd lift a finger to help an enemy? No, I don't think I would."

"You would not show mercy?"

The young woman shook her head. "No. And I don't understand why you would, either."

Anna glanced at Alice, who was being carried away on a stretcher, accompanied by an officer. "Will we not all need mercy at some time in our lives? Mercy we do not deserve? It is a precious gift, and yet it is free. Everyone has the power to give it."

Albert came to Anna, carrying her crying son with a delicate awkwardness as if the infant was a slippery china teacup. Thanking him, she took her baby and bounced him, making shushing sounds.

Penny's nostrils flared at the sight of the child.

"If I were in Alice's place," Anna said quietly, "I would hope to be shown mercy."

Penny turned away, shook her head. She swiped at her cheeks, still shaking her head. "What am I supposed to do now? I have nobody."

"This is only true if you choose it to be," Anna said. She studied Penny, a once assertive girl, who had appeared to know who she was and what she wanted, now faltering. Struggling. Perhaps with disillusionment. Perhaps with the stark revelation of the true ugliness she had based her beliefs on. Anna could almost hear the timbers of Penny's world cracking and falling, crashing down like the burning workshop beside them. The sound of her world falling apart.

What Anna just said about mercy would never be true if she herself could not live it.

She drew a deep breath. "Penny, I believe that if you would choose to have the compassion and acceptance for others that your parents could not, you will never be alone."

Penny did not respond.

Anna looked down. Her son was asleep. She bent and kissed his head, then rose with him and headed for the house. The fire was nearly out, but the smoke was still billowing, and she feared the baby was breathing it in.

"Wait," Penny said.

At the porch, Anna stopped and waited for Penny.

"Sarah Tucker was talking about you one day." Penny looked across the lawn, at the bystanders and emergency workers, at the boys, at Thomas. She straightened her shoulders, then turned to Anna. "She told me, 'Anna's not bad. You just have to get to know her.'"

Anna smiled, bit her lip, then burst out laughing, drawing stares.

Penny scowled. "What's so funny?"

"She said the same thing to me about *you*."

At first, Penny's jaw dropped. Then a faint smile lifted one side of her mouth.

Thirty-Six

1 August

My Love,

First, the bad news: the wood shop was completely destroyed by fire. But Thomas and the boys are rebuilding and will be able to replace some of their tools, with the community's help.

Now, the good news: Corbin's citizens have chosen to remove the biggest seed of hatred in their midst. I think the walls that kept people closed to one another are starting to crumble, and in time, I believe they will fall. As long as they always remember this and never turn a blind eye to bigotry again.

Samuel is stronger. It turns out much of his running was not "away" but "to" a place that holds memories of his mother. A place he still visits. He places whittled figures there for her, in case she ever returns. Just to let her know he is okay. The figures are of Jesus, Thomas, and the other boys. He also left a little Noah and King David. All of his heroes, he says. I think he will be a man of G-d, one day. Or, perhaps...he already is.

Thomas is home with enough money to last a while, so I am preparing to move on. Mary Francis found a lonely widow in Chicago who has agreed to let me room with her for free! She does not mind that I am Jewish and hopes I will cook for her sometimes. Of course! I will do this with joy. See,

I am going to be purposeful in singular moments, as you so wisely urged, and I will look for joy in small things.

I will not burden you with what I am feeling, partly because right now, my emotions are in a constant state of upheaval. The thought of leaving Thomas and the boys crushes the air from me. But I must hope this will one day pass. I am looking only ahead now. I will focus on Papa and the day I can report that he is found, or at least what has become of him. And I am looking forward to the day I might be invited to return home, like Noah's dove, empty-handed. Well, not so empty. I may have a tiny olive branch, perhaps. If by some great miracle, it might now be seen as one. Only time will tell.

Forgive my cryptic messages, dearest. I hope that one day soon, all will be made plain.

On August first, the baby was a week old, and while Anna had already decided there would be no bris, her son still needed a name.

And he ought to receive *some* sort of blessing over his life, especially now that the two of them would be setting out together into the unknown.

She finally decided she would simply have to name him and bless him herself, the best she could.

Sarah knocked at the kitchen door with another casserole and latest news of the Withers investigation. Anna asked her to come outside to where Thomas and the others were working on rebuilding the shop, so they could all hear the news as well. Thomas and the boys greeted Sarah and stopped hammering to listen.

Sarah told them that an exhumation and autopsy by the state police had concluded that Colin Dooley had died of poisoning, and Boyd Withers had been formally charged with his murder. In addition to that, three former Klansmen were willing to testify that he had told them about his intentions.

Thomas and the boys cheered.

"That's the best news I've heard in a long time," Thomas said.

Anna heaved a sigh. "Yes. What a relief to know that the late sheriff will receive justice, and Boyd Withers no longer has the power to harm anyone."

"Not only that," Sarah added, "but soon after Boyd's arrest, the local chapter of the Klan tucked tail and scattered. And Alice's local committees have split up, too."

Thomas and the boys, still discussing the news, went back about their work.

Sarah took the baby from Anna and stroked his cheek. "Funny how nobody wants anything to do with the Witherses, now that they been charged with crimes. Folks are startin' to figure out that all them shockin' stories about foreigners and coloreds don't add up." Sarah kissed the baby, then chuckled. "Well, they *may* be figurin' it out because I been goin' around tellin' everyone that all them stories can't be true, like you said. A whole group of people can't be all bad, or all anything. Each person is just as precious in the sight of God as the next one."

Anna studied her friend, wondering how many ways Sarah would continue to surprise her. "What a wise, bold thing to do, Sarah. You are an inspiration."

"Me?" Sarah smiled and seemed to stand a little taller.

Anna returned her smile. "I wonder what is left for people at the café to talk about *now*."

"How to get along, I guess." Sarah cooed at the baby. "So now what about this handsome little fella? Is he ever gonna have a name?"

Thomas paused his hammering and stole a sideways glance at the baby.

Anna drew a deep breath. "He will be eight days old tomorrow. Since I cannot have a bris, I have decided to name and bless him myself."

"Bless him? Well, you're in luck. You got a minister right there who can do that."

"Minister?" Anna's brows rose. She glanced at Thomas.

Thomas put down his hammer. "I'm...no rabbi, but I'd be honored to say a prayer for him, if you want me to," he said.

Honored? To bless an illegitimate child?

"I'll bring food," Sarah said, eyes alight. "And maybe we can invite the Sisters Mary, too. Might as well make it a full house."

"Yes," Anna said. "Sister Mary Francis delivered him, after all."

Sarah clapped her hands. "It's all settled. We'll be here tomorrow for Corbin's first Jewish, Baptist, Catholic version of...well, I don't know what to call it, but it'll sure be somethin'."

Anna smiled. There was a time she would have thought such an odd collection of faiths strange and pointless. But not now. Those who had been part of Anna's life for the past five months would help her give this tiny boy a blessed start in life, despite how different their beliefs were. This would be the strangest ceremony she had ever seen, and she could not wait to see it.

The next day, the Sisters Mary, Thomas and the boys, and the Tuckers all gathered on the bank of Plum Creek, where Anna had first met the boys.

Anna held her son, and everyone stood around her.

"You'll have to tell us what you want us to do, Anna," Thomas said, apologetically. "I'm a Baptist. We usually do our thing in the creek over there."

Anna smiled at everyone and shrugged. "I am afraid this is new to me as well. We are dissimilar but united, like mismatched cloth from different sources, joined at the edges and stitched together, for one purpose."

"Like a crazy quilt," Sister Mary Agnes said, smiling. "I like that."

"Thank you for allowing me to be part of your lives, if only for a short time," Anna said quietly. "If these past months have taught me nothing else, they have taught me that though I am only a seed blowing in the wind, I must still be fruitful wherever I land. I have learned that wherever we find ourselves, we must have the courage to stretch out roots and produce something useful, even in times of difficulty. We must bloom boldly in whatever field our seed has fallen."

Thomas looked away, past the creek, toward the golden sea of grain beyond the town.

Sarah wiped a tear from her cheek.

Anna turned to Thomas. "I would like to ask the Lord to help me raise him to be a kind, honorable man. Like Gabriel did for you."

Nodding, Thomas said nothing. He appeared unable to speak.

Anna placed the child in Thomas's arms.

Thomas cleared his throat, then prayed a prayer of blessing, dedicating the child to the Lord, asking God to protect him, and to help him grow in favor and knowledge and wisdom, that he might be a steadfast man of faith who follows God with his whole heart.

"I pray that he'll come to know You at an early age, and to be Your guiding light to those around him," he said. "And that he would be a good son and a blessing to his mother."

Blessing...

Tears flowed down Anna's face. For the longest time, Anna would not have called this child a blessing. But perhaps now... She looked up and met Sarah's gaze.

Sarah was crying, but she smiled at Anna.

Thomas handed the child back to her.

Anna beckoned the six older boys closer, knowing they were eagerly waiting for this last part. "There is a Jewish saying, 'With each child, the world begins anew.'" She caressed her son's tiny fist and looked into his eyes. "You, little boy, are the first of my family to be born in America. May you do great things. Only God knows the plans He has for you. Who knows, maybe you will change the world."

She kissed her son.

"Your Hebrew name is Yesha'yahu, which means, 'God is Salvation.' And Shemu'el, which means, 'God has heard.'"

Her gaze remained on her son.

"His English name is Isaiah Samuel..." She swallowed hard, then added, "Chandler."

A thick silence followed.

Anna waited, then finally looked up.

Thomas was watching the child, his face completely unreadable.

"Isaiah...Samuel...Chandler," Samuel said slowly. "God saves, and God hears. Yes, ma'am, that's a real fine name." He smiled.

Thirty-Seven

FINISHED.

This was the word Anna was trying to make her heart accept. Not complete, but finished. Finished with all that she had set out to do in this place, and finished with what she had been asked to do. Any incompleteness she still felt would have to go away, retreat into the dark, quiet corners of all that might have been. She had much to be thankful for. She had grown, and her heart had grown. She had loved.

And now, she had a son, and together, they would set out in a few days, and Anna would be his champion, and Isaiah would grow up to be a good man one day.

If only he would be good *now* and stop crying and go to sleep.

Anna walked her wailing son around the tiny bedroom, shushing him. Exhaustion had set in. The past three nights, Isaiah had cried on and off all night long, and would not nurse, but only grew angrier every time she tried.

The tiny boy did not understand that this was becoming a very bad habit.

She sat in the rocker and rocked him, but his crying only grew worse. He clearly did *not* want her to sit and relieve her tired back. How did babies know?

But the longer she went without sleep, the testier she felt. Sarah had told her the day before to try to relax because babies can tell when their mamas are tense, but this did not help. In fact, she had told Sarah that telling her to stop being tense only made her *more* tense.

She cried fresh tears, miserable that she had snapped at her friend. She tried not to think about it now, as she shushed and bounced the child.

"What do you *want*, little boy?" she whispered. "You are too young to be so dissatisfied with life already. I do not have the answers. I would not have them even if I were *not* too exhausted to think. Please go to sleep, Isaiah."

She walked in circles, bouncing him and crying herself, certain that she could sink into the bed and sleep for a week.

A tap on the door stilled her. "Anna?" Thomas's voice.

"Come in," she said, then continued shushing.

The door opened a few inches and Thomas poked his head inside. "Anything I can do to help?"

Any trick to calming the child at this point was far beyond Anna. She shook her head. "I do not know. I have tried everything. I am trying to fig-ure out what he wants, but with him yelling at me this way, I cannot think."

Thomas stepped quietly into the room. "Why don't you let him yell at me for a change, so you can rest."

Anna stared at him. How long could a man put up with an inconsolable infant? But did she have a choice?

Reluctantly, Anna agreed to let him try and handed him over. She watched as Thomas shushed and patted Isaiah, then carried him out and closed the door behind him.

Too fatigued and too bewildered to worry, and engulfed by the sudden silence, Anna laid down and immediately dozed off.

Sometime later, she awoke. Thomas was in the room, carefully laying Isaiah in his cradle. A *sleeping* Isaiah. Thomas lingered there, his back to her, unaware of Anna's scrutiny. The way he watched the sleeping infant made her heart swell to nearly bursting, threatening to squeeze the air from her lungs. He moved to leave.

"Thomas..." she whispered.

He froze but did not turn.

"I cannot do this anymore." Instant regret seized her. Had she said that aloud?

"You're exhausted," he whispered back, then he turned to her. "It'll be okay. Things will look better after you've gotten some rest."

"No, I mean...I cannot keep living like this." *Pretending that your hatred does not break my heart every moment of every day. Pretending that I do not love you with all my being.*

A strange look dawned on his face, a look of resignation. "I know."

Did he?

Thomas returned to the cradle. "You agreed to stay until Sam was well. That's all I asked of you, and you've done that and more." He shook his head. "I won't keep you any longer. But before you go, if you want to annul the marriage and be free of me, I'll make the arrangements," he said, his voice low. "Or you can leave things as they are and keep my name...if that'll help you and Isaiah have an easier way in life. Tell people whatever you like about being married—the truth, a story, doesn't matter to me."

The words stung as his meaning became suddenly clear. Not only did he have no more need of her, he did not care what she did or where she went from there.

He ran a palm along the polished edge of the cradle. "I never wanted you to feel tied down or forced to stay. You did as you were asked. You're free to go your own way."

Finished, and now dismissed. He wanted her to leave.

Except, what he was telling her now about keeping his name made no sense...

"If I go my own way, as you say," she said, still sorting through his strange offer, "but remain married to you, then *you* would be tied down."

"Don't worry about me." His voice was so low, she could barely hear him.

"But this is not fair to you," she whispered. "Surely you will meet someone, and then you will want—"

"Someone?" He turned to her, his eyes dark and penetrating. Then just as suddenly, he turned his attention back to the baby. He stroked Isaiah's soft hair, his gaze never leaving the child. "You mean someone who knows me like no one else ever has? Someone gentle and beautiful and strong and wise? Who fills me with joy just by being near?"

His whispered words surrounded her like a fog, shifting and indistinct.

Moonlight cast a milky glow around his silhouette. "Someone I think about so much when we're apart that I can't eat or sleep? Someone whose smile grips me, steals my breath away? Who makes me feel like I've finally come home?" Thomas turned to her, his face etched with the anguish of profound loss. "Anna, do you really think I could ever find someone like that again?"

She could not breathe.

His eyes were dark, like a gathering storm. "Heaven help me, but I've loved you since the moment I first laid eyes on you." His voice broke. "And I can't stop thinking about you even though I've tried everything to get you out of my heart and mind."

Joy washed through her like an enormous wave. She did not know where it began or ended. She only knew she could not feel her legs.

He turned away, jaw muscles rippling. The way he looked when he was angry, wounded. Lost.

Suddenly, she understood. He loved her, but he did not *want* to love her.

Tears clogged her throat. "You wish to get me out of your heart because I am immoral. Spoiled." She could barely whisper the words. "Because what I have done is unforgiveable."

He frowned, shaking his head. "No. At first, I was crushed when I learned of your pregnancy. And yes, I was hurt. Deeply hurt. But...I don't hold it against you."

Anna let his words sink into her heart, pondering them. "Then why have you been so distant, so cold? Avoiding me?"

He regarded her carefully. "I'm sorry if I was cold. But what else can I do? How can I be near the woman I love when I know her heart is already spoken for?" He turned away abruptly.

"My heart...*is* spoken for," Anna said, slowly, confused. "Which is the reason that I did not marry the farmer in Ohio. I could not promise to love one man when I love another. But how could *you* know?"

Thomas stiffened. "I know. After you left on the train to Ohio, I found something you left behind." He went to the window and took down a fold-ed paper from the windowsill. "This."

He unfolded the familiar paper, identical to the pages she had been tearing from her journal to write letters. He looked pained as he read it. "'My Love, someday I will explain why I had to leave. Please trust me that it was necessary, and the only choice I had. I am sorry for the pain I have caused and for the position my leaving has put you in. In answer to your letter, my situation is growing more difficult. I would be lying if I said it were not. Do not worry, though, I am well, but since I am being honest, missing you is especially unbearable right now. I long for the day when we can be together again. No matter what happens, you are forever in my heart. -A.'"

His chest heaved, as if saying the words aloud tore something from inside him.

"I was writing to Shayna, my sister." Tears poured down, wetting Anna's face. "I must have misplaced one of my replies to her."

Confusion furrowed his brow. "Your *sister*?" He studied Anna, then the letter again. "Not Isaiah's father?" Bewildered, he glanced away without seeing, as if sorting through a mountain of thoughts. "All these past weeks, I thought you were pining for a lover you couldn't be with."

"I have no lover," she whispered.

"Then...who is Isaiah's father?"

"I do not know his *father*, as you call him. Nor do I ever wish to."

Thomas opened his mouth but seemed at a complete loss for words.

"I made a terrible, foolish mistake." She wiped her wet cheeks.

He went to the cradle and watched the sleeping baby. "Tell me," he whispered.

She drew a deep breath and began with the night she went out with Rosie and her friends, of her arrogance and flattered ego, of her date and the whiskey that kept coming.

Then she rose and went to the window where she did not have to look at him and she continued, telling him how the date had progressed. She could not bring herself to see his expression when he heard the most indecent part.

Thomas said nothing, so she went on quickly about discovering she was pregnant, visiting the Campbell Home, and her mother's ultimatum. Taking a deep breath to keep from crying, she told him of the day she left home, her journey west, and the heartache of knowing she would never see her family again.

He remained silent, which unnerved Anna, given the way she had just bared her soul.

"And then...I met three young truants who were kind enough to share a meal with me."

He still said nothing.

Slowly, she turned to see him. The tangle of emotions on his face was impossible to read. She tore her gaze away. "So there is no lover, no father, only my insolence and stupidity. I have brought shame to my family and a curse on my sisters. If not for my arrogance—"

"No," he whispered.

She stared at him, confused.

He was shaking his head. "Anna, there's something you need to understand. The man who was supposed to be your date was a brute. He knew exactly what he was doing. The whiskey, a naïve girl like you—"

"*I* am naïve?"

"About sex? I hate to say it, but yes, I believe you are." His nostrils flared. "And I guarantee that guy knew it. How much whiskey do you usually drink?"

"None...besides that night."

"I thought so." He nodded. "And how many of those drinks did *he* give you?"

This was not hard to remember. "All of them."

His lips tightened and he looked around the room as if needing something to punch. "He planned right from the start to weaken your resistance so he could have his way with you. It was deliberate. Oh, Anna, don't you see? He got you drunk, then he—" His jaw clenched. "He forced himself on you." His body twitched, nostrils flaring. "What I'd give to be alone with that guy. Just for an hour."

She could still hear her mother's words. "Because I...was alone with him, my mother thinks very differently about it. She believes I am to blame."

"I don't know your mother, but I know you, and you're not immoral."

"But if I had not gone there in the first place, if I had not been acting so childish—"

"Anna." Thomas came to her and took hold of her arms gently, willing her to look into his eyes. "It doesn't matter where you went, you're not to blame for what he did. I understand what you're saying. Sure, it would have been wiser not to argue with your mother. You shouldn't have agreed to go to a speakeasy. Shouldn't have tried the whiskey. You made mistakes. But none of those mistakes make what that animal did your fault."

She stared at him. "But I—"

"You are not to blame for *his* brutality," he said slowly, punctuating each word.

The meaning of his words suddenly became clear. She bit her quivering lips, desperate to keep from crying.

"Oh, my dear Anna," he whispered. "All this time, you've been carrying around an enormous load of shame you don't deserve."

She burst out crying and slapped both hands over her mouth to keep from waking the baby.

Thomas quickly pulled her to him and held her, gently muffling her sobs against his chest, quieting the sounds. Not shushing her, but allowing her a place to release the long-held shame, the pent-up pain, the mortifying disgrace. His arms encircled her lovingly, patiently, with his kind, compassionate strength.

Anna wept against him, against the rapid beating of his heart. She tried to curb the sobs, but the burden she had been bearing all alone had been so crushing, the sudden void it left so intense. The load had been so heavy, so overwhelming, keeping her a prisoner, making her feel so dirty, forcing her to keep her distance from everyone, leaving her so bereft of touch, of life, of love. She gulped air and summoned control of herself.

Thomas released her, then tipped up her chin and looked into her eyes. "I don't know how you got such a notion so firmly planted in your head, but you are not shameful or repulsive or unforgiveable, or any of the terrible things you've been thinking. I know you and that you're none of those things. I hope one day, you'll know, too. And I hope you'll realize that there is forgiveness for the mistakes you made."

"I have not asked for God's forgiveness," she whispered, wiping her eyes and nose. She shook her head. "I did not think He could."

"Oh, He can, and He will. He can do more than we can ever ask or imagine. He loves you, Anna. All you have to do is ask, He's already there, ready and waiting. He longs for you to have a relationship with Him. But there's someone else who needs to forgive you."

She nodded, fresh tears falling. "Mama."

"No. *You.*"

Frowning, she looked into his eyes, but whatever made him so certain of this was a mystery. "I need to forgive myself?"

"Don't you?"

"Perhaps."

"Well, that's a start." He smiled faintly. Yet there was something about him that looked rattled. Unsettled still. He drew a shaky breath. "So, back to the other thing you said. Ever since I found that letter, I've been... Well, I assumed the letter meant that you'd been writing to a lover the whole time you were here. But now I find out all those letters were just...to your sister."

She nodded. "My sister Shayna is also my dearest friend."

"I sure wish I'd known that." He looked into her eyes, searching. "And now you tell me you couldn't marry the farmer because..." He swallowed hard. "You loved someone else."

"It is true, and I still do." She touched his face lightly. "Rather desperately."

He drew a sharp breath at her touch, then studied her, bewildered. "How? After I threw you out?"

"You did not throw me out," she whispered, shaking her head.

"But I let them chase you off like an animal, in your condition, all alone—"

"It did not make me love you any less."

He grimaced. "And the way I've been treating you since you came back, all because I thought—"

"You have been deeply wounded, Thomas. I could understand your disgust with me—"

"No, shhh," he said, shaking his head. His eyes glittered with unshed tears. "No. Don't say that. Don't ever say that."

"But I—"

He kissed her suddenly, gently, his lips warm and tender, and she melted, losing herself in the intensity of his touch. His kiss, so full of love and wonder and complete acceptance, shook her to the core, stole her breath, made her heart soar like a dove in flight, once caged, but now free and heading home.

No, she *was* home. *This* was home.

His hands gently framed her face and he pulled back a little, looking slightly guilty. "Sorry, I just...thought you should stop talking."

Anna stifled a smile. He was handsome even when he looked guilty. "Is this sort of interruption going to become a habit?"

His brows rose. "That's not a bad idea." He sobered. "Anna, there's one more thing I need to know."

She frowned. Had she left something out? What else was there to tell?

He took her hands in his and looked down at them. "Anna, when I was far away and alone, day after day, all I could think about was how empty my life was going to be after you left us for good. And even though I thought you loved someone else, I wished like crazy that you might somehow...change your mind or...find some reason to stay."

He knelt down on one knee and then looked up, meeting her gaze. "Anna, I don't want you to leave. Not ever. I'm in love with you and I want to spend the rest of my life loving you." His expression softened, and hope shone in his eyes. "Will you marry me?"

Her heart did a somersault. She puffed out a breathless little laugh. "I think you have forgotten. I am already married to you."

He shook his head. "I'm not asking you to take care of my boys or my chickens, or to be our teacher, or anything else." He looked at her with a hopeful solemnity that brought fresh tears to her eyes. "I'm asking if you'll have me. I'm asking if you'll be my wife and...let me try to be a real husband to you."

Tears blurred her eyes. "Yes, Thomas," she whispered. "Yes, I will have you. Yes, I love you and I want to be your wife. I can think of nothing I want more than to wake up beside you every day for the rest of my life."

With a sigh, he closed his eyes, then he stood up and tugged her into his arms. He held her so tight she could barely breathe—or perhaps it was the sudden rush of joy that stole her breath. He held her as if he would never let go, and she rested there, in the arms of the man she loved with all of her heart, who knew her and forgave her and welcomed her fully and completely. This was where she belonged.

Smiling up at him, she touched his face again, hoping he did not mind, because she would never tire of touching him.

With a deep sigh, he returned her smile. "Of course, a lot of sawdust and a pack of grimy boys are still part of the deal, but you don't have to—"

She stopped him with a kiss, long and sweet and full of love. All her doubts and all her shame had vanished. All that remained was love. She was going to love him with every part of her, with all the compassion and honor and passion and promise she had within her.

She caressed his face in both hands and pulled him closer, deepening the kiss.

A low sound came from his throat.

She pulled back to see him.

His eyes were still closed. "Wowwwww," he breathed.

"I just thought you should stop talking." She could not repress her smile.

He opened his eyes slowly, and then smiled. "Yes, ma'am," he whispered. "You are welcome to interrupt me anytime."

Thirty-Eight

24 December 1933
Corbin, Indiana

Dear Mama,

It is Christmas Eve and I am sorry to say this letter is long overdue. I am sorry for many things. For not writing sooner. For the things I have done that brought devastating consequences to our family. For all the pain and suffering I have put you through. I hope one day you can find it in your heart to forgive me.

My son was born on the 25th of July, delivered by a Catholic nun and a Protestant corn farmer. He was blessed at eight days old by a Baptist, and he is brother to six older boys, including a Negro.

Life is indeed like a crazy quilt.

If only all of humanity were forced to be likewise joined together by threads of love, without walls or settlements or agendas, and forced to look beyond our minor differences, and if we had no choice but to depend on one another, could such a world succeed?

Compassion is vital if we are ever to have unity. Mercy, grace, and compassion are the key to accepting what we do not understand, whether it be people who are different, or a heritage beyond our choosing, or a Love that gives up what is most precious of all.

I am proud to be a Jew, and I will always be a Jew. I am also a woman who is seeking to understand the sovereignty *of G-d, and to accept that He alone, as the Author of life, love, and all of creation, knows best. If ultimate unity is found in Him alone, I will consider all the aspects of His plan. If ultimate love is found in the ultimate sacrifice, then I will consider what this cross of Christ truly means.*

In the meantime, I am wife to a most kind, wonderful (and handsome) man, and mother to seven unruly sons. Mama, I have new appreciation for what you suffer. Thank you for your love and sacrifice, including many nights without sleep. I remember the child you lost, and I am so sorry. I do not know the depth of your loss and the brokenness of your heart. But I do know that when we are given the chance to redeem a lost relationship, it is a blessing to be embraced.

I love you. And I forgive you. I hope one day to see you again and tell you this in person.

I have not told my sisters and brother about the child. I will leave the telling of this to you, if you wish them to know. My husband and I hope to visit Manhattan in the spring. Whether or not you meet the three of us will be entirely up to you.

Your Loving Daughter,
Channah Leibowicz Chandler

P.S. I am still searching for Papa. I have recently learned that he may in fact be alive. As soon as I learn more, I will tell you.

P.P.S. In case you are curious, Isaiah is a beautiful five-month old boy with big brown eyes who loves his six brothers and his daddy. He giggles at worms, loves chewing on wooden blocks which his brothers make for him, and loves to pull the fur on the neighbor's new puppy, Samson. And he would very much like to meet his grandmother someday.

24 March, 1934

Dearest Shayna,

Finally, the news you and Mama have been waiting for. I have found Papa. He is alive. But there is more, however, so brace yourself. Let me start at the beginning...

Sister Mary Francis is handy in ways far beyond lug wrenches and midwifery. She took Papa's name and made inquiries. Thanks to the help of her friends in prison ministry, we found him. He is serving time at the state penitentiary in Joliet, Illinois, 30 miles from Chicago. When he heard that I was inquiring after him, he refused to see me. But I ignored his wishes, which will not surprise you. My husband accompanied me last month to the prison and I spoke to Papa. More about that in a moment.

Shayna, at the end of our visit, I convinced him to give me a letter for Mama. I will give it to her myself, if she will see me, as we are planning a trip to Manhattan next month. All three of us.

And now that Mama has told you, yes, you will get to meet your nephew, Isaiah, the first Leibowicz born in America. He is eager to meet his aunties, uncle, and bubbe.

I am ignoring Papa's wishes. I told him that he must trust me. Because I, of all people in this family, understand that shame is a great thief. He tried to forbid me to see him, told me to forget about him, told me that he no longer deserves to be a part of our family. He does not wish for Mama or any of you to know that he is alive or where he is. He does not want you to know that he became infatuated with the allure of quick, plentiful money or what he was willing to do for it. He does not want any of you to know the wickedness he is guilty of. He regrets the blackmail and extortion and all of the things he did for the mob. I told him that Mama never stopped believing in him. He said he does not deserve her faith. His regret for his crimes and for abandoning his family crushes him. He wishes to die and end the curse he believes he is to our family.

But I will not allow this. I told him that he is not a curse.

That he is loved, and that forgiveness and mercy are always possible because they are gifts from G-d. We are all capable of choosing mercy. It costs nothing but can mean everything, especially to a remorseful man in desperate need of redemption whose life dangles on a thread.

The prison walls are not the only ones that confine Papa. He is also confined by invisible walls he has built around himself in order to protect us. He feels he is untouchable, dirty.

I know this feeling, Shayna. He is what I <u>would</u> have become, had I succeeded in walling myself off from those I love. I understand what he is trying to do and why. But I also understand that if love is genuine, then compassion must follow, because compassion is the most basic act of love.

On behalf of our family, I offered Papa mercy, forgiveness, and restoration. I hope I acted as you all would have me do. It was difficult for him, and he would not take it at first, but he finally accepted my offered hand.

None of us can ever fully atone for our sins, but we can find redemption in forgiveness. (My husband was the one who pointed this out. See, he is ever the preacher, whether he stands behind a pulpit or not.)

Shayna, I am so eager to see you I can scarcely stand it. I will come bearing Papa's letter, my chubby, drooling "olive branch," and a white flag. I hope she will see me, but if she will not, I will not hold it against her.

All My Love,

Anna

Thirty-Nine

Thursday, April 5, 1934
Lower East Side, New York

THOMAS REACHED FOR ANNA'S HAND AND GAVE IT A GENTLE squeeze.

She tore her gaze away from the third-story window high above them and looked at her incredibly patient husband, suddenly questioning everything about this trip, her hopes, her plan. Her brilliant plan.

What had she been thinking?

Isaiah tugged on her hair and beamed a wide, dimpled smile with all of two bottom teeth. As if to say, *Mama, you worry too much. Look at me! Who would not love this face?*

She transferred Isaiah into his daddy's arms and took a deep breath. "I will call you up if all goes well. Wish me luck."

Thomas kissed her soundly. "I'll pray you find favor," he said with a wink.

Isaiah chuckled.

The tenement had changed very little. She climbed three flights of narrow stairs and stood at the door on the bare landing. She drew a breath, raised a shaky hand, and knocked.

The door opened to loud cries and exclamations. Shayna, Rivka, and Anshel stood waiting, all dressed up and neatly pressed as if going to shul. They rushed to her all at once, nearly knocking her down, talking over one another.

"Hello to you too," Anna said with a laugh. "Can I at least get one foot inside before you toss me down the stairwell?"

They pulled her inside, touching and hugging her. Anna had forgotten their touch, forgotten how much she missed the vitality they gave her.

Smiling, she hugged and tousled and answered and nodded, all the while looking beyond them. Mama did not seem to be at home.

Her heart sank.

She brightened and pulled a penny candy from her pocket and handed it to Anshel. "See? I have not forgotten."

Shayna's eyes glistened. "Oh, how I have missed you, Anna."

Rivka hugged Anna around the middle as if she would never let her go.

"Are you planning on leaving any for me?"

Mama stepped out of the bedroom. And had spoken in English.

Anna gasped. "Mama?"

Her siblings stepped back, and Anna faced her mother.

Tears filled Mama's eyes, and her face threatened to crumple. She rubbed her nose and told the other three to leave them alone for a moment.

Once Anna's sisters and brother had gone out, Mama studied Anna from head to toe. "You look well."

"I am. And you?"

She shrugged. "No use complaining about things I cannot change."

Anna smiled. "You are speaking English now."

Mama shrugged again. "Sometimes, change is necessary. When it is helpful for others."

Anna's brows rose. This was also new. "You speak it well."

"I am working on it. I want to meet your Christian husband. But first, there is something I need to tell you."

Anna stilled.

"When I insisted you go to that home, the one for unwed mothers, when I said..." She frowned, rubbed her nose again, turning it red. "When I said you would have no home with me, I did not expect you to go away. To set off across the country as you did."

"It was an ultimatum, Mama," she said gently. "What else was I to think?"

Mama frowned, her lips quivering. "I thought you were forever lost to me. And any harm that might have come to you would have been my doing. I could never forgive myself."

Anna's mouth gaped. This was not the exchange she had envisioned. Tears stung her eyes. "I am sorry, Mama. For everything."

Mama took a long, head-to-toe look at Anna. "Wait a minute." She turned and went into the bedroom.

Anna glanced around. A mountain of garments still buried Mama's sewing machine.

She returned with a thick stack of envelopes tied with string. She came to Anna with the bundle held close to her chest. It took Anna a moment to recognize the envelopes. They were her letters to Shayna. All of them, by the looks of it. And they were well-worn, as if read repeatedly.

Anna met her mother's gaze, confused.

"Once I discovered you had been writing, I made her read them to me. Every one of them."

Anna gasped. Mama had read *all* of her letters?

"She translated them. And then I learned to read English and read them myself."

"Why did you not tell me sooner? Why did you not write?"

Mama's lips tightened. "I pushed you away, and I lost you. I did not deserve a second chance."

"No, Mama. See? Shame is a terrible thief." Anna sighed. "Here is one more letter for you," she said, handing over Papa's letter. "The one that you have been waiting very patiently for."

Mama's face crumpled. "You are a good and brave woman, Channah."

"So are you, Mama," Anna said, crying.

Her mother's brows rose. She took a kerchief and blew her nose. "We have both made mistakes."

"Yes." Anna nodded, wiping her eyes.

"But now you are back. You are a wife, and a mother. And I am a bubbe. A grandmother." She tilted her head, as if listening to how the word sounded in two languages. "So. I hope to put the past behind and look only ahead."

Anna nodded, and shrugged. "Except when the past contains lessons we can learn from and try not to repeat. But yes, I can put the past behind."

"Good. So where is he?"

Anna blinked, feigning ignorance of her mother's meaning. "Which one?"

With a frown, Mama waved Anna away. "Of course I want to meet your handsome husband, Channah, but I already know what I need to know about *him* from all your letters. Where is the boy? I have waited a long time to meet my grandson."

LETTER TO THE EDITOR
Chicago Tribune

December 1, 2019

Dear Sir,

Folks are always asking what's my secret to longevity. Truth is, I'm still surprised I made it past the age of ten. I don't reckon I would have, if not for a pretty young hobo I met in 1933.

In my ninety-six years, I've seen many things. Things my caregivers say are just twisted bits of memory fluttering like a dove trapped in an old man's brain. But I've seen things these young folks ain't never seen or even imagined. Horrific things that turned my world inside out and silenced my tongue.

I've seen pointy-headed ghosts standing silent in the woods just beyond my home. I've seen flames in the shape of a cross licking the night sky, and I felt the blood run cold in my veins. I've been spat on, cursed, beat, and chased off for trying to go to school with white kids. Years later, I saw my own children spat on, cursed, beat, and chased off for trying to go to college with white kids. Then a preacher named King fought a battle that began to change all that. It was a battle birthed in blood. Yes, I have seen battles won, and I gained a little more hope each time. But even with all those battles won, the war didn't end.

My boy Ezekiel is an old man now, too. He comes to the home every Friday and brings me the Tribune *even though he knows I can't see to read it anymore. And he brings me challah from the kosher bakery even though the boy never understood why I love Jewish Sabbath bread. I reckon that's because I never could explain it. The first time I tasted challah, it filled a hollow place in me that nothing else ever had. Still does.*

There will always be people seeking peace, motivated by

passion or some big ideology. And there will always be people seeking to divide and destroy, powered by hate and fear.
Where you come from, what color your skin is, what you
call the Creator who made us all—that's all it takes to drive
some folks to do despicable, inhuman things. What these
young caregivers of mine don't know is that there was a time
in this country that these despicable, inhuman things were
done by the few and allowed by the many, all in the name
of "America" and "Morality." But the things I've seen are
neither American nor moral.

Lord only knows why He's kept me around this long.
It's only by the grace of God, because if certain folks in my
hometown had gotten their way, I reckon I wouldn't be here
today. I've seen many things I'd just as soon not. But I've
also seen love conquer hate, and I've seen a village turn on
evil and drive it out. I've seen walls of prejudice crumble, and
people step around their fences and come together.

I've seen many things, some bad, some good, and some I
wouldn't trade for nothing.

My first mama was a young colored girl who never had
a choice about anything in her entire life except for asking
Jesus into her heart, and who summoned enormous courage
to give me up so I could have a chance at life, even though it
broke her heart.

My second mama was a wise, stubborn, Jewish girl who
loved me as if I was her very own. Like Noah's dove, she
found herself bid to come into God's saving ark, bid to come
just as you are, and she did. She didn't believe in letting folks
determine who she was or what she could be, and she passed
that fierce belief down to me.

My older brothers were a raggedy bunch of orphans who
refused to be bullied and they taught me the true meaning of
loyalty and brotherhood. To me, those poor white boys were
richer than kings.

But it was my younger brothers—first Isaiah, then the
ones that followed—who gave me something I needed more
than life, love, and loyalty. Because they never saw me as

anything but a true, blood brother, those boys gave me hope. Hope that folks truly can come together as one family, no matter how foreign they may be in their culture or color or way of thinking.

Hope, because from before the creation of this world, the Lord intended on unity for all mankind. With this hope and the voice that the good Lord gave me, I have preached the gospel for nearly seventy years. I'd still be preaching that glorious good news, if they'd let me have my pulpit back.

Shoot, now I'm lucky if they let me have my own fork.

I got no secrets to longevity. But if there is one thing that has kept me waking up each day for ninety-six years, it's the hope of salvation, by the grace of God, for every last child of God, in every color, size and shape, from every nation, language, tribe, and tongue, all gathered together in Him, in complete unity, once and for all. Can I get an Amen?

Sincerely,
Reverend Samuel Lewis Chandler
Restful Havens, Chicago, IL

Acknowledgments

I am extremely blessed with writer friends who offered their valuable insights on this story, including Leslie Gould, Christina Tarabochia, and Cindy Kelley. I'm deeply indebted to my sweet Jewish (and #Hearties!) friend, Donna Cohen, who provided me with personal reflections and thoughts about Jewish life and customs. My knowledge of Judaism is limited, and I am finding that while they are deeply connected, Jewish and Christian thought are vastly different, and understanding one another's worldviews is complicated. But not impossible!

Speaking of Hearties, I am grateful for my fellow fans of When Calls the Heart, the Hallmark Channel series that has given birth a living, breathing community. The friendships I've gained and the interactions I've experienced have helped to inspire the message of hope reflected in this story. That so large and diverse a group can come together and share a common bond has taught me an important lesson about what can happen when people make an effort to employ patience and understanding. Allyson, Debi, Bobbi, and Brian: you exemplify the kind of grace and diplomacy that I believe is key to the unity and harmony our society desperately needs.

Thank you to my publisher, WhiteFire Publishing, for bringing Anna's story to life, to Roseanna White for the perfectly gorgeous cover, and to those who made these pages shine!

I am deeply grateful and indebted to my Pastor, Reverend Jeremy Siebert. His faithfulness, dedication, and diligence to teach the word of God in grace and truth is tireless and unmatched by anyone I've ever known, and his humility, kindness, and selflessness are a faithful reflection of Christ. Jeremy's life is a source of hope and inspiration to me and countless others.

Thank you to my amazing husband, Dan, for all that you sacrifice and put up with so that I can write, and for your faithful love, prayers, and support. Thank you to daughters Janae for your insightful feedback and Kathryn for the enthusiasm and encouragement to write Anna's story.

Thank you most of all to Jesus, my Savior. You not only wrap me in your steadfast mercy, patience, and love, but you exemplify them for me, and you empower me by your Spirit to try to live them out one day at a time. Thank you for helping me arrange words into stories that shine the light of your love and grace into the darkness.

And to you, reading friends: your love of story gives me reason to write. Thank YOU!

Author's Note

Corbin, Indiana is a fictional town set in a fictional county. Places and certain elements in this story have been fictionalized, mainly because I suspect that this story, set in this era, would have to be much darker in reality, and that's not the kind of story I felt the urge to tell. Yet it was a time some don't remember or recognize. As I researched some elements of the era, I came across some information that most people I know were not even aware of, such as:

"Sundown Towns" which existed on a larger scale than most people can grasp, according to the book, *Sundown Towns: A Hidden Dimension of American Racism.* Author James Lowen claims that the existence of these towns (and counties and states) is an ugly reality that few people know about today. The author's premise is that any town that is predominantly white could not possibly be so by accident, and he backs up this premise with overwhelming amounts of evidence.

The Women of the KKK, or WKKK, separate from the KKK, was a strong force with its own agenda, which perpetrated racial and cultural hatred, not with torches and hoods, but with slander, rumor, and coercion. The WKKK—quieter than its male counterpart but just as vicious—used inter-personal connections and rumormongering instead of outright violence. The Women's Klan employed insidious rhetoric that warned women about "racial peril of unlimited immigration and the threat to Prohibition posed by foreign-born residents." Their agenda was calculated, aggressive, and relentless.

Baby Black Market (as suggested by the fictional Campbell Home) was a dark reality in the nineteenth and early twentieth centuries. For further study, look up "Miss Georgia Tann" in Memphis, Tennessee from 1924 to 1950. The institution of orphan asylums also have a dark history until around WW2. They were often places of mistreatment, neglect, abuse, and more.

And Then There's My Own Two Cents, but...

I don't have the answers. I have ideas and opinions tumbling around in my heart and mind, but I've decided to let the characters in this story have their say and leave it at that. Instead, let's talk. Let's explore and discuss possible solutions that begin with each one of us, brainstorm ways we as individuals can engage in toppling whatever barriers to unity exist first in our own hearts, and then in our parts of the world. Let's be Sarahs and refuse to believe blanket assumptions and choose to see every fellow member of the human race as a child of God, precious in his sight.

Maya Angelou, American poet and civil rights activist, recalls an instance from her youth of racist treatment from a white clerk, and her response to it. In *I Know Why the Caged Bird Sings,* she concludes: "I went further than forgiving the clerk, I accepted her as a fellow victim of the same puppeteer."

Ms. Angelou's gracious attitude about mankind's collective flaws gives me hope. At the risk of sounding simplistic, I firmly believe that grace, mercy, and compassion from each one of us, in spite of any cultural bias we've been conditioned to have, are key factors in creating unity, stitch by stitch. And I believe that while grace, mercy, and compassion are, even at best sorely limited in mortal man, with God's help, they are limitless (Ephesians 2).

And with God, all things are possible.

Bread bakers: This is a recipe I've had on file for decades, which I used to make for my kids when they were growing up, long before I knew what *challah* was actually for.

Braided Egg Bread (Challah)
Makes one loaf, begin 4 hours ahead

Dough:
    1 Tb sugar
    ¾ tsp salt
    1 pkg yeast (1 Tb)
    about 3 ½ cups flour
    3/4 cup water
    3 Tb oil
    3 eggs

Glaze:
    1 egg, 1 Tb water, dash salt

In a large bowl combine sugar, salt, yeast and 1 cup flour. Heat water and oil until very warm, 115-120 degrees. With mixer at low speed, beat liquid into dry ingredients just until blended. Beat at medium speed 2 minutes.

To mixture in bowl, add 3 eggs and ¼ cup flour. Beat 2 minutes. Stir in about 1¼ cup flour, enough to make a soft dough.

Knead on floured surface 10 minutes, working in more flour while kneading as needed (about ½ cup). Shape dough into a ball and place in a greased bowl, turning dough to grease top. Cover and let rise in a warm place until doubled, about 1 hour.

Punch down dough, turn onto floured surface, cover with bowl and let rest for 15 minutes. Grease large cookie sheet (or use a double sheet if bottom tends to turn too dark).

Cut 2/3 of dough into 3 equal pieces. On floured surface, with hand, roll each piece onto a 13-inch-long rope, tapering the ends. Place ropes side by side and loosely braid, <u>beginning in the middle</u> and working toward each end. Pinch ends together for now, and place on cookie sheet for bottom part of loaf.

For smaller top braid, cut remaining 1/3 dough into 3 equal pieces. Roll each piece into a 14-inch-long rope, tapering ends, and braid as above. Place small braid on top of large braid. Stretching top braid if needed, tuck ends of top braid and bottom braid under, securing ends beneath loaf. Cover until doubled, about 45 minutes.

Preheat oven to 375. In a small bowl, beat reserved egg with 1Tb water and a dash of salt. Brush loaf with egg mixture. Bake 30 minutes or till loaf is golden. Cool before cutting.

Reader Discussion

- Why do you think Anna resented her mother's old-world ways?

- How was Anna's role in the family affected by the absence of her father?

- How did assuming a parental role with her siblings affect Anna's relationship with her mother?

- How did Anna's view of American culture affect her relationship with her mother?

- Why did Anna feel the need to prove herself an adult?

- What impacted Anna's decisions and actions the night she went out and was violated?

- Did Anna's view of her mother change throughout the story? If so, how, and why?

- Anna began to see shame as a thief, and a barrier between a person and those they love. Has shame ever kept you and a loved one apart?

- Why do you think Thomas's wife left him?

- Have you ever suffered for trying to do the right thing?

- Have you ever broken a rule (i.e. skipped school) in order to support someone who was being mistreated?

- Thomas continually turned down the invitation to be involved with the local Klan. Yet he chose to stay in the community. Would it have been easier for him to pack up his apprentices and live somewhere else? Why do you think he stayed in Corbin?

- What motivates Sarah Tucker's association with Penny Withers?

- In the beginning, Sarah feels her opinions are of little worth. How does this change, and why?

- Sarah accepts the racist propaganda, but only to a point. How does knowing a Jew and Negro impact Sarah's view of the "stories" she hears from the women's organization?

- Penny Withers vocalizes a worldview shaped by her parents. In the end, it seems she is considering the possibility that her parents' views are wrong. Do you know anyone like Penny? Do you think people like Penny can change?

- When Penny first meets Anna, she seems eager to include Anna in her circle of friends, even though Penny suspects Anna is a foreigner. Why do you think she did that?

- When she leaves to marry the farmer in Ohio, Anna realizes she left her heart in Corbin, and feels it would be unfair to marry one man when she loves another. She ditches the plan that would solve her perilous dilemma. Would you have made the same decision she did, in her condition and situation? Why or why not?

- Samuel forms a bond with Anna and soon finds the courage to overcome the fear that paralyzed his speech. What do you think caused his regression when she left?

- When Anna responds to Penny by saying at least she didn't have to wonder if people liked her, what was Penny's reaction? What affect do you think Anna's statement had on Penny, if any?

- Why do you think Anna was willing to offer redemption to her father?

- If another member of the family besides Anna had found him, do you think Hershel Leibowicz would have been able to reconnect with his family?

- What was the significance, if any, of her papa taking Anna's offered hand?

- Thomas tells Anna that she needs to forgive herself. Has shame ever kept you from moving on and aiming for your full potential?

- Anna's father has walled himself off from his family. Is there ever a time when barriers created by shame are a good, healthy choice?

- In the end, Anna and her mother apologize. What might have happened if they had humbled themselves like this in the beginning?

- Anna makes a comment about blind ignorance being a positive thing. What do you think this means, and do you agree?

- In a letter to Shayna, Anna said, *"wherever apathy, superiority, or injustice rule, evil is not far."* What do you think is the danger in apathy, superiority, and unchecked injustice?

- How is Thomas like Christ?

- How is Samuel like the prophet from the book of Samuel?

- In what ways did Anna resemble the dove from Noah's Ark?

For Further Discussion

- Do you think it's a good idea to bring divided people together? Do you think it's possible?

- Why do people construct invisible walls between themselves and others? Do you think people tend to fear or dislike those who are different than themselves?

- Have you ever caught yourself making assumptions about an entire group of people? Do you think such assumptions are helpful in building bridges?

- Is it possible to be "blind" to what is different or "foreign" about others, and to see everyone from every people group as equally valuable?

- Do you think that more mingling with people from different cultures and ethnicities can help dissolve prejudice? Why, or why not?

- Is it possible to grow up with a conditioned bias without actually being bigoted or racist? Is it possible that people are conditioned to feel various types of bias? In addition to racial and cultural bias, are there economic, religious, social status, education, or other types of bias?

- Is there such a thing as *unconscious* bias? Do you think such bias can be eliminated?

- How might rumors and propaganda be used as acts of violence?

- Have you ever heard the phrase "Sundown Towns"?

- For those of us prepared to begin with ourselves, what are some practical ways we might battle prejudice and bigotry in our hearts, homes, neighborhoods, and communities?

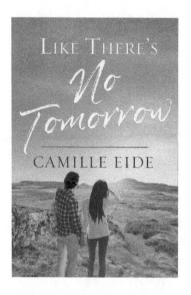

Like There's No Tomorrow

What if loving means letting go? Scottish widower Ian MacLean is plagued by a mischievous grannie, bitter regrets, and an ache for something he'll never have again. His only hope for freedom is to bring his grannie's sister home from America. But first, he'll have to convince her young companion, Emily Chapman, to let the woman go.

Like a Love Song

Susan Quinn, a social worker turned surrogate mom to foster teens, fights to save the group home she's worked hard to build. But now, she faces a dwindling staff, foreclosure, and old heartaches that won't stay buried. Her only hope lies with the last person she'd ever turn to-a brawny handyman with a guitar, a questionable past, and a God he keeps calling Father.

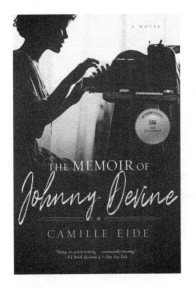

The Memoir of Johnny Devine

In 1953, desperation forces Eliza to take a job writing the memoir of ex-Hollywood heartthrob, Johnny Devine. Rumor has it Johnny can seduce anything in a skirt quicker than he can hail a cab. But now, the notorious womanizer claims he's born again. And so he seems to be. Eliza soon finds herself falling for the humble, grace-filled man John has become-a man who shows no sign of returning her feelings.No sign, that is, until she discovers something John never meant for her to see.

About the Author

Camille Eide (EYE-dee) is the award-winning author of poignant, inspirational love stories including The Memoir of Johnny Devine. Camille lives in the foothills of the Oregon Cascades with her husband and has three adult kids and five grandkids. She loves baking, muscle cars, and the natural beauty of the Pacific Northwest. She also loves the liberating truth and wisdom of God's word, and hopes that her stories will stir your heart, strengthen your faith, and encourage you on your journey.

www.CamilleEide.com

Let's Connect!

Book Bub
https://www.bookbub.com/authors/camille-eide

Goodreads
https://www.goodreads.com/author/show/5356695.Camille_Eide

Facebook
https://www.facebook.com/pages/Camille-Eide-Author/134301859999367

Twitter
https://twitter.com/CamilleEide

Instagram
https://www.instagram.com/camille.eide/

Fiction Blog: Extreme Keyboarding
http://camilleeide.blogspot.com/

Faith Blog: Along the Banks
https://camilleeide.wordpress.com/

CPSIA information can be obtained
at www.ICGtesting.com
Printed in the USA
LVHW011745281119
638726LV00012B/1820/P